PRAISE

Exes and O's

"Unapologetically romantic, wonderfully sexy, always brilliant. . . . With this stunning sophomore novel, Amy Lea has officially rocketed her way into my heart as a must-read author!"

—Ali Hazelwood, *New York Times* bestselling author of
Love on the Brain

"Amy Lea's *Exes and O's* is for anyone who's ever dreamed their book boyfriend could exist in real life. It's a charming and funny friends-to-lovers romance that sparkles with Amy's signature sweetness and steam."

—Carley Fortune, *New York Times* bestselling author of
Every Summer After

"Laugh-out-loud, ardently feminist, and with a hero straight out of a fevered daydream, *Exes and O's* is an outright, unmitigated delight!"

—Christina Lauren, *New York Times* bestselling author of
The Unhoneymooners

"*Exes and O's* is every rom-com reader's dream, a delightfully meta romp with a heroine who loves tropes as much as her readers. Tara's quest to find herself a second-chance romance of her own is swoony, hilarious, and ends in the perfect HEA."

—Emily Wibberley and Austin Siegemund-Broka, authors of
The Roughest Draft

"A gorgeous friends-to-lovers slow burn, *Exes and O's* is filled with fun, charm, and an appealing hero who sees and loves the protagonist for exactly who she is. A perfect mix of relatable characters, hilarious banter, and steam, *Exes and O's* is for everyone who has wondered about past relationships and future loves."

—Lily Chu, author of *The Stand-In*

"I flew through this book—Amy Lea packed every sentence with so much hilarity and heart. Get ready for some trope-y goodness in *Exes and O's*, including a meta awareness of those same tropes that's a blast to read. If you love the roommate vibes of *New Girl*, a heroine who's unabashedly 'extra,' and a hero who accepts her for who she is, you won't want to miss this one!"

—Alicia Thompson, national bestselling author of *Love in the Time of Serial Killers*

"The resulting romance is as sensitive and swoony as it is self-aware, playfully engaging popular romance tropes. This is a winner."

—*Publishers Weekly* (starred review)

"A hilarious, relatable exploration of life and love, filled to brimming with soft moments, small gestures, and a clear love of the romance genre itself. . . . A comically delightful romance about how the best love stories are found where you least expect them."

—*Kirkus Reviews* (starred review)

"*Exes and O's* is equal parts tender and laugh-out-loud funny, with an earnest appreciation for the romance genre singing loudly from every page. With her sophomore novel, Lea proves she's here to stay."

—*BookPage* (starred review)

"The gym has never seemed such a sexy and romantic place as in this book!"   —Denise Williams, author of *How to Fail at Flirting*

"This book's appealing characters and gym-bound setting will resonate with anyone who's ever mentally cursed a fellow gym-goer for failing to wipe down the machine post-use."   —*USA Today*

"A fun, flirty, and hot AF romance."   —Culturess

"Lea's debut romance is a terrific rom-com that offers an essential message about accepting oneself, and it is a pleasure to read."
—*Booklist*

TITLES BY AMY LEA

The Catch

AMY LEA

BERKLEY ROMANCE

New York

BERKLEY ROMANCE
Published by Berkley
An imprint of Penguin Random House LLC
penguinrandomhouse.com

Copyright © 2024 by Amy Lea
Readers Guide copyright © 2024 by Amy Lea
Excerpt from *Set on You* copyright © 2022 by Amy Lea
Penguin Random House supports copyright. Copyright fuels creativity,
encourages diverse voices, promotes free speech, and creates a vibrant culture.
Thank you for buying an authorized edition of this book and for complying with
copyright laws by not reproducing, scanning, or distributing any part of it in any
form without permission. You are supporting writers and allowing Penguin
Random House to continue to publish books for every reader.

BERKLEY and the BERKLEY and B colophon are registered
trademarks of Penguin Random House LLC.

Library of Congress Cataloging-in-Publication Data

Names: Lea, Amy, author.
Title: The catch / Amy Lea.
Description: First edition. | New York: Berkley Romance, 2024. |
Series: The Influencer series
Identifiers: LCCN 2023022198 (print) | LCCN 2023022199 (ebook) |
ISBN 9780593336618 (trade paperback) | ISBN 9780593336625 (ebook)
Subjects: LCGFT: Romance fiction. | Novels.
Classification: LCC PR9199.4.L425 C38 2024 (print) |
LCC PR9199.4.L425 (ebook) | DDC 813/.6—dc23/eng/20230512
LC record available at https://lccn.loc.gov/2023022198
LC ebook record available at https://lccn.loc.gov/2023022199

First Edition: February 2024

Printed in the United States of America
1st Printing

Book design by Daniel Brount

To J: my nature-loving, plaid-wearing handyman of a husband. Thanks for always getting rid of spiders and other equally horrifying bugs on my behalf.

author's note

Dear Reader,

Thank you so much for choosing my romantic comedy *The Catch* as your next read. While this story is generally light and humorous, I would be remiss if I did not include the following content warnings: death of a family member (off page), the associated grief and depression, and an on-page watercraft-related accident. Please take care while reading.

With love,
Amy Lea

chapter one

I F I WERE a character in a classic slasher film, I'd be the first to die. That sounds morbid, but hear me out.

First, I lack the necessary endurance to run long distances without being caught. I have no sense of direction, to the point where I regularly get lost in my own condo parking garage. On any given day, I'm usually alone, leaving the killer ample time to strike when I'm vulnerable. And when placed in high-pressure situations, I tend to make rash, ill-advised decisions.

Case in point: when being pursued, my first instinct is to trap myself inside the tight confines of the condo elevator. Rookie mistake.

"Melanie! Meeelanieee, wait for me!" calls an all-too-familiar, ear-piercing voice.

I frantically press the *Close* button no less than eleven times, heart hammering against my chest wall. Picture the slasher scene where the woman hides in a closet as the killer ponders his next move, mouth-breathing heavily on the other side of the door.

As the *click-clack* of footsteps on marbled tiles grows dangerously near, the elevator doors begin to close. Bless.

Just one more inch.

Half an inch.

And then they stop.

A sliver shy of sealing shut, the doors abruptly reopen like a record scratch. My whole body folds inward, desperate to seek refuge like a turtle avoiding all reality in its protective shell. On second thought, turtles do not have the gift of speed. And in the face of my pursuer's demented smile, one needs to run, or at least power walk.

One could say I'm being a touch dramatic. See, my pursuer isn't really a crazed, axe-wielding serial killer who wants to hack me into tiny pieces. He's my prepubescent neighbor—Ian Montgomery.

"Melanie. You look ravishing."

"Hi, Ian." I summon a sweet smile, taking stock of his short-sleeved button-down. It hangs off his lithe frame, juxtaposed with his creased khakis, which are two inches too short since his winter growth spurt.

A man in tapered joggers takes advantage of the holdup, rushing in behind Ian before the doors close, sealing us in together.

"The color of your top brings out your suntan," Ian tells me, his gaze hovering dangerously close to my cleavage. To be fair, it's at his eye level since he's approximately four feet nine.

I respond to Ian with a low "Thank you," shifting a thick lock of hair over my chest like a protective blanket before shuffling to the right, my Greek take-out bag tucked snugly under my arm.

Ian wastes zero time reclaiming the dead space. "I also liked your bikini photo from the other day."

My cheeks burst into flame when Joggers shoots me an accusatory look over his meaty shoulder. Ian is referring to my latest post—a beach photo shoot wherein I attempted to channel the raw sex appeal of Daniel Craig in *Casino Royale*. Particularly that slo-mo scene where he emerges seductively from the water, beads of moisture shimmering over his taut, suspiciously hairless bod. As it turns out, I have the charisma of a potato compared to James Bond.

"For the record, I did not send this child a bikini photo," I clarify to the back of Jogger's shiny scalp. And it's the truth. The kid keeps close tabs on my social media.

Ian pouts. "I'm not a child. I'm basically a teenager."

"You just turned eleven," I remind him.

Trust, I'm not normally this dismissive of children. But in case it isn't obvious, Ian has been nurturing an unhealthy crush on me since last year when he and his silver fox of a dad moved in next door. Instead of spending his days playing first-person-shooter video games and eating cheese puffs by the bag like most boys his age, he prefers to dream up new and disturbing ways to confess his love for me (including ambushing me in the hallways and writing romantic haikus in my honor).

Of course, I've firmly yet politely explained that I'm way too old for him (*practically prehistoric*) and that his advances are inappropriate. Ian still hasn't accepted this. Either that or the power of agonizing unrequited love has clouded his judgment. I can't help but feel sorry for him. I've never seen him with another kid his age, which is why I try to be pleasant to him despite his overt creepiness. Unfortunately, the nicer I am, the more emboldened he becomes.

Ian leans in to take a dramatic whiff of my Greek food. "Smells good. Is it just for you?"

"Yup, dinner for one," I say proudly, giving the take-out bag a gentle, loving rock, stroking it like it's a newborn baby.

"Greek on Wheels is my favorite," Ian informs me, thick brows bouncing as Joggers exits the elevator on floor six. "And dinner for one sounds like rock bottom."

Damn. This kid went for the jugular. I tighten my grip on my food, hitching my shoulders in defense. "Jeez. Drag me, Ian. And it's really not rock bottom."

Dinner for one has its perks. There's no one interrupting my Zen by chewing their meat loudly in my ear. Or swooping in to steal the best bite I was saving for last.

Ian swings me a knowing side-eye. "No one likes being alone. And you've been alone every night since you broke up with Ronan—the one who was obsessed with cryptocurrency."

Ronan was the last guy I dated. He always pressured me to split my meal because he couldn't choose only one item off the menu. I know what you're thinking: splitting food isn't *that* bad. It's romantic, even. But after a childhood of going to bed on an empty stomach, sharing doesn't exactly evoke the warm and fuzzies.

And if lectures about crypto and meal splitting weren't shriveling my libido enough, I had no choice but to end things immediately when he suggested we take our relationship to the next level and move in together after four months of dating.

I bristle at Ian, unable to suppress the creeping urge to justify my life choices. "I'm not alone. I have friends." I fix my defensive stare on the button panel. Just a few more floors until sweet freedom. "Two friends. Crystal and Tara," I specify. When I say it out

4

loud, having exactly two friends sounds rather tragic for someone with half a million social media followers.

Ian moves on, wholly uninterested in my pitiful social calendar. "I'm going to a poetry reading tonight if you want to join."

"Ian, you're being inappropriate again," I warn, bouncing on the balls of my feet when we finally arrive at our floor.

"Sorry. My dad says I need to dial it back." He jogs to keep up with me as we head down the hallway toward our respective condo units.

"Your dad is right," I say, digging my keys out of my pocket. "Aren't there cute girls or boys your own age you could yearn for instead?"

He averts his eyes to his sockless ankles. "None who will talk to me. Kenna Palmer says I'm a weirdo freak."

"First, Kenna Palmer sounds like a miserable brat. She'll regret that in twenty years when you're a megarich tech entrepreneur with an all-black-interior private jet. And second, you're not . . ." I bite my lip, summoning the most delicate way to get my point across. "Okay, you're a little weird. Maybe a little . . . intense. Overzealous."

He fiddles with the collar of his dress shirt. "Isn't intense and overzealous good?"

"Let me put it this way: You're at high risk of getting your heart skewered over a flaming barbecue if you keep up this type of behavior into middle school. And, if you ask me, love is a burden to be avoided at all costs," I warn. "See you later, Ian."

For the briefest moment, he dips his chin in consideration. "'Hearts are made to be broken,' said the great Oscar Wilde."

"I like being alone. With my heart intact," I call through the crack in the door before closing it completely.

I repeat those words as I face my empty condo.

I like being alone.

The more I say it, the more it will be true.

• • •

MAYBE IAN WAS right. My Greek dinner for one looks depressing at my dining table for twelve.

I was convinced this gargantuan table was necessary for all the wine-and-charcuterie nights I'd host. I never imagined it would be empty ninety percent of the time.

After eating dinner on the couch instead, I commence my sacred nighttime ritual:

1. Send daily check-in text to little brother, Julian
2. Do five-step skin care routine
3. Guzzle three mugs of lemon-ginger detox tea
4. Send another email to my accountant to clarify whether the low-five-digit number in my savings account is a typo
5. Drown out the stifling silence with an old rerun, a faux-chinchilla throw hoisted to my chin
6. Root through notifications on my @MelanieInTheCity account until my eyelids grow too heavy for consciousness

Tonight proves to be another quiet night for DMs, aside from a new demand for my used socks, *worn for an entire week, please and thank you* (yes, my DMs are a terrifying place).

But among some spam emails advertising Viagra and hot-air balloon rides, there's an email from an address I don't recognize.

TO: melanieinthecity@xmail.com
FROM: marketing@seasideresorts.ca
SUBJECT: Collaboration Opportunity with Seaside Resorts

Dear Melanie in the City,

I hope this email finds you well! My name is Shawna and I'm reaching out on behalf of <u>Seaside Resorts</u> in Nova Scotia, on the East Coast of Canada.

I'd love to tell you more about a potential collaboration opportunity I think you would be perfect for. We'd like to offer you an all-expenses-paid getaway experience in exchange for an agreed-upon posting schedule, in addition to video content on your socials.

I'd love to chat further if you're interested, and we can arrange a week for your stay next month, in August.

Best,
Shawna
Marketing Manager
Seaside Resorts
Nova Scotia

The photos on the resort's website boast a boxy white cedar exterior, comprised of a variety of reclaimed wood planks cut into clean lines. The interior is also sleek, the floors a soft seashell porcelain. The modern architecture contrasts with the jagged rocks surrounding the resort like a fortress, protecting it from the frothy sea below.

I reread the email multiple times, shocked I've been offered this opportunity at all.

Your content is stale and a little too curated for our evolving brand. That's what one collaboration partner said when they dumped me after five years. And they were among the many companies moving on to greener pastures, in favor of fresh-faced teens in sweatpants and no makeup crying on live video sans filter. See, at the ripe age of twenty-nine, I'm basically the Crypt Keeper in internet years, teetering on the brink of irrelevance. Without new, exciting partnerships, I'm losing followers (aka my sole revenue stream) at a frightening rate.

This opportunity has to be a sign. A sign that I'm not destined for failure and on track to being broke within a year. That I won't have to find some random job in order to make ends meet and live paycheck to paycheck ever again. With enough new content, I can use the opportunity to revitalize my brand.

Maybe a jaunt in rustic nature (with a luxurious twist) is exactly what I need.

♥ chapter two

One month later

M Y APOLOGIES, MS. Karlsen. I'm afraid I have some bad news," Geraldine, the resort receptionist with a serene spa voice, tells me over the phone.

"Bad news?" I repeat, hauling my luggage to a quiet corner of the airport pickup area. Despite arriving in Halifax bright-eyed and ready to embrace rustic luxury, I've admittedly grown a tad weary languishing on the curb, waiting for the resort shuttle for the past hour.

"It looks like there's some confusion over the booking dates. We have you in for next Friday, not this Friday."

Internal panic ensues. "*Next* Friday? But I'm already here. In Halifax."

"I am so sorry," Geraldine says regretfully. "We have nothing else available until then."

"Nothing at all?" I confirm, frowning. "What are my options? Can I go home and come back next week?"

She hesitates. "As per our policy, we can't cover an additional set of flights. But thanks to a provincial economic development grant, we can offer to expense your accommodations for the extra week."

"Oh, um, well—"

"You're going to have a fabulous stay. There is so much to do here. Nova Scotia really is a lovely vacation spot," she cuts in, tone chipper, as though the resort hasn't completely botched my plans.

I consider reminding her that they're responsible for the date mix-up. But after years of working in customer service and taking the brunt of people's frustrations, I've grown accustomed to being agreeable when on the other side. "So I've heard. Thanks for your help, Geraldine," I grumble, ending the call when it becomes clear there's no alternative.

As I watch a group of burly-looking men in flannel overcoats pile their gigantic bags into the back of a tiny taxi, my phone buzzes with a flurry of texts from my brother.

JULIAN: Hi

JULIAN: Ok plz don't kill me . . .

JULIAN: But HYPOTHETICALLY

JULIAN: If someone were to get pizza sauce on white fabric . . . how would one HYPOTHETICALLY get the stain out??

JULIAN: Also, I can't remember which towels you said I could use . . .

JULIAN: Did you land yet??

JULIAN: I see my msg delivered so I'm guessing you're in
Halifax?? Plz let me know.

Typical Julian. He still hasn't mastered the art of using extreme caution while eating on my white couch. I take in a couple of deep breaths before responding and follow up with a link to a YouTube tutorial on removing sauce stains.

My fingers flex at my side as I consider the reality of being away from him for an extra week while he's staying at my place. But the last thing I want to do is lose this opportunity. Maybe an extra week won't be so bad. After all, it means twice the time for content.

With renewed optimism, I wheel my luggage to a rental car booth, where they give me the very last SUV in their fleet in absence of a reservation: a Ford Flex.

"A Flex? The one that looks like a hearse?" I clarify to the car rental employee.

"It's tourist and fishing season," he informs me, as though I should just *know*.

He isn't wrong. By the time I get into my funeral-chic Flex (jet black for added effect), I've already called seven nearby hotels, all of which are completely booked. Is sleepy Halifax really that happening? I try at least a dozen other hotels, ones that aren't those sketchy roadside motels, to no avail. There's no vacancy for my dates on Airbnb either. This is quickly becoming the trip from hell.

Aside from paying out of pocket for the flight, I have two choices: First, I could camp in the Flex for the week. Though I've seen enough true crime shows to know what happens to lone women who sleep in their cars on the side of the road. Despite my low odds of survival in a slasher film, there's a decent chance I could take a Canadian murderer. I've got a killer uppercut according to my kickboxing instructor. But I'd rather not take my chances.

Or second, I could scrape the bottom of the barrel on Airbnb. When I widen the net distance-wise on the app, exactly one option pops up. It's a bed-and-breakfast located an hour and a half away in a place called Cora's Cove. I click through the photos at lightning speed, terrified if I don't book it now, it'll get snatched up.

A white wraparound porch hugs the entire perimeter of the Victorian-style home, and there's a charming rounded turret, reminding me of the deluxe dollhouse I longed for as a kid, minus the hot-pink exterior.

It's only a week, I remind myself as I click *Reserve*. This will have to do.

The Flex is not the smoothest ride, but at least the drive is scenic. The last few scattered rays of sunshine peek through the pine trees closing in on either side of the freeway. As I pass through countless tiny seaside towns, there are a couple of stretches of road where the vast, dark sea is literally feet away, no guardrail, a cruel reminder of my mortality.

Night has fallen by the time I arrive at the Airbnb. It's a wonder I even made it since my GPS failed on me in the last fifteen minutes.

In the glow of the moonlight, I compare the house in front of me to the photos in the ad. It is not as advertised.

Instead of the cute Victorian dollhouse in the photos, it has all the makings of a haunted mansion. It's large, stately, and nearly swallowed by overgrown vegetation casting uneven shadows every which way. The white double-decker porch is begging for a fresh coat of paint, as is the navy siding.

The porch is littered with pieces of scrap wood, metal debris, a rickety porch swing, and an abandoned green stove from the sixties, rusted burner coils and all. It's only missing a pale malnourished child sitting on the creaky swing who turns out to be a sallow-faced ghost.

I quadruple-check the number on the house to ensure this is, indeed, the correct address. It is. My stomach does a barrel roll.

"Let's hope the inside is better," I say to the crow perched on the tree hanging over my rental car. It's probably wondering what the hell I'm doing here. *Same, bird. Same.*

I haul my luggage to the porch and knock. No answer. Shivering, I rub my palms together and peek through the door's window like a Peeping Tom. The yellow glow suggests someone is inside. At risk of freezing my ass off out here, I walk in willingly, as the horror movie's "first to die" would do.

Inside is an improvement, and by *improvement* I mean it has working electricity, smells like home cooking, and isn't overrun with vines, dead leaves, and dark entities.

A wide, ornate chestnut staircase greets me upon entry. Above me is a six-pronged brass chandelier etched with pretty decorative detail and featuring exquisite glass bowl shades caked with dust.

I tepidly ring the bell atop a wooden desk to my right, half expecting a set of rushed footsteps to follow. Nothing. I go to ring the bell again, but instead I'm distracted by an outdated laptop that can't possibly be from this decade, as well as a wood-carved lobster with bug eyes, wearing an impossibly tiny turtleneck. Next to a lantern, which has been modernized with a light bulb, sits a *Welcome*

Guests sign printed in Calibri font, size 200, with a tiny clip art lobster border.

I lean against my luggage to call the number listed on the Airbnb ad. But before I hit *Call*, my phone starts vibrating with an incoming call. It's Crystal.

"Hey," I croak, taking in the room behind the desk with a grandfather clock, central panel ajar. The room's walls are exposed down to the insulation, wires and all, like someone punctured the drywall in a fevered frenzy in search of hidden bodies or treasure.

"Did I interrupt your sea-wrap full-body massage?"

I snort, mourning my would-be massage at this very hour. "No. I'm not having a massage. I'm not even at the resort."

"What? Was it a scam? You know, my dad was telling us about this scheme where models were rounded up at a supposed photo shoot. Then they got their passports stolen and—"

"No one's stolen my passport. Yet." I take a quick peek over my shoulder for good measure. "The dates of my stay got mixed up. There's no vacancy at the resort for a full week. The only accommodation I found was an hour and a half away from Halifax."

"No! How does that even happen? Why didn't you just come home?"

"Because I'd have to pay for the flight. It's only a week. I'll live . . . I think. Besides, Julian is staying at my place again—" I wince when the words come out, not wanting to burden her with my financial and familial woes. She doesn't need the details about how Julian showed up at my place last week, duffel bag slung over his shoulder, asking if he could crash after his roommate kicked him out for not paying rent.

Admittedly, it was nice to have him back. I'd gotten used to seeing him every day when he lived with me after Dad passed. Dad's heart attack was unexpected and hit both of us hard. Except, where I channeled my grief into my career, Julian became ridden with depression and anxiety. Practically all the things that used to excite him, like socializing, playing sports, and practicing with his band, have fallen by the wayside. Even regular tasks like grocery shopping and driving have become a source of stress.

"So how did you end up an hour and a half away from Halifax? Did you try driving without your GPS again?" Crystal asks.

"Nope. All the hotels are booked for fishing season, allegedly. The place I ended up in is, um, interesting. I'm pretty sure I see a taxidermized moose head above the fireplace." I do a side shuffle into the parlor again to confirm, avoiding direct eye contact with its glossy eyes.

"Sounds . . . rustic."

"I mean, I came to Nova Scotia for rustic . . . but this place is really pushing it. It looks like it's under construction. I'm trying to check in now, but no one's here. I dunno what to do."

"That sounds like a trap. Turn on your geolocation. I don't want you to end up dead in the woods with your kidneys removed."

"Well, if I get gutted and my organs are stolen by a deranged backroad Canadian, I bequeath my handbag collection to you."

"Oh good. I've been eyeing your YSL tassel shoulder bag." She pauses. "In all seriousness, text me every few minutes—"

Without warning, the deep, thunderous growl of a vicious animal sounds behind me. Naturally, I yelp like I'm being brutally attacked, dropping my phone. Consider my motor skills zilch. As my phone hits the tattered welcome mat at my feet, I pivot, shoulders hunched, fists clenched, ready for blood.

♥ chapter three

TURNS OUT, THE growler isn't a wild creature ready to tear my body limb from limb. It's a mountain of a man. A thick plaid flannel button-down covers a barrel chest so broad I doubt I could wrap both arms around him and touch my fingertips. Not that I would dare get within a five-foot radius of someone whose hostile blue stare is so poisonous I think he could vanquish all his enemies with a single look.

His commanding presence freezes me in place. A foreboding sizzle zips through me as I take in the thick, unkempt ashy beard concealing his jawline, barely covering a surly, grim expression. Overgrown dirty blond hair wings out from under his faded and frayed Maple Leafs ball cap, which has seen better days.

"Who the hell are you?" His voice is gruff and terse, as if uttering anything beyond a single syllable is a herculean effort he'd rather not be bothered with.

My body betrays me with a bark of laughter. The moment it spills out of me, I hike my tote over my shoulder, righting my posture in a sad attempt to match his height on the staircase. "Sorry, I didn't mean to laugh. Your voice took me by surprise."

He raises a thick, dark brow. "My voice?"

I blink. "It's just so . . . deep." I wave a hand, trying to unearth the words. "Kind of like an action movie bad guy?"

No response. Just a scowl.

"Um, is this the Whaler Inn?" I ask, despite the Whaler Inn information pamphlet displayed on the desk. Though based on the ad offering a quaint B and B that isn't in the midst of renovations, it's a fair question.

He widens his stance like he's the loyal bodyguard of a young pop star at the height of their fame. "Who wants to know?" His narrowing gaze is so skeptical, I bite my lip to stop myself from laughing again.

"Um, me, obviously. I made a reservation. You're not the owner, are you?" Frankly, I'd imagined a folksy, salt-and-pepper-haired couple in matching knit sweaters. They'd be in their seventies, though they'd intend to keep running the inn until the day they die (on the same day, of course), because it's been in the family for millennia. Upon entry, I'd be offered fresh-baked banana bread and an assortment of senior citizen candies from a crystal bowl. I'd be charmed by their tendency to add an "Eh?" at the end of every sentence while they delight me with tales of merciless northern winters past.

Conveniently, the Plaid Giant fails to confirm nor deny ownership. "You didn't make a reservation," he says matter-of-factly. That flannel is really doing overtime to cover the swell of his arms.

He strikes me as the type who got those Thor-like muscles by doing honest work in the wilderness, trapping animals and hauling timber for the cabin he's building miles from civilization because he clearly hates humanity.

"Actually, I did reserve. For a week." Panicked, I bend over to pick up my phone, which is overturned on the floor at my feet. Crystal has long since hung up, though she's tried to call back four times and sent multiple texts. I pull up the Airbnb email, brandishing the screen at him, as if he can read it from this distance with bionic sight.

A trace of a frown forms under that bushy beard. "Nope."

It's not like I want to stand here and argue, but I've had enough reservation mix-ups for one day. "I have my res right here." I hold out my phone, extending my arm completely, which only results in a deeper scowl.

His frown doesn't budge as he lumbers down the stairs, wood creaking under each heavy step. When he rounds the desk, I catch a whiff. I hoped he'd smell like wet dog or rotting garbage. But instead, his scent is rich and smoky, like a campfire and maybe a hint of leather.

"Is it possible you didn't see my reservation? It doesn't really look like technology is your strong suit." I wave a hand in the vague direction of the clunky laptop.

"Yeah, technology is real hard to come by for kidney-stealing 'backroad Canadians,'" he grumbles, tapping his calloused finger on the counter impatiently as he waits for the laptop to boot up.

Unease settles along my spine as I mentally replay my call with Crystal. I definitely took my sarcasm a little too far.

I contemplate an apology, but before the words come to me, he grumbles something unintelligible and hunches over the keyboard. Whoever constructed this desk didn't take someone of his height into consideration. He stabs at the keyboard with his index finger, squinting at the screen with effort. "You requested the reservation, but it wasn't confirmed."

Crap.

In all the stress, I was thrilled there was any availability at all. I completely forgot about awaiting confirmation from the host, aka this miserable man who single-handedly disproves the theory that all Canadians are nice.

"Can't you just confirm it right now?" I ask, flashing my full-teeth smile, hoping it'll brighten his mood.

His eyes flare with deep irritation. "No. We're not open."

"But you are, according to Airbnb." I point to the ad on my phone screen, which he waves off like a pesky housefly.

"Must be a glitch. Sorry, Your Royal Highness. You'll have to find alternative accommodations. I hear the Ritz-Carlton down the street has vacancy." He conjures up the briefest half-hearted, crooked smile that makes him look more constipated than smug.

What is this guy's problem? I silently wish him a mild case of hemorrhoids, and then I resort to begging. "Can you please just let me stay for one night? I'm desperate."

"No. We're under construction, as you can see. Not open." He gestures to the parlor. His explanation sounds legit, which makes me feel a little better. Until he swaps his baffled expression for wariness. "Wait—you're not some real estate developer, are you?"

"Does it look like I'm in the market to purchase a decrepit—" I bite my tongue when his glare ensnares mine. "An inn in dire need of repairs?"

His jaw clenches. "Why would someone like you want to stay here, anyway?"

"Well, that's the thing. It's not exactly my first choice," I admit. "I'm supposed to stay at the Seaside Resort outside of Halifax. It's a five-star luxury resort."

He treats me to a bored stare.

"I promise to find somewhere else to go in the morning."

"Best of luck with that," he says cryptically. "It's fishing season."

I drop my shoulders. "So I've been told."

"I don't suppose you're here for fishing?" His lips tilt disarmingly, and for a split second I wonder if he's joking. Before I can make a judgment call, it disappears, replaced with another glower.

"Yeah, I'm a pro angler," I say, tone rife with sarcasm. "Look, can you please just make an exception? I have to pee. Badly. I'll pay double," I offer. I even toss in a pouty lip. There goes my last shred of dignity. "You can even have my kidney, struggle-free. I won't fight it."

The joke doesn't land. He's about to wave a dismissive hand at me when a shrill voice bellows from the room off the parlor.

"Evan! Why are you being such a dickwad? This is not how you treat guests." A woman barrels around the corner and gives Evan a smack on the bicep.

She looks about my age, rail thin, with thick, fire-engine-red hair. She's dressed in an oversize sweater with multicolor patchwork that looks like something Crystal and Tara's grandma Flo would crochet.

She must be his wife. Pity overtakes me on her behalf. Having to deal with this man's mood day in and day out would be a special kind of torture. Maybe I should pull her aside and subtly ask if she needs saving. I'd be prepared to smuggle her over the border in the name of sisterhood.

"She's not a guest." Evan crosses his arms, tormented, as the woman sidles up next to him, greeting me with a wide toothy smile that just radiates good intentions.

"I *am* a guest," I retort.

"You're not."

"I am." Jesus, I feel like a small child.

"Just because you say it over and over doesn't make it true," he says, gaze searing.

"Ignore him. He gets like this when he hasn't eaten," the redhead advises with an exaggerated eye roll.

I raise a brow. I get hangry too, and you don't see me lashing out at innocent strangers.

She goes on her tiptoes, extending her pale, bony hand over the desk. She hip checks Evan out of the way in the process, which gives me a pang of satisfaction. Realistically, her tiny size-two frame is no match for him. He moves because she wants him to move, which makes me feel guilty for assuming she's a helpless housewife. She strikes me as a woman who demands to be noticed and gives zero fucks. I like her already.

"I'm Lucy. What's your name and where ya from?" She has a countryish twang in her voice that's much different from Southern accents in the States. It's a little slower, with a heavier emphasis on the vowels.

"Melanie Karlsen—Mel," I say, taking her hand, thankful to be saved from this caveman. "I'm from Boston."

Lucy lets out an impressive whistle. "An American. What brings you up here?"

I explain my reservation mix-up, determined to ignore Evan's scowl. "I'm a fashion influencer. I came to capture some lifestyle content, see the sights, maybe check out some lighthouses."

"Well, you've come to the right place, then. We have more lighthouses in our area than the entire province combined. Hook Lookout just got a makeover by Garth. Just in time for tourist season. Though Ruth Fraser's been lobbying to get it repainted. She claims the stripes are too thin and that it's damaging her retinas," she adds with a slow shake of the head.

Before I can begin to ask what any of that means, she elbows an unimpressed Evan out of the way again and starts typing furiously on the keyboard. Her nails are painted lilac, with the exception of her ring fingers, which are a glittery silver. "Don't mind him. I'm getting you the room with the good lighting, for photos. And it has the best view in the whole house."

Evan casts her a ferocious glare. "Seriously, Luce? Tonight, of all nights?"

"Six nights, you said?" she confirms, ignoring Evan like he's but a speck of dust.

"Yes, please."

While Lucy photocopies my ID and plucks a skeleton key from the corkboard behind the desk, she instructs Evan to carry my luggage to my room. He frowns at my bags like they've been dipped in a radioactive substance before begrudgingly hauling them toward the stairs as though they weigh nothing.

"Oh, um, I can take them myself," I offer weakly, grabbing at my tote and carry-on.

He doesn't seem to hear me as he motors up the staircase, luggage in tow, leading me through a long, narrow hallway lined with doors. To my left, the hallway juts into an entirely separate wing.

The outdated floral wallpaper from the photographs in the ad has been peeled off in the hallway, with random bits and jagged sections still clinging to the wall. It's as if someone ripped it all off in one careless stroke and didn't bother to go back for the smaller, stubborn strips.

"Thanks for carrying my bags. You didn't have to do that," I say genuinely. Despite what he may assume, I'm used to doing things for myself.

Evan discards my luggage with a careless *thud* outside the farthest door on the left. "Your five-star presidential suite awaits," he jeers. The skeleton key jingles in his hand as he unlocks the door.

Bracing myself, I lean forward to peer inside. A tiny shudder runs through me when my shoulder accidentally brushes against his warm, rock-solid chest in the process. Curse him for taking up so much space.

When the door swings open with a toe-curling *creak*, I recoil, failing to mask my cringe. A flick of the light reveals the heavy oak wainscoting, which is the only thing that breaks up the overwhelmingly blue walls. A hefty-looking four-poster bed with turned spindles and a lobster-print grandma quilt sits in the middle of the room. There's a massive window to the right, draped in the heaviest of fabrics, clad with an Astoria valance that belongs to the 1930s and shouldn't have left. I'd have preferred something from this century, but beggars can't be choosers.

Evan catches my less-than-enthusiastic expression before I have the chance to fake a smile. He's surely delighting in my horror. "Glamorous enough for you?"

I spare Evan an indignant look, switching tactics. Being pleasant isn't getting me anywhere with him. Maybe it's time to meet his blatant sarcasm. "It's more than perfect. But please come back in exactly thirteen minutes to run my milk bath. I like it at exactly a hundred and three degrees. Rose petals would be a nice touch too."

His jaw twitches, and for a second I think he's about to throw another jab. But instead he just spins around, disappearing in a blur of fury and flannel.

As I inwardly pat myself on the back for winning that round, Lucy appears. She drags my luggage from the hallway to the foot of my bed, high ponytail bobbing up and down with each step. This tiny woman is freakishly strong. What she lacks in height, she makes up for in boundless energy.

She takes the liberty of flopping on the end of my bed like she's at a slumber party, eagerly spectating as I deposit my things on the upholstered antique ottoman. I plaster on a fake smile and give her an exaggerated nod as I kick my boots off.

"There's a pamphlet if you need ideas for things to do around the village," she informs me, pointing to the stack of colorful brochures in a dusty plastic holder atop the dresser. There's another hand-carved lobster next to it—except this one is wearing a ballerina tutu. I turn it over to find the initials *J. W.* drawn in black Sharpie. "My grandpa carved those lobsters. One for each room in the house," she explains, before continuing on about Cora's Cove. "Anyway, if you run into Ray Jackson at the waterfront, which you will, because he loves newbies, always have an out. The man likes to talk. He'll trap you, and the next thing you know, he'll have told you his whole life story, from his conception over at the old movie theater to his athlete's foot." When she sees the concerned look on my face, she adds, "Don't worry, I'll give you the full rundown tomorrow at breakfast. The week will fly by. You'll see."

"Thanks, Lucy," I squeak, eager for serenity after a long day.

She lingers, running a finger over the edge of the quilt. I get the feeling she wants to stay and chat. As much as I love girl talk, making conversation with a peppy stranger is the last thing I want to do right now. When I yawn and stretch my arms theatrically over my head, she gets the hint, stands, and wishes me a good night.

The moment the door closes, I'm blanketed in uneasy silence.

I can't help but feel guilty for being so short with Lucy. Maybe this is why I have exactly two friends.

To fight the loneliness, I text Julian, How are you? followed by a brief explanation that I'll be staying an extra week.

Within seconds, he FaceTimes me. "You're staying an extra week?" He's flopped on my couch lopsidedly, overgrown blond hair drooping over his left eye.

I grimace. "Is that okay?"

"Why wouldn't it be? Seriously, Mel, don't worry about me. And you don't have to text me every night while you're gone," he points out.

"That's just the price you pay for being my favorite person in the world," I assure him, letting out a tiny sigh of relief. He seems to be taking this news well.

"Aren't you supposed to be relaxing in some darkened sensory-deprivation room? Balancing your chakras? Healing emotional trauma through the chime of ancient Tibetan gongs or some shit?"

"Hey, don't knock sound therapy till you try it. And . . . well, it's a long story." I leave it vague so as not to burden him with my travel complications.

"All I'm saying is, don't drink the mysterious drug-laced smoothies." There's an undeniable glint of Mom in his rueful expression. The flawlessly proportioned features full of clean, angular lines translate differently on him. Where Mom's face is unchanging, feelings veiled, guarded behind velvet rope—even from her own children—Julian is a bundle of emotions, all of which are written on his face long before he'll verbalize them.

Unlike Julian, I don't resemble our mom, or our dad for that matter. My parents struggled to conceive for years before adopting me as a baby from China. When I was seven, Julian, the "miracle baby," was born. But even his big gray eyes and cheeky little smile weren't enough to keep Mom around after they went bankrupt and lost everything.

"I just wanted to check in and see how you're doing," I say, steering the conversation back. Evidently, sibling similarities transcend blood, because we've both mastered the art of deflection, thanks to our parents' influence.

"Let's see, I've already stained your white couch, tossed buckets of baby-puke-green paint all over your closet, pissed off your neighbor . . . Oh, and I've burned the entire place down to a crisp. One or two pairs of your high heels are still intact," he deadpans, smiling only when I give him a stern look. "Kidding, kidding. Well, not about the couch stain. Or the neighbor thing. The little creep called building security on me when I caught him slipping a weird-ass poem under your door."

I sigh. "Ugh. Ian. If he gets to be too much, let me know and I'll call his dad."

"You need a restraining order."

"Trust me, I've considered it. Seriously, though, how are you doing?"

"I'm exactly the same as when you left. Don't stress. You deserve to relax without worrying about me."

"Are you sure? I mean, it's my first trip since . . ."

His pale gray eyes roll so far back into his head, I'm afraid they'll stay there permanently. He does this when I'm acting like an overprotective mom. "I'm not in the same place I was when you went to Spain."

A couple months after Dad died, I got an influencer opportunity to go to Spain for a week. While I felt guilty about leaving Julian, I needed the money to pay my mortgage.

Two days later, I rushed home early after he didn't return my calls or texts for twenty-four hours. I don't know how to explain it, but I knew in my gut something was wrong. My instincts were correct. When I got home, I found him in a depressive state, deep in a grief spiral he only barely climbed out of weeks later.

"You're literally the only other person I have in the world," he'd said to me. Being truly alone had hit him hard because, for the first time, he had to process the grief without me there to distract him. And while I had my own grief to work through, it was easier to focus on *his* instead.

If I'm being honest, over the years, I've relied on Julian for emotional support just as much as he's relied on me. We needed each other, spending hours watching the horror B movies we used to watch with Dad when we were way too young and playing old board games. I thought we were grieving in a healthy way, keeping things outwardly positive, reminiscing about Dad's quirks, like how he used to swear by ketchup sandwiches.

"Do you think you'll try applying for jobs tomorrow?" I venture. Lately, he's been interested in figuring out his career again. His aspirations have ranged from baking to archaeology to high-end real estate.

"Yup. Promised you I would," he drones.

"And remember, I left the passwords to your LinkedIn and Indeed accounts on the scented hot-pink sticky note on your laptop."

"I'm allergic to those scented sticky notes." He frowns, only righting his face when I give him a disapproving look. "Why did you make me new accounts? I already have accounts."

"Your profile was not professional. I had no choice but to start from scratch," I inform him, referring to the five-year-old casual shot of him in a vintage band tee on a sunlit patio, a pitcher of beer half in frame.

"Damn, you're extra today. You're lucky I love you."

I smile. "I love you too."

"And, FYI, I'm doing better than ever. Made a therapy appointment too," he mutters, stretching his arms over his head.

I take a second to collect myself in an attempt to disguise my trepidation. Sometimes when Julian tries to convince me he's *better than ever*, it can mean the opposite. But seeing his grief counselor again is a positive step. "I'm glad to hear. Let me know how it goes. And remember, I'll be back in two weeks, and I'll check in every day," I tell him, even if he'd rather I didn't.

I promised Dad years ago that I'd always take care of Julian. And I don't intend to break that promise.

After we hang up, I commence my skin care routine—the perfect calm-down activity when I'm feeling out of control—swap my travel clothes for my pajamas, and slide into bed. The mattress squeaks with the tiniest movement. It's so firm, it feels as though I've draped myself directly over a box spring and called it a day. Chance of sleep tonight: near zilch. Then again, it's preferable to the alternative—my rental car.

When I close my eyes and take in the quiet, Lucy and Evan's conversation is semiaudible from downstairs.

"What kind of people would we be if we tossed her onto the street?" Lucy asks.

"That's beside the point and you know it." The rest of Evan's response is muffled. The stomp of his heavy footsteps is the last thing I hear before I drift off to sleep.

❤ chapter four

'M A TERRIBLE sleeper in the best of situations, requiring my fan, bamboo sheets, Purple GelFlex Grid cooling mattress, gel sleep mask, and mindfulness meditation audio to even think about getting a wink of sleep.

Maybe it was all the stress of travel, but I slept solidly through the night for the first time in months—until being awakened by the unrelenting, piercing screech of grinding metal. The sound is truly the auditory equivalent of falling from a balcony twenty stories up.

I rub my eyes and squint through the harsh yellow beam of light streaming through a crack in the heavy drapery. On my way to investigate the source of the commotion, my bare toe disturbs a mound of debris next to the bed, which appears to be a pile of dirt and brown pine needles someone swept but forgot about.

Temples throbbing, I peer out the cobweb-laden window, surveying the grassy lawn below.

It's Evan, of course. He's responding to my presence the only way his teeny-tiny brain knows how: by choosing violence in the form of setting up his table saw directly under my window. What kind of sick Airbnb host wakes up their guests at six thirty in the morning with power tools? Something tells me he's doing this on purpose.

My theory is confirmed when he haughtily runs another slab of wood through the saw and angles his head toward my window. When those frosty eyes lock with mine, something snaps in my chest. He challenges my gaze for what feels like an eternity, until he finally shakes his head and grabs a fresh sheet of plywood, continuing on like I don't exist.

He's in plaid again, only today's is green and blue. I could stand here and thirst over the flex of his biceps as he expertly runs a massive hunk of wood through the saw with intense focus, but rugged men like him aren't my type. Besides, I'm too busy seething like the starved wolf that's probably lurking at the edge of the dense forest behind him.

If Lucy hadn't been so kind last night, I'd be tempted to one-star him for poor customer service. Though, if I'm being honest, I don't have it in me to leave nasty reviews after years of being trolled online.

Speaking of, I park myself on the edge of the hard mattress and pull up the Airbnb listing. Upon my hasty booking, I'd noticed it was rated highly but didn't get a chance to read the reviews. Somehow, they're all five stars. Most praise Lucy and Evan for their hospitality. I can't understand who would praise Evan for *hospitality*, of all things. Maybe they just feel bad for Lucy. One review specifically notes how kind Mr. Evan Whaler was, coming to their rescue after the motor failed on their boat rental. Another guest thanks him for driving halfway to Halifax to help change a flat tire. All these reviews read like fiction to me. Evan probably wrote them himself from multiple burner accounts.

How have I made an enemy so quickly? Sure, I might have bitched about the state of the inn last night when I didn't realize he was within earshot. But I didn't say anything that wasn't true, aside from the black market organ thievery. And if you ask me, it's still too premature to rule that out.

As I contend with the shower (with lobster-print shower curtain), which goes from piping hot to frigid every two seconds, I run through various versions of an apology I'm not sure I'll ever say out loud, probably because I have serious doubts Evan even deserves it. I'm here for only a week, after all. Is this dude's uninformed opinion of me even relevant? Besides, who wouldn't be a little emotional when they're on the verge of sleeping in their car in the middle of nowhere in a foreign country?

Things go downhill after my shower when I spot a plump, juicy spider in the corner, curled up near the power outlet where I've plugged in my hair dryer. It's one of those thick-bodied spiders you'd have to crunch with force in order to kill. I shudder at the mere thought.

I haul ass out of the bathroom immediately, closing the door behind me so the eight-legged monster can't escape and plant eggs in my face. Haphazardly, I empty the contents of one suitcase onto my bed and throw on my floral jumpsuit as fast as humanly possible.

The moment I reach the stairwell, makeup bag still in hand, the smell of bacon hits my nostrils. I follow the scent through the construction-zone parlor and through another doorway, which leads to an elegant red dining room connected to a kitchen at the back of the house.

"Boston!" Lucy greets me with a singsong voice while flipping the sizzling bacon on the stovetop like a show-off amateur chef. "Whattaya think?" She does a double pirouette for dramatic flair, grease-dipped spatula in hand. Today's ensemble is hot-pink leggings paired with a green polka-dot dress.

"I don't think there's another soul on this planet that could pull off that color combination," I tell her. And I mean it. While it's certainly not my style, she deserves props. Not everyone would be so bold.

"My ex used to call my style 'unicorn puke.'" There's a sour inflection in her tone.

I don't know how to respond to that, because that descriptor is honestly too perfect. She's basically JoJo Siwa meets Cyndi Lauper.

"I take that as the highest compliment. I really don't care what people think," she says, jabbing her spatula into the air like a sword, red ponytail swishing with every movement. "Okay, well, actually I do care. I really care."

I nod weakly, taking in the kitchen's aesthetic, which is bright and modern compared to the rest of the house, aside from the floral wallpaper on the wall surrounding the window.

In the light of day, the house doesn't look as haunted as it did last night. In fact, it's quite lived in, with lush history seeping out of every dusty crack and crevice: stunning wood carvings and artistic details in addition to the lobsters in wacky outfits in every room. The kitchen's lobster is completely nude, save for its white chef's hat with tiny cutouts for its antennae.

A collection of photos in mismatched frames of various sizes hangs on the far wall above a small cherrywood writer's desk. The photos depict the owner's family from generations past. Black-and-white posed stone-faced couples, then earthy sepia-toned pictures from the mid-nineteenth century, followed by mid-nineties photos of smiling children. I spot Evan straightaway. The penetrating ice-blue eyes are a dead giveaway. There's a photo of him at about ten posing with a hockey stick in an arena, blond hair curling out from under his helmet. Diagonal to it is a photo of him even younger, probably seven or so, fishing on a sun-drenched dock with a boy who's a couple of inches taller. They look alike, though the taller boy is freckled, with a massive, almost devious grin compared to Evan's, which is more serious and contemplative.

A dull ache tugs at my core as I stare at this century's worth of family history. It feels like something greater than me. And I can't imagine what it feels like to be part of it.

"Hey, feel free to take a seat. Food should be ready in five. Or ten. Probably ten." She points to the less-formal farmhouse table in the turret corner with a rounded bench in the interior that has probably always seated multiple people. Not just one, like my sad dining table at home.

"Um, there's a spider in my bathroom," I announce, scrutinizing my surroundings for any sign of it. You can't be too careful. Those fuckers move fast.

"Oh. That's probably Jarvis." Her tone is troublingly nonchalant as she skips to the far counter to sprinkle sugar over a berry-filled mixing bowl.

My body seizes. "Jarvis?"

Jarvis the spider has taken up permanent residence in my bathroom? Over my dead body. I furrow my brow, not bothering to ask why this spider has a name or why it exists at all.

"He lives in that bathroom," she says far too casually, as though this spider is some sentient being with a soul, a wife, and three children.

No. He's a multilegged bug whose sole existence is to torment city girls like me.

"I . . . I don't do spiders. Could you get rid of it?" I probably sound like a mega bitch, so I add a "Please," followed by a polite smile.

Lucy watches me for a moment, as if she's waiting for a punch line. Her brows dip when she realizes I'm serious. "Oh. Um, okay. I'll move him after breakfast. Is that okay? Hey, take a seat!" She points her spatula toward the bench.

As she fills the table with every breakfast food known to man, including but not limited to pancakes, waffles, eggs (scrambled and sunny-side up), toast, and bacon, she rambles about her daily routine, which includes getting up at four in the morning, going for a run, cleaning the inn (allegedly), and then working at the marina.

"Are you a fisherwoman?" I take a seat against the window, delighting in the warmth of the sun on my back.

She shakes her head like the idea is absurd. "Nah. I get too seasick. Prefer to keep my feet on land if I can help it. I manage the marina. It's kinda like being a hotel manager, except with boats. Mostly makin' sure the facilities are running smoothly, that everything is clean for everyone who docks there. You'd think it'd be easy," she adds defensively, "but you'd be surprised what shit people get up to in those three hundred feet of dock."

"That seems like a lot of responsibility. You must love it, though?"

She turns back to the sizzling pan and gives it a shake. "Yup. I started off as an attendant when I was fourteen. When the last manager retired, Harry, the owner, couldn't decide who should take over: me or his son, Damon, who's about as sharp as this spatula. So he made us do rock paper scissors for it, if you can believe that."

I smirk. "Seriously?"

"Yup. I won because Damon only ever chooses rock. Bless his heart. Now I have to boss that nitwit around on the regular."

"That sounds like a headache," I say, already exhausted at the thought.

"Yup. But I can't picture working some depressing nine-to-five. I'd go mad. And to be honest, emasculating fishermen on the daily is a nice perk." She places a heaping bowl of mint-laced fruit salad in front of me. "So I spent my whole run this morning thinking about things you can do in the village. I know you're waiting to go to that fancy resort for social media stuff, but you may be able to get some great pics here in Cora's Cove. Especially in the historic district. There's the fishing museum and the railway museum, though their hours are . . . random. Whenever Noreen wants to be open, really. Maybe I'll tell Frank to give her a heads-up you're coming. And I'm sure folks would be happy to take your picture since you're here all by your lonesome," she says with a pitying glance.

I shake off her comment. "Um . . . sounds great. How big is the village?"

"The permanent population is about seven hundred, though it

doubles in fishing and tourist season." She pushes a dish of home-made whipped cream toward me. I spoon a heaping dollop on my waffle. Might as well embrace the sugar coma.

"What's Cora's Cove known for, tourist-wise?"

"Drunken sailors," she says with a dark laugh. "Just kidding. Well, not really. The fishermen like to have a good time. But the Cove is actually a UNESCO World Heritage Site. Tourists come here just for the hiking and the nature. Oh, and the whales. You can catch them breachin' in the cove this time of year. Roger told me Luna and her new calf were spotted yesterday in the bay." Before I can ask who Roger and Luna are, she continues. "Hey, want me to arrange a whale-watching tour? I can probably haggle a discount for you. I have connections."

I shift forward in my seat. "I'd love that." A mutual travel influencer went on a whale-watching expedition in Tofino, British Columbia, last year. She captured stunning shots on the water. It's not my typical content, but maybe that's the point. Clearly, I need to restrategize. I consider the various nautical outfits I could wear. Besides, whales are animals. Animals that I'm inclined to believe have feelings and families. Unlike spiders.

Lucy grins, pleased she's come up with something I'm visibly excited about. "I'll see if I can get it arranged for tomorrow morning. In the meantime, I wanna hear all about how you use social media. I tried learning it to market the inn, but all the different apps got overwhelming. Gave up pretty quick."

I light up at the thought. "That's my specialty. I can help you with setting up an account for the inn across all the main platforms if you want."

"Wow, you'd really do that?" she asks hopefully.

"Of course! It's the least I can do as a thank-you for setting up the whale watching."

Before I can offer my opinion on which app would be most suitable for their needs, the front door bursts open, followed by heavy-footed stomping that can belong to only one person. Evan barges through the doorway, work boots unlaced, ball cap on backward like a sixteen-year-old boy. Though he certainly doesn't look sixteen. The moment he spots me at the kitchen table, he emits a tortured sigh.

"What's with all this?" He waves his hand in the direction of my makeup bag as he collapses into the chair across from me. It looks like he's trying to squeeze himself into one of those child-size plastic play tables.

"There's a spider in my bathroom," I tell him, popping a strawberry in my mouth. It's not exactly a solid explanation for why I've moved all my beauty products to the kitchen table, but I get a weird jolt of satisfaction from leaving him hanging.

"So?" he asks, eyes fixed on me as he stacks his plate exclusively with bacon.

"She needs you to relocate Jarvis," Lucy says, tone forceful.

Evan resettles in his seat, in no rush to go anywhere. "I don't have time for that kinda bullshit, thanks."

I mentally flush any possibility of apologizing down the figurative tube.

"Again, ignore him. He'll do it after breakfast," Lucy assures me, shooting him a warning glare as she slides in next to me.

Evan grumbles like a petulant child and reaches his monster-size paw over the table to fetch a piece of toast. In the light of day, I can't help but study his eyes. The rings of navy dissolve into azure, fading to a soft silver, all blending into each other like water-color. They'd be beautiful if they weren't streaked with forest-green currents that probably reflect his desire to sweep me underwater and drown me.

"I'm arranging for Mel to go on a whale-watching boat tour tomorrow," she tells him exuberantly, under the delusion that any-thing to do with me is of interest to him.

Evan grits his teeth. "You don't say."

"Hopefully I can get some decent shots." I hold my attention on Lucy, which is difficult given that Evan's obnoxiously large body takes up so much space directly in front of me.

"Water's probably got too much chop for your liking," Evan decides dismissively, jaw fixed as I dip my strawberry in Lucy's homemade whipped cream.

"And how would you know what I like?"

He clamps his eyes shut, probably praying I'll magically dis-appear into the ether by the time he opens them again.

"Mel's going to help me make a social media account for the inn," Lucy chimes.

No response aside from furious chewing.

I tear my gaze away from the thick line of Evan's eyelashes, which are probably as lush as my lash extensions. I wish I could pluck them out one by one.

"I think before we post any content, updating the paint could go a long way. You'd definitely want to keep the original wood and all the historical details," I start. "And I know you've really leaned into the lobster theme, but you may want to tone it down—"

I stop when Evan's stormy eyes meet mine. "We don't need your help."

There goes that.

"I'd like her help," Lucy insists.

He cuts her a glare, and I'm terrified I've started a fight between them. My enthusiasm instantly dims.

"So how long have you two been together? What's your story?" I jump in, desperate to change the conversation.

I've caught Lucy mid-bite of a heaping forkful of eggs. After a forceful swallow, she descends into maniacal laughter, which inadvertently makes me giggle. "Together?"

The table vibrates because, shockingly, Evan is laughing too. Deeply. I didn't think this man was capable of joy. It feels foreign and, honestly, a little uncomfortable. His face is crimson as he slaps his chest. "We're not that kind of backroad folks," he says, still avoiding my eye contact.

Lucy leans in next to me to clarify. "Me and Evan are cousins. First cousins. Pretty much brother and sister."

Wow. I am a complete and total dumbass. I suppose I can see the faint resemblance. The same wide eyes. Dark, thick brows. The slightest dimples shadowed in the morning light.

"My bad. I just assumed," I explain, addressing Lucy exclusively. "Though it makes sense that you're related. I was starting to wonder why someone as lovely as yourself would voluntarily put up with him."

Lucy snickers into her plate and launches into a long-winded explanation of all the things to do in Cora's Cove.

I do my best to evade Evan's incendiary stare.

♥ chapter five

THE CORA'S COVE waterfront is like a living postcard, if you can ignore the malicious seagulls dive-bombing every few minutes in search of food.

Lucy dropped me off for three hours of exploration while she completes the first half of her shift at the marina. While I'm loving the sleepy seaside vibe, I can't help but feel frustrated by my inability to get a good shot in front of the idyllic clapboard buildings along the harbor, which act as little pops of color—red, green, yellow, and white—a contrast to the darkness of the water.

Taking photos would be so much more enjoyable if I wasn't alone, as Lucy pointed out this morning.

That's the thing no one tells you about being an influencer: it's solitary, despite social media's very purpose of facilitating human connection. Nearly everything I do is alone. Photos. Video tutorials. Editing.

Sure, I made some influencer acquaintances over the years. But if I'm being honest, those relationships always felt transactional. Like the people wanted my friendship only for show, as a means to increase their followers. I also never truly fit in with them. I didn't have a trust fund to kick-start my lifestyle brand or a safety net to fall back on. I couldn't drop three hundred dollars on a fancy lunch. I was the girl renting luxury Airbnbs by the hour to make a month's worth of content so people would think I lived the lifestyle I was selling. The one desperately messaging every clothing and beauty brand, restaurant, hotel, and gym to beg for freebies. And the one who broke down crying two years in when I realized I'd made enough money to buy my very own condo.

The prospect of meeting new friends feels like being tasked to engineer a NASA rocket out of a couple of hunks of warped scrap metal. It's partially why I joined Crystal's gym a couple of years ago, to maintain some semblance of regular human contact.

As I watch two seagulls dive-bomb to battle over a limp, squished, oil-doused french fry, it occurs to me that maybe what I really need is some good conversation.

I'm strolling along the marina in search of human life when a cenotaph comes into view. Two Indigenous totem poles stand proudly side by side along the shoreline.

The closer I get to the marina, the stronger the smell. It's briny, a little fishy, but not overwhelmingly so. The pungent scent is cut by the saltiness of the air. The sky is shrouded with clouds and a dense mist overhanging the dark roofs of the large factorylike buildings lining the docks.

After passing multiple closed restaurants suspiciously advertising the *World's Best Lobster Roll*, I stumble upon a café. Vibrant pointy and rounded leaves weave together to form a canopy of greenery around its perimeter, surrounding exactly four tables, all of which are occupied by patrons aged forty-five and up. Even inside, the high-pitched sound of seagull squabbling carries through the breeze.

The moment I enter, the patrons stop midconversation and stare.

"Hi, there! What can I get for ya?" an eager brunette woman calls out from behind the counter. A hot-pink apron stretches across her heavy chest, which reads *Kitchen Bitch* in curly font.

I give her a warm smile while examining the chalkboard menu behind her, which advertises today's lunch special: *Clam Chowder.* Before I can order, she's already leaning over the counter, inspecting my tote bag.

"Holy shit. Blake Lively has that bag. I was just reading a tabloid article about her." She pulls her phone from a front pocket in her apron and clicks around, eventually turning the screen to me. Sure enough, it's a paparazzi picture of the leggy blonde running errands, with my same tote over her shoulder. She leans in conspiratorially. "Okay, truth time. Do you think Ryan Reynolds is punching above his weight? Because I do."

"Totally. Blake Lively is an absolute dime," I agree.

"Gracie, quit scarin' the tourists with that celebrity nonsense," a heavily mustached man in what appears to be a police uniform hollers from the table next to the window.

Gracie shoots him lasers with her eyes. "Fine, Sheriff. But you'll be sorry when I whip your ass in pop culture trivia next week."

This woman's mind runs a mile a minute. And it doesn't stop for the next ten minutes as I wait for my donair and chowder. The townspeople are all incessantly friendly too, unlike Evan. And to my delight, no one presses me for personal information—even Luther, the village sheriff, and his wife, Bertie, who invite me to sit at their table.

Turns out, Luther and Bertie are huge gossips. In half an hour, I find out that Heather and Jacob Gatwick are on the cusp of divorce after Jacob's torrid affair with the owner of another B and B (not Evan and Lucy's). Danielle Dubrow is either with child or has just been wearing unflattering outfits of late. And Matt Paulson is hitting the bottle again (he hasn't been the same since the boating accident last season).

While most patrons seem comfortable lingering long after their meal, I'm still used to the city, where restaurants want you out the moment you take your last bite. Once I'm done with my meal, I bid Gracie goodbye, mildly disappointed in myself for not enjoying the company longer.

As I head back onto Main Street, there's a man lingering outside.

"You must be a newcomer!" he exclaims. The vigor in his voice doesn't match his physical appearance. He's thin, gaunt, and at least eighty, with a weathered, leathery face from many a day out at sea. "I'm Ray," he declares, extending his bony, sunspotted hand.

Lucy warned me about him. She told me to have an out so he doesn't talk my ear off. But when I look at him, he just seems like a lonely old man. Why else would he be desperate to chat with randos on the street? The last thing I want to do is turn him away.

I take his hand and give it a light shake so as not to break him. "I'm Mel. From Boston."

"My great-uncle was from Boston."

"Really? Ever been?"

This is his opening to tell me his life story like Lucy warned me. For the next hour and a half, we walk up and down the docks as he tells me all about his conception during a showing of *Pinocchio* and how he was forced to stop sailing when he tore his ACL. He tells me all about his late wife, Julia, and their three children.

Frankly, I'm a little disappointed when he remembers he has a dentist appointment and heads off with a friendly wave and tip of the hat. It felt nice talking to him and everyone else I met today, even if they did ninety-nine percent of the talking.

For the next half hour, I capture a couple of selfies, running them through my usual filters before posting them in my stories. They don't get nearly the traction that I'd hoped, which only heightens the tightness in my ribs.

The thought of winding up like my parents, who lived beyond their means to the point of bankruptcy, fills me with an over-whelming, soul-sucking sickness.

It's not just the stifling financial implications and my blatant fear of debt and bills. Losing followers and collaboration partners isn't just business. It's personal. Because if people no longer buy into my brand, they no longer buy into me. As a person. And what does it say about me if I can't get people to like me—the best version of me—even behind a filter?

• • •

BEFORE DINNER, I tiptoe into my bathroom to assess the situation, judo-kicking the door open like an FBI agent in an action-packed crime series. I peek into the corner where Jarvis was lurking this morning. He's nowhere to be seen.

Given Evan's disinterest in removing him, the natural conclusion is that the spider is lying in wait, ready to pounce. I back out slowly and hightail it downstairs to the kitchen. Lucy is preparing food while Evan is on the floor, lying on his back, head underneath the sink, long legs extended outward, tinkering with a pipe.

"Did one of you remove the bathroom spider?" I practically scream in a panicked lilt.

Lucy prods Evan's shin with her hot-pink-socked foot. "Did you get rid of Jarvis?"

He mumbles something under his breath, barely audible.

"Well, I don't know where it went. I can't use that bathroom until I know it's gone."

Evan inches out from below the sink to peer at me like I'm flattened roadkill decaying in the sun. The heat from his scowl shoots up my neck, into my cheeks. "You do realize that type of spider can't hurt you?"

"You do realize that phobias are, by definition, irrational fears? Look it up," I retort, hand on hip.

When he rolls his eyes, Lucy gives him a swift kick in the shin again. He clears his throat. "He's gone," he finally says, refocusing on the pipe.

"Yes. The problem is, where? I won't sleep knowing he could be anywhere. Crawling above my head. Dangling from the ceiling. On my face. Burrowing into my skin, laying hundreds of eggs ready to hatch all at once—"

Evan groans. This man is angstier than my preteen diary entries. "Jesus, woman. He's outside."

"Outside?" I look to Lucy for assurance. She looks just as confused as I am. "How would you know?"

He waits a long, frustrating beat. "Because I put him there."

"You touched it? Transported it with your own two hands?"

He emits a maddening sigh. "No, teleported it with my magic powers."

I blink in disbelief, ignoring his sarcasm. "And you just thought you'd keep that tidbit to yourself? Until I made a big deal about it?"

No response.

"Why would you remove it?" I finally ask, twirling my hair between my fingers, an old habit.

"So I wouldn't have to listen to you bitch about it for the rest of your stay."

I cross my arms, unconvinced. "I'm gonna need to see proof."

"Go look for yourself. He's on the porch."

That's still too close for comfort. And, frankly, I'm still not sure I believe him.

"He removed it, Mel," Lucy promises. "If he had the option to keep up the emotional torture, he would have. But Evan doesn't lie."

This is a plot twist. Evan actually removed the spider. I don't know how to feel about it. Do I owe him? Nah. Definitely not.

Lucy shakes her head like a disgruntled mother before clapping her hands toward me. "So, me an' Evan were wondering—"

Evan clears his throat. "You mean *you* were wondering."

"*We* were wondering if you're interested in coming to the Anchor with us tonight. It's totally okay if you'd rather stay in, though. But I thought it might be fun to meet some people from town and grab a drink or two."

"What's the Anchor?" I ask.

"The local pub. They have to-die-for deep-fried pickles. You'll have to try them. And tonight is half-price shots." She gives me an enticing wink.

I'd originally planned to spend the evening brainstorming outfit ideas and vicious insults for Evan. But Lucy looks so hopeful, and I'd feel silly passing on an opportunity to meet new people. I've also never been one to turn down a deep-fried pickle, so I smile and say, "I'm in."

♥ chapter six

THE ENTIRE ADULT population of Cora's Cove is at the Anchor. There's not a square inch of this musky bar that isn't packed wall-to-wall with bodies. Then again, it is the one and only bar in town, according to Lucy.

The walls are adorned with a mix of lifebuoys, rope, and anchor decor; taxidermized fish (all of which are watching me); and license plates from various provinces in Canada, all topped with half-burnt-out, festive multicolored lights unevenly draped along the ceiling. Lively folk music, heavy on the accordion and fiddle, vibrates through the speakers.

As we wade through the plaid-wearing crowd, Evan plows ahead of us. I assume he doesn't want to be associated with me. I watch from afar as he greets just about everyone. The very notion of walking into a club in Boston and knowing literally every single patron is laughable. Halfway through the bar, Evan falls into jovial conversation with a guy wearing a T-shirt with his own face plastered on it. It's shocking that a grump like Evan even has friends.

I stay close at Lucy's heels as we make our way through the small space. She sticks out like a porcupine at a nude beach in her chartreuse blazer with literal shoulder pads and high-waisted plaid pants paired with a chunky belt. Five dollars from Walmart, apparently. One would assume that outfit is the sole reason everyone is turning their heads as we part the sea of bodies.

But no. It's me.

I might as well be from another planet. My pleather skirt and heels probably don't help. And this is underdressed by Boston standards.

Lucy senses my hesitation and tugs me toward the bar.

"I feel like everyone is staring," I whisper. "Are they planning to hunt me for sport?"

"I mean, you're new, you're hot, you're no one's ex, and you're not related to anyone in town. You're basically a fresh, bloody carcass in open waters," she explains, leaning both elbows comfortably on the sticky-looking edge of the bar.

A tattooed young bartender with a soul patch winks at us. "Who's your friend?" he asks Lucy, as if I'm not there. He steals a borderline-creepy glance my way, flirty expression disappearing when his eyes flick behind my shoulder.

"None of your business," a booming voice informs him, minty breath tickling my ear. Evan.

I cast a sour look over my shoulder before defiantly turning back. "I'm Melanie. From Boston."

Before the bartender can respond, Evan inserts himself

between Lucy and me, taking up more than his fair share of space, tree-trunk arms resting over the bar. "What do you guys want to drink?"

"If you're buying, we'll take two Screech Rum cocktails and two shots of whiskey. Oh, and deep-fried pickles," Lucy adds.

Evan smirks. "You really think this girl can handle Screech and whiskey?"

I give him a sharp poke in the ribs, wishing I could summon the courage to jab a little harder. "Again with the assumptions of what I can and can't handle."

"I just didn't take you for a hard liquor kind of girl."

I hold his searing blue gaze. "There's a lot you don't know about me."

He raises his brow in what I interpret as a challenge before turning back to the bartender, parroting Lucy's order. I watch, confused, as he slides a twenty-dollar bill over the bar and refuses the change.

By the time the bartender returns with our drinks and shots, Evan has disappeared into the crowd empty-handed.

"What's Evan's deal?" I ask Lucy.

She gestures for me to lean in closer. "Ryan, the bartender . . . we grew up with him. He's nice, but he can be a bit pervy and desperate with out-of-towners. Evan was just watching out for you in his own weird way."

I nearly choke on my own saliva. *Watching out* for me? Someone he can barely stand to breathe the same air as? Highly unlikely.

Oblivious to my skepticism, Lucy holds up one shot to cheers. I don't want to disappoint her, so I immediately reach for the other shot glass, knowing I'll regret it later.

"Cheers to . . ." I ponder for a moment. "Standing out in a crowd?"

"Hell yes." She clinks my shot glass enthusiastically.

The alcohol burns all the way down. I cringe, shivering as I set it on the sticky bar. Lucy laughs and nudges me to the left toward a semicircular booth, potent-smelling Screech cocktails in hand. In the booth, Evan sits with three guys, all in flannel except one who's wearing a hoodie.

The moment we approach, all of them leap out of the booth (except Evan), hands extended like proper gentlemen, which is pretty adorable.

"Mel, this is the crew," Lucy announces, gesturing like they're a prize on a game show.

She jabs her index finger toward the guy on the far left, who looks like a literal giant even seated. I didn't know it was possible to be broader shouldered than Evan. "This is Kyle. He and I go back to kindergarten, back when he used to eat glue sticks."

Kyle sticks his hand out for a strong shake. "Hey, that was one time. On a dare. I have a sophisticated palate now."

I'm then introduced to Johnny. He's quieter, more reserved than Kyle, but seemingly a nice guy. "From Baw-ston?" he confirms, mocking the stereotypical Boston accent as we shake hands.

"Technically still an East Coaster," I point out, daintily sipping my drink.

A facetious smile stretches across his face as he tilts his hand back and forth. "You're American, though. We'll try not to hold it against you."

Not to be ignored, Kyle leans in again. "I have a distant second cousin who lives in the States. She got her PhD," he explains in the midst of gulping the rest of his beer.

"Looks like the family intelligence skipped right on over you," quips a stocky guy with shaggy, overgrown hair. He extends a hand across the table. "I'm Dustin. With a *D*, not a *J*."

"And you already know Evan," Lucy says.

I toss him a bored side-eye as I slide into the booth next to him. When my bare thigh accidentally grazes his, he abruptly shifts over, less than impressed by our proximity, as if I'm molten lava. "Unfortunately."

Kyle eyes the two of us with a twinkling smirk. "What's Whaler done now?"

Before I can respond with a list of grievances, Dustin leans over Evan to theater-whisper to me, "Whaler's a thirteen-year-old girl on the inside. Don't take anything he says personally."

"Says the guy still living in Mom's basement," Evan chirps back.

Dustin shrugs, unashamed. "Hey, beats doin' my own laundry."

"What do you think of the Cove?" Johnny asks, recapturing my attention.

I don't know how to answer that, so I deflect. "What do I think of the Cove . . . well, everyone dresses the same," I point out, nodding toward his shirt, navy plaid. "I'm a little scared you're all one big cult."

He gives me a throaty laugh. "Yeah. I'm the leader."

Kyle gives him a hard thwack on the head, knocking off his hat. "Fuck off, man. Everyone knows I'd be the leader. I got the charisma."

While the two argue about who is the worthiest of cult worship, Dustin tells me all the things I need to accomplish while I'm here, including but not limited to catching the town's Naked Cowboy in the buff while doing manual labor in his yard, visiting the shoe tree (full of abandoned shoes strung from the branches by their laces), and eating a lobster poutine from Nelly's on the wharf (not Rusty's).

They all talk about Cora's Cove like it's alive. Like it's an entity, not a place. The enthusiasm in their voices and their expressions is contagious. So much so, I'm suddenly very eager and willing to do it all.

At one point, Evan, Johnny, and Dustin disappear and the lights dim. Lucy nudges me when the bartender grabs the microphone to announce tonight's musical entertainment, which he refers to as "the band," no name.

Three band members take the stage. Johnny is first, behind a drum set, followed by Dustin carrying a guitar. A massive dude, also in plaid, is the last to take his position under the glare of the spotlight. I do a double take, craning my neck. Front and center with a guitar is Evan.

I blink multiple times to ensure the alcohol isn't inducing delusions. I didn't peg Evan as the musical type. But he's up there, holding the guitar with so much ease I begin to wonder if he has a more attractive, better-natured twin.

With the first strum of the guitar, the crowd goes wild, cheering, clapping, whistling, and hollering random things that make the guys smile, even Evan. They're playing "Galway Girl"—the original (not the Ed Sheeran version). I only recognize it from *P.S. I Love You*, which Tara made me watch as part of one of her biannual cryfest marathons last year (because "crying is therapeutic").

Turns out, that gruff, harsh voice works when Evan is singing. I'm no musical expert, but I've been around Julian's old band enough to appreciate a strong baritone singing voice. It's hypnotizing. Practically fatal.

Evan's haunting voice booms through my chest, filling me with a cloud of emotion I can't quite describe. There's an almost raw quality to his voice, yet it never breaks unless it's on purpose. It's infinite. Effortless.

In this moment, there's an unfamiliar warmth to him that I can't pinpoint. Maybe it's in the way the spotlight catches the flippy ends of his hair. Or how his ice-planet eyes look more like calm seawater from my vantage point. There's no way someone like Evan could make magic like this—magic that grounds everyone in this bar in one single moment in time.

Our eyes snag for a couple of beats toward the end of the song. I hold his gaze as he launches into the bridge. I'm expecting that cold I-want-to-strangle-you-in-your-sleep glare, but it stays warm, sentimental, as if he's lost in the song.

The rest of the guys chime in, adding some higher falsetto notes, which differentiate the song a bit from the original.

"He's good, isn't he?" Lucy asks. She's giving me a sideways grin, probably because I've been staring at Evan the entire time, mouth open.

I nod reluctantly. Credit where credit is due. Not to be dramatic, but I think his voice may be an assault weapon to my ovaries.

The next song is a Beatles cover of "With a Little Help from My Friends." Everyone vibrates as one, singing along, including Lucy and Kyle, who claims he has no musical talent. In fact, they're singing *at* each other, making eye contact, tossing their arms over each other's shoulders.

When Lucy pulls me in to join their singfest, I feel compelled to sing along. And by the time the song comes to an end, I come to a realization. Sitting here in a dingy bar of strangers in the middle of nowhere is the least alone I've felt in a long, long time.

♥ chapter seven

T'S EVAN WHO hauls me out of the truck, legs first, like I'm a sack of potatoes.

"Ouch!" I scream when he pinches my ankles. "Go on without me. I'll be fine in here." And I'm not kidding. The mere thought of being vertical makes me want to hurl.

I don't know how it happened, but I've had at least ten shots tonight. When the band's set ended, Kyle brought over a tray of shots, followed by another on the house. My eyelids are no longer operating at full functionality by the time Lucy, Evan, and I return to the inn. In fact, the entire ride home was a total blur. Probably because I was in and out of consciousness in the back seat, scream-singing "Hey Jude."

"Yeah, I'm not letting you throw up in my truck," he says curtly, like he's acutely aware my stomach is doing flip-flops at this very moment. Smug in his sobriety, he's certainly relishing my discomfort.

"Mel, do you need a bucket?" Lucy asks. Before I can nod in the affirmative, she's already halfway up the porch. "I'll go get one ready in your room," she says, trotting inside, leaving Evan to deal with me.

He pulls me halfway out of the truck, until my feet are on the ground but my torso is still lopsided against the door. "You're gonna need to stand up," he growls into my ear. The vibration of his voice sends an illicit shiver down my back. Our eyes lock for a moment, and I register that the calm water of his eyes has turned darker in the night, like the depths of the ocean. Who knows what terrifying creatures dwell beneath.

"Um, I don't know if I can stand," I manage, wobbling. These shoes weren't made for gravel driveways. Or drunk wearers.

My ear and cheek graze his chest as I teeter over, stealing a quick sniff of that crisp, woodsy campfire smell. It would be marginally comforting if he wasn't looking at me like he wants to toss me into the ditch.

He lets out a perturbed sigh and does the unthinkable: he swings me over his shoulder and fireman carries me up the driveway as though I'm a weightless doll, despite being north of a size ten. From this angle, I'm privy to a nice upside-down view of his ass. Though this position doesn't do much for my nausea.

"Put me down! My underwear is showing," I demand as a gust of wind hits my ass cheeks. At least I'm wearing a cute lace thong.

"Rest assured, I'm not looking," he mutters as I flail like an eel the entire ascent up the staircase. He doesn't put me down until we're outside my bedroom.

"I'm taking a star off your Airbnb review for manhandling," I warn as he attempts to steady me against the wall just as Lucy passes by with a mini garbage can.

"Double bagged. Just in case. Looks like she might need it," she says, giving Evan a troubled look as she turns to get out of my vicinity. "Sorry, I'm out. I don't do puke. Night, guys."

"I won't puke. I'm feeling fan-tas-tic!" I shout after her with unfounded confidence. I push the door open the tiniest crack, revealing the disaster I left my room in. My cheeks flush with embarrassment. I'm a secret slob—someone who looks neat and tidy to others but is most comfortable in my own chaos (when no one's looking).

"I can take it from here," I assure Evan, righting myself.

His expression is quizzical. "No. You can barely stand."

"I'm *great*. You can retire to your underground candlelit lair now." I take an eager stride into my room, which to me was pretty smooth, but apparently I'm useless.

He leads me to the bench at the foot of the bed, where I proceed to topple face-first into the mattress, legs spread like a mannequin. The compromising position isn't lost on me.

"I feel the need to warn you, I have some pretty lethal hair spray. Just as effective as bear mace, according to *Cosmo*," I say, voice muffled by the mattress.

"What are you gonna do? Blind me with it?" he asks, bending over to retrieve it from under the bed.

"If you try anything, I'll have no choice."

"You don't have to worry about that, Mel." He softens his tone considerably, which is comforting. I'm pretty sure this is the first time he's ever referred to me by name.

Any lingering appreciation is short-lived when he jabs my shoulder without an ounce of delicacy. I must have drifted out of consciousness for a minute or two, because when I open my eyes again, Evan is placing a garbage bin next to me.

"It's right beside the bed if you need it," he says slowly, like I'm a small child. "Do you need me to ask Lucy to help you change? A glass of water?"

"No. I'm perfectly fine," I mumble, flopping over onto my side. He's weirdly attractive from a horizontal perspective, and I don't like it one bit.

He watches me for a couple of peaceful breaths before abruptly pivoting on his heel. "This is going in your Airbnb guest review, by the way."

I glare at him, blowing at the hair stuck to my lip gloss. "The intoxication? Or my veiled threat?"

"Both. Mostly the drunk part. I did warn you about the Screech," he reminds me, hands flexing at his sides.

"It wasn't the Screech. Your friends were the ones pouring shots down my throat. Who am I to deny Canadian hospi-taly?"

He cocks his head. "Hospi*tality*, you mean. And you're wasted."

"Perfectly sober," I mumble, sliding under the covers without taking my shoes off.

"Wears shoes in bed. Another star off," he mutters.

"Mean host. One and a half stars off," I retort, squeezing my eyes shut when the room starts to spin.

"Scratched the shit out of me with those claws. Minus two stars," he says, pretending to rub a hand over his shoulder. I definitely scratched him while holding on for dear life as he hauled me up the stairs.

"Hey, I paid a lot for these nails."

Despite my questionable eyesight in my current state, I'm pretty sure I catch his lips draw upward into the tiniest smile before my eyes close.

♥ chapter eight

E VAN DOESN'T EAT breakfast with Lucy and me.

Lucy spots me eyeing Evan's empty chair across the table. "He's working in town early this morning." She swiftly volunteers this information as if I asked, which I certainly did not.

Personally, I'm thankful for his absence, because it means I can delay thanking him for carrying me to bed, however rough and rude he was. I also look a straight-up mess. It's ten in the morning and I still haven't gathered the strength to change out of last night's outfit.

"What's Evan's day job, anyway?" I swallow my melon with a wince. My head is still throbbing, but luckily that's the extent of my hangover.

"He's a lobster fisherman. Our whole family was in the business. Including our grandfather," she tells me, inadvertently dipping a pom-pom from the sleeve of her oversize sweater in bacon grease. That explains the aggressive lobster-themed decor.

"A fisherman? Really?" Oddly enough, I didn't peg him for a fisherman. Probably because it's hard to picture him doing anything other than haunting the grounds of the inn, terrorizing unsuspecting guests day and night.

She frowns. "Oh, shoot. Sorry if fishing upsets you. If it helps, he's not some huge commercial trawling fisherman destroying the oceans. He does small sustainable catches, mostly for local businesses. Most of his income actually comes from tourism. Fishing charters and stuff," she explains.

I raise my brow. Painting him in an environmentally conscious light does little to save his already waterlogged reputation with me. Though I suppose I can respect the family loyalty. "Are you sure he's not a crab fisherman? It would be more suited to his personality," I say with a dark laugh.

"Sorry about my cousin," she adds with a dutiful nod. "He hasn't been the friendliest. I swear, he's a good guy. But he can be a little touchy about the inn."

"Touchy? Why?"

"It's a long story. Basically, it's . . . on a bit of a hiatus right now."

"A hiatus?"

"We aren't actually open to guests. We've been tryin' to fix it up so we can list it on the market. That's why Evan was giving you a hard time when you arrived."

My stomach dips with embarrassment, recalling how I practically demanded to stay here like a diva. I shift in my seat, suddenly feeling like an intruder. "Oh my god. I'm so sorry. I just assumed Evan was being an asshole when he said the inn was closed, since it was still on Airbnb."

"It's my bad. I forgot to take down the listing. See? Technology is not my strength. It's totally cool, though. We could use the money, and as long as you don't mind the mess . . ." Her cheeks tinge a deep shade of pink.

"Why are you selling this place?" I ask, immediately regretting asking such a personal question of someone I technically just met days ago.

Lucy averts her stare to the stove top. "It's been in our family forever. My mom and Evan's mom are sisters. They haven't spoken in four years. They've been in a legal battle over what to do with the inn since my grandpa died and Nana went into assisted living. My mom wants to sell. His mom doesn't. Unfortunately, no one can afford to keep it. It's a money pit. So Evan and I are kind of . . . filling in until it sells."

"If it's being put on the market, why is Evan bothering to do all these renos?"

"He's still holding out hope that fixing things up will bring in more guests and more revenue and change my mom's mind. That's why I was asking if you could help with some social media marketing. But honestly, I'm not sure there's enough marketing or guests in the world to turn us a profit at this point . . ." She lets out a weary sigh, quickly replacing it with a forced smile. "Anyway, Evan is just weird about outside opinions."

Still, nothing about this long-winded explanation makes me sympathize with Evan. "He sounds like a delightful creature. You're an angel for putting up with him," I say through a sip of steaming green tea.

"That's what family does," she says with a simple shrug.

Something about that statement sits at the base of my stomach. Maybe that's why Evan is so touchy about and protective of the inn. Its deep family history feels special in a way I can't fully understand, probably because I've never lived anywhere longer than single-digit years.

As I help Lucy tidy the kitchen after breakfast, I think about my own family, or lack thereof. How my mom's side outright stopped talking to Julian and me after the divorce. How Mom up and left without looking back.

• • •

FOR TODAY'S WHALE-WATCHING excursion, I opt for a ruffled, striped off-the-shoulder maxi dress paired with a strappy Spanish wedge. Lucy warned me it'll be cold on the water, so I grab a denim jacket before she drives me all the way to the docks, lined with boats of every size and variety.

The shrill call of the seagulls is even louder today as I step out of the car into the harsh seaside wind. The sky is a foreboding steel gray with no hint of blue. This is going to make for a challenging photo session.

"You're getting the VIP treatment today. Personal whale watching. The tour guide will even bring you back home," she says with a wink from the driver's seat.

"Um, which boat is it?"

"That one." She points at the boat to my left.

It's not quaint and postcardworthy like some of the red-and-blue tugboats docked along the harbor. It's smaller than I expected, about forty feet long with an enclosed cabin. A ribbon of navy blue slices the white paint three-quarters of the way down to its aluminum bottom. The name *Fiona* is painted in bold italics along the side.

"Don't have too much fun!" Lucy shouts, like a mom dropping her kid off at their first high school party.

I close the car door and head down the creaky dock toward the boat, spotting the wide back of a man in a thick red-plaid jacket. His bushwhacker-chic distressed jeans are tucked into a pair of hard-core dark green rain boots surely meant for a monsoon.

"Hey, Cap. You must be my tour guide," I call out as I approach.

He stands upright and turns around, thick frayed rope in hand.

A pair of ice-blue eyes greets me.

Evan.

• • •

KILL ME NOW.

Evan is my captain.

"Is there anyone else who can take me?" I gesture toward the dozens of boats moored along the dock. "Literally anyone else?"

His expression pinches. "If there were, you sure as hell wouldn't be getting on my boat in your condition." He swiftly refocuses on the tangled rope in his hands.

"My condition?"

"Hungover."

"I'm not hungover." I definitely am, but he needn't point that out. And now I'm left to wonder if I really look *that* rough.

I slant him a poisonous glare and survey his boat with extra scrutiny, arms crossed. Leaving the relative comfort of this bird poo—covered dock and crossing the threshold onto Evan's boat means entering enemy territory. I don't like it one bit.

"You getting on or what?" he barks, stance wide and hulking.

"That depends. Are you going to toss me overboard?"

He conveniently ignores my legitimate question. How encouraging.

The boat rocks side to side under my weight as I step aboard. Unsurprisingly, he makes no effort to hold his hand out to steady me despite the slippery wet floor. I could crack my skull open and bleed out in front of him, and he'd probably just shrug and go on with his day.

As he settles into the cabin, I conduct a brief inspection. A pile of lobster traps, each big enough to hold a midsize dog, lines the left side of the stern. They sit next to a thick steel arm in an L shape, a couple of feet taller than me, fixed to the right side of the boat. There's an aluminum disc at its base, which appears to be a mechanized pulley system to haul the traps out of the water. Of course, I only know this from watching a ten-hour marathon of *Deadliest Catch* with Julian on the Discovery Channel.

There's nowhere to sit, unless you count the worn, cluttered booth inside the cabin. As I get my bearings, searching for any area of the boat that isn't filled with unphotogenic fishing gear, Evan trudges out of the cabin and thrusts a stained, sun-faded orange life jacket at my chest. "Here."

I crinkle my nose and shield my eyes from the monstrosity. Orange is not my color—or anyone's, for that matter. Especially for photos. "Do I have to wear it the whole time?"

His hard gaze flicks upward, then pins me in place with a stern stare. "Yes."

"I can't take it off for pictures?"

"Put it on and keep it on or we aren't going anywhere. There's too much chop out there today, and I didn't waste my entire morning cleaning this damn boat just for you to fall overboard. I'm not in the mood for a drowning."

"I'm glad my untimely death would be so inconvenient to you. And for the record, I know how to swim, Captain," I say with confidence. It's an overstatement. Probably more of a complete and total lie. I can doggie-paddle around and tread water for a couple minutes, tops. But in the wide-open ocean, I'd be a goner.

"*Melanie*," he warns. At the sound of his voice uttering my full name, however sternly, my stomach free-falls. I don't know how I feel about it. He dangles the life jacket an inch from my face. "Put it on."

I jut my chin toward him. "You're not wearing one."

"Because I'm a professional."

"A professional swimmer? Doubtful. You don't look like Michael Phelps to me."

I'm not sure if he wants to choke me out or give me a swift kick to the shin. Probably both. He lobs his head back and lets out a tortured sigh before stomping into the cabin. I'd bet money he's either giving up entirely or kicking me off this boat. So when he reemerges in a matching life jacket, I nearly dissolve into laughter. The life jacket doesn't look nearly as dorky as I'd hoped on his gargantuan frame.

"Put it on," he orders, pushing the other life jacket toward me for the second time.

"Fine. But for the record, you are so bossy." I groan and take it, strapping it over my dress.

He waits until I'm fully snapped in before jumping back onto the dock to untie the ropes fastening the boat. A gentle wave widens the gap about three times the distance of what it was when I came aboard. I snicker at the thought of him falling in the crack. Unfortunately, he makes the jump with sickening grace and steers us out of the port.

The unsteady sway of the boat nearly topples me. Given my refusal to go inside the cabin with Evan, I'm forced to sit atop one of the cages, gripping the side of the boat as the engine roars at full throttle, jolting us through the rough waters. Once I acclimatize to the motion, I sneak a peek at Evan. He's standing behind the wheel, back to me.

The tense, rigid way he carried himself on land has all but dissipated. His posture is relaxed, grip loose around the wheel. He tilts his head to watch a flock of birds, his gaze tracing their pathway over a rocky bay. Gone is the hardened, knit brow, replaced by softened, weightless peace, reminding me of the Evan I watched singing at the Anchor last night. The mere sight of him like this contrasts with my vision of the reclusive Evan who hates everyone and everything.

"Any sign of whales yet?" I ask, surveying the surface of the water.

No response. He picks up speed through a particularly large crest. The sea spray nearly blinds me, half drenching me in ice-cold salty water. When I scream, he swivels his gaze over his shoulder, the right corner of his lip tugging up ever so slightly, relishing my discomfort.

"Wouldn't be so rough if you'd worn a warm jacket and proper footwear," he calls over the roar of the engine.

I stick out my wedges, admiring them from all angles. "It's a wide heel. It's basically a running shoe."

"So you're gonna freeze your ass off out here just so you look pretty for social media?"

My blood sizzles. I'm not sure I've ever met a more disapproving, dismal human.

"I've never been on the water before. How was I supposed to know how cold it would be? And why are you so hell-bent on being mean to me?" I ask, standing.

He raises a brow as I inch closer to the cabin. "How am I being mean to you? That's the whole reason you came out here, isn't it? Just to take photos of yourself?"

"It's not *just* taking photos of myself. It's my job. I'm selling a lifestyle. Just because I look a certain way, doesn't mean I'm vapid and high-maintenance."

"It's not a matter of opinion. You *are* high-maintenance," he declares, turning his back to me again.

"Please spare me your blatant misogyny."

He turns back around, eyes wide. "Oh, I'm a misogynist now? Really?"

"You think I'm some shallow and vapid waste of space because I promote fashion and beauty—"

"I have no idea what you do or don't promote, or what any of that means, actually."

I ignore him, continuing on. "It's a historically and stereotypically female-dominated industry. Yet there's a bunch of dudes all over the internet doing the exact same thing I do, but with food or tech products. And people don't actively hate them. So why do I get villainized for monetizing my interests?"

No response. The slap of a wave against the side of the boat fills the space between us. I attempt to blink away flashbacks of Ronan calling me superficial when we broke up, to no avail.

"Let me guess, you prefer the girls who *don't know they're beautiful*, who have zero confidence, because women shouldn't be too much—"

"I have nothing against confidence."

"Then what exactly is your problem with me?" I hold my breath, mindlessly smoothing my lash extensions back in place with my finger.

"Not everything is about looks, you know," he says arrogantly, like he's teaching me some noble life lesson.

"Actually, a person's fashion sense is a window into their soul. Sometimes it can be a trick mirror, but at the very least, it tells you what people want you to see."

This amuses him. "For rich people, maybe."

It's on the tip of my tongue to tell him the truth, but the prospect of admitting any of that makes my stomach clench. "Not necessarily—"

"Then tell me, what does your style say about your soul?" He turns and holds my stare, almost like a challenge.

His question catches me off guard. In all my years of being in the fashion business, no one's ever asked me that before. "Well, um, I like bright colors and bold prints . . ." I trail off, unsure what that says about me at all. I've always been drawn to whatever makes me feel confident.

He contemplates that. "Does that mean you want to be noticed?" he asks. While stoic, he isn't staring at me like he wants to roast me over a spit. He almost looks genuinely curious.

I suppose being noticed has always been an inevitability,

especially being a transracial adoptee. I always knew I was going to stand out by default, whether it was because I was Asian or because I was poor, neither of which was in my control. But fashion was different.

I still remember that time in fifth grade when Marissa Rickard told me I couldn't eat at her lunch table anymore because I smelled. I'd been wearing the same hoodie for three days in a row and it hadn't gone unnoticed. After eating countless lunches alone in the stairwell to escape the taunting, I vowed it would never happen again.

That summer before the sixth grade, I did anything I could to make money—like starting a chores business in our apartment building or offering to walk people's dogs even though I was allergic. Hard-earned ten- and twenty-dollar bills and loose change in hand, I'd scour various thrift stores in search of hidden gems or clothes I could revamp and make my own with a tiny used sewing kit our elderly neighbor gave me as a birthday gift. I'd go to the corner store after school and pore over fashion magazines I couldn't afford to buy.

The teenage store clerk let me read the magazines for free, probably because she liked the company. And while she'd drone on about her boy drama, I'd nod and pretend to listen, all while taking mental photos of the clothes in the magazines, challenging myself to emulate these looks with my thrift finds. And the next year, the mean-girl comments stopped. I never fully fit in with the Marissa Rickards of the school, but I knew they respected me. In fact, they envied me, copying my style, assuming I wore vintage thrift as a fashion statement, not a necessity. Everyone at school was under the false impression that I lived some glamorous lifestyle based on some photoshopped pictures online. The consequence of that was keeping friends at arm's length to keep up the facade. Somehow, being envied and alone felt ten times better than fitting in.

I don't say any of this to Evan, though. I don't say anything at all.

Shockingly, he lets it be. "What about me?" he asks, gesturing to his getup.

I make a dramatic show of consideration, stroking my chin like a villain plotting the demise of the human race. "Well, at first I thought your morbid plaid obsession was either a cry for help or a practical choice. But now that I know more about you, I'm developing a new theory."

His eyes darken. "Yeah? And what's your theory?"

"I think you're purposely channeling the lumbersexual vibe."

"Lumbersexual?"

"The ply of your flannels is good quality, so it's not like you're opting for the less expensive brands. You wear different-colored ones every day. And you tend to match the wash of your jeans for every occasion. I think you know what you're doing, rolling your sleeves, flaunting your forearms, strumming your guitar like some tragic Nicholas Sparks character who recently lost his wife and five children in a fire."

A hollow laugh escapes his throat. I'm expecting some cutting remark or insult to follow, but shockingly it doesn't.

"Am I right or am I right?" I probe, praying he doesn't actually have a deceased wife and kids.

He's too stubborn to give me the satisfaction, so he just averts his stare to the water.

We're silent for a few minutes as we curve around an island

dotted with skinny pines, all of which are dead and eroded at the bottoms. It's eerily beautiful, like nature's own artwork. I take my camera out to snap some photos, capturing the vibrant green of the healthier trees behind them.

Evan slows down as we get closer, and for some reason, I feel the urge to address the elephant on the boat. "Look, I'm sorry for making a shitty comment about the inn on that first night."

He shoots me a steely glare over his shoulder, which tells me I probably should have left that in the past. Clearly that weird little moment of peace was nothing but a mirage. "About the inn being disgusting? It's fine. No need to apologize," he says, voice as clipped as it was when I first got onto the boat.

Against my better judgment, I launch into an explanation. "I'd had a long, shitty day of traveling. I felt guilty for leaving my brother to come on this trip." I realize I'm on the cusp of rambling about things Evan definitely doesn't need to know (that no one needs to know, for that matter), so I pump the metaphorical brakes. "Anyway, I thought I'd be sleeping in my car or something. I didn't mean what I said. It's a beautiful property."

He breaks eye contact and angrily stares into the vast distance, probably questioning whether we're far enough away from shore that he can dispose of me. Unfortunately for him, there are a bunch of other boats within eyesight.

"Did you come out of the womb like this?" I ask, unable to leave well enough alone.

He blinks innocently. "Like what?"

I wave a vague hand. "Irksome. Irritating. Generally crappy?"

"Generally crappy, probably." He truly is hopeless.

I grumble and spin back around, assessing the sights. It sounds cliché, but the sea really has a way of making you feel insignificant. Like a mere crumb. The tiniest crumb that isn't worth the effort of cleaning. Based on maps, I always assumed the water was blue in person, but it's almost black—a rippling blanket of darkness.

The shoreline of Cora's Cove is still partially visible until we curve around yet another island. No sign of whales yet, from what I can see. Though even if one were out there, I probably wouldn't see it. My vision is marred by my damp hair whipping every which way in the wind. The extra-strength hair spray holding my barrel curls together is no match for these conditions.

As we bend around the shoreline, a lighthouse comes into view. It's red-and-white-striped, like a sugary candy cane, atop a rocky formation. This is the perfect backdrop. It's exactly what I imagined I'd find in Nova Scotia.

When he slows the boat, I retrieve my camera and unfold my travel-size tripod from my purse. Better snap some shots quickly before my hair is completely destroyed.

Evan, who's still stone silent behind the wheel of the boat, finally speaks. "What are you doing?"

"Taking photos, obviously."

He points to my tripod, which is toppling and skidding around the deck with each gentle wave. "That thing isn't gonna stand."

I've balanced this tripod in dicier circumstances, like in Mykonos, on the edge of a cliff I illegally traversed, so he can bite me.

"Hey, do you mind getting me closer to the lighthouse?" I call over the engine, snapping a few windswept selfies on my phone, noting we have no cell service here.

He pretends he doesn't hear me the first three times before

begrudgingly obliging, cutting the engine. Evan busts out a granola bar, chewing it violently, clearly annoyed with my photo
shoot. I try to ignore him as I examine the shots. The angle is
perfect, as is the light. Realistically, it would be picture-perfect—if
it weren't for the unsightly mechanized pulley system attached to
the side of the boat obstructing the view.

I try moving it over a smidge, but it's locked in place. "Cap, can
you move this?" I ask, my voice divinely sweet.

Evan pretends not to hear me for a solid ten seconds before
placing a hand over his ear. "What? The trap hauler?"

I nod.

"Nope. It stays there."

I could argue with him, but I'm not about to waste any more of
the afternoon's good light. The moment he turns his back again,
distracted by another nearby fishing boat, I take matters into my
own hands.

The trap hauler is heavy, but it has give. While it can't physically
be removed from the side of the boat, it can be swiveled a hundred
and eighty degrees. There's a little rod in the bottom that locks it
into place at certain angles. I move the rod, turning the arm away
from the lighthouse.

Satisfied, I dash over to test the angle of the photo. The pulley
is now completely out of the way and Evan hasn't noticed. Before
he can ruthlessly drive the boat away, I put my camera on the timer
setting and scurry back into place.

As I hold my pose, an afterwave from the nearby boat rocks us
harder than I anticipated, jolting me forward against the side of the
boat.

My spindly tripod skids toward me, crashing into the railing next to my legs. I watch in horror as the top-heavy camera topples straight over the edge.

For a split second, I'm under the delusion that I can save my camera. All I can think about is how many months it took for me to save enough to buy it in cash.

So I lunge for it.

However ideal wedges are for most occasions, they're not the sturdiest. Maybe they aren't like running shoes after all. I bellow a scream the moment my right ankle gives out underneath me.

It's official. I'm going over. My body devolves into a state of emergency. My arms spin wildly like windmills, trying to propel me backward away from the frothy black water below, ready to swallow me into the abyss.

My hands clamber wildly for a grip, but I'm too far forward. There is nothing else to grip but air.

This is it. This is how it ends.

♥ chapter nine

IT ALL HAPPENS in slow motion.

Just when gravity is about to show me who's boss, a deep "Holy shit!" sounds behind me. I'm yanked violently backward by the neck of my life jacket, like a lion cub being plucked up by its scruff.

My legs are no longer my own as I tip backward, landing tailbone first on the deck. At least it's not face-first into the ocean—thanks to Evan.

My body slides along the floor as another wave tips the back of the boat forward, sending Evan stumbling headfirst into the side of the metal trap pulley. I wince at the loud, sickening *clunk*.

His massive body tumbles forward. Straight over the railing he only just saved me from.

In a whirl of plaid and heinous orange, he's gone.

Evan just went overboard.

By the grace of whatever deity exists above, I snap out of my shock, scrambling to my feet. Slipping around the wet floor like a newborn giraffe.

"Evan!" My voice is shrill and hoarse over the water lapping against the side of the boat as I frantically scour the perimeter for any sign of life.

Through my dizziness, I latch my hand over the pulley system for support and crane my neck over the side.

A wave hits, rocking the boat again. Something bobs out of the water, riding the end of the wave. I blink rapidly to ensure my spotty vision isn't playing tricks on me. Sure enough, it's Evan's head, followed by the bright orange of his life jacket.

"Evan!" I call again, desperate.

He must have cut the engine when he left his position in the cabin, because the boat is idling, drifting farther and farther away. He's completely unresponsive to my call, and my gut seizes with dread. When the water turns him over, his head is lolled to the side and his eyes are closed.

No. No. No.

Did I just kill this man?

At the mere thought, my vision blurs from the onslaught of tears and my limbs turn to Jell-O. I could jump in after him, but what good would that do? Despite what I might have claimed, I can't swim for shit. Even in a life jacket, I'd be a useless blob against the brute force of the Atlantic. Besides, the pamphlets Lucy left in my room at the inn detail how frigid the ocean water is, even in the summertime. The temperatures can cause instant hypothermia, rendering even the strongest of bodies virtually immobile.

"Evan!" I scream again, chest heaving.

At the sound of my voice, his eyes flutter open ever so slightly. He registers my voice and turns his neck toward me. Even partially conscious, he still manages to spear me with the world's crustiest glare.

He's alive. With enough wherewithal to recall his severe disdain for me. I've never been more grateful.

"Are you okay?" I call as the boat rocks backward again.

"Does it look like I'm okay?"

I laugh through an exhale, tears burning my lash line. "Try to swim back!"

"I can't! Waves . . . too strong." His faint yell practically disappears into the wind.

It occurs to me that in the movie *Titanic* they used flares to signal for help. I bolt into the cabin to search, despite not having the foggiest idea what flares look like or where to find them. And, honestly, maybe it's for the best, because they scream fire hazard to me. It's also probably ill-advised to base my rescue mission on a Hollywood film set in the early 1900s.

I clasp my palms over my ears and slow my breathing, my mind blanking entirely. Just when I'm about to descend into panic, I spot a megaphone in the corner.

I scream for help over and over until my voice gives out in the cold air, all while keeping an eye on Evan, who's still bobbing along in the water.

Just when I'm about to give up, the rev of an engine tells me a boat is approaching. It's speeding toward us around the island.

The boat, as it turns out, is a recreational fishing boat occupied by two men in their late forties or early fifties. Panicked, I point to Evan in the water.

It takes them a couple of minutes to reach him. As they haul him into their boat, they instruct me to call the coast guard from the walkie-talkie in the interior cabin.

Evan is quiet and sullen as I apologize profusely while we await the coast guard. In fact, he seems more pissed about the fact that the coast guard was called rather than the fact that he fell overboard and bloodied his head.

Within fifteen minutes, the coast guard pulls up in a white-and-red speedboat we're instructed to transfer into. Three men force Evan into a recovery position, moving him carefully into their boat. He isn't a fan, claiming he's perfectly fine to drive the boat back to shore, despite the coast guard's decision to tow his boat behind them.

When I explain that he hit his head on the trap hauler before falling overboard, they insist on calling an ambulance, which is ready and waiting by the time we pull up to the marina.

As the medics fuss over transferring him onto the ambulance stretcher, he shoots a stern glare at the curious crowd of tourists clustering around us. I'm pretty sure one woman has snapped a couple of photos with her iPad.

"None of this is necessary," he barks at the medic as they strap him in, droplets of water running down his forehead. "I'm fine. Seriously. I don't need to go to the hospital."

"Sir, I'm going to need you to have your mantrum elsewhere," the no-nonsense medic rocking a risky burnt orange lipstick responds. Her name tag reads *Reese*. "Lie still and stop resisting or I'll have no choice but to strap you in."

"Evan, stop being an ass and just cooperate," I chide.

He shoots me another look as he finally lies back, unable to control his shivering and teeth chattering despite the foil blanket wrapped tightly around him like a Chipotle burrito. "This is ridiculous."

Reese gives me an eye roll, as though she understands my struggle. "Yup, because the possibility of a brain hemorrhage is so absurd. You need a CT scan at the very least, pal."

He grunts something unintelligible as Jasper, a second medic with a man bun, checks his pulse and blood pressure. Evan grimaces, hands tense at his sides, aggravated by all the prodding—until he's not.

Typically, his stare is pointed. Frosty. But in an instant, it's gone blank. His eyes and lips are twitching, and before either medic can react, his entire body seizes and starts to shake.

"He's having a seizure!" Jasper announces, eyes wide.

My vision tunnels to Evan as the stretcher's wheels hammer sickeningly against the pavement. "Is he okay?" I demand, wrapping my arms around myself.

Neither medic responds. And it's probably for the best. They're in the zone. Reese yells something about Versed, then swiftly appears at his side with a syringe and injects him in the arm. The seizing stops almost immediately, and Evan's eyes loll closed.

"Why—why did you put him to sleep?" I croak, voice breaking midsentence. "Is he okay?"

Reese tightens her orange lips. "We put him to sleep to prevent another seizure. We'll have to get him a CT scan at the hospital in Halifax to see about any internal damage. Seizures aren't uncommon with head injuries, although it could be a sign of something worse."

My chin trembles as the words reverberate in my head. *Internal damage. Seizure. Halifax.*

I watch helplessly as Jasper secures a now-unconscious Evan in the back of the ambulance. Without thinking, I clamber in and park myself on the jump seat next to him, unable to tear my eyes from his unconscious face.

I think about how it could have been me on that stretcher had Evan not pulled me back from the edge.

I can't let him go to the hospital alone.

• • •

"MA'AM, I'M AFRAID you can't enter the ICU unless you're a spouse or immediate family member," the nurse with the banana-print scrubs says sternly, arms crossed, stance wide like a brick wall. She's blocking me from continuing down the hallway alongside Evan's stretcher, which is now plowing forward through a set of double doors.

Spouse or immediate family.

I squeeze my eyes shut, racking my jumbled brain for other possibilities. The entire drive to Halifax, I tried calling Lucy via both the marina number and the inn's number on the Airbnb listing. No answer from either. I don't have her personal phone number, and I don't know any of their family members' names, and certainly not their contact information.

"Ma'am," the nurse says again, smacking her gum impatiently. "Are you a spouse or immediate family member?" she repeats louder as I spin myself into a twister of guilt.

This entire situation is all my fault. I'm the one who stupidly tried to save my camera. I'm the one who moved the trap hauler, causing Evan to hit his head on his way overboard. I'm the one who wanted to go whale watching in the first place. And now he's unconscious, in the hospital, possibly with life-threatening head injuries, with no family, all because of me.

Who knows how long it'll take Lucy to get my messages and drive all the way from Cora's Cove? Until I can reach Lucy, I have a moral duty to stay.

The nurse's flared nostrils tell me she's two seconds away from calling security. In a hazy panic, I say the first thing that comes to mind. "We just got engaged! He's my fiancé. I'm his power of attorney."

She clears her throat, dipping her chin sympathetically. "Go ahead."

♥ chapter ten

WITHIN THE NEXT half hour, I've announced myself as Evan's fiancée to the entire ICU staff, including Dr. Chernoby, who was initially perturbed when I chased the stretcher down the hallway shouting "I'm his fiancée!" at the top of my lungs like a maniac.

"Did I mention we're getting married? Next year?" I ask for probably the third time. It's a nervous reflex, I think, derived entirely from guilt.

Dr. Chernoby gives me a kind smile, adjusting her thick French braid over her shoulder. "You did tell me that. Twice. Huge congratulations. But for now, do you mind telling me the approximate size of the boat? How far he fell?"

Right. We're chronicling the events on the boat.

In between her questions, I keep expecting her to stop and call me out for my big fat lie, but Evan's relationship status appears to be the least of her concerns. She's worried about potential brain swelling and internal bleeding, prompting an emergency CT scan and an MRI.

Thankfully, the test results prove clear.

We're moved to a double room, although the bed closest to the door is currently unoccupied.

"Good news. There's no trace of swelling or bleeding. He has a concussion at the very least, but I'm optimistic for his recovery," Dr. Chernoby explains yet again. She has the patience of a saint.

My shoulders feel instantly lighter. A concussion isn't ideal, but at least it isn't something more serious. "When will he wake up?" I ask, promising myself this will be the last question.

"Probably within a couple of hours, when the medication wears off." She tears her eyes from the scan results on her clipboard and shifts her thick-framed glasses up her nose, giving me a kind, comforting smile. "We'll keep him overnight for observation, just in case. But if all is good, you can go home tomorrow morning. The nurse on duty tomorrow will give you formal instructions for treating the concussion."

"Do you have an insurance form for me to fill out?" I ask, pacing nervously at the foot of Evan's bed. Dad used to get so stressed every time Julian or I got sick or injured. We didn't have health insurance, so every trip to the hospital was laden with guilt and fear over how we'd be able to afford it.

She squints at me. "Form? You mean his prescription?"

I mentally scold myself. I'm in Canada. Health care is free. "Sorry, I'm just a little tired. Never mind."

Dr. Chernoby gives me a quizzical expression. "You should get some rest too, while you wait. If you need anything, don't hesitate. I'll be around to check on him in an hour."

When she exits the room, I flop into the chair and kick my wedges off, muscles weak and exhausted. While I'm stationary, I check my phone again to see if Lucy has called back. She hasn't. In fact, the only person who's blown up my phone in the last twelve hours is Ian, telling me he's keeping a watchful eye over my door deliveries.

A nurse named Stefan lumbers in about fifteen minutes later, asking about Evan's next of kin and if I've already contacted them (standard practice for patients in a coma, apparently).

As expected, I'm a deer in headlights. For fear of Stefan calling me out as a fraud, my only option is distraction.

I place the back of my hand over my forehead and feign dizziness, a move I learned from drama class in high school. Apparently my skills are still top-notch. The traumatized-fiancée act works. Stefan rushes to the bathroom to grab me a cup of water and a damp cloth, ordering me to lie back in the chair and rest.

While I pretend to be out of commission, cool cloth over my eyes, I think about who my next of kin would be in such an event. Given Julian's aversion to hospitals after Dad's heart attack, the last thing I'd want to do is burden him with the duty of being my power of attorney. I can't even count on him to keep my condo clean, let alone sort out my life affairs. And while I trust Crystal or Tara to make decisions in my best interests, is it normal to ask friends to take on such a massive role? The more I think about it, the more pathetic the idea becomes. They probably have a long list of people they'd ask before me.

It must be nice to have people in your life who are biologically obligated to be there for you. My heart pulses with longing for what they have. But before it crushes my spirit entirely, I shove it away.

The hospital room is steeped in shadow by the time eight thirty rolls around. It's quiet, save for Evan's breathing and the muted beep of the various machines monitoring his vitals. I lift the damp cloth to peek at his unconscious hospital gown–adorned body. My glance quickly turns into a one-sided staring contest.

His lack of movement makes my stomach clench. He may be insufferable, but I'd never wish a traumatic brain injury on someone. Especially not someone who saved my life. I'd give anything for him to wake up and give me a stern lecture about how I nearly cost him his life.

I become well acquainted with Evan's face over the next half hour as I cycle through more pointless scenarios. In the absence of a deep scowl, he's annoyingly handsome. It's a shame that such classic Hollywood symmetry is wasted on such a miserable human.

I pinch my wrist before I get too carried away. Thirsting over someone in an unconscious, concussed state is surely unethical. Then again, it's been a long day. I must be venturing into delusion.

"Please be okay," I whisper. My eyelids are sandbags as I fight to regain my focus. Evan's perfectly shaped lips are the last thing I see before my eyes drift closed.

♥ chapter eleven

W HY DIDN'T YOU tell us your own son is engaged?" The whip-sharp voice slices the air, jolting me from sleep.

When I crack an eyelid, a flash of nautical stripes floods my blurred vision. It takes me a couple of seconds to remember where I am. I'm in Nova Scotia. In a dark hospital room. With Evan . . . and others?

A streak of fluorescent light from the hallway illuminates the extra bodies in the room. The owner of the voice looks to be in her sixties with short caramel-colored hair. She tosses a linen scarf over the opposite shoulder in a huff, expression souring by the second at the sight of a bony finger wagging in her face.

The finger-wagger looks around the same age. Only her hair is completely gray, cascading in loose waves past the nonexistent waist of a hemp maxi dress (no bra). Her look is tied together with a tattered pair of Birkenstocks. She's a couple of inches taller than the other woman, broad shoulders blocking my view of Evan's bed. "Does it look like I had any clue? Leave it to you to pick a fight when my son is unconscious in the hospital." Her low, raspy voice contrasts with the other woman's higher pitch.

I make a mental note: the one with the long hair is Evan's mom.

The short-haired woman lets out an exaggerated one-syllable witch cackle. "Oh, that's rich, Nessa. I seem to remember you starting in on me at my son's funer—"

"Fiona, you goaded me into that one and you know it. Stop projecting. It's exhausting."

"For goodness' sake. Stop with the squabbling! You two are gonna put me in the grave if you keep this up." A third woman, white haired, in an oversize canary-yellow button-down blouse with matching pants, shoves her hand in between Fiona and Nessa, pushing them apart with more force than I'd expect from a tiny elderly woman who looks eighty years old at minimum.

Fiona groans. "Mother, you've been threatening death for the past decade. It's getting old."

"Yeah, Mom. Don't act like you're not fit as a fiddle, swing dancing at the hall every Thursday," Nessa adds.

The old woman clasps a hand to her chest, deeply offended. "My rock step isn't what it used to be and you know it."

A man leans in to peer at me, head tilting side to side like a dog. He's tall, with long, untamed hair feathering over his broad, hulking shoulders. There's something different about his demeanor, and it's not just his horrid tropical-print shirt unbuttoned to the navel like he's an exceedingly enthusiastic Carnival Cruise dad. He's smiling jovially, round face lit like that of a pleasant holiday elf. "She's awake!"

All four strangers close in, crowding around my chair. Their eyes bore down at me through the darkness like a band of blood-thirsty trained killers. I shrink back, heart hammering, sweat prickling my temples.

"She looks expensive," the old woman decides, flashing a con-spiratorial side-eye at the man in the tropical shirt.

"What's your name?" Nessa demands.

"Uh, um, Melanie," I respond, voice still gravelly from sleep.

My first name doesn't satisfy her. "How long have you and Evan been engaged?"

"Who—who are you?" I manage, tugging at the collar of my dress, desperate for cool air as my ribs threaten to close in on me. Logically, I know the answer. But I need to hear it.

Fiona steps forward, arms crossed. "Evan's family."

"Soon to be yours too, I hear," the cheerful man chimes in, widening his smile. He looks happy-go-lucky, like the kind of guy who doesn't let anything faze him. Even a room full of angry adults.

Soon to be yours.

My stomach cartwheels.

No. No. No. This cannot be happening.

Evan's family thinks we're engaged.

Itchy hives form over my chest, spiking up my neck as I recall declaring myself Evan's fiancée for the entire ICU to hear. I sup-pose this is a clusterfuck of my own making.

Before I can do the mental gymnastics of explaining myself like any normal human would, my body lurches into flight mode. Bare feet pressed firmly on the floor, I bolt, dodging everyone on my way out like a Black Friday shopper who scored the last cash-mere sweater at Bloomingdale's.

Someone calls my name, but I don't stop running. As I peel around the corner toward the elevator a little too fast, too furious, I slam chest-first into a small redheaded woman in a blinding neon-yellow hoodie.

Lucy.

"Mel?" She stumbles backward, hand to her chest, taking in what I can only assume is my disheveled appearance.

"You're here! Did you get my calls?" I demand, groping at the wall for balance. "I called the inn and the marina like ten times."

She bristles. "The marina phone doesn't work. Hasn't in like four months. But Evan being taken away by an ambulance was the big news of the day. Everyone was talking about it. I drove straight here as soon as I heard. Is Evan okay?"

"He's okay," I tell her, sagging against the wall. I catch my breath before launching into a detailed explanation of the boat debacle, as well as the seizure.

"But the doctor says it's just a matter of time until he wakes up," I emphasize, more to convince myself. "All the tests came back clear. They want to monitor him for the night as a precaution."

Her chest expands in relief. "Thank god. And are *you* all right?" She scrutinizes me the moment I look away.

"I'm fine. I mean, I—well—I fell asleep and woke up to your family arguing and threatening death and—"

She furrows her brow, holding a hand up. "Who all is in there? I only called my aunt Ness."

"She's there. But there's also an old woman, tight white curls—"

"That's Nana."

"Um, and a man in a Hawaiian shirt."

She nods. "Looks like an extra from *Hawaii Five-O*? That's Uncle Ned."

"Oh, and another woman. Kind of ginger."

She sucks in a sharp breath. "My mom. They all came," she whispers in awe.

I lower my voice, matching hers. "Why is that weird?"

"The four of them haven't been in the same room in years. I mentioned before that Aunt Ness and my mom hate each other, didn't I?"

"Really? I couldn't tell," I say sarcastically.

She lets out an exasperated yet resigned sigh, as if that's just the norm. "They *would* bicker at someone's hospital bedside."

"Well, there's more." I take in a deep breath. "They think I'm Evan's fiancée."

Her lips twist in alarm. "Fiancée? Why?"

"Because being his *fiancée* was the only way they'd let me into the ICU," I whisper out of pure shame, hiding my face in my hands. "I know it was stupid, but I couldn't get ahold of you, and I couldn't let him be alone. I fell asleep in the room before your family arrived, and I guess the staff must have told them who I was. They confronted me, asking how long we've been engaged, and I panicked and bolted." Sweat gathers at the small of my back at the all-too-recent memory.

Lucy places her hands on my shoulders to steady me. "Mel, calm down. It's totally fine."

"It's all my fault. I almost got your cousin killed, *and* I reignited a family feud."

"They'd have found something else to fight about if it weren't you." She gives me a sympathetic half smile, eyes falling to my bare feet. "You've had a long day. Go get a coffee and some food downstairs and I'll explain everything to them." She's being far too kind right now, considering her cousin is in a medically induced coma all because of me.

"You're sure they won't hate me?" I ask as my right eye begins to twitch.

"Absolutely not."

• • •

"WHAT'S WITH YOUR hair? You look like that girl from *Brave*, but with a grudge." That's the first thing Crystal asks over FaceTime. She's in a pink workout sweatshirt, dark hair piled on top of her head in a messy bun. Based on the restaurant sign in the background, she's walking home from a late-night gym session.

"It's kind of a long story." I attempt to smooth my hair down, but my finger gets stuck. Not only did the wind render it straw-like and matted, but it's completely damaged my lash extensions. I check myself in the video chat to confirm. Exactly two spindly, stubborn lashes dangle over my left eye, while a clump is still attached on the right. It really adds to my just-came-off-a-ten-day-bender aesthetic.

"I saw your IG stories from the whale-watching excursion. I was worried for you, out in nature," she says, rushed. "But then the video cut to your boat driver. Who the hell was *that*?" She makes an O formation with her thumb and index finger, signaling outright approval.

I level Crystal with a get-real look as I collapse on a bench in the hospital lobby. "Funny you should mention him. He runs the inn I'm crashing at until I go to the resort."

She pretends to fan herself. "I am both concerned and, frankly, a little horny. Tell me everything."

She tugs the crew neck of her sweatshirt over her mouth to conceal her reaction as I divulge the gory details: from the moment my mere presence offended him on that first night at the inn to Jarvis the spider. Then I rattle off the events on the boat, from the life jacket debate to him going overboard, the seizure, the COMA, and waking up to his family midfight.

She takes a minute to digest my harrowing tale before bombarding me with questions, ending with "And you just up and fled the room when you woke up?"

"Okay, cut me some slack. I could have died today." Yet another stark reminder that it could have been me in the hospital if it weren't for Evan.

"Don't you think you should be explaining what happened to his family instead of talking to me?"

I'd rather swallow broken glass or eat expired convenience store sushi. Okay, maybe not expired convenience store sushi. But facing them means admitting that my foolishness put Evan in a coma. And, honestly, their family seems complicated. I don't need that kind of drama in my life. I also don't want to be anywhere near this hospital when Evan regains consciousness and finds out I lied about being his betrothed. I'd probably crumble under his hateful gaze. And maybe that makes me a coward, but so be it.

"I'm leaning more toward Ubering all the way back to Cora's Cove, grabbing my stuff, and going home. Besides, his cousin Lucy just got here. She's explaining everything to the family."

Crystal's face freezes in an unflattering position as she heads up the stairs to her apartment. The exposed redbrick walls tell me she's reached her unit, as well as her Wi-Fi. "It's not as weird as you think," she assures me, removing her shoes on the front mat. "I'm sure they'll be thankful you stepped in before they got there. No big deal."

Her calm tone puts me at ease a smidge. She's not wrong. Despite my poor decisions, I did accompany him to the hospital. That has to count for something, right? "You're probably right. I need to woman up, go back, and explain myself. And then I'll book my flight home."

"You're just gonna ditch the resort opportunity?"

I let out a defeated sigh. "I don't want to. But a near-death experience kind of dampens the mood. I really wish you and Tara were here."

She makes a frowny face. "Same. We miss you."

Things would have been so different if they'd been here. I think about how Crystal would have made fun of Evan behind his back for being so unnecessarily moody. Or how Tara would have probably charmed him somehow, in a way I could never dream of. Not that I'd want to.

I've always been envious of Tara's ability to make friends wherever we go. Her superpower is tapping into someone's deepest desires and making them feel special by divulging her life story to anyone who will listen. And then there's me, brooding in the background, suspicious of everyone and everything. Unlike Tara, I don't inherently trust anyone. They need to earn it.

When I broke things off with Ronan, he launched into a rant in the middle of our favorite Italian restaurant, Mama Maria's.

"I barely even know who the hell you are. I didn't even find out your father died until two months ago." His voice echoed through the restaurant, turning the heads of all the patrons in our vicinity, as well as the waitstaff.

I could have told him it wasn't personal. That I don't tell anyone anything and never have. But instead I just shot him a warning look that screamed *Lower your damn voice, we're in public.*

He continued, speaking over the poor waiter, who'd returned with a bowl of extra Parmesan. "Every single time I ask anything remotely personal, you deflect with some sad, pathetic attempt at humor or sarcasm or whatever the hell you wanna call it."

"Okay, my humor and sarcasm aren't pathetic," I righteously pointed out.

He shook his head, piercing my soul with a look that could only be described as rigid disdain. "You just proved my point. Everything about you is fake. Your boobs, your lips, your social media. Even your personality. Enjoy your cold, lonely, empty existence, Mel."

And that was that. After dramatically tossing his cloth napkin over his half-eaten plate of carbonara, he stomped out of the restaurant, leaving me stunned.

It certainly wasn't the first time a man had weaponized my body against me, demonizing something he'd previously claimed to love. And when I no longer suited them, they'd one-eighty and act as though getting work done makes me a bad person, akin to someone who frequents dog parks solely to kick puppies in the face.

But Ronan's accusation of my shallow and cold personality cut deeper, mostly because I'd gotten closer with him than any previous ex. I'd told him about my brother, for Christ's sake. Besides, he grew up in Back Bay, the son of two lawyers. He'd never understand or relate to my childhood anyway. And why did I owe him the gory details of my entire life? He was my boyfriend, not my therapist.

Then again, this is a continuing pattern. There was Joel before Ronan, and Peter before that, all of whom accused me of being a brick wall.

Evan's hatred of me only confirms what I already know: I'm unlikable and I don't know how to be anything different, which is exactly why I need to leave as soon as I explain myself to Evan's family.

With Crystal's always logical assurance, I finally suck it up and return to Evan's room.

Before entering, I pause in the hallway, straining to listen for drama. There are voices, but they're low and calm compared to earlier.

My head pokes around the corner creepily. People hover around the hospital bed, including Stefan the nurse, who is talking to Evan and taking his temperature.

I do a double take. Stefan is talking to Evan.

Evan is no longer unconscious. In fact, he's wide awake, eyes open, sitting upright. And while he's a little paler than usual, his hair still manages to appear perfectly windswept. I inwardly groan. So much for slinking off into the starry night.

Stefan gives me a polite chin dip as he heads out of the room. The elderly woman in yellow—Nana—high-jumps onto the bed and cuddles Evan, clutching his bicep like a life raft.

This leaves a gap in between Fiona's and Lucy's bony shoulders—a direct line of sight between Evan and me. The moment he spots me in the doorway, he grimaces.

My throat bobs as his family traces his stare in my direction.

Nessa rushes forward, taking my arm. "Melanie, we're glad you're back." In the proper light, the resemblance between her and Evan is clear, particularly in the eyelashes, which are so thick they almost look tattooed. They also share the same dark brows and penetrating gaze, though on Nessa, they're softer, more inquisitive.

The energy has shifted in the room. Any lingering hostility toward me from half an hour ago has disintegrated, replaced with acceptance. They're not mad at me. In fact, they seem grateful that I stayed with Evan until they arrived. Even no-nonsense Fiona's lips flex into a hint of a smile.

Nana whacks Evan on the shin with zero delicacy. "I'll hand it to you. She's prettier than any woman I imagined you marrying."

Evan's eyes bulge with what I can only describe as abject terror. "Marrying?"

I hold my finger over my eyelid to stop it from twitching while I shoot Lucy a stern look with my free eye. Why does this woman still think we're getting married?

"Oh, the poor dear doesn't remember his fiancée." Nana gives him a sympathetic stroke on the cheek, reaching to check his temperature with her wrist. "You must be a little confused from hitting your head. Maybe we should call the doctor back in."

Evan inches away from her touch. "No, Nana, I'm not confused—"

Lucy claps her hands with force, startling everyone, particularly Nana. "Hey! Why don't we give Evan and Mel a little privacy? Evan just woke up and he looks like he could use a bit of space."

No one budges. It isn't until she physically shepherds them like farm animals that they begrudgingly funnel into the hallway.

Lucy fixes her stare at her combat boots, biting her thumbnail as we wait for their footsteps to disappear.

There are a million things I want to say. It's on the tip of my tongue to ask why their nana still thinks we're engaged. But the moment my gaze catches Evan hoisting himself into an upright position in the hospital bed, "You're alive" is all that comes out, because at this point, a flimsy apology hardly seems sufficient.

"Not dead yet, unfortunately for you." He slants me a pointed look that singes my skin.

A dark laugh escapes me. "Guess I should have pushed you a little harder . . ." My voice trails off. That's probably not an appropriate joke, so I settle for "How are you feeling?"

"Massive headache." He pauses, grimacing as he adjusts the thin, crappy hospital pillow behind his back. "I heard you saw the seizure?"

"It was terrifying." I work back a swallow at the all-too-recent memory. When my eyes threaten to well up, I blink rapidly to keep the tears at bay, where they belong.

His face softens for me, probably for the first time. "Sorry you had to, uh . . . see that."

That tight knot in my stomach whenever I'm around him uncoils ever so slightly, and I don't know how to handle it. This whole thing. Seeing Evan confined to a hospital bed instead of stomping around me like a caveman or a petulant child is foreign.

A thick, tense silence hangs between us for a few moments as Lucy continues to chew her nails neurotically.

Evan clears his throat. "Is anyone gonna tell me what the hell is happening here? Why does Nana think we're engaged?"

"It's my fault," I admit. "I panicked and told the staff you were my fiancé so they'd let me in the ICU. They wouldn't let non–family members in."

He tilts his head, puzzled. "And why would you want to come in the room with me?"

"Because," is all I can think to say. "You fell overboard because of me. I couldn't just let you get wheeled off. Even if you are insufferable. Besides, Lucy was supposed to clear things up with everyone."

Lucy guiltily avoids my stare. "Okay, I was about to tell them . . . but then Evan woke up and stole my thunder. The doctor was called in, and everyone was all distracted."

"So sorry for the inconvenience," Evan says dryly. He places a hand over his face, parting his fingers only slightly to shoot Lucy a look. "You should have told them the truth. Nana is going to be pissed, Luce."

We're silent for a moment, and all I can think about is getting the hell out of there. I don't need to be there to witness the dramatic proceedings.

Lucy hangs her head. "I know. I just . . . For the first time in years, our moms weren't at each other's throats."

I raise my index finger to correct her. "They were fighting earlier."

"But they were coexisting *after* Evan woke up."

Evan waves his palm toward the ceiling. "And?"

Lucy plunks onto the bed next to Evan with zero regard for the fact that he's concussed. "Hear me out."

He groans. "I don't like the sound of that."

"This is huge! When was the last time they were in the same room?" Her hands are moving at a rapid speed, which is dizzying.

Evan shrugs, running a finger over his temple. "I dunno. Probably at Grandpa's funeral."

"But what does that have to do with anything?" I demand.

"Before Evan woke up, the first thing my mom did was ask about the wedding and how she could help." She turns to Evan. "She helped raise you like her own son when your mom was working. I guess I just thought . . ."

"You decided it was best not to tell them the truth? In hopes that they'd forgive and make up?" he clarifies.

"Exactly. Think about it. If we tell them the truth when they come back, it's just gonna lead to World War Three. What if . . . what if we didn't tell them for the rest of the night? Just for the sake of peace. Maybe they'll be able to finally work things out?"

Evan blows the air from his cheeks and contemplates. "Easy for you to say. If the roles were reversed, would you lie to Nana and your mom about that?"

"If it meant everyone would finally make up, yes."

"I'm not lying to our entire family, Lucy. Not after everything that's happened. They hate me enough."

"Evan. Stop that. No one hates you." They appear to exchange words telepathically. I'm missing something, but at this point, it doesn't seem suitable to ask.

Evan lets out a strained sigh. "But they're not going to just magically make peace in one day. I'm being discharged in the morning. What then?"

"Maybe that doesn't matter," Lucy hedges. "What if all we need is tonight? Long enough for them to remember how much they care about each other. How much they miss their sisterly bond.

How much time and money they're wasting over this stupid legal battle."

"I don't think this is a good idea."

"But they're already halfway there," Lucy pleads. "You can't deny there was some progress made today. Imagine if we spent the whole night with them? We could even bring up a bunch of memories from their childhood. Remind them of how things used to be when they were best friends. And they're going to want to get to know Mel."

I raise my hand like I'm a student in primary school. "Um, I actually think it's best if I just go home. There's a flight leaving tonight —"

"But your stuff is at the inn," Lucy cuts in. "You can get a ride back with me tomorrow morning when Evan is discharged."

"As much as I'd like to help you with your family reunion, no one will believe we're a couple. It's not plausible," I rightfully point out. "Aren't they gonna wonder why Evan has this supersecret fiancée they've never met?"

"Evan isn't exactly an open book about his personal life," Lucy points out. That makes two of us. "We can tell them you guys met online or something. And that Evan wanted to keep things on the down-low until it got really serious."

Evan is suddenly very preoccupied with a loose thread on the hospital blanket and offers nothing. Not even a rebuttal.

I cut them both a look and gesture to the space between Evan and me. "In case you haven't noticed, Evan and I don't exactly get along. He almost died today because of me."

"But you'd barely have to talk," Lucy assures me. "Or even look at each other. Come on, Evan. If your mom can convince my mom not to sell the inn, this could change everything. If my mom drops the case, we could actually get access to the funds to renovate."

Evan stares up at the ceiling, as if the answers to his problems are up there. "This is so, so wrong."

"Messed up," I add. "Who lies about being engaged? Sociopaths, that's who."

Lucy turns to Evan, brandishing her wide puppy eyes. "All I'm asking for is one night. That's it. We tried to get the inn up to snuff and we failed. I can't lose it. I know it would break your heart too if we lost it. It's all we have of what our family used to be. Please?"

He clenches his jaw with effort, hard gaze flicking back to me hesitantly. "I'll do it. If Mel will."

Lucy exhales and turns to me. "Mel? Please?"

♥ chapter twelve

LYING COMES MORE naturally to some people than others. I would know. My dad used to comfortably glide over half-truths and embellish details because he never wanted Julian and me to know the reality—that we were one paycheck away from eviction.

I suppose that's become my life. Casually omitting truths to avoid a deeper examination of myself. Capturing picture-perfect shots in my living room with the outright mess only inches out of frame. Filtering out any and all blemishes with the click of a button. Showing people only what I want them to see, ever since I was a child, never wanting people to know where I really lived. Even now, despite the lifestyle I've made for myself, I'm still paranoid people can see right through me. That it's written all over my face.

Evan, on the other hand, can't lie to save his life.

Case in point: the moment his family returns, arms laden with cafeteria food and beverages, he becomes C-3PO, only much less delightful. Unnatural upright posture, unblinking. Maybe I should be thankful he's no longer glaring at me like he wants to toss me into shark-infested waters (though I wouldn't blame him for doing so). Either way, pretending to be his doting fiancée is no picnic.

While everything in my body wanted to scream *NO* to this ridiculous scheme and hightail it back to Boston, Lucy's desperation stopped me. Their family must be in dire straits if even Evan would consider a lie of this magnitude. They have so much riding on this. The inn. Their family. And I seriously owe them for causing this whole accident in the first place.

People will do anything for family. I can relate. I'd do anything for Julian, no matter how ludicrous.

"Evan, are you going to formally introduce us to your fiancée?" Nana asks eagerly.

Evan goes blank, mouth open, flustered.

Lucy jumps in to save him. "This is Melanie Karlsen. Mel, this is our nana."

Nana wastes no time folding me into a tight embrace. She's no taller than five feet, but she's got an iron grip. "Even more beautiful up close. You're a Pisces, aren't you?"

Before I can respond and tell her I'm a Sagittarius, Lucy cuts in. "Nana, we'll have plenty of time for astrology later." She points to Evan's mom. "That's my aunt Ness. She's a therapist."

Nessa's layers of thick handcrafted wooden bracelets clank as she leans in. "I specialize in love and intimacy," she explains proudly.

"A sex therapist," Lucy clarifies. I note the tips of Evan's ears reddening.

Lucy moves on to the Hawaiian shirt man, whose shirt is now at least partially buttoned. "That's our uncle Ned. He's a fisherman too. Though he's terrible at it."

I shake both of their hands politely, forcing myself to make eye contact while knowing it's all a farce.

"And this is my mom, Fiona, Evan's aunt." Fiona opts for a soft nod instead of a handshake. She strikes me as the kind of person who doesn't do hugs or human touch in general. Maybe we're kindred spirits.

Once introductions are made, the family clambers to grab extra chairs from the other side of the room. It's like a game of musical chairs, but mostly between Fiona and Nessa. There's only one chair left now, next to Evan's bed, and Nana is eyeing it up.

"Dear, why don't you sit with your handsome sweetheart?" she suggests innocently, patting the side of Evan's bed with a wrinkled hand.

I cough. "On the bed?"

Nana nods. "Well, of course."

"Wouldn't you rather sit there?" I ask, making one last-ditch effort.

Evan wastes no time patting the empty spot next to him. "Nana, there's lots of room for you."

"No, dear, I insist. That bed isn't doing my back any favors." She takes the last chair, all smiles.

If I remain standing awkwardly next to the bed, surely they'll know something is off. I stare at the space next to Evan like it's a wormhole, ready to suck me into the void.

Evan watches me, expression vacant. I can't tell whether he's silently warning me to stay at least five feet away from him or if he's accepted his fate. Either way, we're being gawked at like we're the hot new penguin exhibit at Franklin Park Zoo.

Lucy catches my eye and mouths, *Sit!*

With a gulp, I gingerly perch on the edge of the bed. And by perch, I mean no more than fifteen percent of my butt is actually on the bed. I'm sliding off in an effort to ensure our skin doesn't touch. I can already feel the warmth of his body from the proximity, and I don't intend to get any closer.

I steal a peek at Evan, behind me. Based on his demeanor—jaw clenched, hands tense at his sides—he's repulsed. There's no way his family isn't going to see right through this charade, except for Nana.

"Tell us the story of how you met. From the first moment you saw each other. Don't skip the details." She's fallen for this lie hook, line, and sinker, expecting some love story of the Hallmark variety. My heart twists when I consider how disappointed she'll be tomorrow when I disappear, never to be heard from again.

There's a pregnant pause as everyone awaits a response, metaphorical buttered popcorn at the ready.

I prod Evan's hard forearm. "Yeah, Evan. Tell your family all about how we met."

Now would be an opportune moment for him to take control of the situation. But instead, he just says, "I really prefer it when you tell the story," followed by a tortured forced smile.

A flash of anger sizzles through me. He's chosen violence yet again, throwing me to the wolves.

Thanks for the help, *fiancé*.

At the sight of the entire family's eyes on me, I shift, crossing and uncrossing my legs. "No, I think your family would rather hear it from the horse's mouth."

He gives me horror-movie eyes. "Babe, I'm a little groggy from the drugs. I probably won't get the series of events right."

The little shit.

And then it occurs to me: this is only a one-night thing. I'm leaving tomorrow. Why not have a little fun?

My smile is diabolical as I claw for his hand belatedly. He's going to regret letting me do the heavy lifting. He tries to pull his hand from mine, but I tighten my grip, digging my acrylics in a little as the family leans in, waiting with bated breath.

"About a year ago, Evan and I met online. He found me on Instagram and started messaging me relentlessly. I didn't respond to the first fourteen messages because, honestly, I thought he was a huge creep. You know, guys with photos of themselves holding dead fish as prized possessions are always bad news," I theater-whisper as Nessa chuckles. "Regardless, he persisted, and it was starting to get a bit desperate. So I thought, wow, this guy really wants to talk to me. Then one day, out of pure pity, I responded—"

"She got a little obsessed with me," Evan finally cuts in, face drained of all color. He swiftly rearranges our hands so his engulfs mine. "The moment we started talking, she was already trying to make things official, asking when we'd finally be able to meet. I was scared because sometimes people aren't who they say they are online. I didn't want to tell anyone about her until I knew it was serious. I know she's not everyone's cup of tea, but I—"

"He proposed a few days ago. No ring, though." I pretend to pout, holding my naked left hand up to the fluorescent light. I stare at the empty space on my finger and lower my chin solemnly. "He didn't think jewelry was necessary," I say, eyeing Nana's heavily ringed finger.

Nana lets out a shocked gasp. "No ring, Evan? What kind of man doesn't get their fiancée a ring?"

Evan thunks me on the back with his open palm like I'm a choking victim. "She doesn't need material items to know how much I love her."

"Too right you are, son," Nessa says approvingly. "Jewelry and lavish gifts can't buy true love. I never bought my husband anything over twenty dollars."

"And look at how that turned out for you," Fiona sneers from the corner of the room next to Ned.

"At least I'm not miserable and alone, trying to fill my hollow existence with material—"

She stops when Ned gives her a warning look. Nana stares between the two of them, eyes misty, evidently distressed. There is some serious bad blood between Fiona and Nessa. All the more reason I need not get involved.

Nessa resets her jaw, forcing a warm smile. "So, Melanie, tell us about yourself."

"There's not much to tell about me, really. I'm a bit boring, dull, just how Evan likes it." I flash him a syrupy, borderline-manic grin.

"She's not boring," Lucy cuts in from the empty bed closest to the door. "She's an influencer."

Nana puts her hand to her ear. "What's that, dear? A translator?"

"An in-flu-enc-er. She advertises fashion and beauty products on social media," Lucy repeats, enunciating slowly. When this gets no reaction, she whips out her phone, brandishing my Instagram page full of half-nude thirst traps for the entire family to see.

I'm officially in the pits of hell.

Uncle Ned's eyes widen like pancakes at the sight. He even pulls a pair of wire-frame glasses from the pocket of his tropical shirt and leans in to examine. Nessa looks fascinated, unlike Fiona, whose lips are pressed into a paper-thin line.

Nana gapes at a particularly risqué poolside shot of me in a bikini that displays a healthy amount of underboob. "Oh my . . . very breasty. Evan, is your fiancée a *Playboy* model?"

Cue a violent hacking fit. "Um, no. I'm not a *Playboy* model," I barely manage, grasping for the half-empty paper cup of water at Evan's bedside. There's nothing wrong with posing nude, but the last thing I want to do is send Nana into cardiac arrest.

Surprisingly, Nana swats my words away, chuckling. "Oh, it's nothing to be ashamed of, dear. The photos are beautiful. You know, I once posed nude for a charity calendar, covered in nothing but a bear pelt—"

"Mel is just being modest, Nana," Evan chimes in, brandishing a smile fit for a Colgate advertisement. "I'm so proud of her."

I'm tempted to flee the hospital right now and fly straight home without my luggage. It all sounds like a wonderful plan until I remember my passport is still at the inn. Ears burning, I pinch the skin atop Evan's hand, garnering a wince. "Well, you know Evan. He loves nude models."

"Oh, I remember the internet search history," Nessa confirms with an amused cough from the corner of the room. This gets a chuckle from everyone, except for Evan, who's buried his face in his hands.

"Thanks, Mom. Can we not bring up my teen years?"

"So how will this work? Are you moving here from Boston?" Nessa asks, gesturing between us.

"Evan was actually thinking of moving to Boston—" I start.

There's an immediate shift in energy. Everyone stiffens and gasps, positively alarmed. Of all the outrageous things I've said tonight, this is apparently the most disturbing.

Evan cuts in before Nana breaks down. "We haven't decided yet where we'll live. But Mel knows I'd like her to move here so I can take care of the inn. Mel can do her job wherever, and she's interested in helping with the housework. Scrubbing toilets, laundry—"

Fiona huffs. "No matter. Once we sell it, you won't be tied down here any longer. You can feel free to move wherever—"

"The hell he will," Nessa snaps. "The inn is staying in the family, Fiona. Your own daughter is making a living from it. What kind of mother tries to take that away from her after everything that's happened?"

Fiona points at her sister accusingly. "I'm doing what's best for this family. Not that you know anything about that. Or how much it's going to cost to get that place back up and running. We can't afford it, period."

Nessa stands, hands on hips. "I'd rather go broke as a joke before I sell off our family legacy. But some people don't care about legacy, do they?"

Fiona's face turns nuclear. "Don't you dare bring up legacy."

Nana looks like she's about to cry, as does Lucy, so I clear my throat and say the only thing that comes to mind to shut everyone up. "Evan and I are actually thinking of getting married at the inn."

Everyone goes silent. "Excuse me?" Fiona asks.

I look at Evan, who's gaping at me like I've sloshed him in the face with freezing-cold water. "I— Well, we thought maybe the inn would be a nice place to get married eventually. I mean, the grounds in the back are perfect. It may need a bit of work, but I'd love to—"

"A wedding at the inn?" Nana asks dreamily. "When were you thinking?"

"Not for a *very* long time, Nana. No need to worry," Evan reassures.

"I'm sorry, but the lawyers assure me we'll have it off the books by fall," Fiona announces, tone clipped. "If you want to get married there, you'll have to do it this summer."

I smile at Evan, pinching his veiny, sinewed forearm. "We have a lot to talk about, my love. Maybe we should sleep on it."

"I'm eighty-six, you know. I don't have forever," Nana reminds us. My heart twinges at the thought. She's desperate to see her grandson get married before she dies. I wonder if she's aware of how cumbersome he is and is simply thankful some poor soul (me) has taken the bait. "We have to throw a celebration. An engagement party," Nana decides, eyes twinkling. "We'll make a little family holiday out of it at the inn."

Nessa claps her hands together. "I love that idea. It's been too long since we've been together."

Fiona scoffs. "And play merry family at the inn? No thank you."

I cringe, as do Lucy and Evan. "I don't want to intrude. This seems . . . like a private family matter."

"But you're family now." Nana stands, reaching for my wrist. "Please stay. I haven't had the chance to give you a reading yet."

"A reading?"

"Your birth chart reading," she clarifies.

"Nana's really into astrology," Lucy informs me.

Before I can wrap my head around that tidbit, Evan interjects. "How long would you plan to stay?"

"A week should be enough time, don't you think? Gives us time to discuss the wedding plans," Nana decides. "Besides, Shirley is driving me batty with that damn CPAP machine."

"That's her neighbor in the assisted living facility," Lucy tells me. "Thin walls."

Fiona stiffens, lips thin like a knife slash. "Mom, it really doesn't look like they want a celebration."

"We don't," Evan affirms.

Lucy shoots Evan the same warning look she gave me. "We are long overdue for a family gathering. The Lobster Festival is on Saturday. We haven't gone as a family in years. Besides, if we're really selling this place in a few months, maybe this is a good opportunity to finally discuss dividing the assets—"

"Nana and I will take care of that," Fiona decides, lips pursed like it's a no-brainer.

Nessa scoffs. "And you'll just have first pick of everything you want? Typical."

"I'm the oldest. It's only fair I get first dibs," she shoots back.

"Just like when you had a tantrum when Dad wanted to name his boat after me and not you?"

This devolves into a five-minute-long squabbling session over who gets their father's tiny ship models encased in bottles until Nana yells, "Everyone shut up! I could toss myself in the sea and none of you would even notice with all this bickering. We're spending the week as a family to celebrate Evan and Mel whether you like it or not. I don't wanna hear another word from any of you."

Lucy clears her throat and turns to Fiona, who's crossed her arms protectively over her chest. "It'll just be for a couple of days, Mom. He would have wanted that."

Fiona's eyes mist. "It's a recipe for disaster is what it is."

"Not if we don't talk about selling or who gets what," Ned cuts in, surprising Lucy. "The topic should be completely off-limits."

Fiona, Nessa, and Nana appear confused, like not talking about it is a foreign concept. Based on their bitter expressions, I'm not sure it's even possible.

"It sure would be nice to get to know ya," Nessa says directly to me.

My stomach clenches. They actually want me here amid all this strife? A total stranger?

A balminess tingles the back of my neck, spreading down to my feet, engulfing my body in what feels like an unbreakable group hug. That same warmth reminds me of being eight years old, pre-bankruptcy, sitting in Dad's lap in the living room on Christmas Eve as he read *'Twas the Night Before Christmas*. Mom rocked baby Julian in her arms beside us, just delighted because Christmas was her favorite holiday. It's one of the few happy memories I have as a child before Mom left.

Evan bites the inside of his lip and side-eyes Lucy. *We should just tell them*, he mouths.

Lucy nods solemnly.

"Tell us what?" Nana asks.

My fist clenches at my side as I imagine the looks of disgust on everyone's faces when the truth comes out.

Evan clears his throat. "Everyone, the truth is, Mel is going back to Boston. She isn't actually my—"

"I'm staying," I cut in. I don't know why, but the thought of leaving Lucy and Evan's family in turmoil doesn't sit right with me.

Like a guardian angel, Nurse Stefan pops his head in to announce that visiting hours are over.

"Oh, give her a little kiss, Evan, before we go." Nana watches us, starry-eyed, hands clamped to her chest like she's watching a *Golden Girls* reunion special.

I shoot a fiery gaze over my shoulder at Evan. I expect him to break down and tell the truth so he doesn't have to kiss me. But he doesn't. He just stares at me like I'm nothing but a squished bug on his windshield. There's no way he'll do it.

All my body heat rushes to my face as my eyes fall to his lips, half hidden behind his thick beard. They're perfectly kissable, if not for the stiffness of his mouth. He's hesitant, like he's waiting for some sort of sign.

Maybe it's my extreme fatigue. Or the trauma of the day messing with my mind. Or maybe I'm weirdly thankful for the part of him that saved my life. The part of him that's willing to pretend to be engaged to someone he hates, all for the slim chance it'll repair his fractured family.

The magnetic tug brings me inches from his face. I hover there as a jolt of awareness lights its way down my spine and I imagine what his beard might feel like against my skin. Even after a dip in the ocean and a hospitalization, he still smells like delicious s'mores and wood chips. How is that humanly possible? Simultaneously, we close those last few inches, both pairs of lips pursed like dead fish. It's so unnatural it's almost laughable.

But the moment his lips brush against mine like a whisper, my body quivers unexpectedly. They're as soft and pliable as they look. The searing contact only lingers for a hazy blink before we pull back.

Turns out, being fake engaged to Evan sucks, but kissing him isn't half bad.

♥ chapter thirteen

W AIT—YOU'RE GOING to stay and pretend to be my fiancée? For a whole week?" Evan clarifies the moment the family leaves the hospital room.

"Yeah, I guess I am," I say, second-guessing all my life choices leading up to this moment. "Though I kind of regret going along with it after what you pulled back there," I point out, gathering change from my wallet to grab sustenance from the vending machine.

"And what did I pull?"

I scoff. "You threw me under the bus when they asked how we met."

If I'm being honest, at least seventy percent of my anger right now is blatant jealousy. I'm jealous that Evan has a huge family, as dysfunctional as they may be. I'm jealous that he has a room full of people who dropped everything to come rushing to be at his side. I hate myself for feeling this way.

Evan's thick brows raise in offense. "I'm the ass? You're the one who made me look like a massive creep, telling them I cyber stalked you."

"What was I supposed to do? You left me high and dry."

He tosses both hands in the air. "I can't just lie to my family like that. You could have told literally any story. But no. You had to use the opportunity to make me look like a moron."

"And you thought it was better if *I* do the lying? Unbelievable." I let out a derisive snort. "This was your lie, Evan. And the least you could have done was tell your Nana I'm not a *Playboy* model."

"Hey, there's nothing wrong with *Playboy* models."

"I know there isn't! But I'm not one, and—" I stop myself, sucking in a calming breath. Yelling at each other when Evan is concussed isn't doing either of us any favors. "Can we both admit we embarrassed the shit out of each other?"

"But you did it in front of *my* family. Big difference." He's not wrong. He'll have to deal with the fallout. Not me.

I press my fingers to my temples, massaging ever so slightly to reset. This is petty. Seriously petty, considering all that's happened today. "Let's just pretend this whole day never happened."

"Pretend you didn't nearly kill me? Unlikely," Evan mutters, turning over to face the window.

Any Zen I was reaching for suddenly flings itself out of reach. "Well, guess what? You're very much alive. And I'd appreciate if you stopped bringing up death when my dad died a few years ago, okay?" The jumble of words passes my lips before I even fully comprehend what the hell I've just said.

Never have I ever voluntarily brought up Dad's death to anyone, aside from Julian. See, people react to news of family deaths in a variety of ways, usually involving awkward and uncomfortable shows of sympathy. I'd rather get stuck in an elevator for twelve hours with Ian Montgomery than have anyone pity me for even a second, especially Evan.

Evan turns back to face me, jaw set, stunned.

Thankfully, before he can say anything, Lucy stands, arms stretched on either side to put distance between us. "Guys, let's just chill. We have more important things to talk about." She turns to me. "Did you mean what you said? You're really gonna stay for the week?"

I nod. "Yeah. Unless you want me to leave."

"No! Not at all. This is genius."

Evan glares at me, entirely skeptical, icy eyes locked to mine. "I just don't get it. What do you get out of this?"

That is the question. For a hot second, I was drunk on the delusion that I was part of the family—this family. I pictured myself at the dinner table, passing the butter while Nana spills the tea about the most interesting B and B guests over the years.

If I stay, at least I'll still get to go to the resort at the end of the week. If I went home empty-handed and paid out of pocket for my flight, I'd be alone, which is blatantly depressing. But I'd rather swallow fire than admit that pathetic realization.

There's also the reason I came here in the first place. "My camera and tripod are at the bottom of the Atlantic. I could use a photographer and assistance finding locations for some good outdoorsy content."

Evan narrows his gaze at me, fearful. "I'm not going back on the water with you, if that's what—"

"God no," I cut in. "On land," I add for good measure.

"Evan can do that," Lucy offers keenly. "He knows all the best hiking spots. And I have a DSLR camera you can borrow. Besides, we could still use your help with content for the inn."

"Absolutely. I still owe you that," I note.

Teeth clenched, Evan cuts her a look, as though she's committed the ultimate betrayal.

"I think this is a good idea. They'll implode if we tell them the truth right now," she explains. "They're only doing it for you, Evan. I think we need a couple more days just to iron some issues out. Then we'll tell them. Or you two could stage a breakup after the Lobster Festival."

"I can't go to the festival, though. I'm due at the resort the day before," I point out.

Lucy frowns. "Okay. Understandable. Evan, thoughts?"

Evan runs his hand through his hair haphazardly, face scrunched like he's shouldering the weight of a lifetime's worth of regret. "Okay. Okay, fine."

"Now that that's settled, I have to be honest about something." Lucy pauses, gaze alternating between the two of us. "You closed-mouth kissed like toothless ninety-year-olds. You need to make it more convincing. You're a newly engaged couple who can't keep their hands off each other."

At the prospect, Evan looks like he wants to curl up in a ball in the corner and remain motionless.

I'm tempted to defend that kiss. Closemouthed or not, it was hot. But I keep my mouth shut. "Fine."

❤ chapter fourteen

O F ALL OF yesterday's quasi-traumatizing events—the boat,
the near drowning, the seizure, the hospital, the fake
engagement—kissing Evan should be dead-ass last on my mind.

Only it's not.

I've kissed my fair share of men. And I mean *many*, if you consider the summer after high school. But none have felt like *that*.

I tried not to think about it as I sat lopsided in the chair all
night next to his hospital bed. I tried not to think about it when Dr.
Chernoby discharged Evan this morning with firm instructions to
avoid strenuous activity, manual labor, and screen time. I tried not
to think about it the entire drive back to Cora's Cove, back to the
inn, where Nana, Nessa, Fiona, and Ned were waiting—and bickering.

As it turns out, a couple of hours of forced proximity do not
necessarily yield forgiveness—just the opposite.

"By the way, I spoke to Hank Richards. He's more than happy to come by sometime and assess the inn's condition for resale," Fiona tells us over dinner.

Nessa's face instantly turns crimson. "There are so many things wrong with that statement, I don't know where to begin."

Fiona leans back in her chair, arms crossed and ready for a battle. "By all means, go off."

And they do. Jabs fly back and forth across the table like a pro Ping-Pong match. Nessa calls Fiona out for breaking the agreement we made in the hospital and daring to bring up the resale, as well as Hank, who happens to be her "worst" high school ex-boyfriend.

When Fiona calls Nessa an unrepeatable name, I stiffen at the table next to Evan. We're currently embroiled in our own secret battle: hand-holding (at Lucy's suggestion).

I once read in a corner-store *Cosmo* that there's an art to hand-holding. The dominant one in the relationship typically places their hand over, while the submissive one goes under.

Naturally, Evan and I are both hell-bent on taking the "over" hand position. After multiple pinches and a couple of vicious scratches, which elicited a warning look from Lucy, he finally concedes. If I'm being honest, putting my hand over his feels unnatural given the size difference. His large, calloused hand could probably fit two of mine. But I'll take the win.

Petty logistics aside, the skin-to-skin contact sends an unexpected zip of electricity down my spine. As someone who's always been averse to human touch and unnecessary hugs, this is entirely new territory for me.

"Melanie, dear, have you started wedding dress shopping?" Nana asks over Nessa and Fiona's verbal sparring. She leans over to cut Evan's meat into impossibly tiny pieces, like he's a mere toddler who's only recently been entrusted with solid foods.

Evan makes a pained expression, like he's about to pass out. "No, Nana. We haven't worked out any details yet. It's a little early, don't you think?" he asks me pointedly.

I clear my throat, noting Nana's literal lip pout. "I mean, it's never too early to start thinking about a wedding dress."

At my declaration, Nana's face lights up like a Christmas tree. She shifts forward in her seat. "Will you let me come dress shopping with you?"

"Nana, I'm not sure we'll have time. Mel is only here for a week," Evan says.

"But we can dress shop virtually," I offer before she can respond with disappointment. "Online."

Nana appears delighted at the prospect. "Oh, I hope you won't get one of those poofy numbers. You can't hide that gorgeous figure. Don't you think she has a lovely figure, Evan?"

He chokes on his forkful. His eyes flit over me for a half second, blankly. "Uh, yeah," he finally grumbles. He's not happy about the faux admission. In fact, he looks like he wants to slam his forehead into the table.

My chest twists when I realize I'm holding my breath, bracing for his response. Why do I even care?

Nana slaps his hand. "Men these days have no idea how to properly compliment a woman. You know, when your grandfather was courting me, he wrote page-long poems about my beauty."

"That's so sweet," I coo, pushing my broccoli around my plate as I try not to laugh at the thought of Ian Montgomery's poems.

"Young love," Nana says dreamily. "Anyway, I pray you set

your wedding date soon. Before I die," she adds casually, taking a sip of her wine.

"Mom, don't pressure them," Fiona warns. She's turned her chair completely away from Nessa, boxing her out of her periphery. "You know, I still have my wedding dress if you want to try that?" Her offer to give her wedding dress to me feels like a large gesture, especially coming from Fiona, who I'm still not entirely sure likes me. Or anything, for that matter.

"Um, maybe. I appreciate that," I say with a grateful smile.

"A week isn't enough time to plan your engagement party," Nana complains, shaking her head bitterly. "It's certainly too late notice to send invites out. I'll need to go into town tomorrow to order a sheet cake."

Evan and Lucy shift uncomfortably in their seats. "Nana, we really don't need a cake. Mel hates cake, actually," Evan decides.

"I don't hate cake," I counter. "But we really don't need anything fancy. Honestly. A home-cooked dinner would be perfect."

"And I think it's best we keep this on the down-low. I don't want the whole town in my business," Evan adds.

Nana frowns. "I'll never understand your generation. When I was your age, engagements were celebrated by the whole town, front-page news."

"I'm just glad you'll be here for Lobsterfest, Mel," Nessa says sweetly, to the agreement of the whole family.

My cheeks heat. "Oh, actually, I was telling Lucy and Evan I'll be leaving on Friday. The day before the festival."

Nana drops her fork, aghast. "Dear, you can't leave *before* the festival. The Cove is known for its lobster."

"There's food, vendors, and buskers. Evan's band usually plays too. And there's a big dance. All to celebrate the end of the lobster season," Nessa explains enthusiastically.

"You have to watch the Little Miss Cora's Cove pageant. I was crowned Little Miss in 1972," Fiona tells me, eyes glittering with distant memories of her youth.

"Only because Margaret Price told you how to win," Nessa sneers dismissively.

Fiona flicks her gaze upward. "I won fair and square. You're just jealous because the best you could do was third runner-up—"

This bickering is really getting on my last nerve. Before Nana's welling tears burst over her lash line, I interject. "The festival sounds like a great time. I'll stay the extra day." If one less day at the resort brings this family an iota of peace, it's probably worth it.

Nana pats my hand over the table and smiles at me. "Mel, you are exactly what this family needs, especially after Jack."

Everyone goes silent at the mention of Jack. It's on the tip of my tongue to ask who Jack is, but then I remember I'm supposed to be Evan's fiancée. I should probably know the backstory.

As sweet as Nana is, her statement at dinner puts me in a strange mood. On one hand, I feel even more guilty for this whole charade. At the same time, can I feel that bad for something that clearly makes Nana happy?

• • •

"WHO'S JACK?" I ask. Before I can even hold the question in, it's already out, cutting the air like a knife.

We're washing the dishes in silence. As per Whaler family tradition, it's Evan's job to wash the dishes because he's the last to finish his vegetables. I hung back to help for reasons unknown.

The corners of his mouth tense instantly as he shoves a plate into the dishwasher a little more forcefully than the last. He lifts his gaze to meet mine, and I can see I've made a mistake. "Don't," he says, tone curt and simple.

I should have known. One of the reasons I keep things close to my chest is so people don't bring them up and instantly put me in a shit mood. "Sorry," I whisper, though I don't think he hears it over Fiona and Nessa bickering about selling the china.

Before I can register where it all went wrong, Fiona is already stomping around the premises, scribbling in a notebook and muttering about the extent of the renovations required to get the inn up to snuff and why the only solution is to sell it immediately.

I'm starting to think Lucy was wrong about the inn being the perfect backdrop for the family's reconciliation. Instead of bringing up fond, fuzzy memories, it's brought out the worst in them, despite the plaque made out of driftwood above the mantel that reads *Family Above All Else*.

Amid the strife, I take refuge in my bedroom to avoid all the conflict. After the turmoil of the past two days, I'm grateful for the peace and quiet. I take the opportunity to compile a list of social media content ideas for the inn. Admittedly, the prospect of content creation for the inn is ten times more thrilling than being forced to overshare my life on my own accounts.

Ironically, some of my phone selfies (that didn't perish in the bottom of the Atlantic), including a short video of me getting sprayed in the face with seawater, have gained thousands of likes. They aren't posed or heavily filtered. For once, I've actually gained a couple hundred followers instead of losing them. Maybe switching up my surroundings was exactly what I needed to get out of my rut. Maybe, just maybe, staying was a good idea.

As I contemplate my strategy going forward, a frantic knock sounds at the door. Before I can utter "Come in," Lucy races in carrying an air mattress box seemingly twice her size.

"What's that for?" I ask, although I'm certain I won't like the answer.

• • •

"WE'RE NOT STAYING in the same room," Evan declares, judgy eyes darting to my bra hanging from the bedpost for all to see. Normally, I'd be mortified, but Evan's outright distress is worth it.

I still feel bad for being a Nosey Nancy by bringing up Jack, but I'm not just going to roll over.

"Sharing a bedroom is way too far," I agree. I haven't shared a room with someone since my brother when we were kids, and I'm not about to start now, especially with Evan.

Lucy levels us with a look. "You're supposed to be engaged. What are they gonna think when they catch you guys sleeping in separate bedrooms?"

"That we're respectful? Old-school? Saving ourselves until marriage?" I suggest, frantic. Suddenly, sharing a room with Jarvis the spider is remarkably more appealing.

Lucy snorts. "They'd never buy that. Not with Evan."

He cuts her a dirty look. "Hey!"

"You know it's true. Besides, it's not like you're sharing a bed. Evan will sleep on the air mattress." She pats the air mattress box like it's a trusty dog.

"There's no room for that thing with . . . all this." He gestures at the clothes and shoes all over the floor.

"Evan, don't be petty. Everyone's already seen Mel's stuff in here. Nana came in earlier to snoop at her shoe collection." Lucy points to the lineup of shoes at the foot of the bed.

"As long as you stay on the air mattress," I warn.

"Yeah, because I'm dying to get into bed with you," he mutters before stomping out of the room like a child.

"He'll be back," Lucy whispers.

• • •

WHILE I WAIT for sleep to take me, I make sure to give Julian a call. With everything going on, I haven't been as responsive to his frequent texts as I usually am.

"How are you?" I ask immediately. "How was your therapy session with Hector?"

"Stop worrying. I'm *fine*, Mel," he tells me, clearly picking up what I'm putting down. "You're gonna be proud. I applied to three jobs today."

"Really?" I try to hide my shock. But honestly, I didn't have a lot of hope he'd actually make use of the laptop I bought him, aside from using it for gaming.

Mom claims I'm enabling his behavior by allowing him to be dependent on me, even though she took credit for the idea of Julian moving in with me after Dad. At least, that's what I got from her rant about how "mental health and grief aren't an excuse to put life on hold" five months ago, the last time we spoke on the phone. I probably should have countered with my well-founded theory that Julian's anxiety might stem from the lack of a stable mother in his life, but it would only sour our relationship further.

"Yup. I'm excited about this one. It's remote work. Online customer service support for a sick T-shirt brand. They offer a benefits package, and the guy I talked to on the phone seemed dope." His level of hype is similar to when he invested his meager savings into cryptocurrency (at the ill-fated advice of Ronan) and lost most of it.

"That's amazing. And you wouldn't even have to leave the condo," I say encouragingly.

"Also, I'm pretty sure I figured out what I want to do, long-term."

"What's that?"

"Graphic design. Hoping to eventually design the shirts. I looked into some programs, and I'd just need to build a portfolio."

This is probably one of the first career ideas he's had that doesn't come out of nowhere. He's always been the kid who carried around a notebook, doodled on napkins, place mats, and walls, and obsessed over art projects. It's a shame no one thought of it earlier.

"I can really see that for you. Look at you, adulting without me. Do I even need to come back?"

There's a pause. "Yes. Please. I already ruined one of your expensive pans. And I think I fucked up your fancy washing machine. Does it usually make a crackling sound?"

"Julian, you're stressing me out."

He chuckles. "Kidding. Well, not kidding about the washing machine. You'll need to check that. But I'm fine. Really."

He tells me a bit about how he had another run-in with Ian in the lobby. Overall, it comforts me to hear his voice, especially when he's doing well. There's a calmness and a peacefulness in him when he's not overcome with nerves. He's the carefree Julian I remember as a kid. The one with boundless energy I'd chase around the apartment, making sure he brushed his teeth at night. Not the vacant shell of him I've known for the past few years.

It isn't until around ten thirty that Evan stalks back into my room wearing track pants and a plain white T-shirt that has no business emphasizing his arms the way it does. He's carrying two cloth grocery bags full of what appear to be his belongings and toiletries.

"By the way, we don't have to listen to Lucy. If you don't feel comfortable sharing a room with me, just say the word," he says.

I consider that for a moment. I'm uncomfortable sharing a room with Evan in the sense that breathing the same air as someone you despise is never ideal. But I'm not uncomfortable at all in a primal sense. Evan may think I'm awful, superficial, and generally disgusting, but there isn't an ounce of threat in his eyes. He did save my life, after all.

"I don't feel uncomfortable," I say.

He waits for a moment, belongings in hand, like he's giving me time to change my mind. When I don't, he sighs. "Fine."

"Do *you* feel uncomfortable?" I query.

There's a prolonged pause until he finally mutters, "No."

I glare at him through the darkness as he unpacks his belongings and quietly unboxes the air mattress.

He makes a dramatic show about stubbing his toe on my makeup box. "You didn't clear away your stuff."

"You say that like you're shocked," I point out, unbothered.

"I would have assumed you'd at least try to tidy up before I came back."

It's a fair hypothesis. If I were having company at my condo, I'd never let anyone see it in such disarray. Ronan always used to comment about how clean I kept the place, completely oblivious to the state of it only minutes before his arrival. I'm not sure why it's any different for Evan, a virtual stranger.

"Don't flatter yourself. I don't care to impress you."

He kicks some of my clothes away to make space for the mattress. "I'm very aware of that."

The air pump is one of those electric ones that automatically inflates the mattress on its own. Frankly, it sounds like a dying creature. It's also incredibly loud. I can't help but snicker.

"What's so funny?" Evan asks.

"There's no way the entire house can't hear that pump."

"We'll just tell them you were blow-drying your hair."

"Correction: you were blow-drying yours."

He scoffs, standing when the mattress is fully inflated. It's nearly as big as my bed. I toss him the throw quilt from the end of my bed, along with an extra pillow. When he turns and faces the wall to remove his T-shirt for bed, my first instinct is to dive for cover under the blankets. I'm being attacked, visually.

Tanned linebacker shoulders like these surely don't exist in real life, just in Disney's *Hercules*. In fact, delicious ropy muscle tapering ever so slightly at the waist should probably be considered an international war crime. Just as I slide into a spontaneous fantasy involving running my fingers down the hard planes of that back, he whips around, assailing me with a frontal angle.

This changes my entire worldview. My type has always fluctuated between dad bods and slim builds, nothing in between. Binary options are safe. And Evan has single-handedly created a third, nameless category, which is honestly just rude.

One does not simply get a physique like his by crushing protein shakes and pumping weights in the gym. These aren't your typical washboard, cheese-grater abs. This man is thick, bulky, with a build that's surely capable of wrestling a grizzly bear. How many abs am I dealing with here? I can't be sure. They're vaguely outlined, taunting me, a dense shield of muscle over muscle, hard-earned in the rugged outdoors. From years of hauling sixty-five-pound steel lobster traps out of the sea like it's no big deal. My gaze blazes a path from his barrel chest down to the smattering of light brown hair disappearing into the waistband of his boxer briefs (plaid, of course).

"Holyshitballs," I mutter into the quilt.

"Huh?" he asks, settling onto the air mattress below.

I shrug nonchalantly, pulling my traitorous eyes away. I can't just ogle him with blatant thirst while I'm lying here under the covers in unflattering beige underwear. "You have a nice body. And don't take that as a compliment," I warn.

No response. I just made things weirder.

After what feels like an eternity, he finally speaks. "How was that *not* a compliment?"

"Because there was no positivity attached to the statement. It was simply a scientific observation."

"Okay, then."

We're silent for a solid fifteen minutes as I recover, trying to bleach the visual from my mind by scrolling social media at triple speed.

"So." His deep voice startles me. "You asked about Jack."

My stomach curls inward. "Honestly, it's fine," I say quickly. "It wasn't my place. We don't need to talk about it. Or anything else, for that matter."

The air mattress squeaks as he turns to face me. "You just don't want to talk at all for the whole week?"

"I think we should stick to talking about what's necessary to get through unscathed."

He's silent for a couple of moments. "Well, I'm sorry either way. You mentioned you lost your dad, and—"

His tone sounds like pity, and I don't like it one bit. I feel exposed, despite the heavy quilt draped over me. Why did I have to open this can of worms last night by bringing up my dad's death like a freak? No wonder I don't make a habit of divulging my emotional baggage to others.

"Evan, I just said we don't need to talk about it. We're fake fiancés, not friends. We don't need to commiserate about our loved ones. I'm here to help you get your family on its merry way to reconciliation and save the inn. You're going to help me get good social media content. That's it. Okay?" My tone comes out harsher than intended.

"Right. Okay," he says tersely, flopping onto his back.

"Fine," I add nonsensically. He will not get the last word.

"Good night."

"Good night."

♥ chapter fifteen

EVAN IS UP at three in the morning. The timing makes sense, it being the Devil's Hour and all.

Through my half sleep, I squint in the darkness as he stumbles around, opening and closing drawers in search of his clothes.

When he heads into the bathroom to brush his teeth, I curl my pillow over my ears to block out the *buzz* of his electric toothbrush.

He exits the bathroom after what feels like an eternity, and I grumble, "Why are you conscious right now? Go back to sleep."

"Some of us aren't on vacation. I still need to work," he whispers hoarsely.

"Work?" I lurch to a seated position, swinging my legs out of bed.

Evan's eyes rake up my bare legs before snapping back to my face, leaving a trail of erupting goose bumps in their wake. Then again, maybe it's just the exposure to the cool air outside of the blanket. "Maybe the concept is unfamiliar, but *work* is when—"

I'd rip him a new one if I weren't so alarmed. "You're going back out on the water? Even after what happened?"

He shrugs nonchalantly. "I need to check my traps."

You'd think after nearly dying in the water a mere day ago, one would need to work up the courage to return. Not Evan, apparently.

"You're concussed. Dr. Chernoby said you weren't allowed strenuous activity for days."

He rolls his eyes like a petulant teen and spins on his heel, heading for the door. "It's not strenuous activity. And I feel perfectly fine."

One moment I'm sitting on the side of the bed, and the next, my back is pressed against the door, blocking his exit. Perhaps one of the ghosts at the inn has possessed my body. I'm not sure why I care so much. It must be the all-too-recent memory of seeing him go overboard. Seeing him convulsing on the stretcher. Unconscious in the hospital. I dislike this man with my entire essence, but the simple fact remains: it would be unethical to let a recently concussed individual return to the water prematurely.

"Hauling steel traps out of the water is strenuous. You're not going," I say, jutting my chin up in a poor attempt to match his height.

"You have five seconds to move," he warns, pupils dilated.

I don't budge. Nor does my eye contact.

He takes a daring step forward, his hard chest grazing mine in the process. As he attempts to reach around me for the doorknob,

I widen my stance like a bouncer at an exclusive VIP nightclub for Manhattan's elite, blocking access with my body.

We stay like this for multiple breaths. Chest to chest. Locked in a literal standoff. Like one of those cheesy black-and-white Westerns that Dad used to watch late at night, with me half asleep on his lap. All we need is a pair of smoking pistols and a rogue tumbleweed.

There's no way Evan can get to the doorknob unless he physically pulls me aside. I half expect him to do so, because he can. He has at least seven inches on me. He also hates me. I can tell by the way his brow pinches when he looks at me. In the way his chest rises and falls in rapid bursts.

The faint scent of spearmint from his toothpaste breezes past my cheek, zinging through my entire body, culminating in a dull ache between my thighs. If I really wanted to, I could lean in. Touch his chest. Run my fingers through his thick, dirty-blond beard.

Thankfully, those errant thoughts are depleted by his death glare. He raises a hand, and I'm certain he's going to force me out of the way, once and for all. But he just rests his palm on the door behind my head, inches away from my right ear.

"Why are you being so difficult?" His question comes out in a strained growl.

"Because," I manage, straightening my posture, "you're listening to the doctor. You're resting. For at least two days." I poke him in the chest for emphasis, pushing him backward.

He lets out a caveman grumble, turns, and flops onto the air mattress.

I settle back in bed, heart racing, body far too alert for three in the morning. The sensation flowing through me must be utter shock. Evan Whaler actually listened to me. Praise be. Hallelujah. I was victorious. Though now is hardly a time to celebrate.

Before I turn over and attempt to fall back asleep with a mattress spring burrowing into my lower back, I sneak a peek at Evan. He's flat on his back, covers pulled to his chin, ball cap draped over his eyes as if blocking the nonexistent light.

What a strange, strange man.

• • •

EVAN'S REST DOESN'T last long. By the time I head down for breakfast at nine, he's already in the garage, tinkering away on some old boat engine he and Ned decided to fix.

I spend the afternoon in much more pleasant company, exploring the grassy grounds of the inn with Nana as she tells me all about how nice it is to get away from the assisted living facility. Apparently, Bruce, her tattooed veteran bingo buddy, has taken a liking to her (finally), and she wants to "torture him a little" by being away for the week.

She also takes the opportunity to recount the history of the inn. How her late mother-in-law first came to Canada from Ireland with her sisters, a set of twins who refused to get married because they despised the male species. How she married a Whaler and built the inn with her sisters. They each helped run the place well into their nineties and demanded to be buried in the backyard. She's convinced their spirits reside there.

She leads me down a patch of trimmed grass stretching toward the dense forest (the view from my room), which is mostly flat, only sloping to the right of the inn. There's a narrow pathway dusted with pine needles that leads to a tranquil yet muddy pond straight out of a children's storybook, lily pads and all.

A dilapidated white gazebo sits next to the pond. Its paint is peeled, so much so that *white* is probably too liberal a description. Nana ushers me inside to sit, unbothered by the abundance of cobwebs draped above us from every angle, like a holiday garland.

"Let me give you a chart reading. I do it for everyone in the family," she offers eagerly. "I'd just need your birth date, the time you were born, and the location."

I cringe, cheeks turning pink. "I'd love a reading, Nana, but I actually don't know any of that. I'm adopted, so my birthday is more likely to be before the date they claim it is. Technically I'm a Sagittarius, but I actually think I'm more of a Scorpio."

Frankly, it's embarrassing how little I know about my origins and my past, including my own birthday. I've never felt a strong urge to find my birth parents or anything, but it's another thing to not have that option even if I wanted it.

Nana's thin brows raise as she picks lint off her cowl-neck sweater. "That's okay, dear. I think you're a Scorpio too, which means you're a water sign. My husband was a Scorpio. They're some of the most loyal, ambitious, and protective people. Though they're secretive. Don't like to show weakness much."

I tilt my head in consideration. "Sounds a lot like me."

She leans in. "Now, Evan is a Taurus. Stubborn and bullheaded as they come. The two of you are both strong personalities. Drawn to each other like flies to shit. But you'll really have to learn to make concessions and listen to each other. Compromise is key."

"Sounds like we have a lot to work through," I say, forcing away my wide grin.

"Maybe. But your chemistry is off the charts," she tells me, thin brows bouncing suggestively.

I do my best to mask my nausea. She couldn't be more wrong.

• • •

BY THE TIME dinner rolls around, there's tension over what meal to make. For the sake of peace, I offer to make my "famous spaghetti, an old family recipe."

My spaghetti is not in fact famous. Nor is it a family recipe. It's straight from Google. I don't have family recipes, unless you count the boxed mac and cheese I used to make for Julian when Dad was working late.

I'm on hands and knees, rooting through the bowels of the kitchen cupboards, searching in vain for a jar of Ragu so I can avoid crushing tomatoes like a pioneer, when Nessa comes shuffling in. Her eyes widen in delight when she spots me. She starts by making casual small talk, which somehow turns into a full-blown rant about Fiona and her alleged jealously toward her.

"She's been jealous of me all our lives. Do you know she even cried when I was born? The only way to appease her was by Dad naming his boat after her." She sighs in haughty derision. "It only got worse as we got older, whether it was toys, clothes, grades, boys, you name it."

As a third-party outsider, trash-talking Fiona doesn't seem right. So I just awkwardly smile and nod as she rambles about Fiona's moral inferiority.

"Do you have siblings, Mel?" she finally asks.

"One. A younger brother, Julian."

"It's hard, being the elder sibling, isn't it?"

I nod in hearty agreement. "Sometimes I feel like I'm his mom." The sheer number of times Julian shouted *You're not my mom!* since he was old enough to speak in full sentences is laughable.

The first time he said it was on his first day of kindergarten. I was eleven, old enough to assist with his morning routine like a "role-model older sister," according to Dad. Julian refused to wear the worn, too-large corduroy overalls a neighbor down the hall had donated to us in favor of his favorite Spider-Man PJ bottoms. There was no changing his mind. He was right, after all: I wasn't his mom, despite doing everything a mom should do on paper.

Even now, I find myself falling into the same habits. Today he sent a hasty text requesting I review all his employment and benefits paperwork, which I completed ASAP.

Nessa chuckles. "I hear that. Sometimes younger siblings are worse than your own children."

For reasons I cannot fathom, our mutual experience of having a younger sibling has quickly escalated to "Has my son made intimacy a priority in your relationship?"

I nearly drop the stack of ceramic plates I've retrieved from the cupboard, wholly unprepared to report on my fictional sex life with her son. "Um, well . . . I, uh—"

She steps closer, pulling her long gray hair over her shoulder, wooden bracelets clacking together. "Have you heard of the Erotic Blueprint quiz?"

"Um, no."

"Oh, I'll have to send you a link. I give it to all my clients. It's an arousal map, which tells you what your erotic language is."

I slowly nod, unwrapping a package of button mushrooms. "Oh—"

Before I can get a word in, she begins to explain the erotic languages, direct eye contact unyielding. Frankly, I'm too stunned to digest any of this information. As I stir the sauce, she segues back to Evan. "My son has always been a good lover. At least, that's what I hear around town," she says with a wink, oblivious to how disturbing this is. "I've told him ever since he hit puberty how important it is to make sure a woman finishes first. No matter what. Has he been making sure you finish first?"

I bite my lip. My body temperature has officially skyrocketed from ninety-eight degrees to Satan's Asshole. Before I can respond, a deep voice bellows "Mom!" from the entryway.

It's a very alarmed Evan. I've never been so relieved to see this plaid-obsessed oaf.

"Hi, honey. Mel and I were just talking about—"

"Yeah, I heard. Please don't. Our sex life is completely fine." He gives me the briefest sympathetic look that screams *I am so sorry for my mother* before shaking his head.

Nessa folds him into a motherly hug. "Nonsense. Everyone could use a little improvement. I'm just trying to make sure everyone's happy."

He accepts her embrace, rocking her comparatively slender frame in a way that catches me off guard. I'm not sure I've seen a tender mother-and-son bond up close. My throat tightens, thinking about what Julian missed out on.

"I appreciate it, Mom. But we're fine. Right, Mel?"

She shakes her head. "See, you keep saying *fine*. But *fine* isn't reaching your full potential, is it?"

"Our sex life is . . . marvelous. Transcendent, even," I lie, unable to come up with a word that doesn't sound like I'm a snobby highbrow food critic.

Evan emits a violent full-body cough.

Satisfied, Nessa fusses with the wrinkles on the shoulder of Evan's flannel, attempting to iron them out with her palm. "How did my son become so handsome?"

Crimson-faced, he gives his mom one last squeeze before heading to the fridge. He pulls out the strawberries, grabs a handful, and sets the bowl in front of me wordlessly.

"You know, I'm actually surprised a place like Cora's Cove is a big enough market for sex therapists," I say, dumping sliced veggies into a preheated pot.

Nessa chuckles knowingly, wiping some tomato cores off the cutting board and into the trash. "Quite the opposite. Not much else for people to do here but have sex. Though the downside is half the town doesn't make eye contact with me anymore."

After explaining a couple of awkward incidents—without using names, of course—Nessa finally heads into the family room to sit with Ned. Unfortunately, Evan doesn't slink off into obscurity as I'd hoped.

"Your mom's a delight," I say.

"She can get . . . personal," he finally replies, spectating as I slice garlic, arms crossed like he's Gordon Ramsay and I'm his lowly intern sous-chef. "You don't strike me as the kind of girl who knows her way around a kitchen."

Irritation bubbles inside me. He's not wrong. But it's not because I'm some spoiled brat like he thinks. I'm not afraid of cooking and hard work. It's just that no one has ever taught me how. Mom left before she could teach me any useful life skills, and Dad's kitchen knowledge didn't extend beyond frozen food, hence the ketchup sandwiches he used to love.

"You don't strike me as the kind of guy who knows his way around a clit, but you don't see me pointing that out," I note. I'm flat-out lying, of course. He definitely looks like he knows his way around a woman's body. But I can't tell him that, so instead, I gesture toward him with my garlicky knife like the mature human I am.

It's unclear whether his horror-movie eyes are due to the knife I'm wielding in his face or my causal use of the word *clit*. Either way, he's uncomfortable. He closes his eyes and takes a breath before clearing his throat, resetting.

He watches for a couple more moments as I move on to peel the next clove of garlic. He's dying inside, clearly itching to say something. I can tell by the way he's biting the inside of his mouth. Finally, he does.

"Let me show you." Without warning, he's behind me. The buttons of his flannel press against my spine as his rough hand covers mine in an attempt to gain control of the knife.

There's tension here. Me, pushing down, determined to continue chopping this damn garlic clove solo. Him pulling upward, loosening my grip on the knife.

"It's faster if you do this." His gravelly voice in the shell of my ear weakens my resolve immediately, allowing him to demonstrate. He takes the liberty of picking up my left hand and moving it to the tip of the blade. Then, he shifts my right hand back to the handle. "Don't lift the knife off the cutting board. The trick is a rocking motion."

As he demonstrates, the garlic slices thinly, much more efficiently than my hack job. I'd ask how he learned this if I weren't feeling bested.

Once the clove is fully minced, we move on to the next. And once it's completed, he goes back over it, despite the slices being thin enough. There's a moment where he stops, and I don't know if it's my imagination, but the pad of his thumb does a gentle swipe over the soft skin in the area between my wrist and thumb.

His woodsy scent is all around me now, almost overpowering the fresh garlic. I work down the fireball that's formed in my throat, my body buzzing like a live wire.

It's only when Nana pops her head in the doorway that he startles, releasing my hands.

"Looks delicious. You're lucky you're marrying a woman who can cook," Nana says, prancing over to smell the veggies simmering in the pot on the stove next to us.

"She's practically a chef," Evan says ever so proudly, stepping away from me. "Almost got her own show on the Food Network."

Nana's eyes widen in astonishment. "Did you go to culinary school?"

Irritation bubbles inside me. Maybe I should have used that knife while I had the chance. "Nope. I'm an amateur. Everything I know is self-taught. Evan is exaggerating, of course. I'm pretty average," I say, shooting him a glare.

"Anything but average," he says, planting a chaste kiss on my temple before he trots off.

♥ chapter sixteen

HAVE NEWS," AN excited Crystal tells me over FaceTime.

"News?" The porch swing squeaks under my weight as I bat a pesky moth away from my face.

She pauses for dramatic effect. "Scott and I bought a house." The last half comes out squeaky, like she's just taken a drag of helium. She tilts her phone in the direction of Scott man-splaying on the couch, cuddling with his dog. He gives me an eager wave.

"Hey, Mel! How's Canada treating you?"

"You guys are moving?" I bellow, stunned, not bothering to answer his question.

A wistful smile spreads across Crystal's face. "In a few weeks. You're gonna flip when you see the place, Mel. It's my dream house. Not too modern, kind of farmhouse chic. It has the perfect space in the basement for a home gym. And Scott is really pumped about the backyard. He and Trevor already have plans to build a big deck.

And the best part: it's close to my parents' place." She pauses, awaiting my congratulations.

Her news hits me harder than a wine hangover. My eyes divert to the tiny ants carrying a tiny leaf near the base of the swing in a sad attempt to conceal my true reaction: sadness.

I'm officially a monster.

I should be ecstatic for my bestie right now. She's bought the home of her dreams with her husband, an hour away from the city. And while it's not *that* far, we won't be close enough to have last-minute girls' nights where all I have to do is stumble home a few blocks after three too many cocktails.

My shoulders drop. "Wait, does this mean you're leaving Excalibur?" I ask, referring to our gym. The place we've spent hours together, sweating our asses off, lying on the floor, unloading our personal baggage.

She dips her chin. "Yeah. It's just too far of a commute. But I did chat with the owner of a boutique gym near the new house. She's interested in having me teach there too. I'll miss Excalibur, but it'll be a really nice change."

"Change," I repeat, dazed. "I'll have to go buy you one of those wooden *Live, Laugh, Love* signs for your porch."

She pretends to gag. "I'm already mentally burning it."

Before I let the ridiculously selfish disappointment wash over me, I muster the energy to squeal with the excitement she deserves, *ooh*ing and *aah*ing over the stunning listing photos, which are basically a lifestyle influencer's wet dream.

I ask all the right questions about the neighborhood and potential renovations. She explains how she and Scotty researched nearby shops and how high the school district is ranked. She even promises me first dibs on the spare bedroom. And while I am truly thrilled for her, it feels like the end of something. Like she's moving on to the next phase of life without me.

After our call ends, I head back inside to escape the bugs, only to be summoned into the dining room. Ned wants me, Evan, and Lucy to play a board game called Settlers of Catan.

"Uncle Ned, I don't think Mel wants to play. Board games aren't her thing," Evan says, pleased with himself.

I fake a hearty chuckle and gouge his shoulder with my nails. "Not true. I've always wanted to try it," I lie, not wanting to disappoint Ned.

Turns out, Catan isn't all that difficult to understand. It's a game of trading and amassing finite resources to build roads, settlements, and cities for points. I've quickly deduced two main strategies: either you go for wood and brick to make roads or you risk it with ore, sheep, and wheat to buy development cards. The first player to ten points wins.

Unfortunately, Evan and I have landed on the same strategy. Roads.

The game is long, tedious. But I refuse to lose quietly. Ned and Lucy voluntarily quit, turning in once Evan and I have both taken over territory on the board, locked in a battle to get the Longest Road card. Whoever claims that will most likely take the victory.

Silence pulses between us as we study our next moves with the intensity of the world championship chess tournament in *The Queen's Gambit*.

"When are you going to give up and just trade with me?" he asks from across the table, fanning his cards in his hands like a professional casino dealer.

"Never, because I'd be handing you the key to victory."

"We need to trade for mutual benefit. That's the point of the game," he argues.

I eye him over my cards as I take a sip of beer. "What do you need? You'd have to make the deal pretty sweet."

"I need wood, first of all."

I nearly spit out my beer. "You need wood, huh?"

His eyes snag mine and there's a faint trace of a smile, like he's trying not to laugh. "Are you ten years old?"

I ignore his question, straightening one of my roads, carelessly turning over one of his settlements in the process. "I'll give you your precious wood . . . if, and only if, you give me two bricks and a sheep."

He blows the air out of his cheeks, waving me off like a pesky fly as he rights his settlement. "You're delusional. Not a chance."

"Then we're at a stalemate."

"Looks like we are."

We sit in a stare-off for longer than necessary before he yawns. "Should we call it a tie? It's one in the morning."

"Absolutely not. Why don't you be the gentleman you're not and just allow me, your darling fake fiancée, to beat you?"

This gets a smile. A half-second one, at least. "*Darling*, I would never do that."

"I think you would. If I wore you down long enough."

His brow quirks. "What makes you think you could wear me down?"

"I once read in a relationship advice column that there's always a submissive and a dominant in every relationship." He's already giving me a perturbed look. "And no, I don't mean that sexually.

Relax. I just mean there's one person who calls the shots and leads the pace, while the other is happy to follow and submit."

"We both know I'm not a follower," he declares, eyes glinting in a challenge.

I hold firm. "Do we, though? Because I'm always the leader." I've always been a leader. Consult every personality test. The Myers-Briggs. My Enneagram results. My second-grade report card, wherein my teacher called me "bossy." Nana's recent astrology reading.

"Why do I get the feeling you'd be a nightmare in group projects?"

I tilt my head, lips spreading in a serene smile so as not to show weakness. "Look, Cap, we both can't be the leader for this arrangement. Surely it won't hurt you to stop being a caveman alpha for a couple of days and play the bumbling husband role."

"What's the bumbling husband role?"

I wave my hand dismissively. "You know, the one who follows the antiquated mantra of *Happy wife, happy life.* Brags to his friends about letting his wife watch a chick flick so he can go golfing with his boys."

He mirrors my posture, leaning in ever so slightly. "I don't know about you, but my relationship, fake or not, isn't gonna be a barter system. I like to think I'd be more than happy giving my wife what she wants and needs without expecting shit in return."

"But only if you get to steer the ship and call the shots, right?" I don't mean that question to come out harsh. It's really my way of deflecting what he's just said—about giving his wife what she needs. Something about his statement does something to my already-liquefied insides.

He sits back, folding his elbows on the table. "There's a difference between taking the lead and being a controlling asshole. And when it comes to work, relationships, and sex, I don't take a back seat."

The low, husky way he's just said the mere word *sex* melts my mind. I shift slightly to relieve the tension that's built between my thighs. "Your mom would be proud."

Another half-second ghost of a smile. "She would."

"But just so you know, I don't take a back seat, either."

His stare is heated, prickling the back of my neck. I think he's waiting for me to say something else.

I clear my throat, breaking eye contact as I straighten my game pieces. "In the interest of avoiding a premature fake breakup before Sunday, I think we should agree that we'll be equals in the relationship. Two dominant personalities that will need to compromise from time to time."

He considers that. "Fine. Works for me. But I'm still not letting you win," he decides, gesturing to the game board.

"You sure about that?" I throw down the two brick and two wood cards I've been saving all along. Then I pin him with a righteous smile as I plunk my final two roads down, blocking his entirely. "And that's game."

• • •

"IT'S ONLY FAIR that the victor gets the bathroom first," I say, racing up the stairs, Evan hot on my heels.

I don't know why we're running for the bathroom like children. Maybe it's the lingering effects of the board game's competitive spirit?

"For the record, the only reason you had extra bricks was because Uncle Ned took pity on you as a beginner."

An evil laugh escapes the depths of my throat as we speed down the hall toward our bedroom. "Maybe I'm just better than you at negotiating to get what I want."

He lets out an unintelligible grumble. I find my face split with a smile by the time we reach our bathroom. I dart in, closing the door in his face.

There's an exaggerated groan from the other side of the door before he knocks.

"Excuse you, I'm washing my face," I shout over the running faucet.

"You're gonna take, like, half an hour. I just need to brush my teeth. It'll take me two minutes, max."

I make him wait while I scrub my face with my cleanser, only opening the door once I've slathered myself with my yogurt repairing mask.

In the dim light, his eyes widen and the corner of his mouth tugs upward again when he sees my face. Something about drawing a smile from him gives me a little rush.

He swiftly pulls it back, replacing it with a scowl, brows creased as he slinks in beside me in front of the sink. When his shoulder grazes mine, I'm reminded how small this bathroom is. He could probably touch both walls if he spread his arms out.

When he reaches for his damn electric toothbrush, his forearm accidentally grazes my boob. Thankfully I'm still wearing a bra. He yanks his arm away like he's been branded, leaning as far away as he can without being out of bounds of the sink.

I still have ten minutes before I rinse this mask off, so I retrieve my toothbrush out of my travel bag and slather it with toothpaste. His toothpaste. And we stand in front of the mirror, shoulders just barely touching, brushing furiously.

I brush longer than normal, determined to win whatever new game this is. In an unspoken rule, we've determined that the first to stop loses. But I also keep brushing because I don't know what else to do. My body is a bundle of energy, bursting at the seams with nowhere to go.

We brush and brush until we have no more toothpaste to spit.

Finally, we both telepathically decide it's gone on long enough, and we rinse our mouths. He reaches around me to set his toothbrush on the other side, the side with his shaving kit, which doesn't appear to get much use given the dead-animal pelt on his face.

When his chest presses into my side, his warm, minty breath grazes my neck, sending a tingle shooting down my spine. I idly wonder what would happen if I turned my head. If I pressed my palms against his chest. If I raked my nails through his hair. There's a traitorous part of me that wants to capture those lips with mine. That wants to feel his rough beard against my soft skin.

Against my better judgment, I absorb him, burning a trail with my gaze from the swell of his biceps to his Adam's apple, bobbing ever so slightly. The path leads me up to the squareness of his jaw, somehow visible even under his beard, swooping up to those eyes.

He smirks, like he knew I would check him out, taking his turn to roam my features like a much-needed map to a place he's never been. Unexpectedly, he cups my jaw and my breath hitches.

His grip is gentler than I imagined him capable of, lingering there for a couple of long beats before he smooths his thumb upward. My stomach flips as he studies me, eyes narrowed, assessing.

With a soft swipe, similar to the one I knew I didn't imagine in the kitchen, he wipes a clump of cream from my face mask that's hanging off my jawline, evening it out.

Then, before I can even blink, he abruptly spins around and walks out, leaving me with my chest heaving, bracing myself with the edge of the bathroom counter.

Unsatisfied, I press my nails hard into my palms, forming little half-moon indents. My heart is still racing by the time I garner the fortitude to come out of the bathroom. He's already stretched out on the air mattress, eyes closed.

A wave of relief washes over me as I slide into bed. Am I dreaming, or were we an inch shy of jumping each other's bones in the bathroom? And worse, did I want to?

This cannot be a thing. I know that. Normally, I'm a proud advocate of no-strings-attached, emotionless sex. Maybe it's just my stubborn pride, but the last thing I'm going to do is give Evan a good time, especially after the way he's treated me since the moment I arrived. He doesn't deserve an orgasm. Not to mention, we're sharing a bedroom for an entire week. Besides, I'm here for my business. My livelihood. Period.

We lie in a weird, thick silence as I mindlessly scroll through my phone in an effort to cleanse my mind of intruding thoughts. I stop at a fellow influencer who took some majestic shots with those gigantean ancient moss-covered trees at Yosemite National Park.

"Are you really gonna click around on your phone all night?" he asks in the grumpy tone I'm accustomed to. It's marginally soothing.

"In place of what? Riveting philosophical pillow talk with you?" I ask.

A grunt.

"Do my phone habits offend your delicate sensibilities that much?"

"Yes. One less star."

I roll my eyes in the darkness. "Keep talking and you'll be at no stars. And, by the way, I was promised content for social media. I'd like to go on a hike tomorrow morning."

He responds with another one-syllable grunt before turning over on his side.

I'll take that as a no.

♥ chapter seventeen

E VAN'S FACE IS the first thing I see when I wake up.

For a hot second, I'm convinced I'm in the midst of an erotic dream involving a sexy lumberjack in red flannel, until he whips a Nature Valley granola bar at my face.

"Here. Breakfast for the road," he says, low and gravelly, as the bar bounces off the center of my forehead. "Meet me out front."

Fuming, I fumble for my phone on the nightstand, which confirms my suspicion. It's only five in the morning. At least he's consistent in his primary method of torture (sleep deprivation).

Before I can gather the wherewithal to rip him a new one for assaulting me with processed snacks, he's already stomped out of the room and closed the door behind him. Alas, I'll have to get my revenge elsewhere—by taking my sweet time selecting today's outfit (a bubble-gum-pink spandex workout set).

When I'm finally ready, I find Evan in the garage, already

seated behind the wheel of a gas-guzzling Chevy pickup truck, sipping out of a steaming stainless steel travel mug. He lifts his gaze, scowling when I wrench the passenger door open. I expect to be reamed out for taking my time, but he just watches with subdued satisfaction as I struggle my way into the truck like it's Mount Everest.

Even though I'm in running shoes—what Evan would refer to as "proper footwear"—the sheer height of this truck is daunting. I let out an ungraceful grunt as I hoist myself onto the seat. It smells like Evan in here—like campfire, a hint of leather, and a splash of clean laundry from the Febreze air freshener clipped to the right-side vent.

"We're hiking. Why do you need such a big bag?" He arrows a steely glare at the tote bag at my feet, and I'm inhumanely reminded of last night in the bathroom. When my sexually deprived self wanted him to prop me on the bathroom counter and do unspeakable things.

I promptly submerge those thoughts deep in the murky recesses of my mind. "Why do you need such a big truck?" I counter, unwrapping the granola bar he generously tossed at my face.

No response.

"Trying to make up for some shortcomings down below?" I let my eyes drop to his crotch for a split second, which really gets his temple pulsing.

"I need a truck to haul my boat. And I need the bed space for my fishing gear and equipment," he responds matter-of-factly.

"I need space too. For the essentials." I dig out my selfie stick from the depths of my bag, brandishing it in his face for emphasis.

He shields his face with his free hand as though I'm about to strike him with it. "All right, all right. Put that thing away before you give me another concussion."

. . .

IT'S OFFICIAL. NATURE truly has it out for me.

The prospect of the hike started out promising. Upon studying a three-panel map (color-coded by degree of difficulty) in the gravel parking lot, I selected a route that hugs the water, leading to a waterfall. Waterfall photos are always a hit on social media.

Determined to prove myself, I take off on the packed dirt trail like an explorer expertly tracking wild animals purely based on their droppings and the odd footprint every two miles. To my dismay, the trail is flat for a total of two minutes before sloping upward into a forty-five-degree incline.

My calves are on fire already. See? First to die in a slasher. A shooting pain spikes up the backs of my legs with each crunch of leaves and twigs under my feet and gets progressively worse. Turns out, incline treadmill walking in a climate-controlled gym is no match for this shit. One could argue it's my own fault for choosing a trail labeled *Strenuous* in bold red, the color of fresh blood, but proving Evan right just doesn't sit well with my soul.

Thank god for the canopy of trees above, blocking out the sun. Otherwise I'd probably perish from heat exhaustion. As we trudge deeper, a thick humidity hangs in the air like the faint promise of rain.

I should probably take in the lush greenery. I should appreciate the scatter of tiny forest creatures taking cover in the trees. I should be one with nature. Unfortunately, I'm too busy staring at the ground. The exposed roots and moss-covered rocks are

AMY LEA

proving to be a tripping hazard, jutting every which way from the earth like nature's very own booby trap. There are even a couple of overturned tree trunks to traverse.

Evan offers me a hand over one of the particularly large trunks, which I decline, preferring to struggle all by my lonesome. Of course, Evan scales it effortlessly, climbing and flexing like a genetically modified super-soldier.

Just as we approach an enchanting wooden bridge arching over a burbling stream straight out of a woodland fairy tale, the next bend offers yet another harsh incline. This trail is even narrower and rockier, threading through thick brush. I'm fairly certain I've just spotted a juicy green caterpillar on a protruding branch that nearly took my eye out.

"Glad you didn't bring your purse?" Evan asks behind me, tone gleeful at the sound of my wheezing.

We'd fought about my purse in the parking lot. To be fair, I was being stubborn. According to Evan, my gum, spare makeup, Tylenol, tampons, headphones, mini sewing kit, brush, travel-size extra-strength hair spray, and day planner aren't necessary for the hike. The only thing he allowed me to put in his backpack was Lucy's DSLR camera and my water bottle (because he didn't want to deal with me if I succumbed to dehydration).

I'm thankful I'm not carrying the entire purse, but I refuse to admit that. "I don't know. The extra-strength hair spray could save our lives."

"Please explain."

"It's potent enough to double as bear mace. I read it in a magazine."

"A magazine? Then it must be true," he says, tone laced with sarcasm. "And you threatened me with hair spray the other night when you were drunk, by the way."

A riptide of embarrassment washes over me at the thought of my drunken state after the Anchor. I have no recollection of saying anything about blinding him with my hair spray, though I'm proud of my drunk self for staying feisty.

"If we wind up mauled and bloody like Leo DiCaprio in *The Revenant*, I'm blaming you," I warn him.

"That was a grizzly in that movie. We only have black bears here. They're not known for mauling humans to death. Though they might make an exception for a fancy Boston girl."

Before I can respond, a hard-core couple passes us in the opposite direction. They look straight from the Eddie Bauer fall catalog with their matching windbreakers, bucket hats, multipocketed khakis, and walking poles. Evan and I greet them with a friendly "Hello," because greeting everyone you come across in nature is apparently the thing to do.

There are a couple of forks in the path. On my second wrong turn, Evan wordlessly power walks in front of me with his long stride. With Evan leading, we pick up the pace slightly and head toward a set of stairs going downhill. I let myself relax, taking in the chirps of various birds and the rush of the river running parallel below.

The stairs are short-lived, and we're forced to climb a rocky, jagged slope around another bend. Eventually, the faint roar of the water transitions to a thunderous crash of water against rock, vibrating the earth under my feet.

Just when my ankles are starting to give way, I see it. A rush of liquid silver thunders down in a spray of mist, crashing over the asphalt-colored rocks and decaying logs at the base of the stream. The water below is tinted the most vibrant army green. I'm not sure there's a filter in existence that could improve this view.

Evan has taken a seat on a massive rock, expression neutral, entirely unreadable. I absorb a few serene moments of perfectly imperfect untouched nature before rifling through his backpack, where I stashed Lucy's camera.

"If you could please get some shots from this angle," I instruct, gesturing with my whole arm like a fluorescent vest–wearing aircraft marshal on a runway. "I want the waterfalls in the background."

He cuts me a look, aggrieved as he reaches lazily for the camera. Our fingers graze ever so slightly. I blink away the warmth that spreads through me—similar to when we've held hands in front of his family.

But before I've even angled myself optimally atop the smaller, rounder boulder, he's already started snapping photos, while seated. Not ten seconds after I've finally settled into the proper pose, he stands and returns the camera. The corner of his mouth tugs upward ever so slightly as he pivots to walk away. When I check the photos, the source of his amusement is clear.

There is a special place in hell for those who casually take upward-angled shots of others. They belong in the same circle of fire as the friends who airbrush only themselves in group photos, leaving everyone else with shiny foreheads and off-white smiles. But the upward angle is truly where self-confidence goes to die. And that's not even taking into account the fact that he's cropped the majority of the waterfall out of the frame.

I hand the camera back. "We'll have to take these again.

Getting the falls in the background was kind of the entire point of the hike."

A weary sigh escapes him, as though I've just told him we need to start the hike all over again. "Those pictures are fine."

I zoom in on the shot where my mouth is wide open, midsentence, and my one eye is partway closed in a demented wink. Either I've suddenly become hugely unphotogenic or he's doing this on purpose. I have a sneaking suspicion it's the latter. "You can't tell me this is flattering. I look like a monster from a dark dimension."

He scrunches his nose, trying not to laugh in my face. "It really captures the moment, don't you think? I wouldn't worry about your stink eye too much. You probably have an app to fix that."

"Please retake. You'll have to stand and back up to get the full waterfall in the shot. Probably to there." I point to a bush a couple paces back.

"I thought the point was getting pictures of you, not the waterfall," he shoots back, refusing to take the camera.

"Obviously both. I want to be in the frame in the right-hand corner, not front and center. The waterfall is the focal point."

"But you've barely even looked at it since we've been here."

"I did look at it. A lot, actually. Am I supposed to sit here for an hour just staring at it? That's the point of taking the photos. To preserve the memory. I'm not leaving here until I get a good shot."

He meets my stare in defiance before finally caving.

The next round of photos is a marginal improvement. He's got the frame right this time, capturing the height of the waterfall in totality. If he hadn't been so rushed, capturing the blur of my hand while I was adjusting my braid crown, it would be a half-decent photo.

AMY LEA

"These won't work. Again," I tell him, handing the camera back.

He draws his shoulders back and blows out an audible breath. "You're really killing me here."

I reposition myself on the rock. "If I'm going to be a good fake fiancée, the least you could do is be a good photographer."

"Have you ever considered maybe it's just your face?" he asks flatly.

My mouth goes dry. If I were a cartoon, steam would be billowing out of my ears. "What's that supposed to mean? Are you calling me ugly?"

He runs a hand through his hair. "No. It's just . . . you always look pissed. By default."

"Are you saying I have a resting bitch face?" People have accused me of RBF my entire life. I constantly have to assure people I'm not overflowing with homicidal rage and this is just my regular face.

"Will you push me in the water if I am?"

I jab a finger toward him. "Listen, my bitch face never rests. It's always ready."

"I'll remember that." His deep laugh echoes through the forest.

"Okay, we're going to try something else. You're going to pose for me instead."

His brow furrows. "Why?"

"Because. This way I can show you what I want. The exact angle and frames."

I expect him to put up a fight, but, shockingly, he takes direction well. Admittedly, watching a burly lumberjack in an array of exaggerated poses, including sticking his butt out and holding his hand above his hip red carpet–style, is a sight to behold.

Maybe I'm delirious from an excess of fresh, unpolluted air, but I suspect he's having the tiniest bit of fun with this. I didn't think Evan Whaler was capable of fun, unless you count plotting ways to torment me. I'm not sure how to process this new information, so I bury my face in the camera, scanning the outtakes.

"I think you missed your calling as a model in high fashion," I say, suppressing a giggle at a particularly amusing shot of him holding a crisp maple leaf over one eye like a pirate, while also pouting seductively like a hungry couture model.

"Hey, I only cooperated so we can get out of here. You better delete those. They aren't for human eyes." Based on his scowl as he makes a grab for the camera, Fun Evan has left the building, it seems.

I manage to evade his reach, delighting in his annoyance. "I was actually thinking of making one of them my new lock screen."

This garners a smirk. "Lock screen, huh? Someone's a little obsessed."

"You are my darling after all," I lie, swiftly uploading the leaf picture, along with one that accentuates his ass. For safekeeping, of course, should I ever require blackmail. When I show him my new lock screen, a zoomed-in shot of his pouty face, the corner of his mouth ticks up.

"Noted. You'll be sorry," he says cryptically before we switch places, with me as the model again. He's still no professional photographer, my face is slightly red from exertion, and my braid is a little frazzled, but I can work with these.

I transfer the remaining photos from Lucy's camera to my phone, pull up my editing app, and get to work adjusting the color in my face as well as the shine on my forehead.

Evan parks himself on the rock next to me, ensuring I have a direct view of his brand-new lock screen: the original shot where I look mid-exorcism. I suppose it's only fair.

The idea of anyone else seeing that photo gives me hives, but I make a concerted effort to give him nothing.

Regardless, he appears satisfied, leaning in to observe over my shoulder. "So how does this work? Do you edit your face in every single photo?"

"Yup. I start by editing out small things like blemishes or stray hairs. Sometimes things in the background I don't want, like a street sign or something. For example, I need to give myself eyelashes today."

He blinks. "You have eyelashes."

"My natural ones are super short. And my extensions all came off on the boat." Lash extensions have become part of my identity. The dramatic flair never fails to give me the confidence boost I need to put myself out there on social media.

"Let me see a before and after." When he makes a grabby-hands motion, I hand him my phone so he can flick back and forth between the two. "The before shot is better."

"You're not going to convince me."

"You are very defensive about this," he says, dropping my phone back in my hand.

"I have to be. Online trolls constantly demonize me for it."

"For what?"

I shrug. "For wearing makeup. Having work done. I don't

know." Ever since I started my @MelanieInTheCity account, I've had no shortage of haters in my DMs and comments calling me "fake" and trying to school me into being more "natural."

"Why do people care so much about what you do?"

"People have a visceral reaction to things that make other people feel better about themselves," I say. "They like to make beauty a moral issue. Women who aspire to unrealistic standards are bad. But women who don't conform are bad too. You can't win either way, so I figure I might as well do what makes me happy."

He falters slightly under my stony stare. "I still think the picture is better untouched."

"It is not," I say, zooming back in on the unedited photo.

"Post the original. You'll still get tons of clicks, you'll see."

I raise a brow. "Do you mean likes?"

"Sure. Whatever."

I consider this while taking a panoramic shot of the falls. "Maybe." He's still watching me, closemouthed, like he wants to say something but doesn't. "What? I know you want to make some sort of smart comment. What am I doing to displease you now?"

"Nothing," he mutters.

"Just say it."

"I was just wondering whether you were gonna take photos the entire time or if you planned on actually enjoying the view."

I blink. It's a startling yet fair point. "Oh, I'm going to enjoy it all right. I'm gonna enjoy the shit out of it." As I tuck both the camera and my phone in his bag, I sense him observing me.

"Yup. You look like you're having a grand ole time." He mocks my prim, stiff-backed pose on the rock with a casual smirk.

"I'm actually thriving right now." I make a point of dramatically inhaling through my nose, taking in the scent of the damp earth, remarkably similar to that after-rain smell. I probably wouldn't have noticed it otherwise. When the sunlight catches the water, turning it an almost tawny tone, I second-guess that filter completely. This place is overwhelmingly peaceful, despite the less-than-enthusiastic company.

A maple leaf floating along the top of the stream captures my attention. I imagine the leaf is carrying away all the heaviness inside me. My brain is no longer a jumble of tangled thoughts fighting for my attention. Maybe this is what mindfulness is. I've tried meditating in yoga classes, as well as with various mindfulness audios. But none have ever successfully stopped my racing thoughts. I'm always in panic mode, thinking about what I have to do to ensure I keep making money to support myself and Julian. How I can keep up the perfectly curated lifestyle I've built for myself. Until now.

Just as I'm starting to enjoy the simple act of sitting here in complete silence, Evan casually points to the ground at my feet. "There's a slug by your shoe."

I make a face at him, assuming he's being an asshole.

He is not.

It's shit-brown, about the length of my hand, and juicy as all hell.

"Nope" is all I say before hightailing it back to the trail, Evan's deep bellowing laughter at my heels.

Thankfully, the way back is less intense. Evan lets me guide us in a silent understanding that I prefer to lead. There are still rocks and tree trunks to traverse, but in the absence of an upward incline, I find myself enjoying it, despite the heat.

"So tell me. What was it like to grow up with a mom who's a sex therapist?" I ask, finally breaking the silence.

He takes a couple beats to respond. "It was interesting, if you couldn't already tell."

"I think it would be really cool to have a mom who's so open and free."

"Only if you think it's cool to have your mom guest lecture all your sex ed classes with her trunk full of condoms and dental dams." The color in his cheeks deepens to crimson. It's marginally adorable.

I snort. "A full trunk?"

"Oh yeah. Like a toy chest. But on wheels." He widens his arms to demonstrate, and a bubble of laughter escapes me.

"My dad never even gave me the Talk. He'd get uncomfortable when we watched a movie with a make-out scene."

"I assume he wasn't a sex therapist?"

I cringe at the mere image of tired-eyed Dad even uttering the word *sex*. "God no. But to be fair, he raised me as a single parent. I think the Talk was probably the last thing on his mind."

"Oh yeah?"

"Don't get me wrong. He was still a good dad, though, despite letting me and my brother watch R-rated horror movies in grade school." I press my lips together, forcing myself to stop talking. Why have I just revealed this to Evan, of all people? Nature really is a truth serum.

His brow arches and he gives me a contemplative look. "I get it. My mom raised me by herself too. It was hard on her, even though she never admitted it. It made us really close, though."

"Same with me and my dad. Though he worked late at random jobs a lot," I say, careful with my choice of words. "So when he finally came home, I'd be so excited to spend time with him, even though it was way past my bedtime. He'd ask me those Would You Rather questions until I fell asleep."

Evan chuckles, and the sound takes me off guard. "Like what? Give me an example."

I eye him warily before conjuring one. "Like . . . would you rather your only mode of transportation be a donkey or a giraffe?"

His shoulders lower as he falls back in stride with me. For the first time, we're walking side by side. "Definitely a giraffe."

"Why?"

"Easy. Height and distance. You?"

"You can't ask me the same question. You'll have to ask me another."

He thinks for a moment. "Would you rather everyone in the world have to wear identical clothes, all day, every day, or make two people fight, gladiator style, if they accidentally wear the same thing?"

"What do these identical outfits look like?"

"All-white jumpsuits. Like in those futuristic dystopian society movies."

"Are they shapeless?"

"Like a potato sack."

I consider this. "I mean, I look good in white, regardless. And I'd rather people not be responsible for murder. So the first option."

He swings me a look. "That surprises me."

"Are you surprised I'd give up my passion for fashion for the sake of humanity?"

"Maybe a little. But wait, what if the accidental outfit repeaters are horrible people?"

I slant him a considering glance. "How horrible? Petty crime or crimes against humanity—level horrible?"

"Crimes against humanity."

"I stand by my first answer," I tell him, barely making it over a rotting log.

He reaches out to steady me, hand clasping around my bicep. His touch electrifies my spine, nearly sending me face-first over the log. "Even if horrible people are finished off?"

"Are we really debating the morality of murder?" I ask, somehow managing to restabilize myself.

"Well, you brought it there." A mildly entertained dimpled smirk catches me off guard. I should not be noticing his dimples.

I blink the visual away, turning my eyes back to the ground in front of me. "Okay, my turn. Would you rather have two belly buttons or one nipple?"

❤ chapter eighteen

W E MAKE IT back to the parking lot alive. I may be covered in a sheen of sweat, and I probably smell like a swamp monster or a mildewed sports bra in the lost and found at the gym, but I'm actually feeling . . . light.

Turns out, nature isn't all that bad. While I'll never rest easy knowing bugs exist in this world, this hike restored me in a way that Botox and a steam facial never have. It's as if that waterfall eroded some of that pesky negativity chipping away at my stream of consciousness.

On that walk back, my thumb wasn't itching to check how many likes and comments I'd gotten on my latest post. And mostly, my stomach wasn't in knots over Julian. Instead, all my worries were quelled by a harmony and peace I'd never felt before.

Oddest of all, Evan and I had an actual conversation that wasn't laced with malice. Maybe miracles do happen.

When I finally check the time on my phone (10:30 a.m.), it feels jarring compared to the natural rhythm of nature. I don't know what kind of magic this is, but time seemingly stopped on that trail.

I expect Evan to bring us back to the inn, but instead, he takes a detour—to the marina. The parking lot, more specifically. I'm taken aback that he's brought me to the water after going overboard the other day, until we pull up in front of a tiny yellow food truck. It sits behind a row of at least seven bright blue picnic tables, filled with a mixture of families and fishermen, positioned with a perfect view of the sails of boats bobbing in the harbor.

"Get ready for a life-changing experience," he announces, killing the ignition. A waft of what I can only describe as deep-fried salty goodness hits my nostrils the moment he cracks open the driver's-side door.

I follow warily as he leads me to the food truck window and points to the menu, featuring a photo of a concoction of gravy and lumps of cheese over fries.

"The ultimate Canadian dining experience," he says, arms folded over his chest with pride. "Your reward for surviving that hike."

I shake my head. "Sorry, but poutine does not look appetizing to me."

A family seated at a nearby picnic table sharing one poutine turns, slack-jawed and appalled. Evan joins in, clutching his chest, deeply offended. "First, I'm gonna need you to take that back. It's a delicacy. And second, it's pronounced pou-*tin*, not pou-*teen*."

Before I can protest, Evan greets the food truck worker, an old classmate of his. He gives us a family size, saying it's free "for the extra lobsters last year." Evan insists on paying full price regardless, with a generous tip.

We take a seat at an empty picnic table near the docks. A tugboat tied a couple feet away gently bumps against the dock with each lap of the water. Turns out, there's a reviving quality to the smell of the sea.

Evan passes me a plastic fork while side-eyeing a seagull that is far too curious about our meal. And it's not the only one. There's a full-on harbor seal eyeing us up too, sunbathing on the rock below, catlike whiskers twitching every which way. The white of its eyes is visible from our vantage point, like sad puppy eyes.

"Can those guys eat fries?" I ask, tying my hair up in a thick ponytail so it doesn't blow into my food.

Evan smirks. "Nah. I wouldn't feed him. Mark gets spoiled enough here."

"Mark?"

He nods toward Mark's gray blob of a body. "His name is Mark. He's a regular. Lives off a steady diet of fish guts. The fish-cleaning station is over there." He points to a small pavilion in the distance behind the food truck. "Mark and some of his buddies hang out there waiting for scraps. They prefer fish over fries, but they'll take what they can get."

I can't blame Mark. As it turns out, I was dead wrong. Poutine is the food of gods, and I don't know how I'll return to my normal life without it. I want to eat this golden heap of deliciousness for all three meals, every day of the year.

"I eat my words," I admit, two bites in. Sure, gravy pooled over fries and thick mozzarella cheese curds isn't visually appealing. But it is truly everything.

Evan watches intently as I chew, his eyes glittering, face beyond smug. "Now you owe me an extra star for culinary experience."

I tilt my head in thought, wrists perched daintily on the picnic table as I work down a gravy-laden bite. "Perhaps. Probably. This is amazing."

"Told you. The magic is all in the fry. It has to be fresh-cut. And the cheese curds should be from Quebec."

I bat his hand away when he stabs his fork on my side of the foam container. "Hey, back off."

"That's no way to treat the love of your life."

"Speaking of which, I think your nana is getting suspicious about us," I say, watching a scrumptious-looking bite disappear into his mouth.

He eyes me as he swallows, letting out a low groan that kind of makes me want to strip off my clothes right here, right now. "Suspicious? Really?"

I blink away that pesky errant thought, watching a boisterous group of teens line up at the food truck. "Yesterday she asked me whether you still run in the mornings with Lucy. And I didn't know what to say, because I don't really know much about you at all, aside from the fact that you're a lobster fisherman, have a morbid obsession with plaid, and are musically gifted."

His cheeks swell, flushing ever so slightly at the compliment. "That's basically all there is to know about me," he says with a shrug. "But I'm curious what you told her."

"I panicked and said you've taken up speed walking instead. And you're taking it very seriously," I say, straight-faced. "I told her I bought you one of those aerodynamic helmets for your birthday. She asked if she could chip in. Oh, and she wondered if I was planning a birthday party for you. I have no idea when your birthday is, so I had to awkwardly shrug and say I wasn't sure you deserved one."

He slants me a look, which sparks a flutter in the base of my belly. "Damn. You really went rogue."

"It's not rogue if we had no strategy to begin with," I point out, squinting into the sun. "I think we really need to figure out our plan of action for the next four days."

"'Plan of action.' Sounds very official."

I extract my phone from my purse and pull up my calendar. "Tomorrow we have the engagement party. The next day we do one last outdoorsy excursion. Then Saturday is the Lobster Festival, where we'll have our dramatic breakup. Sunday I'll go back to Halifax to the resort."

"Sounds about right," he says, stealing yet another fry from my side of the container.

"First things first: we need to learn more about each other to prepare for the engagement festivities. Your mom mentioned she was planning some games."

He gives me a bored sigh. "I don't get the point of these games."

"They're to demonstrate how in sync and loved-up the couple is," I inform him, heavy on the eye roll, as a boat passes behind us in the harbor.

Crystal threw Tara's bridal shower a couple of months ago. It included rosé, a balloon arch, multiple variations of How Well Do You Know Your Spouse? games, gift bags, prizes. There was also a fancy wicker chair for Tara to sit in while unwrapping gifts—decked out in eucalyptus, which cost three hundred dollars to rent.

If Tara weren't one of my closest friends, I'd reduce the whole thing to cringey. But the prospect of playing these games with Evan is strangely thrilling. Maybe it's the challenge, or the fact that, as much as I don't want to admit it, I want to learn more about him.

"But it's okay if we're rusty," I add. "It'll be good to foreshadow cracks in our relationship before our big breakup."

He runs his hand over the back of his neck. "I still don't see what the games accomplish. Me knowing whether you're a morning or night person has nothing to do with whether we'd have a successful marriage."

"Hey, it's important to be aware of these things. Like the fact that you take longer showers than me," I say, fork pointed accusatorily.

He snorts. "For the record, I can finish my showers in under a minute."

"I wouldn't brag about finishing things in less than a minute."

A burst of deep laughter escapes both of us, though he reins it in almost instantly, cheeks reddening again. "For the record, I could— Anyway. Never mind."

I break eye contact immediately, piercing the exact fry he's eyeing up.

Evan's eyes dart down to that perfect fry, then slide back up to me as he spears it in a show of dominance, like it's personally wronged him. I'm pretty sure he's dented the container.

We both hold firm, and the fry breaks in half. Exactly in half. We each swallow our half in silence as I wait, hoping he'll circle back to complete that statement. I'm dangerously close to blurting out *You could what?* But I suppress my morbid curiosity as he roots aimlessly, trying to find the crispy fries at the bottom of the container. Note to self: he doesn't actually take any.

Is it bad that the tiniest part of me wants to kiss him again?

"Fine. Hit me with a question," he finally says.

"Let's start with favorite food. I'm gonna make a wild guess that poutine is yours?"

"One of them. Though I try to limit myself. Don't want to clog my arteries." The left side of his mouth quirks up in an easy half smile that's both charming and uncalled for.

As a protective mechanism, I avert my eyes back to my phone, where it's safe, firing off a bunch of questions we need to take stances on. Like who snores (Evan), who hogs the bed (Evan), who made the first move (me), who said *I love you* first (me). Of course, Evan isn't happy that I've elected myself to be the one who made the first moves.

"My turn." He reaches across the table, plucking my phone from my hands to scroll my list. "What's your karaoke song?"

"That's a very specific question, which was not on the list," I declare, taking my phone back.

"That's my question. No passes."

"Fine. 'A Thousand Miles' by Vanessa Carlton."

"Haven't heard it."

"Oh, come on. It's very early 2000s. In the credits of every rom-com. You know the one."

He twists his lips in confusion. "I'm afraid I don't."

"Come on. The one with the piano tune." I do a terrible impression, drumming my fingers against the edge of the table, while humming the opening tune.

He promptly covers his mouth with his fist.

"You don't recognize it?"

"No. I know the song. Just wanted to hear you sing it," he admits with a cheeky shrug.

"I hate you." I shoot him laser beams and scroll for another question. "Not all of us were blessed with the voice of an angel with a head cold."

"I'm not sure if that's a compliment or an insult."

"It's a compliment."

He makes a dramatic show of placing a hand over his chest. "I'm touched."

"Don't get used to it. What's your shower song?" I ask.

He ponders that, stroking his chin like a mad genius. "'It's All Coming Back to Me Now' by Celine Dion."

I choke on my fry, imagining it. "Celine Dion?"

He shrugs, shameless. "Gotta support Canadian artists."

"True. And that song is a banger," I admit. "Did you ever want to sing professionally? Get famous?" I ask, unable to help myself, despite the fact that this is my second question in a row.

"Nope. I don't like that kind of attention," he responds with no hesitation.

"Interesting. Me either."

He eyes me suspiciously. "You're saying you don't like attention? Miss five hundred and seventy thousand followers?"

My jaw unhinges. "You looked at my account."

"I had to do my due diligence when you showed up at the inn late at night. Unannounced," he notes pointedly. "You could have been a murderer for all I knew."

"Maybe I am."

"You do look the part."

"What would my serial killer MO be?"

He strokes his beard. "Wearing your victims' skinned faces."

"A crucial step in my daily skin care routine," I point out. "Your face wouldn't be too shabby, though."

He leans back. "Nah. You don't want my face. Take Lucy's instead."

"Too late. I'm already set on yours," I tease, eyes darting to meet his.

Evan's gaze heats at the contact, and I promptly look away before resetting.

"*Anyway*, to answer your question, I don't like attention, which I know is hard to believe, given that my photos say the exact opposite." I pause, trying to find the words to tell him the cold, hard truth. "You were right the other day, on the boat."

"You'll need to be more specific. I said a lot of things that day," he admits.

There's a moment where I second-guess revealing my hand. I've never admitted this to anyone. Ever. But for some reason, the truth suddenly feels like an anchor on my chest. And I desperately need relief. "That fashion is steeped in privilege. It's true," I confess. "I didn't always have money. Not that I'm rolling in cash now. But yeah."

His brow ticks up with surprise. "Really?"

"Things were fine when I was really young. My parents were middle-class, traveled, had enough money to adopt me, at least. I remember our first house was nice. It was old, but it had three bedrooms and a big backyard with a swing. My dad owned this electronics store downtown, sold radios, CD players, DVD players, you name it. Then the recession hit in 2008. That, in combination with everything moving digital . . . We lost it all. Our house. Vehicle. Literally everything."

His eyes widen. "Wow. Mel, that's . . . terrible."

"I found out later that my parents had been living beyond their means for years, charging everything on credit cards. We had to move to some crappy walk-up apartment in a sketchy neighborhood, and my dad went into a depression over it all." I skip the tragic part where my mom left shortly after the move, making everything worse. "My dad tried getting his shit together by investing in all sorts of random dodgy businesses he thought would make a quick buck. He ended up losing more money than he made."

He lowers his head. "I'm really sorry. I had no idea. You seem so . . ."

"Rich?" I say. My body tingles. But not from embarrassment. From an overwhelming feeling of liberation from the lie I've been living.

He shrugs. "I mean, you showed up in designer everything."

"Most of the stuff I wear, I get for free." I briefly explain the basic ins and outs of how partnering with brands works.

He's silent for a few moments as he works down a bite. "I had no idea there was such a huge business side to it. I thought it was just about taking pictures. I'm . . . impressed," he admits.

"There's this running joke that influencers make all their content one day of the week and spend the other six days sitting idle, but that wasn't me." I tell him how in between working part-time, I'd devise triple the content of all the other influencers. How I'd go above and beyond to satisfy my collaboration partners, ensuring they'd want to work with me again. How, for the first time in my life, I didn't have to lie awake at night, stressing about whether

I'd have enough money for rent. "The long hours and hustling worked—for a while."

Something about that statement clicks for him. "Sounds like fishing. It's feast or famine. Some years we have huge catches. Other years, there's hardly enough to pay the crew. That's why I do whale watching and fishing charters on the side."

"Do you like doing the charters?"

"I do. But I'm having trouble keeping up with the demand. Lucy gets calls constantly. But both seasons run into each other, and lobstering is the priority."

"You could hire someone else to do the charters," I suggest.

He considers this. "I'd need a second boat. *Fiona* is old. Not ideal for tourists, especially city ones like you," he says playfully.

"A boat with a comfortable place to sit would be nice." I flash a teasing smile. "But you should really consider the investment. I think you could make a killing. City people would be lucky to have a guide like you."

He looks down at the picnic table, almost bashful. "You think?"

"You have a special connection to the water. I noticed it right away."

The corners of his mouth curl disarmingly. "My grandpa used to say the water has a way of turning a terrible day into a good one. I don't need much else to be happy, honestly." His statement tugs at my gut. Do I really need money and the material things I have to be happy, beyond the basics? Or have those things merely been a distraction from something deeper?

As I turn those questions over and over in my head, it occurs to me I haven't heard what he's just said. "Sorry, what did you say?"

"I asked if you love what you do," he repeats.

"I did at first. When I started, it was more about me just having fun with fashion and products. I loved the money and the new life it gave me. But once social media got big and being an influencer became a . . . *thing*, it changed."

"How?"

I turn my gaze to the glittering surface of the calm water. "The more successful you are, the meaner people get, whether it's criticizing my face or the fact that I'm not super skinny like the other influencers, literally anything. It's like they don't see you as a human anymore. They don't realize I'm a person behind the account. Brand has become everything. It's all subject to the algorithm. And you have to follow the trends or get left behind . . . Lately, that means giving people raw, unfettered access to your every thought, your private life, your emotions." The more I talk, the tighter I'm gripping my plastic fork.

Evan catches it too, his gaze flicking back up to my face. "You seem uncomfortable with that."

"I am. Photos of me in clothes are easy. But divulging every detail of my personal life? I don't know that it's something I'm willing to give. I share enough of my life, my body. The internet doesn't need access to my emotions and innermost thoughts too."

"You shouldn't have to share anything with anyone, especially random strangers," he says simply.

I know that logically. But it helps to hear someone who isn't part of my world say it too. "The thing is, I also need the money. That's the problem."

"There's gotta be other things you could do that won't make you feel so exposed."

"I don't have a college degree or any other skills, really, aside from customer service," I admit, shoulders sagging when I realize I've dampened the mood. "Anyway, sorry for unloading all that. It's just why I'm so . . . anal about my account and getting pictures right. It's all I really have." I wince when that statement slips past my lips. It sounds sad. Really sad.

He's quiet for a moment before nodding in understanding. "Thanks for telling me that. And for the record, I was also being a dick with that privilege comment on the boat. You were right about the plaid, by the way." He tugs down his flannel.

I raise a brow. "I was?"

"I do try matching my jeans for different occasions."

My eyes light up, victorious. "I knew it."

He gives me a disarming smile. "All right, don't get too cocky. There's more to my wardrobe than just plaid."

"Doubtful. I bet you wear plaid boxer briefs too," I say, not bothering to admit I already know he does.

He makes a zipper motion across his lips, bouncing his brows suggestively. It's comically scandalous.

"I have it on good authority from my friends' partners, both of whom are firemen, that bamboo briefs are game-changing."

His mouth tugs in a wide grin as he stands to toss the now-empty poutine container in the nearby trash. "You really have a grudge against plaid, don't you? What plaid-wearing human hurt you?"

I crush the napkin in my hand and toss it out behind him. "Sadly there's no tragic backstory. I'm just being a good fake fiancée, looking out for the comfort of your balls."

"Please say 'balls' again." He tosses me a devilish smirk over his shoulder as he heads for the truck.

"No. I'm not five."

"Say it or I won't let you in the truck."

"You're evil. I need to lie down." I glance around at families and fisherman merrily enjoying their deep-fried food. The poutine did a number on my stomach, and I could really benefit from being horizontal right now.

He just shrugs, holding firm at the driver's side.

It occurs to me that stubbornness is Evan's dominant character trait. He's enjoying this far too much. We'll be here all day unless I fold. So I do.

"BALLS!" My scream comes out louder than intended, to Evan's shock and delight, as well as the horror of everyone else in our vicinity, trash-mouthed fisherman in shit-kicker rain boots included. "There. Now unlock the door."

Evan's eyes crinkle as his deep laugh carries over the marina behind us. By the time I hoist myself into the truck, I find myself laughing too.

He slants me a far-too-satisfied grin as he backs out of the parking lot. "See? The secret to a successful marriage between two dominant personalities is all about compromise."

♥ chapter nineteen

UNCLE NED SALUTES us from the porch swing when we return. I repay his salute as if I've returned from a bloody battle. It kind of feels that way. Strenuous activity, greasy food, and unloading deep, dark secrets will do that to you.

To my shock, the rusted stove has been moved, replaced by the Adirondack furniture I saw in the listing's photos. Ned must have moved it while we were out. It does wonders for the curb appeal.

"Nice hike?" Ned stretches his arms above his head in a yawn, as though he's just woken up.

I smirk at Evan. I want to shout about how amazing it was. That I'm still reeling from the high, unlike shopper's high, which pretty much ends the moment you get home and take the tags off your purchases. But I don't, because Evan will surely take credit and I'm still unwilling to feed his ego. "That's a loaded question. But it was good."

"Lies. She saw a vicious creature," Evan explains.

Ned sits forward with renewed interest. "Did you see a bear? Heard them black bears are bad this year up around the trails."

"Way worse," Evan says.

Ned's eyes widen. "Worse? A cougar?"

He waits a dramatic beat. "A slug."

"Okay, to be fair, it was humongous." I make an exaggerated distance between my hands.

Evan snorts. "You're delirious. More like this." He makes the tiniest distance between his thumb and index finger, which is about a quarter of the actual size.

"Sorry, we're actually talking about the slug, not your di—"

Evan whistles, playfully covering my mouth with his huge hand as Ned breaks into laughter. "All right. You're drunk on nature and poutine. You should probably take a nap."

Ned smacks the armrest with his fist. "I like this girl," he tells Evan.

Evan just shakes his head, the corners of his eyes still crinkled from amusement as he leans in to kiss me on the side of the head. It's so natural, I almost forget it's fake. "I'm going inside, babe. You good?"

At my assurance, he lumbers inside, the screen door rattling to a close behind him.

"For the record, the slug was about to attack me," I say once the door closes, muffling the sound of Lucy's and Nana's voices inside.

Ned's chest rises with a residual chuckle. "I believe ya. They're tricky little buggers. Damn near destroyed my vegetable garden this summer."

"How rude of them," I mutter.

"Glad Evan's got someone to put him in his place once in a while." He tugs at the front of his halfway-buttoned floral shirt, pulled tight over his belly.

"He needs it."

"Evan's always been a stubborn boy. Doesn't much like to listen to anyone else."

"I definitely noticed," I say, settling into the space next to him. The swing creaks under the addition of another body.

He smirks. "Sorry you've had to deal with us lot."

"Have things always been this way between you guys?" I ask hesitantly, unsure how much he wants to get into the family drama.

He doesn't seem to mind. "Fi and Ness always find a way to fight about something, ever since we were kids. Fi's always been ferocious, urgent, and Ness is more laid-back, marches to her own beat, doesn't like to be told what to do. Both righteous as hell. Kinda like Evan," he says with an affectionate smile. "When Ness met Evan's dad, Kenny, she and Fi had a big falling-out. Fiona didn't like him. Still doesn't."

"Oh? Where is Evan's dad?" I ask. Neither Evan nor Lucy has mentioned Evan's dad. And while I've wondered about him, I haven't had the guts to ask.

"Lives in Montreal," Uncle Ned says matter-of-factly. "Evan was just a little guy, probably about seven or eight, when they split. Kenny couldn't handle living in a place like this. Big-city man. Suit 'n' tie. Met Ness when he came to study at Dalhousie. He took Evan with him for a year or two when he was a youngster, but Ev wanted to come back. So he did."

"Why did he come back?"

Ned shrugs. "Water's in his blood. Like most men in the family. Can't go too long without it."

"Think Evan's a lifer here?" I ask.

"Most people are. Very few leave, aside from going to Halifax for postsecondary. And they all usually find their way back eventually. It'd shock me if Evan ever moved. He's loyal. If you ask me, he's shouldered a lot of guilt since Jack."

I have so many questions, but I tread carefully, unsure what Ned would expect I should already know as Evan's fiancée.

Ned continues. "But we all agree, we haven't seen him happier. In a long time."

I stifle a laugh with a cough. If this is Evan in his happy state, I can't imagine his miserable state. "What do *you* think they should do with the inn?" I venture.

His brows raise to his nonexistent hairline. "You're asking my opinion? None of the women do that in this family."

"Oh, I'm begging," I say with a chuckle.

"Honestly, I agree with Fi. It's becoming a hassle, 'specially since our mom went into assisted living. I think it's also a distraction from the bigger problems goin' on here." He lets that statement hang for a few seconds. "After all these years, I've learned it's best to stay miles away from the inn drama, even though they keep tryin' to drag me in. And a word of advice: you should probably stay out of it too."

"Oh, don't worry, I am," I say, looking away, trying to hide what I'm sure is written all over my face. That I'm part of an elaborate fake-engagement scheme to save the inn. The guilt burrows deeper into the pit of my stomach.

"Our family has always been close. It meant everything to our dad. Still does to our mom. I hope you don't think less of us with all this bickering."

"Not at all," I say. "If anything, it shows how much everyone cares."

He places a firm hand on my shoulder. "Well, we're very happy to have you here, Mel."

• • •

MAYBE IT'S JUST my good mood, but the water pressure in the shower seems much improved today. The hot water drums against my scalp like a spa-quality massage, gushing out in abundance as the steam billows around me.

Lathering my hair, I find myself smiling as I recount the day, from the hike to our poutine lunch at the marina. Full-teeth smiling, in fact. The moment that realization hits, I mentally slap myself for letting my brain run amok. Clearly the steam is messing with my mind, diluting reality.

Sure, Evan and I spent the day together. And yes, we coexisted. We even shared a couple of laughs and divulged some personal things. But the simple fact is, we're both doing this for our own motives. I'm getting good social media content while I wait for the resort in exchange for my part in reuniting his family. That's the deal. End of story.

I reach for my pink-grapefruit bodywash, catching something dark, long, and furry in my peripheral vision. For a split second, I think it's a thick strip of adhesive fake eyelashes. Until it bolts. BOLTS. It's a massive amber-colored centipede, darting across the tiled shower wall at the speed of light.

Get my coffin ready. I am deceased.

With my last kernel of energy, I let out a bloodcurdling scream as the hundred-legged demon from the deepest depths of hell begins its rapid descent down the shower wall, presumably to slay me in cold blood.

In the face of death, it's only natural for instinct to overrule logic. At least, that's what I tell myself when I back up with nowhere to go. My heels hit the side of the tub, sending me toppling backward over the edge.

Everything happens so fast. My fingers clasp the thin, plasticky material of the shower curtain. The entire metal rod rips off the wall, clattering over me.

It's only when I'm upside down, legs in the air, half draped over the tub like I'm giving birth, that I realize my fall has been broken by something warm. It's a body.

"Are you okay?" It's Evan's strained voice in my ear.

My completely drenched, fully naked torso is splayed out in Evan's arms, and we're separated only by the opaque paper-thin shower curtain between us.

If I had to identify the most embarrassing, vulnerable moment of my existence, this must be it. Even more so than the time my faux-leather leggings split on the crowded dance floor while I was getting low at a club.

Lucy skids to an abrupt stop in the doorway, eyes wide, taking in the dramatic sight. "Holy shit, Mel. What happened?"

Nothing comes out when I open my mouth. I'm still immobile from the humiliation of being stark naked, starfishing on top of Evan.

Thankfully, the memory of the creature that is still at large in this bathroom zaps me back to life. I shakily lift my limp hand in the general direction of the bathtub.

"Centipede! There's a centipede in there," I manage to croak as I attempt to wiggle upright, covering my completely exposed nipples with my hands.

From behind, Evan's calloused yet warm hands hoist me upward underneath my armpits, propping me back on my feet. Without eye contact, he makes quick work of wrapping the ripped and dripping shower curtain over my shoulders, covering my indecency.

"You fell out of the tub because of this little guy?" Lucy asks, pointing downward into the tub.

Evan peers over my shoulder to get a good look before the two of them exchange glances, simultaneously breaking into boisterous deep-belly laughter.

The shower curtain crunches as I peer into the tub myself. The monster has now taken refuge near the drain, curled up, probably plotting its next move. "Please don't tell me he has a name too."

Evan shrugs. "I'm open to naming him."

Lucy's eyes light up at the prospect. "He looks like a Bernard to me."

"Guys, no. I'm offended on behalf of all Bernards. Don't talk to me until you get rid of it," I say through a shiver.

Lucy hiccups a laugh, while Evan blasts the beast with water, washing it down the drain. "There," he proclaims, as if it's as insignificant as an ant. "It's gone."

"Nature is conspiring against me. First the spider, then the slug, and now this," I say, suppressing a groan as the residual suds from my hair begin to drip onto my shoulders. "What's next, an anaconda?"

"We do have some garter snakes around the inn—" Lucy starts.

Evan playfully shushes her, covering her mouth. "Let's not scare her away entirely."

"Okay, both of you get out of here before the rest of the family comes in," I instruct, thoroughly traumatized.

Evan shuffles out behind Lucy, but not before tossing me one last shit-eating grin over his shoulder.

chapter twenty

TARA: Mel, I need updates on this fisherman. Are you still
pretending to be engaged? Are you getting along? What's
his family like?

CRYSTAL: A pic wouldn't be too shabby either . . . I didn't see
much of him in that vid from the boat.

MEL: I don't have a pic of him. Sorry!

It's a total lie. I have today's hilarious waterfall pictures. But for
reasons unknown, I have this strong, selfish urge to keep them for
myself. For now, at least.

CRYSTAL: Take a sneaky shot!

MEL: I can't just take his pic without permission!

CRYSTAL: But it's for science.

MEL: Anyway, status quo. We're still breaking up in a few days and I'll head to the resort.

TARA: Really? That's all we get?

MEL: Ugh. Fine.

MEL: He saw me naked today . . .

CRYSTAL: EXCUSE ME.

TARA: Hello??

CRYSTAL: ????????????

TARA: Wtf Mel. You can't just drop a bomb like that and ghost.

MEL: Lol sorry. I've gotta go help him prep for dinner. But just so you know, it's not what you think. I fell in the shower. There's nothing between us. It's just business. A business arrangement.

TARA: I'm interpreting your short tone and harsh overuse of punctuation as defensiveness. Denial.

CRYSTAL: Same.

MEL: 🤦🏽‍♀️

• • •

I HAVEN'T RECOVERED by the time dinner rolls around. Neither has Evan, apparently.

When I broached the topic in the kitchen, he theatrically squinted out the window and pointed to a microscopic dot in the sky, claiming it was a hawk. I suppose concocting nonexistent birds of prey beats looking a quasi-stranger in the eye after seeing her va-jay splayed to the ceiling.

As everyone eats dinner quietly and gossips about a woman who's back in town after taking off with a rumored organized crime boss, I grow curious about the photo in the parlor, perched atop the mantel. It's an eight-by-ten black-and-white photo of a family of four, cheesing at the beach. Upon first sight, I wondered if the boy and the girl were Lucy and Evan, until I realized both children have dark hair. The mother and father in the photo don't resemble the rest of the Whalers, either.

"Who are the people in the photo above the fireplace?" I ask, breaking the silence.

Ned and Nessa exchange the briefest of glances, while Fiona tugs at her collar and takes a large bite of her meat loaf. Even Lucy and Evan shift in their chairs slightly. For a moment, I think I've hit a nerve, until Ned clears his throat. "Those are our cousins."

"Cousins?"

Nessa jumps in. "Yup. The woman is Cher. Our cousin on our dad's side. And that's her husband, Sonny."

My brow quirks. "They're named Sonny and Cher? Really?"

"Yes," Fiona confirms. "No relation to the musical duo. But yes. They met at a nude beach."

"A nude beach," I repeat, looking to Evan for clarification. He just nods, like this is totally casual information.

"Sonny was an Elvis impersonator from time to time," Ned continues. "Did children's birthday parties when he and Cher moved here."

"Didn't quite get used to livin' in the sticks, though," Nessa adds. "Lost a toe hunting once."

"Oh yeah. Never walked the same after that. And there was the time he got attacked by a hawk when he went hunting with Dad and Uncle Earl," Fiona adds.

I slow-blink, unsure how to respond. "Does he . . . live in Cora's Cove?"

"Nope. He got into some sort of illegal exotic pet trade business and took off to South America," Lucy explains. "We're not sure exactly where."

"We think it's probably Peru," Evan tells me.

Nana nods. "Somewhere with lax laws. I heard a rumor he may have opened up a strip club."

My brow furrows. "Do . . . Cher and the kids still live here? Or did she go to Peru with him?"

Nessa shoots Ned a look, and Fiona abruptly clears her throat. And suddenly, everyone at the table is busting a gut.

"That was one of the better ones," Nessa says, high-fiving Ned and, shockingly, Fiona.

"Better what?" I ask, horribly confused.

Evan nudges me gently in the ribs with his elbow and leans in. "Sonny and Cher. They're not real."

"What? They're not?"

"The photo is a random stock photo," Lucy explains, still wheezing for breath through her laughter. "Nana got the frame as a gift forever ago from Grandpa. She never replaced the stock picture, and it kind of just became a thing."

Nana shakes her head with a loving smile. "Every time someone new comes over, we make up a random story. They've been astronauts, monks, you name it."

"Just be thankful we didn't keep it going as long as we did for my ex," Lucy whispers. "He waited for Joey the ghost-hunter cousin to show up to every family holiday for a solid year."

"That was the last time we did it, I think."

"Thanks for that," Fiona says. "And welcome to our family."

I shake my head, jaw still open. Despite being the butt of the joke, I feel like it's a necessary hazing. It makes me feel oddly welcomed, even more so than before. And even better, the picture has somehow broken the tension between everyone, including Fiona and Nessa, who are happily rehashing childhood memories.

The rest of the evening is spent playing games in the kitchen and dining room area by candlelight. Great Big Sea is blasting through the speakers, though everyone is singing louder than the actual band, particularly Evan and his mom.

"Cheers to your first East Coast kitchen party," Lucy whispers, tapping my red Solo cup with her own.

"Kitchen party?"

She shrugs. "It's just a thing on the East Coast. People tend to congregate in the kitchen. Probably because it's close to the food," she explains, nodding toward Ned, who's sifting through the fridge while singing.

The awkwardness of the shower incident fades over the course of the evening. Evan is more comfortable with me tonight than ever. The odd side hug or hand squeeze for the family comes with ease. At one point, he even sets his hand over my knee under the table, a gesture that isn't visible to anyone else. I chalk it up to the alcohol.

I'm the first to turn in to bed tonight. Not because I'm not enjoying myself, but, frankly, the opposite. I'm enjoying myself too much. The day with Evan's family was like being draped by a warm, plush blanket when I didn't know I was shivering.

In the still darkness, I replay Ned's words on the porch earlier in my head. *We're very happy to have you here, Mel.*

When I first agreed to this charade at the hospital, I had no inkling the Whalers would accept me, let alone embrace me as one of their own. The guilt of our lie settles in the pit of my stomach like a small pile of rocks. I don't know if I'm capable of adding to the pile.

Unable to sleep, I roll over and check my Instagram, which I haven't done since we returned from the hike. Being unplugged has actually been quite nice.

The unedited photo I posted earlier today has gotten a ton of engagement. I've even gotten multiple DMs asking where the waterfall is.

With renewed confidence, I post a series of completely unfiltered shots, even some of the ones where my posture isn't perfect, or my face isn't exactly right. Maybe this whole authentic thing isn't so ridiculous. A week ago, posting an unedited photo would have given me hives. But right now, it feels freeing. It feels more me than ever.

Another hour passes and Evan hasn't come to bed yet. The chatter between Lucy and Nessa fades and is replaced with the soft strum of a guitar drifting through my open window. It's haunting and beautiful in the darkness. I tiptoe downstairs toward the source.

Evan is strumming his guitar on the porch, looking straight out of a country music video. The sight of his flannel sleeves rolled up to display thick, corded forearms temporarily blurs my vision. I had no idea forearms were capable of sabotaging my senses.

He dips his chin when I sit on the step below. The guitar is the perfect companion to the sounds of crickets and frogs, which would have been a lot more disturbing to me a couple of days ago.

I even find myself admiring a moth fluttering under the porch light, its iridescent wings glowing yellow.

I don't recognize most of the songs he's playing, though the rich chords strike me deep in the chest, one after another, steadying my heartbeat. It's soothing, turning my muscles limp. After about four songs, he sets the guitar aside and gestures for us to relocate to the porch swing.

The swing glides back and forth at an easy pace that could lull me to sleep like a baby right here and now.

The breeze dusts the skin that my pajama shorts don't cover, leaving me with tiny goose bumps. I pull my bare knees to my chest for extra warmth. Evan notices and removes the flannel button-down over his T-shirt, promptly draping the soft, thick fabric over my legs.

"Would you rather say aloud everything you read, or sing everything you say aloud?" I finally ask.

"Definitely sing," he says. I don't bother to ask him to defend that. Who wouldn't choose to sing with a voice like his?

"How long have you played guitar?" I ask, instinctively draping half the flannel over his legs too, like a blanket.

"Since I could read. My grandpa taught me. Here at the inn."

"My brother, Julian, plays in a band. Well, he used to, at least." It's on the tip of my tongue to explain that he hasn't played since Dad, but I leave that part out.

Evan's brow quirks with interest. "Oh yeah? What kind of band?"

"Mostly punk rock. A lot of screaming," I say, cringing at the visceral memory of listening to his band practice in the community room of our old apartment complex.

"You sound like Nana."

"I'll take that as a compliment. Your Nana is cooler than I'll ever be."

"You guys seem to be getting along." His observation comes out almost like a question.

"She's quite the fashionista. Actually, she offered to show me her cat costume wardrobe," I brag. The moment Nana found out I like to sew, she busted out her photo album containing nothing but photos of her various tabby cats in hand-sewn costumes (including a taco) in front of a stark white backdrop. The very same tiny costumes the hand-carved lobsters are dressed in.

His eyes widen in genuine surprise. "She showed you the cat album? That means she really likes you."

My smile wavers as fast as it came on, swallowed by guilt. She shouldn't like me, because I'm lying to her. To all of them. I swallow the lump in my throat. "You know, it's really interesting to me that your family would drop their lives to stay here at the inn just to celebrate your engagement." There's that jealous pang in my gut again.

He shrugs, like it's no big deal. "That's my family. It's mostly Nana, though. She's the mastermind. She also uses any excuse to get out of assisted living," he adds.

"Still. I can't imagine what lengths they'd go to for an actual wedding."

"I can't even remember the last family wedding."

"I guess that's why your engagement is such a big deal?"

He nods contemplatively, expression undecided. "Why are you still up? Can't sleep with the mess in our room?" he teases.

I bump his shoulder with mine, though he doesn't move an

inch. "I have a hard time sleeping most nights. Plus there's a lot on my mind," I admit.

He tips his head to the side, studying me. "The lying is getting to you too?"

I shift my gaze to the darkened driveway, suddenly paranoid he can read my thoughts. "How'd you guess?"

"Just a hunch. It's been on my mind too."

"I didn't think it would faze me because it's not my family. But the more I get to know you all, the worse it feels. Is it bad I'm kind of looking forward to our fake breakup?"

"Same. I keep going back and forth, thinking maybe we should tell them the truth. It all just snowballed so fast, and now I'm scared it's gone past the point of no return." He lets out a heavy sigh. "Do you think we're bad people for lying? Lucy and me?" He's watching me intently, like he's desperate to know how I truly feel.

I let his question marinate for a few moments. Sure, I feel guilty as hell for my part in it. But when I really think about it, this whole thing was concocted with the best of intentions. "No," I say sincerely. "Your nana is so happy. And your aunt and mom were civil tonight. It's something. Even if it's morally dicey."

He lets out a long sigh, extending his legs to slow down the swing. "My friends are pissed at me too. Especially Kyle. They think I kept you a secret from them." I can tell by his clipped tone that he hates this—hates lying to his best friends.

"In your defense, you're not obliged to tell your friends every single thing about your life," I point out, thinking of all the things I don't tell Crystal and Tara.

"We don't do secrets."

"Never?"

"Never. That's important, especially when we're out on the water. We have to be able to trust that we have each other's backs in case shit goes wrong, which it inevitably does," he explains.

"I get that. But you mean to tell me there's absolutely not a single fact about you that they don't know?"

"Not a single one. And vice versa."

I call his bluff, more out of my own insecurity than anything. "So you could tell me, right now, exactly how many scars Kyle has on his body?"

He doesn't even hesitate. "Three. One on his shin from a leg surgery. One on his ear from a boating accident. And one on his ring finger from a poker incident gone wrong. Long story."

"Wow" is all I can say.

Evan's open-book relationship with his friends strikes me. It isn't necessarily the lack of secrets part. But more the fact that they're comfortable enough to reveal every part of themselves to each other, even the parts that may be hard to digest. I've never had a completely open relationship like that with anyone. A current of envy hits me. What I wouldn't give to have someone I could tell anything to, without overthinking it or worrying about what they'll think of me.

When I don't say anything else, he fills the silence. "And when you live in such a small town, it's kinda hard to keep anything from each other."

"What if you told them the truth? Swore them to secrecy?"

He ponders that for a moment. "Nah. I don't want them to have to be part of the lie. And even if I did, Kyle has too big a mouth. The guy can't keep a secret to save his life."

"Well, on the bright side, once I'm gone, you can tell them how terrible I am and what an awful experience it was being fake engaged to me," I say with a wry smile.

"It's not completely awful." He meets my gaze, lowering his hand over the tiny part of my knee that isn't covered by his flannel. For a second, I think he's wiping away a bug, until he drags the calloused pad of his finger in a soft swoop that makes my body short-circuit.

"It's a little bit awful," I manage, despite his touch rendering me practically comatose. When I stiffen, he lifts his hand and pauses. It's like he's awaiting my permission. Instinctively, I shift closer, craving his touch more than I care to admit.

"Even if you're a pain in the ass, it helps to remind myself it's worth it. To save this place."

"Is there a way you, your mom, and Lucy could go in on it? Buy Fiona out?" I ask.

"We don't have the money to do that. My mom has this habit of not charging her clients. Lobster isn't what it used to be. And Lucy's job doesn't pay nearly what she deserves. We barely have enough money to run the place as it is. Sometimes I think my aunt is right. Maybe it's better to just sell it, divide assets, and move on."

"Move on from . . . Jack?" I venture.

He nods wordlessly, brows pulling together at the mention of Jack.

"I know I said I didn't want to talk about anything personal," I start. "But I'm here if you ever want to tell me about him."

"Thanks, Mel. I appreciate it. And same to you."

"For what it's worth, I don't think you should give up on this place. I know it's easier to just wipe your hands clean and move on.

But . . . there's beauty in holding on . . . as long as you're not trapped in the past," I manage, trying to keep my composure as his thumb swirls along the soft underside of my knee. I force down a swallow, unable to think clearly as all the blood in my body flows toward my core. How can the smallest touch make me ache with need in an instant? Am I really that hard up?

I shift the flannel a few inches to cover his hand, as if protecting this moment like our little secret. Unlike the rest of our touching over the past few days, this isn't for show. At least, it doesn't feel like it. Not when we're out here, just us two, with only the crickets and the dull twinkle of the stars bearing witness. Maybe if no one sees it, it doesn't count. It doesn't mean anything.

"You think?"

"There may be some small things you guys can do that wouldn't be that expensive," I say, trying to keep a straight face as his hand glides higher and then back down in a calming rhythm.

"Maybe. Though if we get it looking too good, Fiona will be rushing to sell the place."

"That's why you need to make it lucrative. Attract so many guests and turn such a good profit, she won't be able to argue the value. Advertising is expensive, but even local ads with high-quality photos and a write-up that isn't from the eighties might do the trick."

"See? You have skills beyond marketing just yourself. Maybe that's something you should consider. Doing marketing for run-down inns," he says, his fingers sending tiny jolts of electricity twirling over my skin.

A tiny laugh nearly escapes my lips as I consider the paradox of our conversation. Here we are, talking about renovations and marketing. And yet, under the protective fabric of the flannel where he's touching me, we're in a different world. A world that feels far from our reality.

"I'll think about it," I say seriously. He does have a point. I do love the creative side of marketing and social media, so long as I'm not the product.

"Thanks, Mel. For staying and going along with all this," he says genuinely, hesitating before swirling to my inner thigh. "You're . . . different."

"Different?" I whisper, relishing his touch.

"From what I thought originally."

"Is that a good thing?" I hold my breath as he trails one finger dangerously close to my bikini line.

"Yeah. It's a good thing." When he removes his hand from under the flannel, there's a moment of disappointment. A moment when my body physically aches without his touch. It's only when he drapes that arm over me, pulling me snugly into his side, that all is right again.

I find myself shifting closer until I can feel his breath dance against my neck. Until we're pressed so close, not even a feather could slip between us.

Eyelids heavy, I nuzzle into his collarbone. The paces of our breath meld together, slowing by the second as I drift in and out of consciousness, the chirp of distant crickets lulling me to sleep.

• • •

I WAKE UP to the feeling of being lowered onto a soft surface. When my eyes flick open, all I see is Evan. The glow of the moonlight casts a dull, silver-blue hue over his face, rudely reminding me of those dimples that make him look faintly approachable through his typical hard scowl. And that's when it occurs to me. Evan has a resting bitch face too—albeit an adorable one. Maybe we're more alike than I thought.

I search the depths of my soul for the disdain I felt for him when I first arrived in Cora's Cove, but come up with zilch. Then again, it's hard to hate a man who's carried me to bed like a princess. A man who is leaning over me, quite literally tucking me into bed.

"This is the second time you've had to carry me to bed," I mumble through a stretch, half conscious as he begins to bed down on the air mattress below me.

He lets out a soft chuckle as he strips himself of his shirt. "You better remember this service when you write your review."

"Oh, I will," I promise, squeezing my eyes shut. It's not that I don't want a peek of Evan shirtless. Quite the contrary. But after tonight, after the way he touched me under our makeshift blanket, I'm not sure I could handle it. In fact, I'm scared I'd lose all control. "I might even consider that tiny little thing you did on the boat too."

"And what was that?" he asks over the creak of the air mattress.

I turn over, propping myself up on my elbow to peer down at him through the darkness. "You saved my life."

His eyes remain closed, and he shrugs like it's no big deal. Just a normal day in the life of a maritime lobster fisherman. "Minor details."

"No. It is a big deal, Evan. Thank you. Really."

"Well, we're even. Because you saved mine too," he says in a voice just barely above a whisper.

chapter twenty-one

MEL: Hey, haven't heard from you in two days. How are you?
JULIAN: Good!
MEL: Just good??
JULIAN: Yup just busy w/job.

Julian's texts have been sparse and uncharacteristically short lately. Sure, starting a new job is hectic, but a few more updates here and there would be nice. I try giving him a call, but it won't go through.

"Is anyone else having trouble getting signal?" I ask, holding my phone up to each living room window for better reception.

I'm probably overreacting, but it's admittedly a good distraction from thinking about last night. When Evan and I fell asleep on the porch swing. When he carried me to bed. When I didn't wake up again until he left at four in the morning to set traps with

Kyle. He was confident about beating the storm and returning for our engagement celebration tonight.

"All the lines are down," Ned informs me, peering out the bay window in the kitchen to assess the sky. "Storm's coming in fast."

"Looks worse than the forecast," Nessa points out. She's stationed at the breakfast nook, pulling a whole chicken apart for her contribution to tonight's festivities: buffalo chicken dip—a family crowd-pleaser.

With each roaring gust, the entire house creaks, a stark reminder that it's almost a century and a half old. The sky is an ominous gray, marred by dark tunnel clouds determined to swallow everything in their wake. The rain that was pattering against the porch has turned horizontal, pelting the side of the house, fighting for dominance over the rustle of tree branches scraping the siding. The sound reminds me of Scott's dog's nails clattering against the hardwood floor in Crystal's apartment . . . which will soon be empty.

The thought of going back to Boston after all this, sitting in my empty apartment at my table for twelve, and having to drive an hour away to see her feels grim. I'm not ready to think about it, because I'm not lonely—yet. Not while I'm here with the Whalers, despite the fact that Evan is back out on the water today after a mere three days off. It strikes me how Evan can have a near-death experience one day, and days later risk it all like nothing happened.

"Do you think he'll make it back in time for the party?" I ask no one in particular over the melancholy Anne Murray playlist on loop (Anne Murray is God, according to Ned). I'm furiously whisking the cake batter into oblivion out of pure anxiety.

Nana rips the bowl from my hands before I botch it entirely.

"I've tried texting him and Kyle, but my messages aren't delivering. Both their cells are out of range," Lucy explains, stuffing a bowl of broccoli salad in the already-packed refrigerator to cool.

"He'll be fine," Nana assures me as she hovers over Nessa to ensure the chicken is pulled "thin enough."

"I take it you've played the waiting game a lot in your life, huh?" I venture.

"Oh yes. My husband, then Neddy, and both grandsons. It never gets easier, every time they go out. Eventually, you'll learn not to let your nerves get the best of you, or you'll spend your entire life waiting for the worst to happen."

"Man is no match for the sea, though, no matter how confident," Ned adds. "No matter how long they've been doing it. The best fishermen know that. Evan is one of them."

Ned's assurances aside, my stomach is still in knots as the hours pass by. Once most of the food is prepared, the family scatters to deal with their nerves in their own way as they wait to hear from Evan. Nessa even convinces Nana to take an afternoon nap, leaving Lucy to tidy the kitchen while I edit a couple of promotional videos of the inn's grounds and gardens from footage I shot while exploring with Nana the other day.

"You're nervous, aren't you?" Lucy's question comes out accusatory, even though it isn't.

My cheeks burn and I keep my gaze to my phone. "No. I mean, yes. But no more than anyone else." My mind won't stop replaying the sight of Evan falling overboard. The sky was even relatively clear that day. I can't imagine how bad the waves could get in a storm.

She smiles at me knowingly, letting it go. "Nana's been up since six in the morning cooking for the party," Lucy says, passing the broom over the crumbs and flour sprinkled on the floor. "She's going all-out to impress you."

"Impress me? Why?"

"I think she's worried the potluck-style engagement party isn't fancy enough for you. She really wants you to like us."

My heart twinges at the thought of Nana worrying that all this effort isn't enough for me when it's the complete opposite.

"Honestly, I already told Evan this is beyond what I'd expect. I feel so bad everyone is putting in so much effort, especially when this isn't . . . you know . . . real."

Lucy smiles ruefully. "Trust me, if she had her way, we'd be inviting the entire town. This is very scaled down compared to what she used to drum up back in the day. When I was a kid, she'd cook for days getting ready for her big summer parties. And she refused to get anything catered."

"She's pretty incredible."

"It's killing her to keep the engagement party within the family, though. She's asked Evan twice now if she can invite her friends."

"Why can't she?"

"Because if we let her invite people, then my mom is going to insist on inviting people, and so will Nessa, and it'll be this big thing. Evan's already gonna have to answer to the entire town as it is once you leave."

I hadn't thought about the aftermath for Evan. "I guess being publicly engaged kind of cramps his style with the ladies in town," I hedge, entirely aware I'm pathetically fishing for information like I'm in middle school.

Lucy raises a brow as she sweeps the flour into the dustpan. "He dated around a lot when he was younger. But he hasn't been with anyone since his last girlfriend about three years ago. She was from out of town. Between you and me, I think they were too different. She didn't really understand his obligation to be on the water. Or the work he had to put into the inn."

"Sounds like a lonely life for his spouse. Though I'd assume there's lots of women in town who understand that lifestyle?" I ask, pondering the possibility of using this exact reason as plausible grounds for our breakup.

"It's pretty hard to date in this town. Everyone's already married with kids."

"Even all your dude friends from the Anchor?"

She leans in, eyes wide. "Why? Are you interested in any of them?" she whispers conspiratorially.

"No," I snort. "I was wondering if you've ever been interested in any of them."

She nearly chokes, bracing herself with the broom handle. "Like, romantically?"

I nod.

"God no." Her tone tells me my suggestion was wildly absurd.

"Why not? They're all decently good-looking guys."

She stares at me for a couple of moments before turning to close the dishwasher. "They're basically family. Not to mention, they all have wives except Kyle. And he's destined to be a perpetual bachelor."

"You're saying you never crushed on any of them growing up? You must have a type."

"Do you have a type?" she counters.

"I'm . . . open to all types. City guys mostly."

She smirks. "What about country guys like Evan? Do you find him attractive?"

I blink like I've just been smashed in the face with a basketball. How dare she ask this perfectly legitimate question? "I think any human with the gift of sight would consider Evan objectively attractive. I don't get why he's single in a small town like this," I say, voice low.

"I mean, he's my cousin. I'm forced to love him. But I can see why he'd be more of an acquired taste."

"What about you? What's your type?" I scan her blank face for a moment. "Let me guess. You're into the alternative type. Kind of artsy?"

"More like geriatric. Wispy white hair. Mega rich. On their deathbeds," she deadpans.

"Ah, black widow. I like your style. It would make you feel a little better about your own looming mortality."

She chuckles. "Just kidding. Honestly, I'm into everyone and anything. Guys, girls, I don't discriminate, so long as their names aren't Stan or Evvie. They also have to be into running, turtles, and watching UFO documentaries unironically. Oh, and willing to sit in the nosebleeds with me at concerts without complaining."

"Those are oddly specific yet completely understandable criteria."

Before she can respond, Nessa yells "Guys!" from the window in the parlor.

The distant hum of an engine is audible amid the steady downpour outside. When I reach the window behind Nessa's shoulder, my chest expands.

I've never been happier to see Evan's foolishly gigantic gas-guzzler of a vehicle.

• • •

EVAN DOESN'T SEE me at first. He's too busy hurriedly hauling his gear from the truck bed in a whirl of flannel.

The rain is coming down now in a heavy sheet of silver, like someone took a knife through the sky and split it open.

Once he's unloaded his toolbox, he spots me, eyes partially covered by the shadow of his worn Maple Leafs ball cap. The corners of his mouth tug upward slowly in that trademark smile that made my blood boil only days ago.

It occurs to me that he's probably amused I'm outside on the porch steps, barefoot, my cashmere sweater and light-wash bootcuts sticking to me like a second skin.

Either way, an otherworldly spirit takes over my body. That's the only logical explanation for why I'd run into his arms like the second-to-last scene in one of Tara's sappy rom-coms. I've managed to wrap my limbs around his solid mass, hanging on like a koala bear.

For the briefest moment, his body stiffens in my embrace. And in a blink, he's matching my enthusiasm, hands locked under my bottom to hold me there. It's a welcome warmth from the icy chill of the rain. When I unwrap my legs to stand on solid ground, his arms stay in place on my waist, rocking me back and forth like a soothing wave. I breathe in his salty ocean scent as he presses his face into the crook of my neck. His soft lips graze the sensitive patch of skin behind my ear, sending a chill careening down my spine.

I step out of the hug and scrunch my face up at him.

A quizzical look flits across his face. "You put on a nice show for the fam," he says casually, nodding toward the Whalers crowded on the porch, watching us from afar.

I give him a pathetic punch in the chest. "It's not a show. I was worried. You were supposed to be back hours ago."

He digs his ancient, cracked phone out of his pocket, flashing a blank screen toward me. "Shit. I turned it off when we lost signal. Was trying to conserve my battery."

"Everyone was really worried," I say sternly.

He reaches forward to move a strand of hair plastered on my forehead, gently placing it behind my ear. "I'm sorry. Really. I've been in worse storms than this one. And besides, I had to make a special pit stop." He opens the truck door, reaching for a plastic grocery bag on the driver's seat.

I take it tentatively. It's peculiarly light. "What is it? I don't like surprises."

"Just look and see."

My breath catches. Inside the bag sits the last thing I would have expected. At least ten different plastic containers of adhesive fake eyelashes of all varieties. Some are ridiculously thick costume ones, while some are tame, for everyday wear. They aren't the same as lash extensions. In fact, they're not at all the brand I would buy if I needed glue-ons, but the very gesture hits me deep in my core. It's like I'm peering into a bag of gold. "You got me . . . eyelashes," I manage through my shock.

"You were complaining about losing them on the boat the other day, so I thought you might like new ones for the party to-night." He rocks on his heels, lips pressed tight, awaiting my reaction.

"I messed up, didn't I? I didn't know where to start in the store, so I panicked and got them all. The cashier told me to get that glue too. Are they even the right ones? Probably not—"

I cut him off mid-ramble with a surprise hug. We're both entirely waterlogged now, but I don't care. This is the nicest thing anyone has ever done for me. It's not just the eyelashes. It's the fact that he remembered something so seemingly insignificant and trivial to anyone else, particularly someone like Evan.

"Thank you," I say as he pulls me tighter. "I can't believe you'd do that for me."

"Anything for my fiancée." I study his face, searching for a small smile to indicate he's joking. He moves in slightly, hovering dangerously close to me, beard hair tickling my cheek. But from this vantage point, he doesn't look like he's kidding in the slightest.

Through the rain, our eyes meet in a heated glance. I'm now acutely aware of my own heartbeat. Instinctively, my eyes dart to his lips, which are parted ever so slightly. I desperately want to kiss him. And not for show.

Someone, probably Ned, does one of those finger whistles from the porch, where the entire family is huddled, watching us.

Even Fiona jumps in, pumping her fist *Jersey Shore*–style. "Come on, give us a kiss!"

Evan tosses his family a derisive headshake, motioning for them to go back inside. And they do.

Once we're in private, Evan's lips turn up in a challenge, encapsulating the ongoing game between us. Who will reign supreme?

Just when my mind is ready to take control, show him who's boss, my body betrays me entirely, freezing. He squints at me, puzzled when I don't match his challenge. Instead of rising as a worthy opponent, I'm staring at him like a glitched-out, malfunctioning robot. I half expect him to call me on it and gloat about his victory. But he drops his figurative weapons and just takes my hand, giving it a confident squeeze as if to say *I've got you*, like we've dropped our warring flags and melded into one team.

His shoulders drop in relief when I inch closer, armor stripped, heartbeat hammering so loudly he can surely hear it.

Evan runs his thumb across my cheek and down my jawline to cup my chin, and everything blurs. The trees, the gust of the wind, the feeling of the gravel under my bare feet.

I press my palm against the curve of his neck, feeling the drum of his pulse, in sync with mine. When he lifts my chin with only his finger, eyes searching mine, everything goes quiet.

It happens in segments. Like camera stills. His hot breath against my mouth. The faintest of head tilting. The drizzle of rain from the cloud that's opened above us. The slightest brush of my bottom lip with his. The scruff of his beard, rough against my skin as his lips capture mine fully. The first, sweet slide of his tongue, so perfect I think it was made for this exact purpose. The delicate press of the pads of his fingers against my cheek. The hitch of my breath as he deepens the kiss, melding us together as one unit.

The whole thing is PG-13, though it feels anything but. His grip tightens around my waist, fingers roaming up and down my back and up through my hair. I kiss him back desperately, like we're on the clock. Like we have only a minute left on this earth.

"Wow. That's quite the welcome. You must have been *really* worried about me," he murmurs in between kisses. "Maybe I'll have to plan more near-death experiences."

"Shut up. I can't take any more risks." I press the softest bite onto his bottom lip as punishment, and he lets out a soft groan that makes me ache with need.

"You sure about that?" Fueled by my enthusiasm, he backs me up into the side of the truck, gaze searing. His hardness against my thigh doesn't go unnoticed as he rocks against me, kissing me hard until my lips go numb. Pulsing vibrations spread to the forgotten corners of my body, lighting my insides with a feeling I don't recognize.

The sudden *squawk* of a distant bird makes us both pause. We stay forehead to forehead for a couple of long beats, exchanging shallow breaths, before I pull myself away with a staggering step to the side. Evan tilts his head, lips still parted with surprise at my abrupt departure.

Chest heaving, I come to a realization: I have a very inconvenient crush on Evan, who I'm breaking up with the day after tomorrow.

♥ chapter twenty-two

"**A**RE YOU EVER going to tell me where we're going?" I prod from the passenger seat.

Evan drums his fingers on the leather steering wheel to the beat of a Tragically Hip song filtering lazily through the speakers. "No. That defeats the purpose of a surprise, doesn't it? Besides, if I tell you, you'll just complain the rest of the way."

I shoot him my best evil eye. In turn, he assaults me with an adorable side smirk before turning his gaze back to the open road. "I won't complain," I assure him.

"You absolutely will. I know you." He says it with an absurd amount of confidence for someone who's known me less than a week. And yet I'm starting to think he might know me better than I know myself.

After all, the Mel Karlsen of last week is not the type of girl who paces around, waiting with bated breath for her man to return from danger. She's not the kind of girl who runs into the rain, barefoot, for a passionate embrace. And she's most definitely not the type of girl who spends her backyard barbecue engagement party in a torn toilet paper sash that reads *BRIDE* written in Sharpie. Or is she?

That very thought sends a zing of warning through me. Suddenly, this maddeningly massive truck feels far too small.

"We need to plot our breakup today" is all I can think to say, pressing the button to lower the window a crack. I feel like a panting dog in a parked vehicle on a hot summer's day. Technically, I'm not wrong. Tomorrow is the Lobster Festival—the day of our breakup. And thus far we have no idea how it's going to go down.

Evan's jaw visibly tenses. "Do we have to?"

His response catches me off guard. It sounds . . . genuinely reluctant. "We do," I tell him.

"You don't *really* want to break up with me, do you?" He flashes me a childish faux frown, which looks hilarious on a man his size.

I squeeze my lips together, blocking any honest response from escaping.

He answers for me. "I don't think you do." There's that effortless confidence again. He knows I don't want to end . . . whatever this is.

But I wish I did.

A maddening sigh arises from the depths of my core as I study his profile. The gentle slope of his nose. The perfect shape of his lips, which are far too soft for someone who spends his days at sea in the harsh wind. I've never wanted to kiss someone again so badly in my life, and I don't like it one bit.

One could blame the anguish of awaiting Evan's safe arrival

yesterday morning. Maybe it warped my perception of reality. But I'm fairly certain Evan wants to kiss me again too. And maybe more. The man did travel through a storm to buy me fake eyelashes.

Of course, we haven't discussed the kiss. At all.

And then there was the rest of the day. I didn't expect to have so much fun at the engagement party. Nana went all-out with white balloons and a food spread that included cheese platters, meats, dips, battered and fried halibut, and crab legs. It felt elaborate to me, though according to Fiona, it's just typical afternoon barbecue fare at the Whalers'.

The best part? Nana, Fiona, and Lucy wore glue-on eyelashes "in my honor." Nana chose the extra-dramatic faux-mink triple-thickness falsies and informed everyone of her intention to wear them daily from here on out. She is truly a woman after my own heart.

Sure, it wasn't the Pinterest-perfect aesthetic. There was no rosé or massive flower wall for photos or tray of blush Persian macaroons. Ned cranked his country playlist so loud it scared a flock of birds resting in the maple tree by the side of the inn. And I wouldn't trade it for anything.

I try to let myself enjoy the simple beauty of the skinny pines dotting each side of the tiny gravel road we've turned onto. It ribbons through even denser trees, leading to a secluded lake.

Unlike the ocean, this body of water is statue-still, peaceful, and serene. There's nary a boat in sight. Its color mirrors the broad span of azure sky speckled with cotton candy clouds. The shoreline is grassy with just a small clearing of rippled sand. A cluster of thick, mature trees provides ample shade from the beating sun. It's so majestically soothing, it looks like a naturalesque oil painting you'd find in the lobby of a hotel.

Evan parks two lawn chairs along the sandy shoreline before heading back to the truck.

"What kind of fish are in this lake?" I ask, snapping a few wide shots with Lucy's camera.

"Trout, pickerel, perch, and the odd bass," he calls over his shoulder.

The fish species go over my head entirely. "You're not using real bait, are you?" I ask, quivering at the thought of wriggling earthworms.

"Not after your ferocious centipede attack." His cheeks are pink when he returns with his fishing pole and tackle box. "Lures."

He takes in the untouched beauty of his surroundings like it's a drug, scanning the water and sky. With his flannel sleeves pulled to his elbows, there's a haze of ropy, thick muscle flexing and twisting as he roots through his tackle box in search of the perfect lure. He looks like a sexy young country star in a music video for an upbeat song about leaving his villainous wife for his first love—fishing. It's only when he slants me a quick pearly smile that I realize I'm white-knuckling the cracked armrest of the lawn chair as though I'm seconds away from public electrocution.

I cross and uncross my legs to relieve the sudden tension as he attaches the lure to the rod. I feel an urge to do something with my hands. Capture this on film. But no camera will do this visual proper justice.

On the cusp of losing myself entirely, I give my cheek a mental slap. No more lumberjack fantasies. No more touching. No more cuddling. No more kissing. Definitely no more kissing.

Back to business. I lean forward in my chair and clap my hands together, as if I'm washing the slate clean. I'm leaving in two days, after all. "All right, breakup planning time."

There's a delay as he casts the line into the water with a smooth *whoosh*. "You're really hell-bent on this breakup, huh?"

"What choice do we have? Unless you want to tell them I got eaten by a rabid raccoon, we need a plausible story for my exit."

The resort has confirmed twice that they're expecting my arrival on Sunday. At the prospect of finally going, I find myself frowning. I don't know when it happened, but leaving has lost its luster. Even the promise of deep pampering and ultimate luxury isn't lifting my spirits like it should.

Despite my feelings, maybe leaving is a good thing. The safety and serenity of the resort where I can be alone with my thoughts might be lonely, but at least it's familiar. It's nothing I can't handle.

Besides, after last night, I no longer trust myself. After the engagement festivities ended, Evan and I had another heated moment in our bathroom.

"You okay?" he'd asked, leaning against the doorway, forearms flexed purposely to weaken my resolve.

"More than okay. Why? Do I not seem okay?" I asked, gripping the edge of the counter to stop myself from grabbing his face and finishing what we started in the driveway.

He watched me for a moment, a mixture of concern and amusement. Like he knew how much I wanted him. "You seem . . . jumpy. Do you want to talk about . . . today?"

The fact that I nearly spontaneously combusted when you humped me against your truck? I was tempted to say. Instead, I opted to plead ignorance. "What about it?"

Before he could respond, Nana waltzed in without knocking and asked me for a tutorial on how to take off the false lashes. I had enough wherewithal to take the interruption as a sign, put on my ugliest PJs, and tuck myself into bed. Solo. Things have been a smidge awkward since.

Evan doesn't tear his eyes from the water, so I let my gaze rest on his profile. His mouth is turned down in the slightest frown, probably because I'm distracting him.

"Don't worry. You don't even have to do much. I already brainstormed some potential reasons for our breakup."

He leans his weight on one foot for a moment, seemingly uninterested. "Let's hear 'em."

I consult my phone, pulling up the note I prepared early this morning. "First option: growing apart."

"That won't work," he claims. "We told my family we've only been together a year."

"Length of time doesn't really matter. Maybe in the year we were together, you felt like you didn't know who I was," I explain, not at all drawing inspiration from past relationships. Not at all.

"After the other day—when you fell in the shower—I feel like I know all there is to know about you."

I hide my face behind my phone. "How much did you see?"

He lifts a hand from the rod and makes an infuriating zipper sign over his lips. "I'm not at liberty to disclose."

I swat him on the bicep. "Tell me. What did you see?"

"Everything." His low, gruff tone sends a quiver working its way down my back, settling in my lower belly.

RIP to me. I'm internally screaming. I've never been so thankful to be in a seated position. "I'm sorry I ruined your shower curtain and fell on you. Naked. Not my finest moment."

"It's fine, Mel. Don't worry about it." His mouth softens, notably more neutral than it was a few minutes ago.

In order to distract myself from the smidgen of disappointment I may or may not feel about his lack of enthusiasm for my naked body, I distract myself with the next possibility. "How about fundamental differences in worldview? For example, I can't get on board with your dedication to flannel."

"Nah. Not convincing. You secretly like it."

I avert my stare. "Nope. Okay, third: lack of communication."

"I communicate," he assures me, reeling in the line to recast.

"Do you, though? Because you're a man of few words."

No response.

I'm not in the mood for debate, so I continue down my list. "Fine. What about trust issues? It's an easy sell. I always have guys in my DMs when I post my thirst traps. Maybe you can't handle it."

He shakes his head vehemently, eyes simmering. "Nope. What kind of man would get pissed if his girl posted pictures like that?"

I'm unsure if he's referring to my pictures specifically, or just scantily clad photos in general. "My last ex, for example. He'd get really jealous about my DMs. Which is ironic, because we met after he slid into mine."

He gives me a knowing look. "Sounds like a familiar tale."

"I may have borrowed bits of my past experience for our fictional backstory with your family, yes," I admit.

"Well, this ex of yours sounds like an insecure asshole."

"He was fine at first," I note. "He was super complimentary

about the way I looked. But when we started seeing each other more seriously, the jealousy came out. He'd ask me to delete the pictures. And when we ended things, he told me he thought everything about me was fake."

His shoulders drop. "You're a lot of things, Mel, but you're not fake."

"You don't think? Even with all my edited pictures?"

His face cracks in a grin, summer-sky eyes snagging mine, holding me hostage. "I'm just going by what I see in front of me. And your true emotions are pretty much written all over your face, whether you like it or not."

I scowl, trying to wipe whatever expression he's reading off my face. I shan't be perceived by him anymore. "All right, so you're not down with this one." I consult my list again, sweeping to the bottom. "What about one partner doesn't feel seen? Maybe you spend too much time on the water for my liking. Maybe I come to the dramatic realization at the Lobster Festival that I'm not cut out to be a fisherman's wife."

He scowls. "I don't like it."

I drop my phone in my lap, aggrieved. "Evan, why are you being so difficult? We need a plausible breakup reason, and that's the most believable."

No response.

"See, we should just go with the lack of communication one," I suggest. "Either that, or I got kidnapped by a pack of wolves."

"I just don't think being a fisherman's wife is that bad," he says, fully ignoring my joke. "I'd never be one of those men who stay on the water for days at a time. I'd never put any job or anything before my wife's happiness. Ever."

I blink away his hard stare. "That's a nice sentiment. But it's not realistic."

"How is that not realistic?"

"Because. Men aren't like that in real life."

"Well, I'm real last time I checked. And most of the guys on my crew feel the same way. So maybe it's less about men in general and more about the fact that you haven't met any decent ones."

My stomach flips. He's not wrong. But I'm not about to explore my misguided dating history. "It's not as simple as you ensuring your wife's happiness. It's about whether you can compromise. If your wife can't handle the lifestyle, the worrying, then it means you're not a good match. It's not necessarily a failure on your part. Or hers."

"I like to think I could come up with a compromise to make sure she's still happy. I'd do whatever it took," he tells me.

"Evan, this is fictional. Your Nana thinks I'm a nude model, for god's sake. You can bend a little."

"It just doesn't feel right to me," he says, eyes fixed on the water.

I suck in a calming breath and exhale slowly. Clearly Evan isn't in the mood to do anything other than fish. "Okay. We can park this conversation for now, but we need to come up with something. Tonight."

"Sure, no problem," he says stonily as he changes the lure on his rod.

We sit in silence for a while. There's something about being near water that magnifies sound. I can hear everything. From the echoing *caw* of a flock of birds overhead to the *plop* of water when the fish jump for a cluster of flies. Even the rustle of leaves swaying in the warm summer breeze above.

"Want to try?" Evan asks out of the blue, gesturing to the rod.

I blink. "Try fishing? Me?"

There's that charming smile again. "Who else?"

"I mean, I don't really like the idea of injuring fish for sport," I say hesitantly, batting away a pesky mosquito.

"I don't do it for sport, Mel. Anything we catch, we're bringing back to the inn to eat," he explains, reeling in his line.

I stand, cautious, as he hands me the pole. "Lucy did say you were an ethical fisherman."

He laughs, positioning himself behind me, chest spanning my shoulders to demonstrate how to cast the line. He even carefully moves my hair over my shoulder to ensure it's out of the way, thumb grazing the back of my neck in the process. I shudder. This doesn't bode well for my *no touching* promise to myself.

He grabs my index finger, holding the line in front of the reel before placing his hand over mine to tip the rod back, releasing as we cast. I get a tiny jolt of satisfaction when the bobber soars and lands in the water with a *plop*.

"I don't know if there's such a thing as a fully ethical fisherman," he starts. "But I try to do things right. My grandpa always taught us to respect the fish and the water. If you wanted to get him riled up, all you had to do was mention commercial trawlers. He freakin' hated them."

I smile instinctively. "How long have you fished?" I ask, relishing the vibration of his voice against my back as I reel in the line. *This is innocent. Nothing more, nothing less*, I tell myself.

"Since I was old enough to hold a rod," he says, stepping back from me, confident in my rod-holding ability. The distance isn't nearly as appealing as it should be.

"And you still find recreational fishing fun even though it's your day job?"

His eyes light up as he settles in the lawn chair. "Oh yeah. There's nothing like it. Even work—sure, it's stressful. Like I said, the money is hit or miss. But being on the water with my crew, who I hand select, doesn't really feel like work. Fishing in fresh water is a nice change, though. I like the challenge, the feeling of the tug on the line. And it's relaxing in a different way. No need to stress if I don't catch anything. Though I always do," he adds with a cocky half grin.

"I'm sure you do," I chide with a gentle headshake. "Did you always know you wanted to be a fisherman?"

"Oh yeah. Except for the week in first grade when I wanted to be an astronaut."

"I could see that for you."

He laughs. "Nah. The idea of space is kinda freaky, don't you think?"

"You'd rather face the potential prehistoric creatures that lurk in the depths of the oceans instead of space?"

"Prehistoric creatures over aliens a hundred percent. In space, it's infinite dark nothingness, black holes, and no normal sense of time," he says, sure of himself. "Sure, eighty percent of the ocean is unexplored, but at least it's on Earth."

"That's true." I take in his relaxed demeanor, a tinge jealous at how comfortable he is in nature. "It's like you were born for fishing."

"Jack and I always knew. We never wanted to do anything else. I don't think anything could take me away from the water."

I note the way he says *Jack and I*, as though they're a duo.

He lifts his head, eyes flicking to mine, like he knows what I'm thinking. "In case you didn't already gather, Jack was my cousin. Lucy's older brother."

"Tell me about him." I bite my tongue to stop myself from the onslaught of questions that have built within me since day one, since the first mention of Jack.

"Jack was two years older than me. He and I were basically like brothers. Larger-than-life personality. Outgoing. Funny. Everyone loved him. He made people feel important, like they were his best friend. He was always getting up to shit in town as a kid, stealing from people's gardens, riding his bike recklessly around the marina, scaring the tourists. And somehow he charmed his way outta everything. He'd give the shirt off his back to anyone who needed it. He was just the kind of guy everyone wants to have around, you know?" I note how his entire face lights up when he talks about Jack.

"He sounds like he was a really good person. Just like you."

"He was. I wanted to be like Jack so badly. But I was always more reserved. Shy, I guess, despite always getting into trouble too. When he started going out fishing with my grandpa, I had to learn too. When he got a dirt bike, I had to get one."

"Sounds like he was your idol."

"Kind of," he says, eyes brimming with nostalgia. "Though I never would have admitted that. To be honest, I was pissed when our grandpa left the boat to him. He made him the captain when he retired."

"Really?"

He grins. "I was a shithead, to be fair. Thought I was a better leader. Never liked taking direction from anyone."

"Not much has changed, I see."

"It made sense, though, in hindsight. Jack had the most

experience at sea. We spent so many damn hours out there to-gether. Knew each other better than anyone. We'd tell each other everything. Never let the drama with our moms get in the way of our relationship. And then one day he went out alone to set some traps and got caught in a storm." My gut twists at his words. "I shoulda been there that day. But instead I slept in, hungover from going out the night before. I still hate myself for that."

"Evan, I'm so sorry . . ." It strikes me now why he was so mili-tant about wearing a life vest on the boat that day. "It's not your fault. The sea is treacherous . . . for everyone."

"That's what everyone in the family says . . . even though no one has looked at me the same way since. Especially Fiona. The whole family kind of fell apart after that. Everyone stopped doing holidays together at the inn. They stopped coming to the inn al-together, actually."

"And you stayed."

"No. I avoided it for years with everyone else. Until my grandpa passed and Nana moved out. I felt like I had an obligation to keep it running . . . almost as a way of making up for what happened, I guess."

"Evan, it wasn't your fault. None of it. You're not responsible for how people reacted to a fucked-up situation."

"It doesn't feel that way, though. Even all these years later," he says, face twisted with anguish. "The anniversary of his death was actually the day you showed up. I spent the entire day on the water just to feel close to him."

My insides hitch at the admission. "Really?"

He nods. "Yup. I was in a hell of a mood. I'm sorry about that. It's not an excuse for the way I treated you."

I hang my head and lower the rod, replaying the first night I arrived when I was on the phone with Crystal. The look of disdain on his face that night is burned into my mind. Sure, he shouldn't have treated me that way. But now I know that anger was a side effect of pain. It's oddly relieving, knowing it wasn't all because of me.

"I'm an asshole either way. I'm so sorry, Evan. I shouldn't have said what I said about the inn."

He waves my words away. "For what it's worth, you're completely right. It's outdated. A total mess. Even without the construction zone. I was embarrassed about it. That I let it get to that state. My grandpa would be horrified to see it as it is. It used to be beautiful for guests when I was a kid. Or maybe I just thought it was."

"But in your defense, you also weren't expecting guests that night," I say, letting him off the hook. "And I rudely barged my way in and demanded to stay."

He drops his serious expression, the corners of his eyes crinkling with the slightest smile. "True. But I'm thankful you did."

Before I can respond, there's a strong, unexpected tug on the line that nearly causes me to drop the rod entirely. "Oh, I think we have something!" I shout, heart pumping, body zipping with adrenaline.

Evan rushes over, enveloping my body again from behind, placing both hands over mine. "Hold on," he instructs as we whip the rod up to set the hook. "Okay, time to reel it in."

We crank the reel in unison, keeping steady tension on the rod until a silvery-green fish with a gaping mouth eventually surfaces.

"Nice job! You got a bass," he exclaims as he retrieves it by the mouth with his bare hands.

I hop from one foot to the other, unable to stay still in my ela-tion. Evan was right—there is no better thrill than the tug on the line. I squint, stepping closer to inspect. "That's a bass? It's so ugly."

He holds it up for me, admiring it before shooting me a mega-watt smile. "Nah. She's a catch."

♥ chapter twenty-three

EVAN IS NOT wearing plaid. I repeat: Evan Whaler is not wearing plaid today. This feels like a monumental occasion. A rare sighting of an endangered species in the wild.

Instead, he's opted for a fitted navy blue T-shirt with the marina logo. I curse the way it stretches over his biceps. He really needs to cover those arms, for the sake of humanity.

I should be distracted by the Lobster Festival. By the fact that the entire Main Street of Cora's Cove is closed to vehicle traffic, blocked by barricades. I should be enamored with the vibrant colors. The pops of red and blue tents lining the crowded street selling food and one-of-a-kind, locally made clothing, jewelry, and crafts. The laughter and excitement of the crowd milling about, in no rush to be anywhere but here. The salty wafts of ocean breeze, battered and fried fish, punctuated with tangy hints of lemon and vinegar. But instead, it's Evan who's captured my full attention.

"You're strangely quiet today." He flashes me an adorably hesitant smile as we snake through the crowd toward a glittering Ferris wheel, his arm hooked around my waist like it belongs there.

I match his smile by reflex, despite my vow not to let him dazzle me. "I don't mean to be. Just taking it all in."

He surveys me for a moment, ultimately deciding not to press it. We're breaking up today, after all. What more is there to say?

The Ferris wheel pod sways as we take our seats side by side. Evan wraps an arm around the back of the seat, though he doesn't pull me close. As we ascend, we're blessed with a full view of the harbor, which is alive and bustling. There are hundreds of feet worth of floating docks, as well as various wharves jutting out at angles, lined with boat after boat of all different sizes and shapes. Evan points out one ship currently unloading a fresh seafood catch. Most striking is how the marina is dotted with the vibrant pops of color from the buildings. It looks even more picturesque from here than it does up close. I snap a mental photo for safekeeping, somehow already missing this place before I've even left.

My spirits rise again ever so slightly when we find the rest of the Whalers in the beer tent, merrily socializing over the crack of lobster claws, the sizzle of butter, and the hiss of steam in the back cooking area. The long cafeteria tables are laden with tray upon tray of fresh, buttery lobster, flaky golden buns, and coleslaw.

A Celtic fiddle-and-accordion tune echoes from the stage to the right. In front of the band are three young girls partaking in some traditional maritime step dancing.

"This is where the dance is going to be. They move all the tables when it gets dark," Nessa explains as we join them.

The Whalers appear to know everyone in town. Countless

people swarm within minutes after we sit down, eager to get the latest gossip on what's happening with the inn. But most of all, they're eager to introduce themselves to me. Each handshake and "congratulations on your engagement" chat further reminds me just how deep this lie has seeped into Cora's Cove. I've always known this felt wrong, but never has that nagging prickle at my deceitful heart stung more than right now.

"It's okay," Lucy says, giving me a pat on the arm and a tight-lipped smile before sipping her foam-topped beer.

"Don't you feel . . . kind of bad?" I ask, tone hushed.

"I do. But I also look at my mom and Aunt Ness getting along . . . and it feels worth it, you know?" Any lingering remorse temporarily dims at the sight of Fiona and Nessa across the table, both of whom are cackling over a pitcher of amber-colored beer. Gone is any evidence of a long-standing feud. Deceit aside, it feels good knowing our elaborate scheme wasn't for nothing.

I'm mid-bite of my lobster roll when Kyle squeezes his massive body in between Evan and me, a tornado potato skewer in his right hand and a beer in his left.

Evan shifts over to make space, his eye narrowly dodging the pointy end of the skewer. "You remember Kyle?"

"'Course she does," Kyle cuts in. "I'm kind of famous in Cora's Cove."

"Famous for your criminal record, maybe," Lucy teases from my other side.

Kyle's brows bounce knowingly. "What can I say? Girls like a bad boy."

"What did you do?" I dare to ask.

"He spray-painted penises on all the boats at the marina when we were teenagers. Got slapped with a vandalism charge," Evan explains.

"Fuck sakes, Whaler. How's a petty charge supposed to impress her?"

Evan gives the brim of Kyle's tattered ball cap a swift flick. "Impressing my fiancée is dead last on your list of things to do, bud."

Everyone goes dead quiet for a moment, waiting for Evan to crack a smile or concede to the joke. But he doesn't. Admittedly, he plays the jealous fiancé well.

"This one's always been possessive of his toys." Kyle reaches to give Evan a retributive slap on the back of the head. "So tell me, how and why did this dickhead keep a beautiful woman like you a secret for so long?"

Panicked, Lucy jumps in, rehashing the same general story about us meeting online that we told the family at the hospital, minus the jabs and the embarrassment. Everyone within earshot strains to eavesdrop, including the Whalers.

"Guess you'll be movin' up here, right?" Kyle confirms.

"Um, that's still something we need to—" I squirm in my seat, eyeing Evan for help. Bold as Kyle is, he's actually given us the perfect opening to sow the seeds of our breakup, which we discussed last night before falling asleep. And by *discussed*, I mean I told him we were going to argue about relocating while he lay in silence on the air mattress, offering exactly zero feedback except for a grumpy *All right, sure* before turning over to sleep.

"Of course she's moving here," Evan cuts in, tone terse and convincing.

I play along, tossing him an exaggerated expression that

screams *Let's not fight in public.* The irony. "We may have to be long distance for a short time, just while we figure things out."

Evan shakes his head vehemently. "I'm not going to be nine hundred kilometers from my fiancée."

It strikes me that he knows almost the exact distance between Cora's Cove and Boston. Maybe he took our conversation more seriously than I thought and prepared ahead of time.

Sensing the tension at the end of the table, Ned jumps in and proposes a toast. "To the future Mr. and Mrs. Whaler, wherever they may end up."

We don't get the chance to resume our fight, because Evan is summoned to prep the band for the dance. I'm left to deal with the abundant yet incredibly generous offers to help with our wedding from townspeople. Venue, catering, you name it. They have it covered. My chest feels fizzy as I register how genuine everyone is. How they're willing to go out of their way to help make someone else's big day a reality, without expecting anything in return.

Soon the crowd erupts in applause as the DJ appears onstage, starting off the night with a classic Journey song, evidently a crowd favorite based on the whoops and hollers.

Lucy buries her face in my arm as we wade through the crowd to the dance floor. "Oh god. See that woman on the table?" she asks, peeking through splayed fingers.

"The one slow-grinding with the dude in the trucker hat?"

She nods gravely. "That's my fifth-grade teacher, Mrs. Hilliker. Evan had her too. She hated him. Always put him in detention," she says as we watch her husband accidentally lose the contents of his pitcher on her shirt. "Told ya. Lobsterfest is wild."

She's not wrong. Even Nana, Fiona, Ned, and Nessa are letting loose dancing.

A couple of drinks in, I fancy myself a skilled, near-professional dancer, spinning arm in arm with Lucy to some sort of jig. We've quickly attracted a crowd. They circle around us, clapping to the beat, heartily cheering as we twirl each other around and around until everyone's smiling faces are a complete blur.

When the beat slows and the song ends, I spin into someone's barrel chest. "You're not Evan," I say, registering a familiar face.

It's Kyle. His chest shakes with a grumble of a laugh. "Unfortunately for you. Fallin' for him, huh?"

I draw my brows together, heart rate spiking. "Consider me already *fallen*. We're already engaged."

He tilts his head, as if to say *The jig is up*. "It's all right, Mel. I know."

Heat crests my cheeks. "He told you?"

"Nah. But I know Whaler like the back of my hand. Known the guy since we were in preschool. I haven't put all the pieces together yet, but I figure it has something to do with his family. He wouldn't lie unless it was important."

Impressive. I nod, confirming. "He's planning to tell you everything tomorrow. Until then, promise you won't say anything?"

He places his hand over his chest. "I solemnly swear on my boat—which is my prized possession, by the way—to keep . . . whatever this is a secret."

My shoulders drop slightly at the reminder. As though he recognizes my disappointment, he leans in to whisper in my ear, "But I will say, I never thought I'd see Evan Whaler in the makeup section at a Shopper's Drug Mart for half an hour with a basket full of stick-on eyelashes. You've left an impression on him, that's for sure."

"Really?"

He nods. "He hasn't been the same since Jack. It's only since you've been here that I'm finally starting to see glimpses of the old him."

I barely have time to process this over the roar of the crowd when Evan and the band appear onstage, steeped in a spotlight. Their first song is "I've Just Seen a Face" by the Beatles. Evan finds me in the crowd after the first line, zeroing in on me like I'm the only one in the audience.

They cycle through a bunch of crowd favorites, mostly songs with an East Coast / Irish flare. By the time the band breaks and the DJ takes over again, I meet eyes with Evan as he heads offstage.

"Nice pipes," I call out.

He flashes me one of his charming smiles. "My arms or my voice?"

"Both," I say boldly. The alcohol is definitely getting to me. And I'd be lying if I said Kyle's comment wasn't an added boost of confidence.

Based on the glint in his eyes, he likes my forwardness. "Having fun with Kyle?"

"Oh yeah. He's telling me all your darkest secrets. And he's an excellent dancer," I toss in, just to gauge his reaction.

He raises a brow. "Not sure how I feel about another guy dancing with my fiancée." There's something about the way he says it, low, husky, eyes locked to mine as the music crescendos around us.

"*Fake* fiancée," I remind him. Against my better judgment, I run my index finger down the soft inside of his forearm. His muscle flexes under my touch, and his breathing accelerates, matching mine.

Evan mirrors me, trailing the rough pad of his finger down the inside of my forearm in an identical swoop. "I dunno. This feels pretty real to me."

His words suck the last of the air out of my lungs as he closes the distance. His massive hand fans my waist, sending a thrill of electricity humming to the base of my stomach.

"Hey, let's take a break," he says, as though he can tell I'm in overdrive.

"A break?"

"Come with me."

♥ chapter twenty-four

E VAN LEADS ME to a field behind one of the canneries. The deep-fried scent is less pungent here, only to be replaced with the salty smell of buttered popcorn.

"You haven't bit my head off in a full day. What's up?" Evan asks over the crunch of gravel under our feet.

"I'm just tired," I say, avoiding all eye contact in favor of looking at the hills and rock formations ahead, which tell me we're close to the sea. Though I can still hear the echoing screams and the *whoosh* of air brakes from the festival rides behind us.

He lets it go, leading me by the hand up a rocky incline. It isn't until our destination is in clear view that I understand where we're going.

"Is this the . . ." My voice trails off, but what I mean to say is *Is this the lighthouse I was taking photos of when you fell overboard?*

What I thought was a vibrant candy cane garland of red-and-white paint from the boat is a bit duller in person. Despite its weathered paint, it's beautiful. The fading sun bathes it in a yellow glow reflecting off the dark water, juxtaposing with the luminous sky.

"The very same," Evan confirms. "Figured you still wanted some nice pictures in front of it before you go."

"We really don't need to take photos."

"You took an hour to get all dolled up in that fancy little outfit and you don't even want photos?"

I flash him an indignant look, gesturing to my knee-high camel suede boots, white jeans, and blue-striped asymmetrical top with tiered ruffles, all pulled together with my brown YSL shoulder bag. "It took forty-five minutes, actually."

"Look, I didn't boat through a storm to get you those eyelashes for nothing. I won't let them go to waste," he says, tossing me a smoldering smile.

I'm not feeling up for a photo shoot. But the view is incredible, and part of me wants the photos for memory's sake. To remind me this was all real.

Shockingly, Evan is patient today, unlike with our photos at the waterfall. And by patient, I mean he only rolls his eyes at me once while snapping the shots at all the right angles. He's managed to remember the tips I gave him, framing me in the bottom left-hand corner.

I make a come-hither motion. "One more."

He gives me a quizzical expression. "You want a close-up?"

"No. Get in the photo with me," I demand.

"You want *me* in a photo *with* you?" he asks, wide-eyed.

"Relax. I won't post it. It's just for me," I reassure him.

His shoulders lower slightly as he sidles next to me. I press my cheek against his as we smile for a selfie. His beard tickles my cheek as I snap a couple of shots, not wanting to linger too long. Too many hits of his scent and who knows what feelings will crop up out of the blue.

Evan, of course, looks perfectly photogenic. His smile radiates confidence, with that pain-in-the-ass twinkle in his eye. Meanwhile, my left eye is halfway closed, and it isn't the most flattering of angles. But secretly, it's my favorite photo of any I've taken this whole trip, even if it makes me a little sad.

"Way to make me look bad." I let out a heavy sigh, turning my phone to show him the selfie.

He leans in to examine it. "Is that your weird way of complimenting me?"

"You're photogenic," I say nonchalantly.

"So you think I'm attractive?"

"Photogenic and attractive are different things. But yes. You'd fall into both categories," I say, against my better judgment. "Why are you so surprised? I already told you I'd wear your face."

He laughs. "True. Though you have spent a ridiculous amount of time trying to tear down my ego."

"Because your head would burst otherwise," I point out. "And you weren't exactly pleasant the first few days."

He laughs softly, tilting his head in admission. "How are you finding me now?"

Charming. Irresistible. Either of those would do. But I refuse to go there. I clear my throat, squaring my shoulders. "You're tamer. You still need some work, though."

"Fair. I can be an asshole sometimes." He nods toward my phone. "Anyway, send me that photo, okay?"

My fingers tingle as I text it to him. Before I can torture myself thinking about Evan keeping a photo of the two of us, I wave a hand toward the lighthouse. "Come on. I don't wanna stand here all day taking photos," I say, mocking him.

Evan drops his phone in his back pocket, happily leading me inside and all the way up the winding interior stairs.

"Jack and I used to come here when we were kids," he tells me, resting his forearms on the railing, watching the frothy waves slap against the rocky shoreline.

I peer down, morbidly imagining how easy it would be to accidentally go right over the railing. "This feels like a dangerous hangout spot for children."

He laughs. "We were teens, technically. He'd load his truck with beer and we'd just come up, sit right here in this exact spot, and goof off, shoot the shit, write swear words in Magic Marker on that wall." He points to a section on the lighthouse that appears to have been painted over, sloppily, with ten too many layers. "Had my first kiss up here too," he adds, eyes twinkling playfully.

I place my hand over my mouth, mocking scandal. "Details, please."

"Jack really liked this one girl at school, Doris." He glances at me, holding back a chuckle. "Yeah, I know. Not a sexy name. But he was straight-up in love with her. Constantly hit up the ice cream shop she worked at in the summer. He'd get cone after cone, multiple times a day, just to see her. And he was lactose intolerant."

I smile. "Wow. He must have really loved her to put his bowels through that."

"Oh yeah. This went on all summer. I was getting pretty damn sick of hearing about her. Finally, he got the courage to ask her out.

And she said she'd only go on a date with him if she could bring her cousin Juliet. An out-of-towner." He bounces his brows. "Anyway, it was kind of a fail. We clanked teeth and agreed never to kiss again. We held hands a lot that summer, though."

"That's the picture of a summer-fling romance right there. Fresh meat is a hot commodity in Cora's Cove, I hear."

"Oh yeah. Dating in town is impossible. Unless you wanna risk dating your second or third cousin," he says, maintaining a straight face.

This garners a snort out of me. "The royal bloodline is full of intermarrying. And look how they turned out. Prince Harry is pretty sexy."

"Harry made out okay. But didn't some of the royals have deformities? Wonky jaws and shit?" He pauses, squinting into the distance. "This convo took a really weird turn."

"It did. But thank you for bringing me here, Evan. It's a really special place."

"It is. I miss him. A lot," he admits, eyes swimming with all the memories this place holds.

I grit my teeth as I reflect. No wonder he was miffed by my desperation for lighthouse photos on the boat that day, all for aesthetics. Just to show people I'm well traveled, to give the illusion I'm so adventurous. But now, just knowing what this place means for Evan, and probably for many others who knew Jack, the lighthouse takes on a whole new meaning.

"Can I ask you something?" he says.

"Sure."

"I overheard you talking to your brother on the phone a couple of days ago. It sounds like you two are pretty close?"

That was the last conversation we had, about his work papers. He's barely texted me at all since then, which has been weighing on me more and more over the past few days.

"Yeah. He's had a rough go of things since our dad passed." My shoulders sag with the relief. I've never told anyone else about Julian. Not in detail, at least. Not only because his struggles never felt like mine to share, but also because unloading that baggage would require me to be open about my own life by extension.

Somehow, confiding in Evan is freeing. As I tell him all about Julian moving in with me after Dad and what happened when I went to Spain, there's no judgment in his demeanor, or ill-judged suggestions to help Julian deal with it because *everyone has depression these days*. He just listens and takes it in.

"What about your mom? She's not in the picture?"

"My mom . . . well, she can't really be bothered. She blames my dad for going bankrupt all those years ago and thinks Julian is exactly like him. She doesn't even know Julian, really. She moved to Portland and remarried after they declared bankruptcy when he was only a toddler."

"Wow."

"Yup. After my dad died, I called her. My dad always told us that she remarried, and that was it. And I always kind of thought maybe there was more to the story, you know? How could a mother just voluntarily leave her two children?" I pause as Evan places his hand over mine. "Anyway, she told me she was unhappy and had to leave. And that was it. No remorse, really. Just nothing. All that to say, that's why I do so much for my brother. Because I'm all he has."

He hangs his head. "And it sounds like the responsibility is all on you."

"Yeah. I guess it is."

"You're a good sister. A good person in general. I mean that. What you've done for me and for my family, even when you hated me, is . . . something I'll never forget. You're the best." He curls me into his side, arm heavy and protective, palm smoothing comforting circles on the small of my back.

"I could be better."

"Nope. Already perfect. See, look." He pulls his phone from his pocket with his free hand to show me his new lock screen. Gone is the hideous photo of me at the waterfall. Instead, it's replaced with the selfie we just took together in front of the lighthouse.

I blink at it, shocked. "Why?"

"Oh, I just really like my own face in that picture," he explains with a teasing nudge that tells me maybe, just maybe, it's more than self-admiration.

In a show of appreciation, I promptly also change my lock screen. "I like your face in that picture too."

A wide smile spreads across his face as he stares into the sunset. I'm not sure I've ever seen him look so peacefully content, with the exception of being on the water. After a couple moments of quiet, he turns to me, eyes searching mine. "I'm going to ask you a question I've wanted to ask you for days now."

"I don't like the sound of that."

"Do you want to leave so soon?" he asks, gaze so earnest it physically hurts my chest.

I fix my eyes on the blood-orange sky, blinking away the tension hanging between us like a heavy fog. There's no way I can admit there's a part of me that's burrowed myself in Cora's Cove.

In him. How can I have let myself get to this point after only one week?

He's waiting for my answer expectantly, but I can't seem to pin my feelings down. "Does it matter? We're breaking up. Tonight," I manage, cringing at my own statement.

He narrows his gaze, staring me down in a challenge. I don't know if he's plotting my demise or wanting to rip my clothes off. "Impossible. We're *lock screen official* now."

I can't help but snort. "Sorry, but I don't think that's a thing."

"It is for me. Once something goes on my lock screen, it stays. Until I drop my phone in the ocean and need a new one." His warm eyes conduct a thorough scan of my face. "And I get the feeling you don't want to leave, either."

"How would you know what I want?"

The yellow fairy lights above illuminate the vibrant aquamarine flecks of his irises. "Because you're looking at me like that."

I knit my brows together. "I'm not looking at you like anything."

"You are. But I'll be nice and let you win this one. You know why?"

Jesus. His voice alone is going to be the end of me. "Why?"

He leans in close to my ear, his chest brushing against me. "Because I want you to stay too."

The simple declaration sends me rocketing out of orbit. My gaze locks with his, unblinking, as he sweeps a strand of hair from the crest of my cheek. "Kiss me."

And I do.

❤ chapter twenty-five

MY LIPS SETTLE against his, just barely. I suck in a sharp inhale at the warmth of the contact, like the softest wave.

"You call that a kiss?" he whispers into my mouth, eyes sparkling, matching his smug grin.

Our eyes lock as he silently tells me he's going to show me. I pop onto my tiptoes, ready for his challenge. I breathe in his scent and savor it, wrapping my arms around his neck. His jaw twitches as the planes of his chest press against me, molding to me until we're flush against each other. He threads his fingers through my hair, cupping the left side of my face.

My vision blurs at the rough contact of the pad of his thumb against my cheek as he presses me against the railing. Suddenly, we're not at the lighthouse, overlooking hundreds of laughing, dancing people. We're far away from the pulse of the music and the shouting. We're alone, just Evan and me, and it feels utterly right.

This kiss is anything but introductory and shy. His lips feather my neck, upward around my jaw, dragging to the corner of my mouth. He presses firmer and firmer until he's biting my bottom lip with just the right amount of pressure, claiming me. A soft moan of relief escapes him, vibrating through me, exploding in tiny riptides.

I inhale that woodsy campfire scent, desperate to memorize how this feels. How incredible it is to be so connected and in sync with someone else. I'm not sure it's humanly possible to forget this kiss. Ever. This man kisses with his entire damn body. I am officially ruined for all kisses from here on out.

He tilts my hips toward him, rolling against me at just the right angle. I have to pry my eyes open to confirm we're technically in public, albeit a hundred feet from the ground.

I give his lower lip the softest bite before he eases the pressure, pulling back.

"We should probably stop," he murmurs in my ear. "There may or may not be people down there."

"People ruin everything." I bristle, pressing my head into the crook of his neck, not ready for this moment to break.

He checks over his shoulder, evidently not *that* concerned about onlookers. And, frankly, neither am I. My hands play out my fantasies, sliding through his coarse hair. I tug ever so slightly, which he likes, based on the low growl in my ear.

Without notice, he spins us around, clamping both my hands to pin them above my head against the side of the lighthouse. I've never relinquished control like this. Ever. Then again, I'm not sure I've ever encountered someone who made me want to surrender so badly.

"You have no idea how long I've wanted to do this," he says, breath ragged against me.

"How long?"

"Since that first morning. At breakfast."

"What?" I recall that first breakfast the morning he woke me up with power tools, back when I still thought he and Lucy were a married couple. "I was convinced you wanted to murder me with your fork."

"Only because you were driving me crazy eating those strawberries, licking the whipped cream off your lips across the table."

I search his face for any morsel of deceit but fail to find one. "So let me get this straight—the scowls, the stomping around, weren't all because you hated my guts?"

"I hated the idea of you. But you're so damn charming and you don't even know it. And after seeing the way you are with my family ... I could never hate you. No matter how hard I tried. And I did try," he adds with a wicked smile, running his thumb tantalizingly slowly along my bottom lip, as though we have infinite time.

My heart thuds loudly in my ears. Half of me is flooded with relief, knowing he never hated me. The other half is terrified. My trusty defense mechanism kicks in, and my eyes narrow to slits. "I don't know if I believe you."

"Whale watching. Lucy was gonna ask Arnold Yates to take you. I volunteered to do it. I planned to apologize to you that day on the boat. But then ... well, the first thing outta your mouth was, and I quote, 'Is there anyone else who can take me?' So I chickened out and assumed I'd already fucked things up."

"But you still hated my shoes, though. And my clothes," I blurt out, trying to make sense of his maddeningly confusing self.

His brow quirks as he releases my wrists. He drags his hand down my neck, playing with the hem of my blouse. "Don't you get it? I love the way you look. I love that you get all dolled up every day to do nothing. You're stunning. Always. And anyone who's made you feel otherwise is a fucking waste of space."

No other compliment has ever made me feel this full. This genuinely happy. The type of happiness that's so fierce, it scares me. At his admission, I raise up on my tiptoes again and press my lips against his. He groans in relief, tongue sliding against mine, demanding, fighting for dominance in a way that's so inexplicably *us*. Somehow, he knows exactly what to do, like he's always had me to begin with.

It's bittersweet. This kiss. How did we go from our rocky meeting to aggressively making out at a lighthouse at the Lobster Festival, of all places? My heart aches, speculating about what could have been, had we not wasted all that time as adversaries. And tomorrow, it will be nothing but a memory when I go back to Halifax.

He releases my hands, his thumb slipping underneath the waist of my jeans, grazing the lace of my panties. Every touch, every ragged breath feels downright illicit. Probably because it is. Anyone could look up and spot us at any moment. That risk only serves to heighten my senses tenfold.

"Can I touch you?" He pauses, waiting for my verbal *yes* before unbuttoning my jeans, shoving the lace to the side.

"Yes. Touch me," I demand.

He grits his teeth, like he's fighting to contain himself. "Open your legs wider." A hot string of curse words flows out of him as his finger glides against me, exactly where I want it. "Shit, you're wet."

"All because of you," I whisper as he works his magic of slow circles and swipes. As the tension builds and builds, my head falls back with a moan that's carried away by the wind.

"Have you imagined this?"

"Yes," I admit.

I can tell he likes that response by the way his eyes gleam. "Tell me what you've imagined."

"I've thought about you fucking me in every way possible, making me scream," I manage, back hollowing as he slides one finger against me.

"Jesus," he groans.

"Don't stop," I pant, arching into his hand.

He treats me to a wicked smile, sliding just the tip of his middle finger inside me. "Fuck. How are you this tight?"

The heat blooms in my stomach, strumming through me in small pulses with every brush and flick. "Evan, what—what if I didn't go to the resort tomorrow? What if we didn't break up?"

He pulls back to take me in, scrutinizing my face for any sign of bullshit, all while winding me up with just the right amount of pressure. He is truly a gifted multitasker. "Are you telling me you want to stay?"

I hold stubborn, closing my eyes as the feeling builds inside me, threatening to erupt. When my legs vibrate uncontrollably, he stabilizes me, expertly steadying me with one hand while pleasuring me with the other.

"Tell me or I won't let you come," he whispers, breath urgent as he moves a second finger lower, brushing against my entrance. Teasing me.

I'm trembling, teetering at the edge of a cliff, grasping for something to hold on to. Anything. "You're such an ass," I say, even though I know full well I'm staying.

He laughs, sliding his thumb against my clit. "An ass who can make you come harder than you ever have in your life."

"So confident."

"I just speak the truth." His brow arches. "Look at the way you're fucking my hand. The way your legs are shaking. You're about to lose it. Now tell me you're staying."

"I'm staying." The words pour out of me fast, because I mean it.

"Good." His chest expands with relief. With one smooth motion, he sinks the second finger deep inside me, relishing the look on my face. "Now come for me."

I can only nod, losing all resolve with each second. I'm weightless as my inner walls pulse around his fingers. He curls them, hitting me exactly where I need it, before adding another. He takes his time, savoring every moment, testing, coaxing as many moans and trembles from me as he can. His expression is one of pure satisfaction when I tell him I'm close. He's reveling in the power he has over me, and I don't know if I've ever been so turned on in my life.

The buildup is fast. Intense. It hits me hard, mid-gasp. He watches me, forehead against mine as I plummet over the edge. It's personal in a way I've never experienced before. And when I let out that last cry, he presses his mouth to mine in a lingering kiss. We stay still for a solid minute, exchanging short bursts of breath.

When he releases me to button my pants back up, I sag against the lighthouse, body recovering from the throbbing aftershocks as he presses a kiss to my neck.

"That was . . ." I can't even complete my sentence.

He gives me his trademark smug smile. "Told you I don't take a back seat."

"Neither do I." I hook my finger on a belt loop of his jeans and tug him closer. There's no hiding his enthusiasm for the situation. And I'm determined to take care of that ASAP.

He smiles, relinquishing control.

I advance tantalizingly slowly, trailing a hand down his chest, over the hard ridges of his lower stomach, swirling back upward every so often to torture him. Shockingly, he's patient, waiting for whatever I have in store. I'm not sure I've ever seen Evan so easy and compliant. His Adam's apple bobs, jaw flexing when I hover close to where he wants me, as if my touch is an open flame.

When I pull him out of his jeans, I nearly laugh out loud, just like when I first heard his deep voice the night I showed up at the inn. It should be used as a model in anatomy textbooks. Or as my new lock screen.

He pauses. "Should I be offended?"

"The opposite. Sorry," I say, unable to pull my eyes away from its glory. "You're just—huge."

He smirks as I kneel in front of him, coaxing a couple of low groans as I softly run my tongue around the head. He threads his fingers through my hair, pulling it gently to one side. "I've never seen a better view than this. You on your knees for me." With a near-violent shudder, he drops his head against the wall, not holding back, telling me how good it feels, how much he loves my mouth, as I take him deeper and deeper. "Fuck. Just like that," he hisses.

And just when he nearly loses control, reaching to angle my head, that's when Lucy finds us.

"Hey! There you two are—"

• • •

LUCY APOLOGIZED FOR cockblocking Evan about fifteen times. He's okay with it, or so he says, because he has plans for me later tonight.

Unfortunately, I've had a few drinks too many by the time the night is over. Maybe it's the music. Or the fact that East Coast drinks contain far more alcohol than Boston's (just my theory, not scientifically proven). Or maybe it's the peer pressure. East Coasters can party. They could probably drink anyone under the table. I am not on their level.

Evan notices my visible sway as we clamber into his truck. "Jesus, how much more booze did Lucy funnel down your throat tonight?"

I hold up three fingers. "It's my heels. I'm not that drunk," I lie.

He chuckles softly as he turns his key in the ignition. "Am I gonna have to fireman-carry you up the stairs again?"

"Not necessary," I assure him, missing my seat belt buckle for the fifth time. "Though I won't turn down the prospect of being carried everywhere."

"If you wore proper footwear, you wouldn't need to be carried, sweetheart," he informs me, flashing a teasing grin.

His chiding encourages me to prove him wrong when we get back to the inn. And I do, just barely. I make it three-quarters of the way up the stairs while he walks close behind, only intervening when I start to turn like it's a spiral staircase and not the perfectly straight set of stairs it actually is.

When he plops me onto the bed, I pounce like a feral bobcat, practically climbing him like a tree. He meets my lips with a quick peck before leaning back with a cute smile. "Believe me when I say I want to fuck you more than anything right now."

"I want you to. So badly," I whisper.

His face looks tortured as he pushes my hair back over my shoulder. "But we aren't doing anything tonight, okay?"

"Why? I never finished repayed-ing you," I slur.

"I hate myself for saying this, but you're not coherent, and I can't let you do anything you might regret," he responds earnestly, holding firm, like nothing I say will change his mind.

Must he meet the bare minimum requirement of being a decent human being? I press my cheek to his heart. The vibrations are comforting. "I won't regret it. I still know what I'm doing. I fully consent."

His chest vibrates with a low rumble as he lifts my chin, cupping my jaw. "I bet you do. But when we fuck for the first time, you're going to remember it." His tone sends a shock rippling through me. I could listen to this man talk about the weather and still get off.

I stay splayed on his chest like a flying squirrel as he pushes my hair out of his face every two seconds.

He collects all my hair in his hand, his breath skating against my neck. "You have a lot of hair, woman. It's real, right?"

"All natural," I mumble. "It has a mind of its own."

He fumbles in the darkness on the bedside table and grabs a

hair tie. His abs flex as he sits up to pull my hair back into a sad, floppy ponytail. "That's better."

I snort, using the last of my strength to retie it into a high messy bun. The man can't do hair to save his life, but the gesture melts my insides all the same.

As I change into my tank and sleep shorts, he goes to fetch a glass of water for me from the kitchen. We settle in a spooning position, with him curved around me, his arm protectively snug, folding me into him.

And tonight, for the first time in forever, I fall asleep quickly. I fall asleep with the comfort of knowing this is no longer my last night here. I fall asleep feeling safe.

♥ chapter twenty-six

THERE'S NOTHING WORSE than sharing a bed with another human (yes, even on a king-size mattress). There is no hope for sleep when someone is facing you, breathing directly in your face. Or pressing the entire surface of their warm, sweaty bod against yours like a gigantic hot water bottle from the pits of hell. And let's not forget the blanket thieves who leave you shivering in the night.

I've spent my entire adulthood avoiding sharing a bed. In fact, in the few relationships I've had that progressed to sleepovers, I'd inevitably sneak onto the couch the moment they fell asleep to avoid the aforementioned problems.

That's why waking up being spooned by Evan, legs intertwined, with no desire to lurch out of bed like the house is on fire, is nothing short of a miracle. Somehow I've even managed to sleep solidly the entire night.

The morning light streaks through a crack in the heavy drapery, illuminating him and his adorably tousled hair in a comforting golden haze. I trace the smooth lines of his face, committing it to memory.

"Morning," I whisper, voice hoarse and raspy in a very non-sexy way, a result of scream-singing last night at the festival.

A soft grin spreads over his face. "How are you feeling?"

I rub my eyes. "Sober. Very sober. Thanks for fending me off last night," I say, suddenly thankful for his self-control. I probably wouldn't have been of much use in my state last night anyway.

"Don't thank me for not taking advantage of you."

I nod. "Noted."

"But since you're now of sound mind, I need to ask. Did you mean what you said last night?" he asks, a serious expression replacing his soft gaze.

"You'll have to be more specific. I said a lot of things," I say, sliding out of bed to brush my teeth. Is this an avoidance tactic? Probably. I know he's referring to me staying. To the fact that we're no longer fake breaking up.

He lets me off the hook for a few moments as he comes in to brush his teeth too. But my reprieve lasts only so long. "Are you still staying?" he asks again as we both slide back into bed.

I press my lips together and stare at the ceiling. I don't know why the question scares me so much. I know the answer, and yet navigating my feelings seems like an insurmountable possibility right now. "I am staying," I say cautiously, cocooning myself under the covers.

His eyes light up as he runs the rough pad of his finger across my lip. An unhurried kiss follows, unspooling the spindle in my stomach that's been wound so tight my entire life.

As he deepens the kiss, we don't talk about what my staying means. We don't talk about it as he curls my hair around his finger, giving it the tiniest playful tug, backing me into him. And we definitely don't talk about it as his fingers feather over the bare skin of my ribs, dusting over the soft undersides of my breasts, lighting a trail of goose bumps wherever he touches.

I arch my back and he pulls me close against him. We're touching everywhere. Literally everywhere. From my shoulders against his chest to my ass rocking back, chasing the hot friction.

With each press against me, warmth pulses between my thighs, pushing away any pesky lingering thoughts that will talk me out of this.

He lets out a defeated groan from deep in his throat when I circle my hips in a soft rhythm against him.

"Christ, I could come just like this," he grits out.

When I reach back to trace the waistband of his boxer briefs, he takes control again, moving over me, pressing me onto my back, forearms caging either side of my head.

His eyes drag down every inch of my body like a map of the sea, lighting up at every beacon point. He slides his finger over my trembling leg, under my silky sleep shorts, circling around my inner thigh. "Your skin is ridiculously soft. What's your skin care routine?"

We dissolve into a fit of laughter, his chest heaving against my stomach. I'm cackling so hard, I let out the most unattractive snort, which only makes us laugh harder.

I take a moment to marvel and appreciate his ropy biceps. His chest labors as he runs his finger along my seam, drawing a moan from the back of my throat as he pushes the tip of his middle finger inside me. "I love feeling you clench around me. You're soaked already," he says, eyes sparkling.

I rock against his finger, praying he's about to give me a repeat of last night until he unexpectedly maneuvers me by the legs onto all fours in one fluid motion.

My legs prickle with warmth when he pulls my shorts down and runs his hands over my ass. I shiver, breath uneven, when he presses leisurely kisses from the sides of my breasts to my hips and down. And when he runs his thumb over my seam from behind, followed by a generous sweep of his tongue, my legs give out.

His fingers dig into my stomach as he reaches to stabilize me, keeping me in place. "You taste so fucking good." He mutters about how good I taste, how he could do this all day, how much he wants me, and something I can't fully hear, though I'm pretty sure it's along the lines of "I'm going to fuck you, okay?" I'm dizzy as he runs himself along my entrance, teasing. The rumble of his groan vibrates through me.

I nod as he seamlessly shifts over to grab a condom from the pocket of his pants, strewn atop the air mattress below. Once it's on, his fingers lace with mine and I brace myself as we join together, him entering me from behind.

A gasp passes between us as I take a second to adjust to his size. "Oh, fuck, Evan."

He senses my hesitation and leans into the shell of my ear. "Does that feel okay?"

As I grip the sheets, I manage to mumble something close to "More than okay. Keep going."

"God, I love the way you sound." His breath stills as he reaches forward, gently angling my chin back to study me. His finger traces my temple, my cheekbone, my lips, as though each curve reveals my inner thoughts. There's something about his expression that liquefies me from the inside out. It's hunger and need like last night at the lighthouse, but it's also something else I can't put my finger on. Something different. An intensity I've never felt before. I couldn't have prepared myself for it, despite building my entire life around protecting my heart. It's already slipped past my defenses.

Before the gravity of that thought fully settles, he tilts me upward where he wants me. "I can't believe we waited this long," I rasp underneath him.

"It was worth it. And besides . . ." He rocks in and out of me, hitting me at the perfect angle, filling all the empty parts of me. At my moan, he speeds up slightly, but only for a brief moment. It's as though he wants to savor the slow, measured rhythm. "I would have waited forever for this. I've never felt anything so fucking perfect."

"Evan" is all I can say, and his grip around my waist tightens. No one's ever spoken to me like this in bed before. Never.

When I shift myself back into him, taking him deeper, he thrusts harder. The heat radiating from his body feels like desperation, like he needs this as much as I do. It's taking all his effort to hold back, and I'm more than happy for him to let go. His hand reaches forward, tugging my hair with just the right amount of pressure.

He turns my head again. "Mel, I need you. Look at me," he commands. His heart hammers against my back, and when our eyes lock, it occurs to me that mine has fallen in sync with his.

His lips collide with mine in a frantic kiss that makes me clench, and he feels it. "Your pussy is so fucking tight. It's just throbbing around me," he says into my mouth. "I—I don't know if I can hold back much longer."

"Don't hold back," I urge. "Please don't."

With one fluid motion, his right hand reaches forward, sliding exactly where I need it. Neither of us can contain our volume as it builds. Our bodies crash together at a pace that's more erratic than controlled. The buildup is fast, erupting in little bursts that make me see a blur of white spots in the morning sunlight. Just when I'm sure I can't take another second, he's a goner too. The blood pounds through my ears and I can barely catch my breath as he pulses over me, pulling me close, holding me like I'm about to slip away.

We collapse onto our sides, entirely out of breath as the aftershocks pulse through me. "I— That was—" I start, unable to find the words. "Five stars."

He shudders with laughter, and the room quite literally gets brighter, sun streaming in to halo his face like an angel. "Plenty more where that came from, sweetheart. I'm yours."

He tucks me snugly into his side, and I clamp my eyes shut to hold on to this moment of utter, complete bliss for as long as possible.

I must have drifted into sleep, because when my eyes snap open, I'm alone in the bed and there's a loud knock at the door. The sound of water running tells me Evan is in the bathroom.

"It's Ned!"

"Just a minute!" Evan calls out in a panicked lilt, turning the tap off and racing back to dive under the covers next to me.

Not a second after he manages to pull the duvet over my naked body, Ned waltzes in.

He's in a green Hawaiian shirt today. I'm not sure if it's more Joe Exotic or *Ace Ventura*. He smiles as he settles onto the end of the bed, proudly thrusting a box with a handle toward us. "Canadian delicacy," he announces. Either he's completely oblivious to what Evan and I were doing, or he simply doesn't care. I can't tell which.

Cheeks burning like the fiery flames of hell, I hesitantly reach for the box while clutching the duvet to my chest, lest my left boob pop out. "What is it?" I ask, praying it's not some dead animal.

"Open it," he instructs.

Lucy, in a neon T-shirt about five sizes too large, appears behind him, followed by Nessa and Fiona.

Everyone watches in amusement as I open the box and peer inside. "You got me donut holes!" I say, feigning enthusiasm.

"Do not call them *donut holes*," Evan warns, pressing his palm to his chest dramatically. He promptly reaches over my shoulder to pluck a glazed one from the box.

"What do I call them then?"

"Timbits. They're called Timbits," Nessa calls from the entryway.

"Timbits," I repeat.

I watch as Uncle Ned rifles through the box, finally emerging with a chocolate one, popping it into his mouth whole.

Lucy makes herself comfortable on the end of the bed and starts rooting through the box.

"You seriously need to not touch every single Timbit," Fiona says, slapping her hand.

I work down a hard swallow. The entire Whaler family is sitting on the edge of our bed. While I'm naked and sweaty. Underneath this blanket.

Lucy raises her hands in the air. "I have no choice! The birthday cake ones are always on the bottom. I had to get them before everyone takes them."

"It's Canadian etiquette rule number one: never touch all the Timbits," Evan says in vigorous agreement.

Uncle Ned shakes his head. "Well, it had to be done."

I lean forward to pick up the box. "Could you not just shake the box? Get the one you want to come to the top?" I ask, closing the lid to demonstrate.

They all tilt their heads in amazement. "I suppose so. Never thought of that before," Ned says.

"See? The American has strategies too," I tease.

"By the way, Nana made a special goodbye breakfast for Mel. It's ready in ten," Fiona announces.

"We'll be, um, right down. We have something to tell you all," Evan says, eyeing everyone with a heavy silence. I assume he's referring to the fact that I'm staying.

It works. Everyone scampers off downstairs, even Lucy, who hung out for a couple of minutes to regale us with town gossip about who hooked up with who last night at the festival. When neither of us responds with the level of enthusiasm she was hoping for, she gets the hint and leaves, taking the Timbits with her.

I roll onto my back. "Your family really has no boundaries, do they?"

chapter twenty-seven

MEL: Hey Julian, you were supposed to update me on how
your job is going. I'm free this morning for a call but will
probably be out of service later today. Going camping . . .
pray for me.

"You're staying at the inn for another five days? With the fisherman?" Tara repeats over the crunching sound of a chip bag. She
dumps Doritos into a mixing bowl with a truly frightening raven-
ous glint in her eyes.

"Yup," I say, collecting myself after being viciously attacked
by a ladybug on the porch. I explain the harrowing tale—how
I caught the ladybug creeping up my neck moments before our
call.

Unfortunately, Tara isn't interested in my ongoing battle with
nature. She's fixed on my travel itinerary.

She slaps her hand over her mouth. "Oh my god. I'm so excited about this. How did the family react?"

"They were thrilled." So thrilled, they all decided to stay a few extra days.

"And you're canceling on the resort?"

"Yup. Already canceled it."

"You should have asked if I could take your place. I could use a massage. I've been guilted into prepacking Crystal's apartment, and I think I messed up my lower back. This is what happens when you turn thirty," she warns. "Soon, I'll be buying Metamucil in bulk and installing a grab bar in my shower."

The reminder of Crystal's move tugs at the base of my stomach. While their closing date isn't for a few more weeks, they have to be out of her condo two weeks earlier.

"Hey, if you have a bad back, maybe you can get out of helping on moving day," I point out, keeping my tone light to conceal my disappointment. I doubt I'll even get to see Crystal's condo one last time. Things will be so different when I get back to Boston, and I don't like it one bit.

"Good point." Tara pops a chip in her mouth. "Anyway, you've changed the topic ten times now, and I'm not having it. You and this fisherman. What's the deal?" She's not wrong. Every time she's broached the subject, I've expertly pivoted, getting her to talk about herself, which is, frankly, easy to do.

"We're . . . I don't know what we are."

"Boyfriend and girlfriend?" Tara asks.

"No." Sure, I have a massive crush. And sure, I've extended my stay. But it's five days. Not forever.

Tara crunches another chip. "Friends? Fuck buddies?"

I repeat the word *friends,* and it feels like sandpaper on my tongue. I think about the way he looked at me the morning after the festival. The way he saw me. Truly saw me. *Friends* feels wrong. But because I'm me, I have no idea how to articulate any of that. So I default to deflection, my go-to coping mechanism. "I wish I could say fuck buddies. The universe doesn't want me to have casual sex. It's made that pretty clear."

Unfortunately, we've had zero luck for the past two days. I give her a run-through of the multiple times Evan and I were interrupted yesterday.

Exhibit A: After the Timbit delivery, the moment Evan and I started getting hot and heavy again, Nana came upstairs with a full breakfast tray and gave us our daily astrology reading.

Exhibit B: Evan was just about to step into the shower with me when his mom pounded on the door demanding a lawn game rematch.

Exhibit C: During a midafternoon make-out atop the kitchen counter, Lucy decided it was as good a time as any to ask for makeup advice.

Exhibit D: A crow dive-bombed us while I was dry-humping Evan on the patio chair in the backyard.

We cannot find any peace. And neither can our libidos. I suggested taking a drive down a desolate road, but Evan refuses, claiming he doesn't want to do it in his truck like teenagers. We're at an impasse.

So when he jokingly suggested we go camping today, I jumped at the opportunity. While the mere thought of sleeping in a tent, with only the thinnest fabric separating me from bears, wolves, and god knows whatever else lurks deep in the forest, I'm willing to risk a brutal mauling if it means time alone with Evan. Maybe nature will have mercy on me today.

Tara gives me a knowing look. "This is classic. Fake dating always leads to true love. Fact. I don't make the rules."

"Yeah, in your books." I lower the volume on my phone so no one overhears. "Fake dating is not something normal people do. And trust me, it's not all it's cracked up to be. It's exhausting lying to everyone, even if it is for a good cause."

She flaps her arms, pointing at me. "And that's exactly how I know you're more than just friends. You're awfully invested in this family parent trap thing you're doing."

"Okay, but even in the hypothetical scenario that we'd be more than friends, there's no realistic way we could be together. We live in two separate countries."

"So? Look at Claire and Jamie from *Outlander*. They're separated by *time*. Hundreds of years."

"You know you'd make a much better point if your examples weren't fictional characters from a historical fiction fantasy novel."

"Whatever. My point still stands. The best love stories are hard-won."

While I appreciate Tara's insight, my self-protective mechanism takes over, disallowing me to even consider a stretch of time past the next week.

You don't need to think about the future. Just enjoy the moment, I tell myself. I repeat the sentiment all morning. And again as Evan weaves us through the lush forest trails on the back of his ATV. I practice logging every moment in my mind, the way the sun feels against my skin, the earthy scent of fresh rainfall, the stunning red woodpecker eyeing us up as we pass by. And for once, these moments aren't for my followers. They're just for me.

In the past few days, I've barely been on my phone, aside from checking to see if Julian texted. I seldom log in to my social media. It doesn't even register that I should check how many followers I gained or how many likes I got on my last photo. There's a freedom to it that brings me a peace I didn't know I had in me.

Even through Evan's thick flannel, I can still feel the outline of his abs. Unable to help myself, I press tighter, clinging to him for dear life as he navigates the ATV up a steep incline, leading to a clearing with a view to a gently flowing river.

"Here's our spot for the night," he declares.

"Have you been here before?"

"Only about a hundred times. My grandpa used to bring Jack and me here when we were kids. Learned to fish in that river, actually." He tells me a bit about summers past as a kid, coming to this very same camping spot, and all the antics he and Jack used to get up to in the river.

It warms my heart that he's willing to share these special places with me. Then again, he's opened his entire family up to me, a virtual stranger.

I spectate as Evan pitches the tent (yes, I make plenty of lame jokes). Despite my offers of assistance, he assures me it's easier without my help, particularly after a blunder wherein I nearly poked his eye out with one of the stakes. I've now been relegated to collecting long sticks for roasting marshmallows.

It's nearly dark by the time he cooks our dinner, including freshly caught pickerel, veggies, and potatoes. It's simple, but it hits different over a crackling fire. Amid distant sounds of leaves rustling and crickets singing.

When we're finished eating, I settle on a mossy log, watching the embers flicker and the silver smoke disappear into the vast marble-black sky specked with iridescent dots like tiny snowflakes. I've never seen the stars so bright before, so uninterrupted and unmarred by human life. It's so vast, and yet it brings me a sense of comfort. Just like Evan does.

It's another moment with this man that I want to live in forever.

Evan wraps his thick jacket around my shoulders from behind, gently lifting my hair from the collar. "It's weird seeing you like this. No fancy clothes, no phone glued to your hand."

"I'll have you know my sweater is cashmere," I tease. "But yeah, being unplugged feels nice."

He wraps an arm around me, pulling me into his side, hand resting gently on my upper thigh. I nuzzle my head into his chest, comforted immediately by his body heat. "Can confirm. I don't have social media and I don't intend to."

"Not even Facebook, huh?"

He smirks, his fingers tracing tickling doodles over my leg. "Facebook is the absolute worst."

"It's true. Full of random people from high school trying to con you into an MLM."

"I'd probably follow you into an MLM if you recruited me," he teases, the corners of his eyes crinkling adorably.

"Though I have to say, the fact that you don't exist anywhere online, it's a little suspicious." I press myself closer, desperate to feel the vibration of his voice against me.

"Oh, so you googled me?"

I poke him with my marshmallow stick as a defensive reflex, and he shifts my legs, pulling me onto his lap. "Maybe I did. But you looked me up too, so we're even."

"Touché. Not gonna lie, I'm a pretty big fan of the bikini shots," he admits, positioning me so I'm straddling him, one leg on either side of his torso.

I raise a brow, running my hands through his hair. "Oh yeah? Which ones?"

A low moan rises from his throat at my fingers against his scalp. "I might have a thing for the one in the bikini with the underboob. You're in a weird position." He tries to copy it, twisting his body in a way that makes me shudder with laughter.

"I must warn you, you have some serious competition."

He sits up a little straighter, pulling me flush to his chest. His face is cast in a golden hue that accentuates his cheekbones. "Oh yeah? What am I up against?"

I pull my phone from my pocket and pull up Ian's profile. I go to a picture of him dressed in his white lab coat from a science fair. "This fine fellow."

His lip quirks. "Hate to break it to ya, but you might get arrested. And I don't know if I want any part in that."

"He's a kid who lives in the unit next door to mine. He's got a massive crush on me. He writes me poems. Kind of gives your singing-and-guitar schtick a run for its money."

"Poems? Like what?"

"The last one went something like 'Hair as dark as midnight. Eyes like a raven. Skin pale as a ghost. Melanie, your beauty is what I love most.'"

Evan vibrates underneath me, nearly folding over with laughter. "That's . . . many shades of disturbing." He pretends to check over his shoulder. "Is my life in danger? Should I be worried?"

"He once threatened to call 911 on a guy I was seeing last year for loitering outside my door," I warn, pressing my forehead against his. "You may want to watch your back."

"Sounds like a delight."

"Speaking of kids. Nana has been asking me when we're having them." Just yesterday, she cornered me in the dining room to let me know she hopes our first is a girl.

"Of course she did. When are you having my hypothetical babies, Mel?"

I side-eye him evilly. "I'm already with child. I think it's quadruplets."

He dips his head to the side, feigning understanding. "Quads sound easy enough. Who needs sleep or sanity?"

I snort. "The truth is, I don't know if I even want kids." I lean back with a wince, bracing for his reaction, even though his reaction shouldn't matter to me. I know I'm not obliged to tell him this, but it just feels like the right thing to do. Maybe it's the fact that nature has a way of making me reveal my innermost thoughts. Or maybe some part of me is trying to ward him off from wanting anything more with me.

"No?"

"Maybe it's because I'm paranoid I wouldn't be able to take care of them financially? I don't know."

To my surprise, he doesn't respond aversely. He doesn't even flinch. Instead, he just gives me a curious look. "I get it. And after seeing how hard it was for my aunt Fi after losing Jack, I don't know if I could ever set myself up for something like that."

"Understandable. I mean, I have Julian. Not that he's a burden in any way. But having someone else depend on me would just feel like . . . a lot."

There's a pang of guilt when I say it, along with an outpouring of anxiety I've been holding in all day.

"I'm getting really worried about him," I confess, explaining how Julian hasn't responded to my texts or calls in two days.

"You haven't heard a single peep from him in two days? Is that not normal?"

"Nope. Normally he texts me all day, every day, though he hasn't lately. I just . . . I have a bad feeling. Like when I went to Spain. Only worse." As much as I've let myself enjoy Cora's Cove to the fullest, I can't help but lie awake at night, playing out various scenarios in my head about Julian. None of which are good. "I've been thinking . . . about going home to check on him," I finally confess.

He smooths a calm hand down my spine. "You could. But you could also ask one of your friends to drop by your place and check in? That way you don't have to fly all the way back if you don't need to."

I consider that. It's never felt like an option to ask someone else for help, especially with something so personal. But after spending so much time here, I'm starting to feel like that's a possibility. "You know what . . . you're right. I think I'll ask Crystal to check in on him if I don't hear from him by tomorrow or the next day. Thank you."

"Of course."

"Anyway, sorry to derail the kids conversation. I did actually consider kids for the first time when I was at your bedside in the hospital."

His brow quirks. "Yeah?"

"I was imagining it was me in your place. And I wondered who the hell would even come. Maybe my brother . . . but I think it would stress him out more than anything. I guess your children would be obligated to come, but being alone is probably a horrible reason for considering parenthood, isn't it?" I pinch myself on the thigh when the admission slips out.

Evan tucks a thick lock of hair behind my ear, dragging his thumb down my neck, over my collarbone, and back in a way that makes my skin prickle. His gaze locks with mine, finding *me* yet again. "You're never alone in this world while I'm in it, Mel." There's a conviction in his words that makes me feel grounded, tethered in a way I've never been able to grasp. I've never told him I'm lonely. Not explicitly, at least. Yet he's managed to tell me exactly what I didn't know I needed to hear.

The night air crackles and sparks between us. I'm frozen, the rush of emotions turning inside me like a hamster wheel spinning too fast to jump off safely. My legs tense around him, and my ribs feel like they're closing in on me. And suddenly, all the fear I've tried so hard to bury deep down within me the past few days has popped up to say, *Hello, remember me? We need to rebuild those protective walls. ASAP.*

I shift myself off his lap, blinking the budding tears away before they make their way past my lash line.

"Mel? You okay?" His thick brows meet in a frown, and he's rightfully taken aback.

"I'm great," I lie. "Just need to pee. Did you bring toilet paper?" I ask, sufficiently sabotaging the moment.

"No," he says, righting his posture in the absence of my weight.

I groan, standing to avoid his gaze. He's far too good at reading my mind. "What am I supposed to use?"

He looks me dead in the eye. "Leaves."

"Seriously?"

The corners of his lips curve upward ever so slightly, quietly reveling in my horror. For a brief moment, it brings me back to our old dynamic, which is, frankly, comforting. "I told you we were having an authentic camping experience."

I spin around, ignoring his rumble of laughter, and trudge deep into the darkness of the woods. Despite his warning not to venture too far, I keep walking. The last thing I need is for him to see me in an unflattering squatting position, pee ricocheting off the ground.

Coming from Boston, I had no concept of how dark nature gets in the absence of electricity. Even with the flashlight on my phone, I can only see about a foot in front of me, enough to ensure I don't walk into a tree.

When I've reached a sufficient distance away from our campsite, I grab a handful of leaves and do my business, only narrowly avoiding peeing on my right ankle.

Crack.

I screech at the not-so-distant sound of a twig breaking behind me as I pull up my leggings. It's probably a squirrel, but I have no desire to find out for sure. So I bolt, running at full tilt toward the glow of the campfire.

When I return, fully out of breath, Evan's still got that stupid smirk painted on his face. "You're alive. You didn't even need your bear hair spray. Don't go so far next time, though."

I resettle on the log. "I didn't want you to hear me pee."

"Come on, Mel. Everyone pees." He stands to tend to the fire, moving the logs around with his bare hands.

"Obviously. But I don't want you to hear it," I say, leaning back as the embers spark.

"Why?"

Because I might have fallen for you. Completely fallen.

I freeze the moment my mind registers that thought. It's not a surprise, really. Yet my body has the knee-jerk reaction to kick this thought to the curb immediately. I cross and uncross my legs, unable to find an ounce of comfort.

All the while, in my periphery, Evan is looking at me with that crooked, knowing smile, like he's waiting for me to say it out loud.

"You good?" he asks.

"Never better," I mumble, squirming. I stand momentarily to pace around the fire. Maybe the roughness of the log is irritating my skin, because I'm itchy. Increasingly itchy. Yet, even standing, the itch isn't going away.

"Are you okay? You look uncomfortable. We can go back to the inn—"

"No!" I snap. Discomfort aside, I desperately want to prove to him and myself that I'm okay with nature. That I'm okay in his element. And, realistically, I have been enjoying myself. The campfire smell is more soothing than any fancy spa or candle. The stars dotting the sky in abundance are more beautiful than my closet wall of designer bags in Boston. I know I'd be thoroughly enjoying these things if my downstairs wasn't burning.

He runs a gentle hand over my back when I sit back down. "Seriously, Mel. Camping is a lot. I won't make you do something you're not comfortable with."

There's no way in hell I'm going back to the inn tonight. We're having filthy sex. In the tent. It's happening.

"I appreciate it. But, honestly, it's—" I pause to wince through the burn. This is not normal. "I'll be right back." I head to the tent, halting before going inside.

"What's up?" he asks. "Want me to check the tent for bugs?" he offers earnestly.

"I'm good," I assure him. As much as I'd love and appreciate him scouring every inch of the tent for bugs, I'm in dire straits. The moment I'm alone in the tent, I use my phone's front camera to assess the situation.

Fuck. My. Life.

I am a red and inflamed mess. Muffling my cry, I google *red and inflamed vagina*. None of the results are helpful. It's official. Nature fucking hates me.

This is just my luck. It's our first opportunity to be alone and my vagina implodes. I wonder if this is a sign from the universe, telling me I don't belong. That I should cut my losses and go back to Boston.

"You okay in there?" Evan's voice is slightly muffled outside the tent.

He starts to unzip the tent when I shriek, "NO!"

"Why? Are you changing?"

I clear my throat. "Um . . . no."

"You sound weird. What's going on?"

I let my head fall back in anguish. "I may be having an allergic reaction."

"Shit. Can you breathe properly?"

"No. Not that kind of reaction. Um . . . down there."

He's silent for a moment. "What did you use in place of toilet paper?"

"Leaves. Like you told me," I say, just barely hiding my bitterness.

"What did they look like?"

"I don't remember, Evan. Green. With a pointed tip."

"Were they by chance in bunches of three?" he asks.

I squeeze my eyes shut, trying to recall. It was dark. I was basically groping blindly for the nearest bush. Though the description does sound vaguely familiar. "I think so?"

"I think you might have had your first run-in with poison ivy," he says delicately.

"Of fucking course," I mutter, eyes brimming with tears. "What do I do now?"

"Can I come in?" he asks calmly.

"No!" I shout, grabbing the zipper from the inside to stop him from coming in. "You're not coming in here."

"Please? I need to see how bad it is." It's a perfectly reasonable request. But I can't think of anything more humiliating.

"I'm not letting you see it like this," I groan. "This isn't how it was supposed to be." I let my hand fall from the zipper. He opens it slowly, expression sympathetic yet calm.

He inches into the tent, sitting beside me tentatively. He levels me with a knowing look. "First, who cares what it looks like? You have nothing to worry about. I've seen it already and it's perfect, just like the rest of you."

"Really?" I whine.

He places his hand over his heart. "Promise. I've taken too many cold showers trying not to think about it," he starts. "And second, there is nothing to be embarrassed about. I once got stung on the dick by a bee after pissing on its nest."

I start to laugh, even through the tears burning underneath my lids. "How old were you?"

"I was seven or eight. It was a school field trip. So that was fun." He moves closer, folding me into his side. "Seriously, Mel. Just let me take a look. I need to know if we have to head back home or not."

I sigh, shifting back to let him see.

He takes a quick look. His expression is impossible to read, though I think he's trying not to freak out for my sake. "We should probably head back to the inn. You need Benadryl," he finally decides.

I frown. "You hate me, don't you?"

He runs the pad of his thumb over my cheek, cupping my jaw. "Why would I hate you?"

For sabotaging everything, of course. I toss my hands in the air, spiraling. "Because. We're so different. I'm obviously not your normal type—"

"My normal type? Sorry, I don't remember telling you what that is," he says as he starts folding the sleeping bag back up.

"Well, definitely someone who doesn't rub poison ivy all over her vagina the one night we're going to have privacy."

"Mel—"

"Probably someone who doesn't collapse in the shower when she sees a bug," I continue.

"None of that matters to me. And we don't need to have sex."

I tilt my head. "We don't?"

He pauses in folding the sleeping bag and sits back on his heels with a grim expression. "Is that all this is to you?"

I let out a long-suffering sigh and finally come out with it. "No. It's not. I wish it was, though."

"I don't." His tone is unwavering, which fills me with both warmth and fear at the same time. He senses it, because he sharply looks away. "But right now, let's just focus on getting you back to the inn."

♥ chapter twenty-eight

HATE EVAN WHALER.

I hate the way the right corner of his mouth quirks up when he's being a smug asshole. I hate the way he can read my every expression with complete and total accuracy. I hate the way he's nursed me back to health, supplying me with the proper doses of Benadryl to relieve my poison ivy–induced itching and swelling.

I hate how he brought me a Boston cream donut in case I was homesick. How every night, he makes a point of scouring the bathroom to ensure there aren't any spiders or centipedes, an act which is successfully eroding my resolve. I hate how he puts everyone else before him. How he makes sure everyone in his family has water or is fed before himself. How much he cares about the inn and his family's legacy. How he's always tinkering away around the house, doing everything he can to make his grandfather and Jack proud.

I hate the way that, despite these massive losses in his life, he still has space in his heart for me. To give me a soft place to land when things feel out of control. The way he's comforted me over not hearing from Julian for the past four days. The way he's reminded me to lean on the people who are already in my life, like Crystal. Earlier this morning, Crystal agreed to check on Julian tomorrow night on her way to the gym while rejecting my offers to do all her chores for a week when I get back.

I hate how, every night, Evan does exactly what he said he'd do that day we discussed breakup scenarios. He does everything in his power to ensure I'm happy by coming home early to spend extra time with me. His first order of business is a shower, where he belts out Celine Dion's greatest hits at the top of his lungs. Then he emerges, fresh and energized, to take me for walks on the trails behind the inn, along Main Street to peruse the shops, and back to Gracie's café to chat with the locals.

And most of all, I hate that I can't bring myself to hate Evan. Not one bit. Not when he's all giddy and childlike, showing me the run-down one-story redbrick elementary school he attended from first to eighth grade.

"See that big cedar tree by the fence?" Evan extends his pointer finger out the windshield of his truck. "That's where I caught Kyle kissing Lucy."

I audibly gasp at the scandal. "What? Lucy and Kyle had a thing?"

He smirks, reaching over the center console to thread his fingers through mine. It's stunning how natural this feels, driving through the Cove, holding hands like some happily married couple. "Well, in fourth grade. He hasn't tried anything since."

"Why not?"

"Because I decked him, which was terrifying considering he had a good twenty pounds on me, even back then. We both ended up in detention. He begged me the whole time not to tell Jack, who would have properly kicked the shit out of him."

"Did you tell him?"

"Nah. Kyle bribed me. Said he'd give me the snack in his lunch every day for a week if I kept it a secret. So I did."

"Damn, Whaler. I didn't know you were so easily persuaded by snacks."

"Oh yeah. Kyle's mom packed him all the best snacks my mom never let me have because they weren't *organic*. Dunkaroos, Fruit Roll-Ups, Gushers. Oh, and Twinkies."

I snicker, mostly at how his face lights up like the sun when he talks about his childhood. How he squeezes my hand tighter when he laughs that booming laugh that feels too big for even his massive truck.

No matter where we go in this tiny village, there's a story to be told. Like the lopsided, weathered corner store he and Kyle stole candy bars from. The bent stop sign on the corner of a random street where he got in his first fistfight waiting for the school bus. The hill outside Dustin's house where he fell face-first Rollerblading too fast. The dilapidated tree house he and the guys slept in on prom night after being chased by the cops for sneaking booze into the dance.

"This was Lucy and Jack's childhood house," Evan tells me, pulling up to an old white farmhouse with green shutters that reminds me of a smaller version of the *Anne of Green Gables* house. "I spent more time here or at the inn, actually, than my own house."

"How come?"

"My mom did her therapy sessions in our living room. She didn't want me around for those, so I'd go to the inn or Aunt Fi's after school."

"I bet the three of you got up to a lot of trouble," I chide.

"Me and Jack, mostly. Lucy tried following us around when we were really young, but of course, at that age, you think you're *too cool* to hang with your little cousin."

I make a pouty face. "Aw, poor Luce. And look at how she runs your show now," I tease.

Evan barks a laugh. "Yeah, I won't deny that one. She terrifies me."

"Have you ever wanted to live anywhere else but Cora's Cove?" I venture.

"When I was a kid, I honestly didn't think much about anything beyond here. Beyond Nova Scotia. Though I found out about the rest of the world pretty quick when I moved to Montreal with my dad when I was in high school."

I nod, recalling what Ned told me. "Do you see your dad often?"

"He used to visit about once a year when I was younger. Hasn't in a while, though. I think he's secretly kinda bitter that I don't go to see him more often. That I choose to be with my mom instead."

"How come you don't visit more?"

Evan shrugs. "Whenever I go, he tries to impress me by taking me out to fancy restaurants and shit. Like he's trying to show me what I'm missing out on. He's been doing that ever since I decided to move back."

"It's nice to know he cares enough to want you to be closer to him," I point out, thinking about my own mom and her total indifference to me and Julian.

He tilts his head to the side. "True. I'm lucky that way. He's a good guy, even if we're totally different people."

"Moving to Montreal as a teen must have been a huge shock, though. Going from a place with no traffic lights to a big city."

We make our way down a small, quaint street dotted with colorful historic homes that beg to share their stories. They're all shaded with dense, mature foliage. As we pass by, Evan waves to all the townsfolk relaxing on their porches, in no rush to be anywhere. Then again, no one is. Over the last week, I've learned everything here can be categorized as *slow*. The cars, the people taking leisurely strolls, the service at any given store, even the kids pedaling their bicycles up and down the narrow streets.

"Oh yeah. I hated Montreal," he declares, eyes on the road stretched in front of us. "Too big. Too loud. Too many options. I hated going into a restaurant and not knowing anyone. No one you passed on the street would even make eye contact. That's why I came back as soon as I could. I could never live somewhere like that."

My stomach pinches with something that resembles disappointment. "Somewhere like Boston." The words float past my lips before I even realize I've said them out loud.

"Boston must be nice, though. With the sea?"

"Don't get me wrong. I do love Boston. But I've never really felt a sentimental attachment to it."

"No?"

"I don't know. I grew up in a lot of crappy apartments. I was always scared we were gonna be evicted. Even my condo now . . . Logically, I know I own it. But I still have that fear, you know? I guess I don't really feel a sense of home anywhere."

He watches me for a moment, the light dimming in his eyes. "I can't imagine what that must be like."

"Is it that sad?" I ask, and it occurs to me how opposite we are. I have no sense of home, while he's defined by his home. Every square inch of it.

"Everyone should have a place they feel safe and at home."

"Maybe it's an adoption complex. I don't know," I chuckle nervously. "My therapist back in Boston says that adoptees sometimes have a hard time grounding themselves anywhere."

"Have you ever wanted to go back? Find your birth parents?"

"It's complicated. A lot of people assume all adoptees want to find their birth parents. But not all of us do. I mean, when I was younger, I did, especially after my mom left." I pause, watching a wave strike the rock below as I reveal what I've never admitted to anyone before. "But as I've gotten older, I'm not sure what good it would do, dwelling on a past I had no control over, wondering what my life would have been like. I feel better about moving forward with what *is*, if that makes any sense."

"It makes all the sense in the world," he says without hesitation. "I do hope you find it, though."

"Find what?"

"Your home," he says simply, pulling my hand over the console, close to his chest.

"Me too," I whisper. My eyes begin to well at the steady thump of his heart under the back of my hand. I keep my eyes trained out the open passenger window, unsure where to put all the extra feelings that continue to surface, no matter how hard I try to banish them.

I didn't know I was humanly capable of the depth of feelings I have for Evan in such a short amount of time. Logically, it makes no sense. We've only known each other a total of nine days. And yet, after touring this magical little village that's made Evan the kind, salt-of-the-earth man he is today, I feel like I've known him for nine years.

It scares the shit out of me, because now I can't picture how I'm going to return to my life in Boston.

♥ chapter twenty-nine

"WILL YOU BE ready in fifteen?" Evan asks from the bedroom doorway.

"Half an hour," I tell him, running the curling iron through my hair.

He smirks, eyes twinkling like they always do when we're negotiating. "Twenty minutes."

"Twenty-three."

"Fine. See you downstairs in exactly twenty-three minutes," he concedes, with a smile so adorable I nearly scald my ear with the iron.

Evan has a surprise for me this afternoon. The only thing he's told me is I need to dress warmly and wear flat shoes.

Shockingly, I'm ready in twenty. While I wait for him on the porch, I mindlessly edit the photos of the inn I took yesterday to update on the Airbnb ad. I tactfully avoided all the areas under construction, focusing on the cute little reading nook in the family room beside the stone fireplace, the Adirondack chairs on the porch, and the stunning wood detail in every corner.

"The pictures look nice." The voice startles me. It's Fiona, peering over my shoulder. She's wearing the same nautical-striped linen blouse and white scarf she wore that day at the hospital.

"Thanks. It's really all about the filters," I tell her, showing her a before and after. "Makes a huge difference for the aesthetic. People are visually attracted to high-quality lighting."

She nods her head in approval, lowering herself into the chair next to mine. "It's certainly an improvement from the current photos." I expect her to launch into a lecture about how keeping the inn doesn't make financial sense. But she doesn't. "Thanks for doing this, by the way. We're all really happy you decided to stay until the end of your trip."

Her words catch me off guard. While I've spent hours with Nana, Nessa, and Ned, Fiona is the one family member I haven't had much of a chance to connect with. In the rare moments we've been left alone together, it's mostly been generic small talk.

"It was an easy decision. It's been really lovely being here with you all," I tell her honestly. Too easy. Especially over the past few days. No one has talked about the divide that's plagued them for the last few years. No one's dared to bring up selling the inn. And while I'm thankful for the peace, there's a palpable unease. It's like everyone's treading carefully, waiting to see who will broach the topic before the bubble bursts.

She moves her bangs from her face and leans forward. "This was actually the first time I've been back to the inn. Since Jack."

I dip my chin. "Evan told me you stopped coming shortly after he passed."

"It was too hard, you know? I couldn't be here without feeling so angry."

"I understand that. After my dad died, I had a really hard time. Not as hard as my brother . . . but it was little things I never thought would bug me. Seeing a certain kind of cereal in the grocery store that he ate every morning. Advertisements for old horror movies he loved. Any reference to old technology or gadgets he used to show me in his store. Or Dolly Parton songs. He loved her. I'd barely ever heard her music before he died. And then she was randomly on the radio all the time. Or mentioned on TV. It was like the universe was purposely being an asshole."

Fiona peers at me hopefully. "Or maybe it was a sign? A message?"

I shrug. "I don't know. Maybe. It was hard, though. I know it's not the same as losing a child, but—"

She mindlessly massages the inside of her left wrist. "Grief is grief. I mean, it's taken me this long to come back to the inn. Everywhere I look in this house, I have a memory of him here, you know? Running up those stairs as a toddler in his little Velcro shoes. Getting in trouble for bouncing his basketball in the foyer. Stealing all of Lucy's dolls and hacking their hair off with the garden shears. He hid the doll hair in that big porcelain vase in the entryway. Thought we'd never find it."

My chest pinches for her. Sitting side by side like this, I can feel the ache radiating from her body. "Is it painful? Being here again with the memories?" I ask.

"I convinced myself it would be," she says. "Which is why I've wanted to sell it so badly. I was so angry that the rest of the family didn't care about how this house made me feel. Especially Ness. You know her and her therapy spiels. She thought I needed to be here to deal with it. But she didn't understand how it felt to have lost a son and see him everywhere."

"I can't imagine how awful it must be."

I expect her to nod in agreement, but she doesn't. "The truth is . . . being back has been . . . good for me."

For the first time, I think I'm seeing a sliver of who Fiona really is underneath her icy exterior. She's sensitive and kind, even though she doesn't want to be. "Really?"

"I haven't cried so much since it happened. But I feel connected to him here. I know that sounds ridiculous—"

I place my hand over hers. "It doesn't sound ridiculous at all."

She wipes a teary eye with the back of her free hand. "Jack loved it here so much. I'd forgotten that. This reminded me how special it is. It brought Ness and me back together. For the first time in years. So thank you, Mel."

Her words bring me comfort. Although she seemingly still wants to sell the place, at least she seems more at peace with the idea of making amends in the family. Even if they don't have the inn, they'll have each other. And that's all that really matters in the end.

• • •

"YOU'RE ACTUALLY BRINGING me back onto the water?" I ask, baffled, as Evan holds his hand out for me to step onto the boat. I'd assumed coming back on the water with me was an automatic no. And, to be fair, I've been a little wary of the idea since last time.

Evan takes my hand as I make the jump from the dock to the

rocking boat. "As long as you promise not to push me." He promptly hands me a life jacket, which I'm more than willing to wear. "But if you're nervous, I understand. We don't have to go out if you don't want to. Just thought you'd want another shot at seeing some whales."

He gives me a hopeful, earnest look that threatens to melt me on the spot.

I cast my eye out to the sea. I'd hate to give up an opportunity to go out one last time. "I do. I really do," I tell him, zipping the life jacket.

The engine roars to life, and Evan steers us out of the marina and into open waters. Unlike the last time we were out here, there's not a cloud in the sky. The water is calmer, I'm in flat shoes, and I'm behind the wheel with the captain.

Watching Evan in his element is an experience. Somehow the water heightens his sex appeal at least ten notches. There's something about his demeanor, his confidence out here. The way he surveys the other boats, waves to the other fishermen he knows. The way he can point out any fish, any type of boat. There's no doubt this is what he was born to do.

The first whale we spot is a humpback breaching with its calf. The haunting sound of their breathing is both mesmerizing and humbling.

"That's Melon. She hadn't been spotted with her baby until last week," he tells me as they dive back down into the water with a shockingly small splash for their massive size.

I'm captivated by their slow, graceful movements, beyond grateful to get to experience something like this. "How do you know it's her? Don't they all look kind of the same?"

"Her tail. They all have different markings and shapes." He waits for a moment, scanning the water. "The baby's tail hasn't been captured in photos yet for official record. At least not that I know of."

I hold my breath, scanning, waiting for them to come back up. And within three minutes, they do. I snap multiple pictures in succession and successfully get a shot of the calf's tail. "There, now it has," I say, examining the photo.

Evan wraps his arms around my waist from behind, resting his chin on my shoulder. "You know, traditionally, whoever gets a photo of the tail first gets to name it."

"Yeah?"

"Any ideas?"

I shake my head, unable to come up with anything on the spot. It feels like a massive undertaking.

"How about Melanie? Melon and Melanie sounds like it has a good ring to it," he suggests.

The gesture is consoling, knowing I'm leaving a mark, however insignificant, here in this ocean.

We spend at least twenty minutes watching Melon and Melanie breaching while Evan explains how they migrate back and forth between Greenland and the Caribbean for breeding.

When they relocate to hunt, Evan steers us into a little rocky bay that appears to be home to a group of seagulls. From here, there's a partial view of the clapboard houses along the waterfront. According to Evan, they were strategically painted bright colors so the sailors could see them from afar.

"Bet you'll miss this view," he says into the shell of my ear as we stand against the railing, gazes wandering along the glistening surface of the water.

"I will," I admit. The moment the words come out of my mouth, a heavy band of silence falls between us. I let out a shaky sigh, trying to push that thought to an abandoned corner of my mind. I'm not at all ready to leave this place yet. I love how no one pretends to be anything they're not. Not even me. Sure, I'm a complete fish out of water here, but it's the most accepted I've ever felt. Anywhere.

After a few long moments, the tension snaps when he backs away from me. "Look, I know you don't want to talk about what this is between us—"

"It's scary," I admit. "I don't let people in. Ever."

He studies me for a moment as he rakes a hand through his hair. "I get it. Believe me. The last thing I ever expected was to end up here. Not just with you, but with anyone."

"Really?" It hadn't even crossed my mind that he could be just as scared as I am.

"I didn't think I deserved to be happy again after Jack. I pretty much stopped dating entirely and threw myself into work," he explains. "But . . ."

"But?"

"But then you showed up on the anniversary of his death. I can't help but feel like that's . . . that's gotta mean something, right?"

My heart lodges in my throat. Sure, maybe it does. But that doesn't change the reality of our two completely different lives, almost six hundred miles apart. I reach for his hands and squeeze them, unable to tell him what he wants to hear.

"I was thinking about what you said the other night when we went camping. About how we're different. What did you mean by that?"

I level him with a knowing look. "I mean, we're complete

opposites. In almost every way. You're a fisherman from a small town where everyone knows everyone. You love the outdoors. You name the spiders in your house, for god's sake. And I'm . . . a high-maintenance girl from the city who can barely be without her phone for two minutes and is terrified of nature. And that's just the tip of the iceberg. We don't . . . fit together, on paper at least." I hate the way that statement sounds out loud, but it's the cold, hard truth.

"So what?" His shoulders rise and fall in frustration. "None of that even matters at the end of the day."

"How does it not matter?"

"Because I love everything about you. The real you. Not this . . . facade you've constructed for yourself on social media."

I squint at him, taking in that earnest expression. "And who's the real me?"

"The person who's worked her ass off to give herself a better life. Who cares so much about her brother that she's sacrificed part of herself to make sure he's okay. The type of person who goes to the hospital with a complete stranger—who, by the way, was a total prick to her and didn't deserve her at his side."

I can't help but laugh at that one, despite his conviction.

"Are you a little high-maintenance? Hell yes. Seriously high-maintenance. And I don't give a shit. I like you exactly how you are. No matter how many ridiculous outfits you wear on my boat. If that means you need a little extra attention, I'm more than happy to give that to you. I want you to stay. And not just a few extra days. I want to give this a real shot, because there is no reality in my mind where I can let you go."

His admission leaves my vision spotty. It's like my body can't handle the information overload. Evan wants me to stay. And not just temporarily. "Insult my clothes one more time and I'll end you," I warn, poking him in the chest, deflecting.

He gives me a stern expression, taking a seat on two piled lobster trap cages. "Are you gonna knock off the jokes and admit you want to be with me or what?"

I suck in a sharp breath, letting it out slowly. The admission is lodged in my throat, desperate to be freed. Before the words can make their escape, my chin dips in admission. "I do want to be with you. And I hate it." The words barely scratch the surface of how I really feel about him, but I don't think I have the strength to say anything else.

From his seated position, his eyes quite literally sparkle at the admission. "Was that so hard?"

"Yes." I cover my face, breaths coming a little easier. "It just all feels . . . complicated." And I mean that. Every time I start to think about how fulfilling a life with Evan would be, a warning voice inside my head reminds me that this bubble of simple happiness is a lie. A farce. I can't help but wonder how things will change when we tell the Whalers the truth. Lucy, Evan, and I have collectively decided that in the absence of a fake breakup, we have to come clean about our relationship charade tonight, at our very last dinner before everyone leaves to go back to their regular lives.

"What's complicated?" he asks.

"Everything. Staying here for real . . . like, actually moving here? Full-time?"

"You know I don't believe in long distance," he reminds me, taking me back to our conversation at the Lobster Festival.

"That's no small decision. I'm not sure I can give you an answer right now," I say truthfully.

He dips his chin. "Fair. You don't need to make a decision right this very moment. Telling my family the truth tonight is enough for now. Okay?" He reaches for my hands and squeezes them, pulling me into the space between his legs.

"Good, because I don't know if I'm ready to unpack all of this right now," I admit.

He smooths his left hand down my spine, eyes flicking up at me mischievously. "What am I gonna do with you?"

"I can think of some things," I say, dancing my fingers along the broad width of his shoulders.

With one tug, he pulls me over his lap, knees snug on either side of him. His eyes flare as I settle over him, feeling his excitement underneath me. Before we can go any further, he stabilizes me, gripping my hips to slow the motion. "You sure everything is . . . okay down there?"

"All back to normal," I tell him truthfully, mentally thanking whoever invented antihistamines.

"Still trying to be in charge, huh?" he asks, lowering his shoulders, loosening his grip, like he's giving me the reins.

"I told you, I like to lead," I tell him, feathering my hand over his cheek, over his hard jaw, partially obscured by the thick beard I've come to love.

"Maybe I'll let you." He leans back, just far enough so he can look me in the eyes before moving my hair behind my ear, letting his fingers fall through the silky strands. And when he scrunches his nose in that adorable way he always does when he's amused, there's a flicker of something in those crystal-blue eyes. Something inherently good. Something that tells me I'm safe with him, treasured, loved in a way I've never been before.

I slant my lips over his, utterly hungry for him. A sound escapes me when he moves under me in response. He likes it. I can tell by the way he's chasing my kiss hungrily. His teeth graze my bottom lip, the pressure of his bite filling me with pleasure.

"What if someone sees us?" I ask, lips swollen against his as I skate my finger down his throat, feeling the ripple of his swallow.

His fingers trace my thigh, moving over my ass, clutching my flesh in his palms. "No one will see us. You can scream as loud as you want out here."

"What makes you think you'll make me scream?"

He gives me a look as if to say, *Really?* Under my life jacket, he twirls my nipple between his thumb and index finger so expertly, I fight my losing battle to the sound of pleasure halfway up my throat as the sensation rockets between my thighs, slowing time entirely. "Fuck. I love the way you sound," he whispers.

He temporarily unfastens my life jacket and slips my dress over my head, unhooking my bra at the same time. His breath hitches as my breasts spill out.

"You. Are. Perfect," he whispers, tracing his tongue from my neck, slowly making his way down.

Desire pools in every inch of my body. I arch my back and roll my hips against his, aided by the rock of the boat. His throat bobs as he pulls my thong to the side and runs his thumb over me exactly where I want it. "Does that feel good?"

I nod, moving faster against him, desperate for the friction, for him, heat building by the second.

He swirls his finger exactly where I need it, winding me up like a children's toy before shifting me off of him to stand, propping me up on the side of the boat.

"And what if I fall in?" I ask, peeking over my shoulder at the sea below.

"If you fall in, at least you'll have had a good death."

I softly punch him in the chest, quickly pulling him closer to me.

"I won't let you fall in, Mel. I promise," he says with conviction that's impossible to deny. He tightens his grip before he kneels down, nudging my knees apart. His lips blaze a hot trail from the inside of my knee, up the inside of my thigh, straight to where I want him. I laugh a little from the tickle of his beard against my thighs. My legs completely fall apart at the first swirl of his tongue, intent on sucking the life out of me.

Maybe it's the thrill of hanging off the side of the boat with only his hair to grip between my fingers. Or maybe it's the gust of wind. But all the factors add up to a truly lethal combination. My blood rushes straight to my center, throbbing and pulsing.

He holds my legs open wide despite my instinct to squeeze them shut.

I'm wholly unprepared for the tide building inside me so violently my legs begin to shake uncontrollably. He holds my left thigh down, making me shake even harder, drowning me in pleasure to the point that cries are spilling out of me, echoing across the sea. His tongue does some unexplainable things, coaxing wave after wave out of me until the tremors finally lull.

As I recover, he makes quick work of removing his pants. Then he motions for me to sit back on top of him. My breasts graze his chest as his lips meet mine again, starved, his teeth nipping at my bottom lip. His hands scrape down my back, over my ass, gripping until he rocks me against him in a rhythm that threatens to detonate me.

I tease him, brushing my hand along him, dragging a moan from deep in his throat. He looks like he's in pain. I love seeing his face, watching him shake, desperate and undone. "I'm gonna come if you don't stop doing that," he warns.

"I want you to," I murmur into his mouth.

He lifts me up momentarily, grabbing his discarded pants to retrieve a condom from his wallet.

"How do you want me?" I ask, swallowing a newly formed lump in my throat.

He rolls his eyes. "Don't pretend you don't want to be in control," he says, scooping me up to place me back on top of him.

Our hands join, palm to palm, fingers sliding seamlessly together. "Admit it. You like me on top, don't you?" I ask.

"I may be a stubborn ass, but I'm not dumb enough to pass up having your tight little pussy all over my lap." His eyes lock to mine as I lower myself over him, taking him inch by inch.

"Told you I'm a born leader." I unhook our fingers to grip his shoulders for balance.

"You're the only one I'm letting take the lead." His eyes flutter as I settle over him, hand roaming down my back to cup my ass, angling me to take him deeper. He presses his head into the crook of my neck, teeth pushing into my shoulder ever so slightly as I sink lower. "Jesus Christ."

I gasp as he fills me, mini quakes rippling inside me with every inch. "Is it in yet?" I ask into his ear, just to get a rise out of him. Meanwhile, my body is like a live wire with him inside me, stretching me completely.

He leans back, pinning me with a searing gaze as he works me over him so he hits me at a deeper angle. "Can you feel me now?"

Aside from a whimper, I can barely respond as I take in the brunt of his size. "Mm-hmm."

He pulls my head forward by a thick chunk of my hair until our lips meet, the slight pain translating into pleasure. He bites and sucks on my lower lip, breath hot as he rolls his hips below, moving in and out of me, claiming me without words.

We take turns leading the charge. Sliding in sync with each other like it's second nature.

"Fuck, you feel so good. I—I don't want this to end," he says as I move faster and faster over him, arms clinging around his neck to brace myself. We're moving like frenzied animals as he buries himself in me with renewed urgency.

A powerful wave hits me, pulsing over and over, slamming me home, dragging me under until I can't feel anything at all.

"Holy shit," he manages. His body seizes underneath me, hot breath coasting over my shoulder as he follows me over the edge with a strangled moan. "That was . . ."

"Six stars," I say with a shuddering laugh, still limp. Evan's lap is now my new favorite place in the entire world.

"Six stars? Is that even a thing?"

"You get a bonus one for location."

He laughs into my mouth, pulling me flush to his chest, and holds me there like he's never letting go. "All the fucking stars."

♥ chapter thirty

'M ANXIOUS, WAITING for Crystal's update on Julian. Just when I'm considering texting her, Nana appears in the doorway, batting her faux lashes.

"I have a fashion emergency that requires your assistance," she says, enigmatic as hell, before trotting off.

Hair half curled, I follow her into her bedroom. It's spacious, with a Victorian four-poster similar to mine, along with the inn's signature heavy drapery and quilted bedspread. Of course, her room is much tidier than mine.

"Where's the fashion emergency?" I ask, lingering in the doorway.

She waves me into the room from the dresser. I sit gingerly on the tufted bench at the foot of the bed. Eyes wide and eager, she sits next to me, clutching a polished lacquered cherrywood jewelry box. There's an inlaid veneer in the design of an intricate white floral pattern on the lid. The inside is lined with a stunning ruby-red suede interior reminiscent of the inside of a vintage Louis Vuitton.

It's a literal treasure box, filled with brooches of various colors and designs. There are at least ten rings that glitter and sparkle with even the slightest tilt of the box. Hanging from tiny hooks along the back are some of her more delicate necklaces and chains.

"These are stunning, Nana," I say breathlessly, running my index finger along the smooth, rounded edge of the box.

She smiles and sets it on the bench between us, taking out a particularly large brooch in the shape of a fish. It's filled with blue, red, and green jewels that sparkle like a stained-glass window in church with each tilt in the sunlight. "My mother-in-law gave this to me a month before I got married. It was a tradition to pass it down to the women in the family marrying fishermen, for good luck." She drops it in my palm.

I weigh it in my hand. It's as heavy as it looks. "It's beautiful," I say, shocked that fish jewelry could look anything but utterly ridiculous.

"Fourteen-karat gold. And the eyes are emeralds. I reckon it's worth a couple thousand nowadays," she says proudly.

I hand it back to her. "I'd imagine. It's a work of art. Truly."

She rifles through the box, showcasing some particularly blingy pieces she knows I'll appreciate. Finally, she settles on a ring. It isn't until she hands it to me that I'm able to examine it in greater detail. It's a flower, with a one-carat diamond in the middle, accented by three smaller diamonds on either side in a beveled leaf motif. The band is dainty and intricately designed, with tiny millegrain detailing all the way around.

"This is beautiful," I say simply. No descriptor in the entire dictionary could do it justice. And it's the truth.

"It was my grandmother's. She was a fashionista. Just like you. Always decked out in the flashiest of jewels. She never left the house without every one of her fingers covered in rings. All us kids thought we'd inherit her jewels when she passed, but she had the last laugh by requesting to be buried with them. Except for this ring," she says wistfully. "When Jamie asked my father's permission to propose, he didn't have the money for a diamond ring. So my mother gave him this ring."

When she tells me this, the weight of the ring sinks in. This ring has history. It quite literally symbolizes love. Family. Traditions. Everything I don't have.

I turn it over in my palm, holding it to the light. "It's in impeccable condition."

"We've had it refurbished a couple of times since then," she says with a soft chuckle. "One of the diamonds on the side fell out about ten years ago, and Jamie had it replaced as a surprise."

"It must be so special to you. Do you still wear it?" I ask, peeking at her left hand, adorned with a simple gold band.

"It's gotten too large for me. Fingers are too bony nowadays," she laments, eyeing her wrinkled hand. "I've been too afraid to get it resized. And I've been hoping to pass it down one day."

"Lucy will love it."

She gives me a hesitant look. "I'm not so sure. Lucy's never been too interested in jewelry. Fiona and Ness never cared much for it, either. Same with Ned's kids' wives." She pauses. "And you remind me of my grandmother in some ways. With your fancy clothes and all. So, it only seems fitting that you would have it."

My jaw practically unhinges. The dust swirling in the sunlight over the bed freezes in time. Nana says something else, though her voice is marred and echoey, like I'm in a fishbowl. "You—you want *me* to have it?"

She gifts me a smile so warm and genuine, my eyes instantly well. "Of course. I can't think of anyone who would suit it more. Besides, my grandson never gave you a ring, for goodness' sake. And I don't want him losing you. I can't think of a partner more perfect for him."

I cough as something twists in my chest, clawing at me from the inside. "Really? We're so . . . different."

"Everyone thought Jamie and I were doomed," she says. "Opposites, the two of us. I wasn't a local."

"You're not?" Seeing Nana now, I never would have guessed she wasn't born and raised in Cora's Cove.

"Lord no. I'm from Halifax. Jamie and I met in the strangest of circumstances, really," she tells me. "I was a nurse at the time. He was rushed into the hospital that day."

"Was he in a fishing accident?" I ask.

She smiles wistfully, brimming with fond memories. "Oh, no. The silly man got hit by a car. Broke his femur. Was all bruised up. He'd been in Halifax for a fishermen's convention. Wasn't used to the big city. It was probably one of the handful of times he'd left the Cove in his life. Anyway, there he was in that hospital bed, smiling and charming all the nurses with his head all bandaged up. Everyone said Jack got his personality from Grandpa Jamie. He was inherently good. Kind to everyone he came across."

I smile, remembering how Evan mentioned the same thing.

"But I shit you not, the moment I came in the room to check

on him, he started complaining, going on about the pain. I thought he was being a bit of a wimp. Needed constant attention for that whole shift. He was supposed to be discharged the next day, and you know what he did?"

"What?"

"He waited. Spent an entire day in that waiting room, waiting for me to come back for my shift. Told me he regretted not having the courage to just ask me out that first day. He was feeling perfectly fine, he'd said. But he wanted an excuse to get my attention. We spent two days in Halifax, just me and him. They were the best two days of my life. We fell in love, fast. And he asked me to move to the Cove. The city wasn't for him, getting hit by that car and all," she says with a soft chuckle.

"So, wait, you left your entire life for a virtual stranger? After two days of knowing him?"

"Lord no." She lets out a witchy cackle. "I told him to kick rocks. To go home. That I couldn't leave Halifax for a village I'd never been to. I couldn't leave my parents. My friends. So he left." Her eyes dim slightly. "Months passed, and I carried on with my life. But I couldn't stop thinking about him and those two magical days together. So I packed everything I owned and came to the Cove."

My breath hitches. "Did you call him first?"

"Dear, this was the fifties. He never left his phone number. It was my only choice."

"You weren't scared you wouldn't be able to find him? Or that he'd be with someone else?"

"Oh, I was terrified of that. But I was even more terrified of never seeing him again. Otherwise I'd live in regret. I'd live in a state of limbo never knowing what could have been. So I went. I showed up in town and went straight to the harbor, where I knew he'd be. And sure enough, one nice young man took me to his boat."

"He was there?"

She nods. "Mm-hmm. And his first words to me were 'Took ya long enough.'"

I laugh heartily, as does she before continuing. It sounds exactly like something Evan would say.

"No one, and I mean no one in town thought I'd last here. It was worlds different from what I was used to. It didn't have a lot to offer me at first. But I learned to love the people. The water. The smell of the sea. The Cove has this way of sucking you in and keeping you if you let it."

"Do you ever regret your decision? To leave it all and move here?"

"Never," she tells me, voice unwavering.

My throat closes at the sight of her luminous, eager eyes. Being a part of this family has been everything to me—but it's not real. The truth is on the tip of my tongue, ready to be divulged. She'll find out at dinner tonight and absolutely hate me. "I absolutely love the ring, Nana. But I'm so sorry. I can't."

Defiantly, she slips it onto my ring finger. And it fits perfectly. Too perfectly. "It belongs on your finger, dear."

When she pulls me in for a hug, my heart pounds so hard from the guilt, I'm shocked she can't hear it. I'm swimming in an entire ocean of it now, ready to drown.

• • •

I FIND EVAN on hands and knees in the garage, working on an old boat with Ned. The moment Ned sees my face, he understands I need to speak to Evan. Urgently.

"You look like you've got a lot on your mind. I'll, uh, walk myself out," Ned says, tipping his hat.

I thank Ned with a silent chin dip. The moment he leaves, I extend my hand to Evan. He sets his wrench on the workbench before taking my hand, brows raised in confusion.

When his finger grazes the ring, he does a double take.

"Nana gave me this," I inform him.

His eyes widen. "Is that—"

"The family engagement ring. It was her grandmother's. She wants me to have it."

He runs his thumb across my ring finger and over the diamond ring. His gaze glides from the ring to my face, expression uneasy. "What did you say?"

"I told her I couldn't accept it, obviously. And . . . she wouldn't let me say no." I scrunch my face at the memory.

"You definitely don't look like a woman who just got gifted a diamond ring." He gives me a half-hearted smile.

I level him with a stern look. "Because I can't keep lying to them like this." When he sees the tears sprouting from under my lids, he presses his thumbs to either side of my face to wipe them before pulling me in. His embrace makes me cry even harder.

He presses a soft kiss on my forehead, rocking me back and forth. "I know. This all got complicated really fast. But we're telling them tonight. I promise."

♥ chapter thirty-one

HAVE SOMETHING TO tell you," Evan announces, setting his cutlery on his plate with a soft *clink*. I note that he says *I* and not *we*. He's taking full responsibility for this, even though it's not just on him. He gives my hand a firm, protective squeeze under the dining table.

My knee won't stop shaking, an aftereffect from the quiet anticipation of the past half hour. Evan has been waiting for Nessa and Fiona to tire of their childhood stories. It feels almost cruel to destroy this fragile new dynamic.

Everyone straightens in their seats, awaiting Evan's announcement.

I brace myself for all hell to break loose. They're going to hate me, I'm sure of it. Who wouldn't?

As much as it felt good to pretend, the simple fact is, I'm not a real member of this family. I'm an impostor.

Before Evan can confess, Nessa clears her throat and exchanges a knowing look with Fiona across the table. "Actually, we have something to tell you too."

Evan leans forward in his chair with renewed curiosity. "You first."

Fiona delicately dabs the corners of her mouth with her napkin. "We've decided collectively that . . . we won't be selling the inn."

The reaction to this announcement is mixed. Lucy spits her sip of water across the dining room, eyes wide in pure shock. Nana clasps her chest, brimming with relief. Evan lets go of my hand to clink glasses with his mom on his other side of the table before Ned stands to bring them into a hearty group hug.

Before I know it, I'm being embraced by everyone, as if keeping the inn is just as much a life-changing decision for me as it is for them. Each hug adds a layer of guilt. I feel like I've snuck my way into an intimate family moment I have no right to be a part of.

"When did you decide this? What made you change your mind?" Lucy asks Fiona as everyone resettles in their chairs.

"This afternoon," Fiona tells her, before pausing to offer me a small smile. I think about the chat we had on the porch before Evan and I went out on the water. Sure, she was emotional about the inn, but I had no inkling she was going to change her mind entirely. "That said, we have a lot to discuss as a family regarding the path forward. I still think it's a huge financial risk. Everyone is going to have to give their all to make this work. But we have to try."

Various conversations spark at once. Plans for renovations. Ideas for marketing. Whether or not the inn should be used for weddings, and who is best to take over that part of the business.

Fiona and Lucy are going down a rabbit hole about which of the two main contractors in town is more reliable when Nessa settles everyone down.

"Let's put a pin in that. Plenty of time to figure all of this out." She gestures to Evan. "You mentioned you had something to tell us."

Nana inches forward, delighted. "Mel is pregnant. Isn't she?" She presses her hands to her cheeks in delight. "Oh, having babies out of wedlock is my most favorite sin."

"No, Nana." He sucks in a breath, letting it out slowly as he does one last scan of everyone. He gives my hand another squeeze under the table, as if to tell me everything is okay. "This is going to be tough for everyone to hear, but the truth is, Mel and I aren't . . . engaged."

My body tenses when he says it. And while it's the truth, something about those words breaks my heart. My chest feels empty, drained, nostalgic for something we didn't actually have. Not really, anyway.

Everyone is slack-jawed and confused, as if we've just told them we're extraterrestrials. There's a collective murmur of "What?" before Nana pushes her chair back and stands.

"What do you mean you're not engaged?" she asks, hand over her chest.

"I mean . . . we lied about our relationship," Evan admits, jaw flexing. The confession is painful for him, as evidenced by his rigid posture.

Fiona stands, chair legs scraping against the dining room floor. "Tell me you're joking."

"Why would you lie about something like this?" Nessa asks in disbelief.

Lucy stands too, matching Fiona's height. "It's all my fault. It was my idea," she explains, compulsively twisting the thick sleeve of her oversize fuzzy orange sweater.

Evan gives her a silent look, as if to say, *It's okay. You're off the hook. I'll take the blame.* "It's not Lucy's fault."

"Then who the hell *are* you?" Nessa asks me at a decibel barely heard by the human ear.

"Mel was a guest at the B and B. An uninvited one," Evan says bluntly. "She showed up on the anniversary of Jack's death, actually. And the day I ended up in the hospital . . . well, she saved me. She told the staff at the hospital she was my fiancée so she could come in with me. And it all kind of snowballed from there."

A heavy silence falls over the dining room as everyone struggles to digest the sequence of events.

"As I said, it was my idea," Lucy pipes in, apparently not wanting Evan to go down without her. "I saw how well you guys were getting along when you found out Evan was engaged. And I guess I just thought it would be an opportunity for reconciliation. It was only supposed to be for that night. And, well . . . then you wanted to come to the inn, and . . ."

"So you just thought you'd let this charade continue?" Ned asks simply, lips like a knife slash. I'm not sure I've ever seen him so angry.

A barrage of accusations follows.

How could you trick us into getting along?

Who would do such a thing?

How could you lie to your family like this?

And while it's scary to be yelled at, their anger is completely founded. All I can do is nod and take it.

"Don't blame Mel or Lucy," Evan pleads once the accusations die down. "It's on me. I did it because I felt like it was my responsibility to bring everyone back together . . . after everything."

"But why would that be your responsibility?" Nessa asks.

"Because it's my fault Jack died."

The statement sparks silence.

"I should have been there with him on the boat that day. If I had, none of this would have happened. You two wouldn't be fighting. I guess I thought this could be my opportunity to fix that . . . though now I know there's nothing I can do to fix it."

Fiona stiffens at the mention of Jack, eyes misting. "And you really thought Jack would have condoned lying? To your whole family?"

"Lucy and Evan only wanted the best for you and the family. They did it with the best intentions," I cut in, finally finding my voice. It's important for the Whalers to know that. I saw firsthand how difficult lying was for Lucy and Evan, two people who are so loyal to family, they'd pull off an elaborate ruse in the tiny hope they could bring everyone back together. And that's part of the reason I fell for them in the first place.

"Are you and Mel even together at all?" Nana asks, holding her breath.

Evan's stare burns my profile. He's waiting for my response.

Truthfully, I don't know how to answer that. We've mutually admitted we want to be together. But we also haven't discussed how that's going to work logistically—if it even can. And I know that mere wanting and cold, hard reality are two separate things.

"We're . . . trying to work that out," I say, unable to hide my hesitancy with the statement.

Evan stiffens next to me, steely gaze fixed upon a dent in the table.

"But, Mel, why would you go along with this? What was in it for you?" Fiona asks.

The room falls so silent I can hear the blood rushing through my ears. That's the question I've asked myself over and over since I set foot in the inn. And while staying that first night was a necessity, I just as easily could have flown home the next day.

But I didn't.

I could have called every hotel and motel in the city the night Evan was hospitalized. I could have gotten the hell out of there when his family arrived.

But I didn't.

And when the resort was ready, I could have packed my bags and driven straight there.

But I didn't.

Because of Evan. Because of Lucy. Because of the entire Whaler family. Because of the inn.

I bow my head. "You can't understand how sorry I am for my part in this. I hate that I had to lie to you. But the truth is . . . I stayed because I care about Evan. A lot. And turns out I care about you all too. Your family is special. I never had an extended family like this, and as stupid as it sounds, I guess I just wanted to experience it for myself." I meet Nana's eyes, which are wet with tears. "I fell in love with all of you, and that's why I can't accept the ring, Nana." I begin to pull the stubborn ring off my finger. What was a perfect fit has now, somehow, shrunk. Eventually I manage to pry it off and set it on the table, pushing it back toward her.

She stares at it as if it's lost its luster.

Upon a quick scan, it's clear everyone is angry. Faces red, shoulders hunched, arms crossed. When Nana's wrinkled hand reaches across the table to take the ring back, something inside of me breaks.

Holding back the onslaught of tears, I bolt upstairs to the relative quiet of my room, closing the door behind me.

I collapse onto the bed and hide my tearstained face under the covers, utterly crushed. And that's when my phone vibrates with an incoming call on the bedside table. It's Crystal.

I launch upright, body already in flight mode. "Hello?"

"Hey. So I'm at your place now. I grabbed your key under the mat . . ." She pauses.

"And? Is Julian there?"

Another pause. "No."

Everything in me freezes. "What? Did you check the spare room?"

"I'm looking now. There's some laundry on the floor . . . but the drawers and closet are empty."

I shudder. Julian brought over all his clothes the night he showed up. I remember standing in the doorway, asking him about getting kicked out of his apartment, while he shoved his clothes haphazardly in the dresser drawer.

Crystal does a walk-through of the rest of the place. "Honestly, it doesn't really seem like anyone's been here in a while. There was a pile of your neighbor's love notes at the door too."

My blood runs cold. Julian was collecting them for me. And a pile at the door confirms he hasn't been there.

If Julian isn't at my place, where is he?

♥ chapter thirty-two

EVAN SITS NEXT to me on the edge of the bed, concern creasing his face. "Was he at your place?"

"No. Crystal said most of his stuff is gone. I don't know where he is, and he won't answer my texts." I bury my head in my hands. "It's my fault. If I'd been there to make sure he was okay, this never would have happened."

Evan holds his arms out to pull me into a hug. I settle against his chest as he brushes my cold arms with his knuckles. "How is this your fault?"

"Because when he came to stay with me again, he wasn't in a good place."

He pins me with a sympathetic gaze. "Mel, think about it. The last time you talked, he didn't give you any sign anything was wrong. You can't jump to any drastic conclusions."

"But that's the thing. He never lets on that there's anything wrong . . . until suddenly there is. It was selfish of me to come here knowing that. It's like every time I go away, something bad happens."

"No. You couldn't know how things would go when you were gone. And you should be allowed to leave Boston when you want to. You can't blame yourself for living your own life." He grabs my hands. "For being here. With me. Because you want to be."

"But I'm supposed to be there with him. We're all each other has." I gesture wildly to nothing.

"So that's just it, then? You're leaving?"

I nod. "Tomorrow. As soon as possible."

He's quiet for a span of three breaths before finally nodding, working out the logic in his head. "Okay. I get it. You should go and make sure everything is okay. But if—" He pauses, stopping himself.

"But if what?"

"Nothing. Let's get you packed." There's an edge in his voice as he stands, running his hand through his hair haphazardly. His knit brow and the rapid rise and fall of his chest tell me he's conflicted.

"Were you going to ask what happens next?" I wager.

"No. Not really. I mean . . . I guess I can't help but wonder . . . if you find him and he's all right, what then? Would you come back?"

Any remaining glimmer of hope in his eyes fades the longer I stand there, wordless, like a wild animal caught in headlights. Even the buzz of insects and the squawk of birds from outside the open window fall silent, as if nature is bracing itself.

"Did you mean what you said on the boat today? That you want to make this work?" he asks, eyes searching mine for an answer.

"Of course I *want* to make it work, Evan. But I have a whole life back in Boston that you're just casually asking me to give up on a whim."

"It's not just a *whim*. You fit in so well here. My family loves you—"

"They absolutely hate me now."

His face twists with torment, and he doesn't deny it. "They'll forgive us. It'll just take time."

"How can you be so sure?"

"Because that's what family does. They love you unconditionally." His statement is simple, yet unfathomable to me. I'm not certain I even deserve their forgiveness.

My face stays stiff, concealing the tornado in my mind.

Evan fills the silence. "You've said it yourself. You don't have many attachments in Boston. It doesn't feel like home to you. My family loves you, despite what happened. Everyone in town loves you. I fucking love you."

At his admission, my entire body seizes. My heart folds itself inward, back behind the stone fortress, where it should have stayed all along. Safe and secure. "And you think it's as simple as that? That I relocate my entire life from Boston to be here, in this . . . this village that doesn't even have a Walmart? Just give up the life I worked so hard to build all on my own to be with you? Forever?" I suck in a breath, fully aware I've practically yelled that last question.

"Why not?" he asks simply, voice breaking.

"Because! We've known each other less than two weeks. Do you know how insane that sounds? To give up your entire life for someone you just met?" Suddenly, our fake breakup scenario is playing out in front of us. For real.

"Sure. It sounds fucking ridiculous. But why does it matter if I've known you for a day or a decade?" He places his palm over his chest. "I live my life going with my gut. For everything, even fishing. And I know I want to be with you. I can't explain it. But I know. I can see our life together as plain as day. Running the inn together, going for walks by the ocean. You said you loved it here. I just thought—" His tone is rife with conviction. I wish so badly I had an ounce of it.

My lip trembles. "Evan, I would never ask you to move to Boston with me, because I know how miserable you'd be. You'd resent me for taking you away from your family. So please don't do that to me."

"But it's not the same thing, me moving to Boston."

"How is it any different?"

"Mel, my job is here . . . And the inn. And my family. I thought you understood that."

"So my life and family are less important? Just because it's only my brother?"

He shakes his head. "No. That's not at all what I'm saying. I just— You know your brother needs to step up and start taking care of himself. You said it yourself."

He's not wrong, but the statement unleashes something inside me, bringing me back to all those conversations with Mom. The lectures about enabling Julian. How I'm making things worse. I narrow my gaze. "Don't talk about my brother like you know what's best. You have no idea what he's been through. Okay? None."

His hands fly up in surrender. "I'm sorry. I know. It's not my place to tell you what to do about your brother. And, trust me, I love how loyal you are to him." He sighs, pausing, brow contemplative. "But would you really be that miserable here? With me?"

Logically and objectively, the old Mel would undoubtedly hate it. There's no shopping, aside from the no-name value brand. There's no entertainment. No concerts. No clubs. But in my heart of hearts, I'm not so sure any of that stuff matters—if it ever mattered. I worked so hard to afford those things in Boston, and yet they've never made me truly happy. They've acted as a distraction. But the prospect of putting all my happiness into one basket— Evan and his family—sets off alarm bells deep within me. If I lost them, I'd have absolutely nothing. And what if Evan eventually loses interest in me? Just like all of my followers? My mom? His family already has, after our bombshell revelation.

I can't set myself up for that kind of heartbreak. The risk of losing everything all over again. I don't know if I could survive it. So I suck in a shaky breath, meet his eyes, and tell him, "Yes. I'd be absolutely miserable."

The swirl of light in his eyes dims. If there's a visual of a heart breaking, this is it, right in front of me. "Okay. Then it's settled. We'll get you home. For good."

"I'm sorry, Evan," I say before I collapse into his chest.

• • •

WE FALL INTO bed in a tangle of desperate limbs one last time. Because we both know this is it. There's nowhere for this— whatever this was—to go from here.

My palms are on Evan's chest, and I don't know if it's because I have half a mind to push him away from me. He senses this, jaw ticking as he pulls back, eyes searching mine. I don't know what compels me to remove my hand, but the moment I do, he rolls over me, pinning both my arms into the mattress above my head.

His lips work their way down my body, taking control, enveloping me in a warmth that I hope stays with me long after this is over. My thighs part as he settles himself over me. He watches me for a moment, eyes burning a trail from my belly button to my face, as if locking my features into his memory.

"Are you okay?" I whisper, feeling the way his back muscles flex, tensing underneath my fingertips.

He nods, pressing his forehead against mine. My eyes instantly tear up. I know he's not okay. And I don't blame him. Because neither am I.

"I just don't want to say goodbye to you," he whispers.

The intensity of feelings in this tiny space between us is beyond what I ever thought possible within two weeks. As a person of logic, I never knew it was possible to feel this much for someone in such a short amount of time. And maybe that's why everything feels so heightened—it's a lifetime of love packed into mere days.

I push through those feelings, pulling him closer, saying goodbye in every other way as I move my lips down his neck, over the ridges of his shoulder. He says goodbye too, running a hand down my breasts, over my stomach, along my waist, following up his touch with gentle kisses all the way down to where I need him. My body isn't ready for the feeling of his tongue against me, engulfing me headfirst in what feels like freezing cold water. He's intoxicating, as he's always been.

I tug at his hair, desperate to pull myself closer as he works his way over me, circling until I can't handle the pressure anymore.

He comes back up, skating his teeth along my bottom lip, crushing me to him as our lips fuse together, fierce and deprived. He kisses me with so much emotion, with his entire body. I mold myself to him, as if it was meant to be this way.

He's talking to me, whispering in my ear as he guides himself into me. "You feel so, so good. Like you were made for me."

My breath comes in gasps as he pulls my thigh up to hit me at just the right angle, shooting heat through my entire body. He closes his mouth over mine to stifle my volume. He keeps pumping into me, hot breath against my neck. I try to memorize how it feels. All the garbled sounds he makes as he tells me he's close. The heat builds in my center and my legs begin to shake again. I can feel he's close too as I clamp around him.

He sinks me deep into the mattress, corded forearms caging me in place, watching me come undone for the last time. As the elastic band snaps between us, I cling to him like he's going to disappear. Because he is. Being with Evan is not like anything I've ever experienced. It's a wholeness I've never felt with anyone before.

When it's done, he folds me into him, arm tight around my waist, chest pressed into my back, the smooth release of his breath warm against my neck. Our hands are linked, fingers tight. And it crosses my mind that he's let my hand go over his.

He's compromising for me in the small ways he can. And I guess he has since I arrived.

I love this man. I know it in my heart. And as good and whole as he makes me feel, I can't give him what he needs.

I do everything in my power to hold the tears in. I take in his scent, a mixture of woodsmoke and salty air, branding it into my memory.

His heart beats slowly against my back, and it's not in sync with mine pounding in my chest. Not anymore.

I brace myself to be okay without him. To breathe without him without my chest caving in on me. To be okay knowing I can't have this connection day in and day out, no matter how much I want it.

I have no idea how I'm supposed to move on with my life after this. I've done the unthinkable. I've let someone else into my life who's not permanent.

And I have to let him go.

♥ chapter thirty-three

THE NIGHT MOM left, she woke me up from a dead sleep and told me she was taking a long trip. By the way her eyes glittered at the mere prospect of leaving and starting over, I knew she wasn't coming back.

I would have preferred no goodbye at all, honestly. Because watching her walk out the door without looking back as I sobbed at the foot of my bed, begging for her to stay, ruined all goodbyes for me.

Not to blame my blatant cowardice on deep-seated abandonment issues, but I think about that night often. The flashbacks bombard my mind as I carefully lift my last suitcase down the inn's porch steps.

Leaving Cora's Cove in the cloak of darkness while Evan is still sleeping is another level of savage. But I can't look the Whalers in the eye, one by one, and take the brunt of their anger toward me. I can't let that be my last memory of them. I can't say goodbye to Evan like that. It would officially shatter my heart to smithereens.

Unsurprisingly, the inn is loyal to the family. During my time here, I thought I'd identified which floorboards and stairs creaked incessantly. But no matter how careful I am, every step and movement is amplified with a harsh *creak*, hell-bent on revealing my quiet escape.

It's a wonder I've made it as far as my car before Evan catches me.

"Mel!" Under the glow of the porch light, his hair is tousled, messy. His forehead is creased with a pained expression I assume matches my own. The buttons of his flannel are askew and the laces of his boots are still untied. He rushes down the driveway toward me. "What are you doing?"

I can barely look him in the eye. "You know I have to go."

The expression on his face drills straight through my chest, piercing my heart.

"Why are you looking at me like that? Please don't make this harder," I plead.

"You didn't tell me you were sneaking out at two in the morning. That you weren't even gonna say goodbye to anyone. To me."

"You said last night you didn't want to say goodbye."

"I don't. I really don't. I just—" He runs his hands through his hair and sucks in a breath, like he's trying to rein himself in. "I wanted to apologize. I should never have guilted you like that. Not when all this is going on with Julian. I had no right to put that kind of decision on you. It was fucked up of me to do, and I'm so sorry."

His apology doesn't sit right with me. I place a hand on his forearm. "Don't be sorry. I'm the one who's sorry I couldn't give you what you wanted."

"You already have, Mel. The inn was a ghost before you came barging in. And you breathed life into it again." His gaze softens encouragingly.

"Even if I destroyed your shower curtain? Or made you relocate all the inn's resident creatures?"

He laughs softly, nodding. "I can't thank you enough for everything. I'll miss you so fucking much." His eyes meet mine with such honesty, my chest flutters. "This . . ." He gestures to the space between us. "This was real, though, wasn't it?"

I can only nod, because if I open my mouth, the floodgates will open.

I don't cry as we hug goodbye, as he rocks me back and forth with a strong, all-encompassing hug that reminds me of being on the water. I commit to memory how his solid chest feels against me. How his calloused fingers press into my back, steadying me until my heart slows to a steady pace.

He lets me out of his embrace for a split second, his hard, broken gaze scrolling over my features. He brings both hands to cradle either side of my face, the pads of his thumbs sweeping across the crests of my cheeks, just hovering like he's not sure whether to turn around and go back inside.

And then he pulls me in. And I don't cry as his lips meet mine one last time.

It starts off sweet, almost reserved, like he's promised himself it'll be quick. And then his tongue slips past my lips and everything spins. I press myself against him, hungry, desperate to eradicate any last ounce of his sadness.

The kiss grows slower, sweet again. Softer. Eventually, we stop, still against each other. The dread builds inside me before I open my eyes, like pouring rain flowing over the edges of a bucket. Because this is the end.

I'm still poker-faced as I drive away in my funeral-chic Flex in total silence. The entire drive back really does feel like mourning.

It's only when I'm seated on the plane that it all comes pouring out. As I watch Nova Scotia get smaller and smaller from the window. When it's lost in the clouds, I let out a tiny sigh of relief.

Evan was right. The prospect of staying is ten times scarier than leaving. Not that I even had a choice in the matter. My place is with Julian. And if there's one thing spending time with the Whalers reinforced, it's that family comes above all else.

• • •

UGLY CRYING IN public while compulsively eating plane pretzels is not a good look. One of the two might be borderline acceptable, but not both.

The curly-haired flight attendant is concerned, based on her perturbed glances in my direction and her indiscreet whispers to her coworker with the pink lipstick. The concern extends to my fellow passengers, many of whom have kindly offered me their pretzels after my seatmate, Marjorie, guilt-tripped everyone with a speech that went something along the lines of *This beautiful young woman is having a crisis! How can you sit there and do nothing? If you want peace on this flight, hand those pretzels over.*

Something about the inflection and tone of Marjorie's voice reminds me a little of Nana, which does little to quell the emotional wreck inside of me.

By the end of the flight, Marjorie has scared seven people into donating their pretzels, despite not knowing what's wrong. Not that she didn't ask five times. I never really answered her, aside from vaguely responding, "Breakup," before violently blowing my nose.

I'd gotten used to talking back in Cora's Cove, revealing the unfiltered, messy underlayer of myself. But I'm not there anymore. And it seems my guarded layer of protection has returned.

By the time the plane lands, I dab my tears and check my reflection in my compact mirror. I'm barefaced, mostly because putting on makeup in the dark without waking Evan up wasn't exactly an option.

Scary, blotchy red face aside, I straighten my shoulders and draw in a deep breath. I have from exactly now until I deboard this plane to pull myself together.

I, Melanie Karlsen, do not cry over men. Especially not in public. Once my feet are planted firmly back on Boston soil, my emotions will be restored to their natural order. Right?

♥ chapter thirty-four

THERE'S A PILE of folded notes with doodled lopsided hearts stacked on my kitchen island when I get home. Crystal already warned me they're more notes from Ian, because of course they are.

On a normal day, I'd read them for a laugh and confidence boost. But I'm too fragile right now.

Just like Crystal said, the spare bedroom is empty aside from some stray socks and a wrinkled hoodie strewn across the bed. I toss myself on the couch and check my phone. While going through customs, I messaged all of Julian's friends to see if they've heard from him. Some of the responses are coming in now, including one from an old band buddy of his, Rodney.

RODNEY: I saw him last night. At a concert.

I nearly cry when I read that. Sure, it doesn't make up for the fact that he's otherwise MIA and not returning texts, but it's something. He's alive, at least.

MEL: Was he okay?

RODNEY: I think so? Seemed to be in good spirits.

I let myself relax, but only slightly, my worry transitioning into frustration and anger. It strikes me as uncharacteristic. Julian refuses to go to the grocery store because of crowds, let alone a concert. And if he's out and about at pubs, why can't he take two seconds to let me know he's okay? I contemplate whether I did or said anything to make him mad. Then again, he isn't the type to hold a grudge. If he's annoyed with me, he usually tells me right away and we move on.

While I contemplate my next steps, I check the flurry of notifications on my socials. I'd posted some photo and video content from the lighthouse, as well as the camping excursion a couple of days ago, and they're still getting hits.

My inbox is also flooded with emails from brands and companies eager to partner with me. There's a casual wear brand. A rain boot company. Even an offer for a glamping experience in Northern California.

After the past year of professional disappointment when I was desperately trying to regain my momentum, I should be ecstatic about the potential money and the followers. But instead I'm staring at my screen, feeling empty.

It must be the fatigue, I tell myself. That's surely to blame for my salty thoughts about Julian and my disinterest in work. I try to give myself some grace. I didn't get any sleep last night, and, realistically, my eyes are too sore to stare at my screen for longer than five minutes. Once I've had a good night's sleep, my drive will return. I know it.

I set my phone on the coffee table and just let myself feel the silence.

The distant honks of horns and the wails of sirens used to be a daily comfort. Now I feel more detached from the outside world than ever. While the traffic was mild in the Uber on my ride home, it felt overwhelming, almost suffocating compared to the quiet streets of Cora's Cove. The moment the comparison registers, I stuff it away and bury it. I just hope the grave is deep enough.

The quiet is grating without the soundtrack of nature I'd gotten used to. I never realized just how empty my apartment is. And I don't mean empty of furniture and decor but of memories. Sure, I've spent many a night laughing, sitting on the floor, eating pizza with Crystal and Tara. But it's not the same.

Sure, this condo is glamorous. It's everything I ever wanted for myself when I was a kid. And yet it doesn't hold decades of memories and history. There's no telltale creak of the stairs or those few loose floorboards. No rushed footsteps of Whalers barreling into my room without bothering to knock. No haunting strum of Evan's guitar. No singing and laughing.

The quiet is so suffocating, I fall asleep with a Netflix reality show on in the background.

• • •

IT'S DARK BY the time I wake up. There's a tall black figure hovering over me, draped in shadow like the Grim Reaper. Have I died? Am I being welcomed into the abyss?

Before I can muster the strength to scream, the figure closes in. I jolt upward into a seated position, shielding my face with a tasseled throw pillow. At the same time, the figure flicks on the side table lamp.

"Mel! It's me."

I recognize his scratchy voice instantly.

"Julian?" Still stunned, I squint through the blinding light to confirm, decoding his features through my spotty vision. He's in a black hoodie that only a stereotypical burglar would don, paired with the track pants I bought him last Christmas.

"Jeez, who else would it be?" He blinks rapidly as his pale blue eyes adjust to the light.

I clutch my throw pillow to my pounding chest. "Why the hell are you standing in the dark watching me sleep like a murderer?"

"I just came by to grab some food from the fridge. Didn't know you were coming back early. Was trying not to wake you up." I can tell he's revved up with energy by the way he's bouncing on the balls of his feet. "Guess what?" he asks, tossing himself on the couch next to me.

"What?"

"I went to a concert last night," he announces proudly, picking at a tassel on my pillow. I slap his hand away so he doesn't inadvertently pull it off.

"How was it?" I ask, not bothering to feign surprise.

"It was sick. It was this grunge band Sera loves from overseas. You shoulda heard the lead singer. He's the next Dave Grohl. Sera loved him too—"

My mind goes into overdrive as the timeline slides into place like a puzzle. "Wait. Who is Sera?"

"My new girlfriend," he says, chipper.

I blink, startled. "Hold up. You have a new girlfriend?"

I listen as Julian tells me all about her. According to him, they have tons in common, including the same taste in music and a specific love for pierogies. He even has me look her up on social media. Her latest photo is her and Julian at the concert he was telling me about.

Sera is quite stunning in the photo. Thick, shiny auburn hair. Large, luminous dark eyes. She's rocking a maroon lip and knows how to do a good contour. Julian's face is pressed against her cheek. He's full-teeth smiling. I'm not sure I've seen his pearly-white front row of teeth in years. Gone are his typical worry lines. His heavily creased brow. In fact, he looks entirely at peace. Blissful, even.

My eye twitches with a tangle of conflicting emotions. On one hand, I'm thankful and relieved he's out and having fun. At the same time, there's a tendril of resentment slithering its way up my throat. I left Cora's Cove in the middle of the night because Julian needed me. At least, I thought he did.

He's on a ramble about how they're basically the same person. How they can be together 24/7 and never get sick of each other, which is why he's been staying at her place all week.

I should be happy for him. Grateful he's content. Grateful my worst fears haven't come to fruition this time. But my mind is in overload, and all that comes out is "Why haven't you been returning my texts and calls?"

He pulls his phone out of his pocket, revealing a shattered screen. "Broke my phone a couple days ago and haven't had the chance to get it fixed." He shrugs it off like it's no big deal.

"Are you kidding me right now? That's why you've been MIA for five days?"

"I told you, I don't think we need to do these daily check-ins anymore."

"I never agreed to that. I even had Crystal check in to see if you were here. You could have been dead in a ditch somewhere for all I knew."

He leans back against the armrest, turning his legs away. "Woah. That's really extreme, Mel. I thought you'd be happy for me."

"Of course I'm happy for you!" My voice comes out louder than anticipated.

"Really? Because you're kind of yelling at me."

"I've only ever wanted you to be happy, Julian." Everything I've done has been for him, ever since we were kids, when I was staying up late into the night doing his science fair projects or reading his books for English class so I could give him the CliffsNotes version the next day at breakfast.

I think about the hours I used to spend making his costumes for school plays. All the homemade Valentine's Day cards I wrote on his behalf for his classmates. I'm the one who made sure he finished his homework. That he studied for tests. Went to school in general.

And when Dad died, it was on me to make sure he had food and shelter. That his bills were paid. That his taxes were filed. Hundreds of hours of work, all to make his life easier. To ease the burden of grief. "But you scared the crap out of me."

"I literally told you I was okay a couple days ago. How do you go from that to thinking I'm dead? Have you heard anything I've told you since you've been gone?"

"*Okay* is pretty vague, Julian. I was thinking the worst. Like last time when I went to Spai—"

His features twist with a blend of emotions, none of them good. "Mel, you have it in your head that you know best, but the truth is—" He stops himself. "Look, we're both pretty heated. Clearly you're tired from traveling, and I need to get back to Sera's. Can we talk after we've cooled down?"

"Yeah. Sure," I mumble, watching as he heads out the door.

I hate leaving things unresolved with Julian. A wave of embarrassment and shame washes over me. I've only just gotten back, and he already needs a break from me.

But as I stare at the closed door, it occurs to me that for the first time, maybe I don't know best. Maybe I need to listen to him. Truly listen.

♥ chapter thirty-five

STOLE ONE OF Evan's flannels, which probably makes me a supervillain. It's the green one. The softest, thickest one in his collection. It was my favorite on him because it brought out the pine specks in his eyes. It smells like him. Like campfire. Ever since my fight with Julian two nights ago, I've been living in it.

I don't know if Evan knows I stole it, given that he hasn't texted me about it. He hasn't texted me anything since I left, for that matter. Not that I blame him. Continuing communication is a surefire recipe for regret and potential disaster.

Crystal scrutinizes the shirt as I kick my booties off on her welcome mat, confused. "Is this a new trend? You look . . ."

"Like a Home Depot manager?" I say, reaching to give an eager and excessively slobbery goldendoodle a pat on the head. Even having paired the shirt with a tan suede miniskirt and knee-high riding boots, I'm aware I don't look like one of those cute, dainty girls in their boyfriends' clothes.

Crystal's expression softens. "I was thinking more along the lines of a hot Tractor Supply Co. model. Let me guess, it's Evan's shirt?"

I conveniently ignore her question. I haven't told Crystal or Tara that leaving Cora's Cove nearly wrecked me emotionally. That I've done nothing but sulk on the couch and impulse-purchase random shit I don't even need just to feel a little something. I also haven't told them that Julian and I got into a tiff and haven't spoken since. And I certainly haven't told them how alone I feel as a result.

There's a thickness in my throat that won't go away. A heaviness in my chest that now feels like a permanent ache. Nearly everything—including an episode of *90 Day Fiancé*—makes my eyes well up with tears before I can will them back in.

"Wow, you already packed most of your stuff," I say, surveying Crystal's nearly empty, barren apartment. There's more exposed brick on the far wall than I remember.

With Scott's dog following, panting at my heels, I do a semicircle in the living area, where her big forest-green couch and antique coffee table used to sit. Her place used to be filled with jewel-tone furniture, pillows, bold rugs, and paintings. While it's not my style, it always made me feel like I was in the condo of a trendy Brooklyn textile dealer.

And now its emptiness nearly matches the hole in my heart. For tonight, she's kept one of her end tables as a makeshift coffee table and propped up some stacked gym mats as chair substitutes.

It's not the same. Then again, nothing is, even the fresh laundry–scented candle that flickers in the corner, which has replaced the cinnamon-scented one. I'd hoped coming here to see Crystal and Tara would lighten my mood. But now I'm not so sure.

"I really didn't have that much stuff to begin with," Crystal tells me. She's delusional. "When Scott moved in, we got rid of a lot. Though Grandma Flo stopped in earlier today and tried giving me a bunch of crap for the new house, like an ancient toaster with a broken electrical cord and a thirty-year-old Crock-Pot she swears by. I told her to donate it all. Tara packed up my kitchen all wrong, and I'm pretty sure she forgot to use packing paper for my plates."

The moment Crystal suggests that theory, Tara comes trotting down the hallway from the bathroom like she's been summoned by the mere mention of her name. Her dark eyes light up when she spots me. Immediately, she comes hurtling toward me, arms outstretched for a bear hug. She's a touchy-feely person. The type who will just climb into your lap and stay there until you force her off. It took some getting used to when we first met.

I accept her hug, wrapping my arms around her tiny frame, cushioned only by her chunky baby-blue knit sweater. It actually feels nice to hug someone again after daily hugs from Evan and Nana at the Whalers'.

When we pull back, her eyes go wide in awe. "Wow. Did you just hug me back?"

"Don't get used to it," I warn.

"You smell like . . . s'mores," she says, taking a liberal sniff.

"Evan's shirt," Crystal whispers.

Tara nods like she understands, then hightails it to the kitchen. She returns with a fabric bag overflowing with what appears to be an entire grocery shelf's worth of chips of all flavors. We park ourselves on the gym mats in the living room with our chips and wine, catching up on the last two weeks.

Some points of note:

Another one of Grandma Flo's TikToks went viral. This one was about whether Tara, an avid erotica reader, can be saved.

Tara thinks she's found the perfect wedding dress. As per the photo, it's a soft, romantic tulle A-line with off-the-shoulder drop sleeves and a waistband adorned with little pearls. It's absolutely perfect. So perfect I'm a little disheartened they went dress shopping without me. Then again, it sounds like it was a family event, and, frankly, it would only remind me of dress shopping with the Whalers.

She definitely senses my disappointment, because my face is a traitor and reveals all, like Evan told me. "I'm sorry you couldn't be there. It's just the only time all the aunties could be there. And, honestly, they were obnoxious as hell anyway. They won't be joining in on any future wedding things." She tells me about how they took it upon themselves to try wedding dresses on as well, each trying to outdo the others with a more elaborate gown.

"They were more dramatic than me trying on bathing suits in the JCPenney dressing room in eighth grade. You dodged a bullet," Crystal informs me.

"But I did want to see if you were free to do dress shopping next week, just us three. Because"—Tara gives Crystal a conspiratorial side-eye—"I'd love for you to be part of my bridal party. You're one of my best friends, and—"

"Are you kidding me? Of course I'll be your bridesmaid," I practically scream. My face hurts, and I realize it's because this is the first time I've smiled in days. I think it's probably the best news

I've gotten in a long time. While I'm not exactly family, it shows she values me as an important person in her life, and I couldn't be more grateful. I place my hand over my heart. "I'll wear whatever you want me to. Even if it's heinous."

Tara pulls me in for a side hug. "I was thinking everyone would be in different colors. Crystal in mustard yellow. You in Grinch green," she deadpans.

"Heeled BeDazzled Crocs too," I add, pulling my phone up to google a truly eye-watering example.

After a few moments of gut-busting laughter over the ridiculous abominations of footwear, Crystal claps her hands together, eyes narrowing on me. "Oh, also. I've been waiting until you got back to tell you. Scott was talking to his friend Justin Kuntz from the gym, and—"

I let out a loud snort. "Sorry, did you just say his name is *Justin Kuntz*? Like *just in cunts*?" I clarify. That tells me all I need to know about him.

These random offers to hook me up with one of Scotty's or Trevor's friends are becoming increasingly regular. Just last week, Crystal proposed a couples trip in the group chat, adding, "Don't worry, Mel. We'll find you someone before then."

"Mel, it's not Justin's fault his parents were reckless. Don't be so judgy," Crystal advises.

"Stupid name or not, I don't want to be set up right now," I say before she goes any further. "I appreciate it, though."

Luckily, Crystal doesn't push it. Much. "All right. Fine. But just so you know, Justin is a great guy. He's a publicist in the tech industry. I went to his place for drinks with Scotty and did a little digging. I'm happy to report he doesn't own a single pair of cargo shorts. He also has a real bed frame, and he's close with his mom—"

I squirm, burying my face in my throw pillow. "My ex Peter, the one you guys hated, was close with his mom, and that woman was a nightmare from hell. Hard pass. Unless he's down for a bang." That last bit came out more for posterity than authenticity. The thought of sleeping with anyone other than Evan makes me sick to my stomach.

"Anyway, I want to hear about the end of your trip," Tara demands, popping a barbecue chip in her mouth.

I tell them more about Cora's Cove, the people, the marina. I tell them about how it felt to be in nature. The feeling of morning dew on my skin. I tell them about the inn. The Whalers. How free I felt not being glued to my phone. After being alone in my condo for days, there were moments I started to question whether any of it was real. Despite my sadness, talking about the Whalers brings them back to life in my head.

I tell them about Jack and how the inn was a pinch point in the family. How Nana gave me the family ring. And how we had to come clean about the charade.

I cover everything. Except my feelings for Evan.

"Were they pissed that it wasn't real?" Crystal asks.

"Absolutely. They hate me. And rightfully so," I say through my remaining guilt. "Wouldn't you be pissed if someone did that to your family? Like, imagine if you two were feuding."

"If it was to bring us back together, I wouldn't be mad for long," Crystal admits thoughtfully.

Tara nods in agreement. "And their anger just shows how much they loved you," she adds optimistically. "If they didn't care, they wouldn't be angry."

I bow my head. "Maybe."

Tara places a hand on my knee. "It's okay to admit you miss them."

"He told me he loved me," I admit instead.

Tara drops her bag of chips, placing her hands over her mouth, while Crystal half chokes, mid-guzzle of wine.

"Evan dropped the L-bomb?" Tara confirms.

"He wanted me to stay," I explain. "Asked me to pack up my entire life and move there. Wild, huh?"

Crystal contemplates this, pulling her arms over her head like she's stretching before a workout. "It feels a little fast. You've only known each other, what, two weeks?"

Tara cuts in. "Hard disagree. Love isn't on some timeline." She resettles, stretching out onto her stomach on the floor. "What did you say?"

"I said no, of course. Can you imagine me just leaving the country? Living the rest of my life in a village of literally seven hundred people and no high-speed data?"

Crystal presses her lips together, like she wants to say something, but refrains.

"No. It doesn't sound like you at all," Tara admits. "But . . . did any part of you want to? I mean, you looked beyond happy in your IG stories and pictures. Happier than I've ever seen you, honestly."

"Part of me did . . . still does," I manage. "But you know when you come home from vacation and you're feeling nostalgic? Maybe that's it. I'm sure it will pass." It has to. Or else I don't know how I'll cope in the long term.

Tara shrugs, unconvinced. "Maybe."

"Either way, it would be ridiculous to make a decision like that so fast," I say, more to assure myself.

"Do you love Evan back?" she asks.

My mind wrestles with the truth. I've come to terms with the fact that I love Evan. But saying it aloud is another thing.

Luckily, Tara doesn't make me say it. She squeezes my thigh, like she's giving me an out.

"It doesn't matter anyway," I continue. "Besides, it would mean I'd be leaving you guys, and I can't give up *Bachelor* nights."

Crystal levels me with a knowing look. "We know you hate *Bachelor* nights, Mel."

I blink, startled at the callout. "What?"

Tara nods in agreement. "We know."

"How?" I ask, suddenly paranoid. I grab a handful of chips for no good reason other than to distract myself from the discomfort.

"You look like you want to poop yourself whenever we bring it up," Tara says.

"Okay. It's true. I hate the show with a burning passion. But that's not the point. I'd still miss you guys too much. My life is here."

"Is it, though?" Crystal asks.

"Do you really think I could survive in a tiny fishing village for the rest of my life? Give up everything I worked so hard to build? Risk it all for one person?"

Crystal tilts her head back and forth, considering. "I mean, don't get me wrong. I'd be devastated if you left. But I want you to be happy. You're not happy here, if we're being totally truthful. And you could move anywhere with your job. Your mom lives across the country, so really, it's only your brother here, right?"

I suck in a breath. I need to tell them. "You know how I said Julian relies on me for a lot of things?" They nod simultaneously. I explain why Crystal had to check on him. I tell them about Julian's battle with grief and depression, just like I explained it to Evan.

"I had no idea he struggled. He always seems so happy-go-lucky whenever I've seen him," Crystal says.

"He puts on a bit of a mask for people," I explain. "Anyway, we got in a fight about it when I got home. He left before things got too heated, and we haven't talked since."

"I'm so sorry," Crystal says. "Why didn't you tell us sooner? We could have come over or talked."

I shrug. "I just . . . hate burdening people with depressing news. And I didn't want to be a charity case or make you guys feel obligated."

Tara places her hand on my shoulder and gives me a small shake. "Mel, we don't feel obligated to do anything. You're our best friend. If there's anything we can do to help, just say it."

I bow my head. "Thank you. Really." I always assumed admitting I needed support would feel scary and vulnerable. And I've always known Crystal and Tara were good friends. But having their support right now means everything, even if they're both on the brink of starting shiny new chapters in their lives.

And then there's me. From the outside, my life is the same as it ever was. Yet, on the inside, everything has changed.

♥ chapter thirty-six

START MY DAY with breakfast at CLINK, then get a lash fill and a fresh wax, capping it off with a shopping spree, all in an effort to remind myself that this is my lifestyle now. That I've worked too damn hard to get here. And yet I don't feel any better than I did downing pretzels on the plane.

All the days flow into each other, one after another. Logically, I know it's only been five days since I got home, but it feels like a hundred.

My follower count continues to rise, as do the number of DMs in my inbox. The comments and messages used to fill me with a false sense of validation, popularity, and acceptance. It was like one big distraction from the emptiness in my life. And now, somehow, it just makes me feel more isolated. Because these people don't really know *me*.

Even the ocean doesn't hit the same in the city. You can't

escape the muggy skies. The smell of sewage. The people who don't even bother to look you in the eye as they rush by. And I can't seem to escape my dreams at night. It's just Evan. His smile. His voice singing to me. The way his hair shines blond under the sunlight. How I felt when he pulled me onto his lap and made me the center of his world. The light flickering in between the leaves as we weaved our way through the trails, me holding on to his waist for dear life. Maybe I should have held on tighter.

I spend the entire afternoon on a bench at the waterfront, trying to feel closer. Trying to imagine that Evan's touched this very water. Trying re-create the feeling of being in Cora's Cove. But it's impossible. It's the same ocean; I know that. But it feels meaningless here. Different. Then again, *I* am different. I'm not the same person I was before I met him.

I can't pull free from the crushing ache whenever I see a couple holding hands as they pass by. It's like I'm wandering, aimless and alone. And as I stare at the waves slapping against the rocks, I pinpoint the feeling flooding through me. It's a feeling of being incomplete. Of being straight-up lonely, even with Crystal and Tara in my life. And I don't know whether location has anything to do with it. If it ever has.

All the sadness plaguing me feels like too big a mess to solve right now. Except one thing: I've been thinking a lot about my talk with Julian. After seeing what a yearslong feud did to the Whaler sisters, the last thing I want to do is waste time holding a grudge. So I text him, asking him to meet me at my condo.

He swings by after work. His expression is somber, not angry. Not like he was the other night. We make jilted small talk about the rain as I invite him to take a seat on the couch.

"Can I say something before we start?" he asks as I park myself on the chaise diagonal from him.

"Um, yeah. Of course."

He looks me square in the eye and drops his shoulders. "I'm sorry. For ditching our conversation the other night—"

I hold my hand out. "No. We would have ended up fighting if you stayed. You did the mature thing by taking a pause. I wanted to apologize to you, actually."

He stiffens. "Can you not wait until I apologize to you first, or do you always have to have everything your way?" He holds his ultraserious face before we both break into laughter. "Are we actually fighting?" he confirms through a smirk.

"We might be," I say, relieved that the tension has loosened ever so slightly. "But I'm sorry for cutting in. You go first."

He folds his hands in his lap, moving one thumb on top of the other. "I wanted to say it was wrong of me to accuse you of not being happy for me. I know it's the opposite. I know you care about me, a lot."

"A little too much, as I gathered the other night?"

He gives me an impish smile. "I get it. I've gone to dark places. I was really, really depressed after Dad. You've seen me at my worst, like when you went to Spain. You've always . . . done everything."

"No—"

"Look, I know I have a rosier memory of Dad than you. I know I've always been defensive of his memory. But I do know things weren't great growing up, and it's not lost on me that it was always you who made sure we were taken care of. That we had food on the table. And you're the one who has things taken care of before they even cross anyone else's mind. I guess I've just gotten used to that—" He stops himself. "Ever since Mom left. You've been taking care of me my whole life, really."

I nod, grateful for the acknowledgment, even though I don't really need to be thanked.

"But in the past year, I've made a lot of progress, even though it may seem like nothing—"

"It doesn't seem like nothing," I tell him. "I've noticed."

He gives me a weak smile. "I don't think I'll ever be . . . you know . . . back to normal, whatever that means. But I do think I've gotten to a better place. And I feel like I can do a lot more than you think I can. I know I should have told you forever ago how I was feeling. And so I'd like to ask that you trust me. Trust that I know what I need and that I can do things myself."

He's entirely right. I've been holding on to him like a lifeline, terrified of letting him go. "I get it. Completely. I've been too much," I admit. "I've gone too overboard. I haven't even given you the chance to do things on your own. I'm just sorry I let my fear guide our relationship and stress you out even more. I'm sorry for not seeing *you*, as a person. Because you're amazing, and I'm such an asshole."

"You're not. You've just tried to protect me. Always."

I squint. "I do have to ask, though, did you practice this with Sera?"

He rubs his palms over his knees. "Sure did. You can be kind of scary."

"Yeah, so I've been told." I can't help but laugh. "So, Sera, huh? I take it you really like her?"

"I love her," he tells me proudly. He looks giddy, like a little puppy dog. "We told each other on the phone before we even met, actually. I think we might even move in together. Which you'll be happy about. I'll be out of your way."

"Don't you think it might be a smidge too soon—" I stop myself so as not to be overbearing.

He shrugs. "Not in the slightest."

I try to smile, though it quickly morphs into a frown.

He eyes me knowingly. "You look like you're about to cry."

I sniffle. "No, no. I'm totally fine. Just pollen, you know . . . allergies."

"You're not okay. You look miserable. You know, you coulda stayed longer. With your sexy fisherman."

"Ew. Don't call him sexy, please. That's weird."

"Fine. Your unsexy fisherman."

I don't know why, but the tears flow out. For the first time since the plane. Julian looks horrified. He leaves the couch to give me a hug. It's unfamiliar. Him comforting me.

"Jeez, Mel. What's wrong?" he asks, passing me the Kleenex box.

It all spills out of me. Everything I told Crystal and Tara about Evan and Cora's Cove.

"Wow. I . . . Why didn't you just stay?" he asks.

I snort. "Stay? I'm perfectly happy here, with you, with my friends, in Boston. I finally have the life I always dreamed of. Evan was never going to fit into my life here. And I would never fit into his life there." I try to convince myself we were just two lost, lonely souls. Sure, he was surrounded by family. But he was isolated by his own guilt. And I saved him from that. He saved me too. Teaching me how to open up to someone. Teaching me how to live in the moment, not caring about what people think.

"I don't think that's entirely true."

I give him a knowing look. "Me, move there permanently? No. There's no way. I mean, everything is here. And you."

"You mean you felt obligated to be here with me, in this life you decided you wanted years ago when we were dirt-poor, eating Betty Crocker icing out of the can for dinner."

My face goes hot. "No. That's not it. It's not an excuse, but Dad made me promise forever ago that I'd take care of you. Honestly, ever since I can remember, I've been terrified to lose you. I *am* terrified to lose you, especially after Mom left us. You're the only family I really have, and—" My voice cracks when it hits me. "Maybe I didn't leave Cora's Cove solely for you," I admit. More to myself than to him. "I mean . . . I convinced myself you were the reason, when really I was just scared."

"Scared of what?"

I sigh. "I don't know. Something."

"Of losing someone?" he asks.

"Maybe."

"I've noticed, even when I was a kid, you keep everyone at arm's length. You didn't really have a lot of friends. And the ones you did have . . . you never really told them anything about yourself. And all the guys you've dated the past few years. I feel like they were always really surface level."

I digest his words for a couple of breaths, thinking about everyone who's ever been in my life. Julian is completely right. I've avoided letting people in, telling them personal things about myself, even Crystal and Tara.

It was easier for me to blame Julian for my choice to leave Cora's Cove, because I liked being needed by him. Keeping him close was my way of making sure he'd never leave. Maybe I've just been terrified to be alone this whole time. Leaving was easier than admitting that I'd fallen in love. The whole time, I was less scared about Julian and more scared of being vulnerable. Of letting someone in. Not just Evan, but the entire family. Giving that many people the power to hurt me was too overwhelming to bear.

But maybe I did have people who cared about me all along. Like Julian, Crystal, and Tara. And I never let them, because my automatic assumption was that they'd always leave. Like my birth parents, my string of meaningless relationships, Mom, and Dad.

I raise a brow. "So you're saying I'm that Hallmark heroine who can't form close relationships because her mom bounced on Christmas Eve twenty years ago?"

He snorts. "Basically, yes. Cue the sad violin."

"Why are you so smart?"

"Lots of time in therapy," he says with a cool smirk. "Speaking of, our parents really fucked us up, didn't they?"

I snort, making a mental note to book a session with my therapist. "Yup. Sure did."

"We should send Mom our therapy bills."

"She'd love that."

Julian laughs. "So tell me more about the hot fisherman," he prods.

I tell him about Evan and the Whalers, leaving out the gory details about the fake-relationship charade. "You'd really like him. He's into music too. Plays in a band."

This piques Julian's interest. "Oh yeah? What kind of music does he play?"

"Mostly classics. Covers and stuff."

"Sounds like a cool guy."

"He was the best. His family too. It was the big overbearing family we never had," I say with a wistful smile.

"You know, just because you loved being there doesn't mean you can't still be here for me too."

"But that's the thing. If I choose him, I lose you," I say, voice shaky.

He reaches to take my hand. "You won't lose me, Mel. I'll be here. Whenever you need."

I nod, in awe. The Evan stuff is still a jumbled mess in my mind, but I've come away with some clarity here. I've been so wrapped up in fearing the consequences of Julian's grief that I became overbearing, blinded by how far he's come.

He squeezes my hand, strong and firm. And it occurs to me: my little brother is stronger than I ever gave him credit for. He was brave enough to get help. And now he's managing it day by day. He was even strong enough to tell me to back off.

Julian doesn't need me. And perhaps he hasn't needed me in a long time.

♥ chapter thirty-seven

AFTER MY TALK with Julian, I feel loads lighter as I head to my very last workout session with Crystal.

She's promised to go easy on me for this session, though I'm not naive. She mentioned sled pushes and assault bike rounds—my two biggest weaknesses. I know that's code for her most difficult session yet.

It's bittersweet, knowing we'll never work out together at Excalibur again. We'll never again lie on those mats by the window swapping Instagram tips or rehashing the drama on our favorite shows. Crystal claims she'll come out of the suburbs all the time to visit, but we both know this is the end of an era.

As I hit the elevator button for the lobby on my way out, a door creaks open down the hall. The familiar *click-clack* of boys' dress shoes against the ceramic tiles tells me Ian is afoot.

He makes it into the elevator just before the door begins to close. Today he's dressed in an argyle sweater-vest and a short-sleeved dress shirt in a muted orange.

"Oh, hi, Melanie, I didn't see you there," he says, pretending to be startled by my presence, as if he didn't hear me exit my apartment and run after me in pursuit. He gives my red workout set a once-over, ending with an uncharacteristically casual chin dip. "You look lovely."

"Thanks, Ian. How are you?" I don't have the energy to be snarky right now. And to be fair, his squirrely demeanor is making me feel a little guilty. For the past week since I've been back, I've been avoiding him, mostly because I haven't had the mental capacity to deal with him. I haven't answered the door when he's come by. On one occasion, I even opted to take the stairs when I spotted him waiting for the elevator.

"Very busy. School started this week," he tells me.

"Right. Can't believe it's already September," I say, like a sixty-five-year-old whose life is passing her by at warp speed.

There are a couple beats of heavy silence before he asks, "Have you gotten my poems?"

"I did. Sorry. I've been really busy unpacking and stuff," I explain, shifting my gym bag higher on my shoulder.

Disappointment flashes across his face. "Did you read them?"

"Not yet."

He rocks back and forth on his heels. "Oh. Well, if you did, you'd know I've moved on."

I blink, confused, as the elevator reaches the lobby. Like the gentleman he is, he ushers me ahead of him. "Moved on?" I repeat once we're in the lobby.

Ian directs me to one of the leather chairs near the door. I feel like I'm having a conversation with a business associate, not an eleven-year-old.

"Melanie," he starts, lowering himself into the chair next to mine. He sucks in a deep breath before continuing. "I've recently fallen in love with someone else." He quickly misinterprets the look of pure shock on my face, adding, "I'm sorry."

The declaration catches me so off guard, I smack the armrest of the chair with far too much enthusiasm. In love with someone else? I have so many questions. "Ian, I'm so happy for you. Can I ask who the lucky new soul is?"

"Her name is Padma." A massively toothy smile stretches across his face the moment he says her name. If Ian were a cartoon, tiny red hearts would circle around his head like a halo. It's marginally adorable—when the passion isn't directed toward me, that is.

"Padma," I repeat. "How did you meet?"

"We met in science class."

"Oh, is she your lab partner?" I ask playfully, matching his smile. I can't help myself. I'm grateful, not only that I don't have to put up with his advances anymore but because he seems genuinely happy. And that's all that matters.

He shakes his head. "No. But she did tell me she thinks I'm gifted. She asked to have a meeting with my dad about putting me in the advanced program, and—"

My throat swells. "Wait. She's not a student?"

He shakes his head, confused. "No. She's my teacher."

My eyes bulge. This was too good to be true. I quietly send mental strength to this poor teacher. She's in for a treat. "Oh, Ian. That's not appropriate."

"Dad said the same thing," he says. "But I can't help how I feel. I figure I'll tell her maybe next week."

I just nod, because he's certainly not about to take my advice.

"Anyway, the reason I wanted to talk was to tell you . . . I'm not sure it's appropriate that I continue speaking to you regularly. I don't want to ruin my chances with her if she thinks I'm still in love with another woman. Especially someone as beautiful as yourself. She could be threatened by you."

I nod, trying to resist the urge to laugh. "That's understandable. I certainly don't want to stand in the way of your happiness. You know, I've always admired how you just . . . go for things."

"Isn't that just what you do for love? Go for it?" he asks simply.

"Sometimes it's a little more complicated than that. Sometimes there are things that get in the way, like distance, or timing, or age," I say pointedly, fiddling with my Fitbit.

"What's the issue with the new guy?" he asks.

I contemplate playing dumb, but Ian is too smart for that. "Distance, mostly. I broke his heart when I left."

He squints at me, utterly confused. "If you broke his heart by leaving, wouldn't you unbreak his heart if you went back?"

Oh, Ian, you sweet summer child. If only it were that easy. "It's a little more complicated than that. I don't know if it would work out for me, moving somewhere so different from Boston. And his family is mad at me," I say, shaking my head as the boulder of guilt drops in my stomach. I messed things up with the lie. With leaving. How can I just show up expecting everything to be fine? To be forgiven?

He arrows a look at me. "You're making excuses."

I stiffen. "Excuse you. I'm just stating the facts."

He shakes his head. "Sounds like excuses to me. Go back."

"And do what? Declare my love?" Am I really allowing myself to get schooled by a child right now?

"Yup. I can help you write a poem if you want," he offers.

"Thanks, Ian. I appreciate it. But I don't know."

"Well, if you change your mind, I think you should surprise him. The element of surprise is key."

I sigh. "Ian, you're going to make an excellent boyfriend one day, you know that?"

"So you've told me."

"You'll find someone age appropriate who appreciates you."

He smiles. "You'll always be my first love."

I smirk. Funny how a fifth grader already knows he's in love, and I've only just realized it at nearly thirty years old.

I think about the life I could have with Evan back at the inn, and all I feel is the warmth of pure joy.

It may not be what I pictured. But maybe it's exactly what I need.

♥ chapter thirty-eight

"THIS IS A terrible idea, isn't it?" I ask for the fifth time in the last four minutes.

Crystal is unable to respond. She's exerting all her superhuman strength to flatten my suitcase, allowing me to pull the stubborn zipper completely closed.

Tara cracks her knuckles before turning to the second suitcase. "Nope. Stop trying to talk yourself out of it. You're taking the advice of the little creep next door, and that's that."

After my conversation with Ian yesterday, somewhere between a harsh round of burpees and sprints, I decided to go back to Cora's Cove. Tomorrow. Crystal was initially hesitant, cautioning me to think on it for a couple of days before making a hasty decision. But truthfully, I'd already made up my mind.

It's hands down the most terrifying thing I've ever done, including getting a poodle perm five years ago. For all I know, Evan could turn me and my excess baggage (literal and figurative) away. His family could still hate me. I could wind up back in Boston, heartbroken and crying in the dark, listening to Adele.

But like Ian said, maybe that's just what you do for love. You put yourself out there, even when there's a high likelihood of getting irreversibly scorched like a marshmallow over an open fire.

Before I risk it all, I'm throwing a small gathering. I've invited Crystal and Scott, Tara and Trevor, and Julian and Sera for wine and charcuterie. I'd be lying if I said having them here to assist with closing my overflowing suitcases wasn't an ulterior motive.

"So, Mel, walk me through the plan for tomorrow," Trevor requests. He's a man of precision, detail, and facts, which I first learned during an apocalypse-themed escape room we did together when he first started dating Tara. I still credit him for getting us out of the room alive without having a full-blown panic attack.

"Once I get there, I'll get a rental car and just . . . show up, I guess?" When I say it out loud, it sounds absolutely ridiculous.

Trevor tilts his head as he zips the suitcase with ease, thanks to Tara's full body weight draped over the top. "Do you know if he'll be home? Isn't he a fisherman? Don't they go out on the water for days at a time?"

Tara gives him a gentle slap on the bicep. "Trevor, don't scare her with logistics. The element of surprise is key with grand gestures."

"I think it's brave as hell," Scott declares from the kitchen as he peruses the meat-and-cheese selection. "I mean, you're flying to a different country, only to risk—" He stops himself when Crystal gives him a warning glare.

"Sorry, what Scott means to say is that it's an expensive risk.

When I apologized to Scott at the gym, if he'd said *Nah, I don't forgive you for being terrible,* I'd have just walked home. But you'd have to fly all the way back, and—" She cringes. "That isn't really helping matters, is it?"

"Not in the slightest," I confirm.

Tara shakes her head. "But you have to do it in person. There's no other option. Imagine doing some weird virtual grand gesture. You'd probably freeze mid-apology because they don't have high-speed Wi-Fi—"

A knock at my door interrupts her.

"It's the pizza," I say, springing to my feet. When I pull the door open, it's not the pizza. It's Julian and Sera.

It's my first time meeting Sera. But the moment she walks in the door and compliments the BeDazzled lapel on my leather jacket, I know we're destined to be friends.

While Scott, Trevor, and Julian bro out in the living room over a football game, Crystal, Tara, and I get to know Sera around the kitchen island. I can see why Julian fell in love with her so quickly. She's outgoing, unafraid to introduce herself to everyone with confidence. She has a positive, bubbly energy about her that makes her impossible not to like.

Apparently, she used to have a beauty blog on YouTube, which immediately bonds us. She can do a mean winged eyeliner and promised to show me her tricks.

"I'd already followed your @MelanieInTheCity account for years. You were the one who gave me the confidence to wear a crop top," Sera admits, spreading cheese over her cracker. "Before I even started talking to Julian. I was floored when he told me you were his sister."

"You didn't see the family resemblance? We're basically twins," I tease, jabbing my thumb backward toward Julian in the living room. There's a knock at the door. "It's the pizza. Finally." Stomach growling at the prospect, I shuffle over to the door, careful to sidestep my suitcases.

Turns out, it's still not the pizza.

Six faces smile back at me.

It's Evan.

And the Whalers.

♥ chapter thirty-nine

OING SOMEWHERE?" EVAN asks, nodding at my luggage.

"I— Oh my god" is all I can muster. At the melodic sound of his voice, I think I'm having an out-of-body experience. Is it possible I'm having cheese-induced visions? I blink rapidly as Evan steps toward me, hands in the pockets of his dark-wash jeans, which are paired with an orange-and-blue flannel.

I think my heart just stopped. It feels like my body has ceased functioning after years of struggle, aimlessly adrift in the frigid sea. Something warm and fizzy expands inside me, extending to every limb like little pops of light, showing me the way.

"Surprise?" His expression is a puzzle I can't quite decipher.

"What are you all doing here?" I ask, scanning the familiar faces behind him. Everyone is smiling. Full-teeth beaming at me. Nana, Fiona, Ned, Nessa, and Lucy. Uncle Ned even has a box of

Timbits in his hands. It's a far cry from the anger and disdain that plagued my nightmares.

Evan glances back at his family. "Um . . . well, we collectively decided—"

"We miss you," Nana shouts, tiny body barely visible behind Ned's broad shoulders.

"But . . . I lied to you. I lied to all of you," I say.

"We know you kids had the best intentions. Especially you. I mean, doing all this for a bunch of strangers . . ." Fiona says. "And anyone who makes my son so happy is someone I can't stand the thought of losing."

"Besides, the inn just isn't the same without you," Nessa adds, flashing a kind smile.

"We love you," Nana tells me.

Their words strike me. After all I put them through, they've still found it in their hearts to forgive me. And love me. The tears begin to well. I do my best to force them down, but they spill over my lash line.

"Hey, we agreed I'm supposed to do the talking," Evan gently reminds them. "Can you please . . . give us a minute?"

"You guys are welcome to come in," I say, stepping aside for them to pass.

Uncle Ned is the first to head in, proudly depositing the Timbits box in Evan's hands on his way.

"If you need us, we'll just be giving ourselves a tour of your condo while eavesdropping," Lucy says, flashing me a wink while visually assaulting me with a Pepto-pink crocheted grandpa sweater.

"You brought Timbits?" I ask through a sniffle as everyone follows Ned, who is not-so-stealthily hiding around the corner.

Evan's right shoulder lifts. "Uncle Ned smuggled them on the plane for you. I know it's not the same as poutine. But gravy and cheese don't exactly travel well."

I blink, thoughts swirling in my head too fast to follow. "I was going to go to Cora's Cove. Tomorrow."

"And you were going to bring *all* of this?" He points to my luggage, the tiniest smile quirking the corner of his mouth.

"I was hoping my apology would be good enough for you to let me stay, yeah."

"Let's hear it, then," he says, leaning against the door, arms crossed with that cocky stubbornness I fell for.

I'd planned to practice the shit out of this on the plane. But now that I'm on the spot, looking into Evan's eyes, it all comes flooding back to me. "I'm so sorry for leaving like that. For telling you I couldn't give you what you wanted. I've regretted it since the moment I drove away—"

"Mel, Mel. I was just kidding. You have nothing to apologize for. Really," he says, taking a step forward when he sees my face crumple.

I hold my hand out and he takes it, threading his fingers through mine before dropping his hand back at his side. His touch, however short, gives me the courage to speak from the heart. "No. I do. The whole thing took me by complete surprise. I went there with the goal of working. Developing content. Transforming my brand. I never expected to wind up in Cora's Cove. And I definitely didn't expect to meet you and your family." I suck in a shaky breath. "I fell for you so hard and so fast. I fell for everyone. And it scared me because I'm not the kind of person who lets people in. I haven't let people get too close to me, ever since I was a kid. And when I realized how I felt about you, I guess I just froze and took the first excuse I could find to flee. I'm sorry for that."

"No, Mel. I asked you to give up your entire life to be together without even thinking about how I could fit into yours. It was beyond selfish, and I've been beating myself up about it ever since you left. And it wasn't just me that was devastated. It was all of us." He gestures over my shoulder to the wall the Whalers are waiting behind, shamelessly listening to every word. "I told you . . . the night we met was the anniversary of Jack's death. I was having the shittiest day, trying to figure out how the hell we were going to pull together and save the inn. The family. And then you came barging in, and I was so fucking mad at you." He pauses, letting out a small laugh. "And it was the first time I'd felt anything but numbness since Jack. There's no way that was a coincidence. Jack brought you to me. To all of us. And I'd be a fool not to follow you wherever you go."

That fizzy feeling inside overflows, filling and mending every crack and crevice in my heart. I would probably fall to my knees, weeping at his words, if it weren't for a teen in a backward ball cap and a Domino's delivery uniform with a stack of pizza boxes creeping up behind him. He tiptoes cautiously toward us like he's just entered a secret society.

"Um . . . I'll just leave these here?" he says, stopping five feet away. "This sounds like an important conversation."

"It's all good." I flash him a weak smile. My eyes meet Evan's as the delivery guy just stands there, unsure who to give the pizza to.

"I'll take 'em," Julian says, sneaking into the narrow space between me and the doorway to take the pizzas. He gives Evan a polite nod, clutching the boxes to his chest. "Nice to meet you, man. I'm Mel's brother."

Evan returns his chin dip. "It's really nice to meet you too."

We both wait in a bubble of awkward silence for the delivery guy and Julian to back away before recommencing the conversation.

"Anyway, I was thinking about how you said you didn't want to be alone. That you were scared you'd have no one beside you in the worst moments. That you'd have no one to make decisions for you if you were ever sick or in the hospital. And it broke my heart to hear that, because that's what I want to be for you. I want to be your rock. The one at your side, always."

I blink, startled by the gravity of his words. "You want to be my power of attorney?"

"Of course I want to be your power of attorney." I think this is the single most romantic thing anyone has ever said to me. "I want to be everything to you, Mel. And I know it's not as simple as that. You were right. Back at the inn," Evan continues. "We each have an obligation to our families. We live different lives. We can't just uproot completely."

"So what are you suggesting? I thought you didn't do long distance."

"I would rather have you half the time than not at all. But I think I have a better solution."

"And what's that?"

"We compromise. Find something that works for both of us?

Maybe spend spring and summer in Cora's Cove for fishing and tourist season, and fall and winter here in Boston? I'm willing to do anything," he declares in earnest.

The prospect of splitting our time between Boston and Cora's Cove fills me with overwhelming joy.

"Let's do it," I say effortlessly. I've never been so sure of anything in my life.

He blinks. "Really?"

"Of course. I love you. My home is with you. And I know how ridiculously cliché that sounds, so don't you dare laugh," I say, instinctively reaching to pull him closer, over the threshold.

A massive grin spreads across his face as he draws closer. "I love you too. Now get over here."

He makes me close the rest of that distance, which I suppose is only fair. Then again, nothing could pull me away from him and those clear blue eyes beckoning me back to him. His fingers intertwine with mine as he cups my jaw. He tries to kiss me, but I'm too busy smiling against his mouth, raking my fingers through his hair, trying to cement this moment in my mind.

He presses his forehead to mine and lets out a shuddering breath, blending with mine until the steady, synced rhythm is all I can hear.

When our lips finally meet, they melt together like a warm, gentle wave. For the first time, I kiss him with ease. With simplicity. Gone is the lingering fear in the back of my mind that he could hurt me. That this could all be temporary. That I need to run while I still can. Right now I'm utterly grounded by him, heart and soul. This is it. My end and my beginning.

I think about what he said to me the night we went camping. That I'd never be alone in this world as long as he was in it. And for the first time, I truly believe it.

When we pull away, the Whalers funnel out from their hiding spot around the corner and join in our embrace, piling over each other in the messiest, clumsiest way to join our group hug.

By the time we go inside, Tara already has the wine poured. Crystal is on the phone, ordering more food. Scott, the gentleman that he is, pulls out chairs, offering Nana, Nessa, and Fiona seats.

Evan is introduced to everyone individually, though he's apparently already met Crystal via DM.

"I needed your address, so I may have slid into her DMs," Evan admits.

Crystal snorts, pulling her phone up to show me. "And get this. He had no followers and no profile photo, so I didn't even bother to look at it for days."

"So you knew they were coming?" I ask.

"Yup. It was awkward yesterday when you decided mid-workout you were going to book your plane tickets."

Her hesitation makes complete sense now. "That's why you didn't want me taking the red-eye."

"I sent him an SOS message as soon as you left the session," she says.

Evan wraps his arms around me from behind. "I had to make sure I got here first. Couldn't let you beat me to an apology."

I can't help but laugh, entirely blissful at the sight of everyone I love in one room. My family.

With Evan at my side, I watch as Julian whispers something into Sera's ear. Tara plops herself onto Trevor's lap and feeds him a bite of her pizza slice like a child as he chats with Ned about a fire call. Fiona and Nessa are at the end of the table, mid-guffaw over Nana, who's sipping her wine like a queen, fluttering her faux lashes at Scott, who she's taken a particular interest in, to Crystal's amusement.

And for the first time, I realize, my absurdly large, waste-of-space dining table for twelve is entirely full. I even need a thirteenth chair.

❤ epilogue

Two years later

EVAN

Morning, beautiful,

*Meet me at the docks today at 5 p.m. And no, not 5:30. Or
5:15. I will accept 5:05 but no later.* ☺

Love,
E

I do a brief reread of my chicken-scratch Post-it before sticking
it to the bathroom mirror like I do every morning before a long
day at sea.

"You really don't have to write me a note every single day you go out," Mel insists regularly, even though I know she keeps every note in the drawer of the bedside table.

As a suprise to absolutely no one, my stubborn ass doesn't listen. Leaving a note to let her know I'm thinking about her is the least I can do, especially when I spend more time on the water than at home during busy season. I try to make up for it at night by doing all the things I promised we'd do: exploring the trails behind the inn, going on poutine dates, taking sunset walks along the harbor, going to the Anchor on Fridays.

Mel says she misses me but assures me she's never lonely. Not while helping Lucy with the steady stream of inn guests. And certainly not while entertaining my family, who've made a regular habit of dropping by unannounced, sometimes multiple times per day. She's also keeping busy with her role marketing the inn as well as my whale-watching and charter-tour side businesses, both of which are thriving thanks to her genius.

Over the past two years, the Whaler Inn has been completely transformed. Under Mel's design direction, we've renovated the parlor, modernized all the bathrooms, and added new touches like automatic blinds to replace the heavy drapes. We've updated the bedding and painted the walls and exterior siding, all while keeping its original charm. We've also replaced the wonky plumbing so she can take showers longer than two minutes.

Of course, it's been a family affair to get everything done on time for this year's fishing season, with everyone, including my crew, pitching in to help with the labor. Even Nana is helping to rejuvenate the gardens around the grounds.

But no one has worked as hard as Mel. Nothing makes me happier than watching her cultivate a new passion. She's had a hand in just about every step along the way, from taking a sledgehammer to the drywall herself (while in heeled boots) to documenting the entire renovation on her new social media account, @MelanieIn TheWild, which has replaced her old fashion and makeup account.

She's drummed up such a big following, furniture and decor companies from all over the world want to partner with us, offering to send us free items. Our Airbnb page is flooded with inquiries on a daily basis. And within one week of advertising the inn's renovations, we were booked solid from May to October. Nana says in all the years the inn has been open, it's never been this busy.

We haven't opened the inn for weddings yet, but that's on Mel's to-do list for next year. Ned and I plan to build a small honeymoon suite in the back.

Spoiler alert: Mel and I will have the first wedding to take place next year at the inn. She proposed last month at the lighthouse, surprising me with a picnic setup at sunset. Great minds think alike, I guess, because Nana's ring had been burning a hole in my pocket for weeks. I'd been waiting around like a lovesick chump for the perfect moment to ask her to be my wife—for real this time.

Thankfully, she didn't steal all my thunder. Because I have a surprise up my sleeve for tonight.

Of course, it's been a bitch to keep this a secret. If there's one thing folks have a special talent for in Cora's Cove, it's talk. I've had to remind the guys at the marina about a hundred times to keep their big mouths shut whenever Mel is around.

"Glad you're finally showing her the surprise tonight. I don't know how you expect me to keep this shit to myself," Kyle tells me on the way back to the marina with the day's catch.

"Oh, I don't expect you to keep anything to yourself. You already told your girlfriend." For the past few months, Kyle has been happily dating Paige, this new city girl from Toronto. He says he's taking a page out of my book.

"I didn't say shit, asshole." He blushes guiltily, hiding his bearded face with his massive hands.

"Lying doesn't suit you. I know you." And it's the truth. I know everything there is to know about him. He's basically family. He was always hanging around me and Jack as kids, and we had many a detention together after school. And many more hours being lectured by our parents for doing the dumb shit kids do, like stealing candy or leaving construction pylons on people's doorsteps. We got in trouble together pretty much everywhere we went. "It's cool, though. I'll forgive your sorry ass this time."

He lets out a resigned sigh. "Fine. I told her, okay? But the wives don't count."

I cock a brow in his direction. "Referring to her as your wife now, huh? Things getting serious?"

He shrugs, standing to drop the fenders as we near the dock. "Wishful thinking. Tryin' to convince her to stay. Haven't been successful so far."

"Sounds familiar," I say, docking *Fiona* in her usual spot.

"It's only been a couple months, though. Maybe it's too soon."

"Nah, man. When you know, you fucking know." I sure did. Within a week, I knew Mel was it for me. She owned me from that first snarky interaction. Sure, she infuriated the shit out of me with her clothes, her attitude, and a sense of humor sarcastic enough to go toe-to-toe with me. But I think that raw, visceral reaction was my first sign that she's more than meets the eye.

It didn't take me long to notice the way she holds her hands over her mouth and squeezes her eyes shut when she's laughing, like she's trying to contain her joy. How she notices small things about everyone in the room and listens to them. Really listens. She easily puts everyone else before herself, like she does with her brother. Like she did the day of my accident. She could have left us high and dry and gone home. But she stayed. For us. A bunch of strangers.

I've never met someone so hardworking, strong, and—most of all—someone who challenges me like she does. Despite all those things, she has a vulnerable side. A part of her that needs stability. A rock in unsteady waters. I intend to spend the rest of my life being that for her.

Kyle lifts his chin in an upward nod in the direction of a sight I will never tire of. "There's your girl."

MELANIE

I'm exactly eleven minutes late, but I can't help but stop to say hello to Mark the seal, who's sunbathing his plump gray body on a rock below, blissfully content.

"There you are," a familiar voice calls.

As my eyes adjust to the sunlight, Evan comes into sharp focus. He's exiting the *Fiona* in the cozy red flannel button-down I bought for him, windswept hair contained under that frayed Maple Leafs ball cap.

I close the distance between us, unable to stop full-teeth grinning. An unfortunate symptom of being near him in general, especially after a long day apart. "Sorry I'm late. But I have a good excuse. Two, actually."

A soft smile flirts at the edges of his mouth. "Let's hear 'em."

"First, there was a spider in the lilac room. It took me the better part of the afternoon to strategize how to get rid of it before our VIP guests arrive tonight." Crystal and Scott are coming for a weeklong stay for their babymoon, and I've been buzzing with excitement over it for the past month. It's only been two months since we last saw them, but since Crystal is pregnant, I've been dying to see her, especially since I probably won't be back in Boston until the baby is born.

In order to ensure I don't miss out on city life, Evan and I have upheld our compromise. We're spending the warm months in Cora's Cove and the cold months in Boston, where I can get my fix of shopping and time with Julian.

Aside from not understanding how to cross a busy intersection, Evan adapted to city life much better than expected, enjoying the vast food and entertainment options. It also helps that Scott and Trevor have massive man crushes on him and have welcomed him into the fold.

"Spider in the lilac room," he repeats. "You mean Mateo?"

"Lucy put him in the backyard," I tell him before he gets too concerned about the eight-legged monster's well-being.

He runs his hand over the back of his neck, relieved. "Okay. Glad he's been safely rehomed. And your second excuse?"

"I got stuck behind Susan Blake on the way." No elaboration necessary. Everyone in town is well aware of Susan, a ninety-eight-year-old who regularly cruises through town at a speed of approximately five miles per hour.

"In that case, I'm shocked you're only a couple minutes late. But now that you're here, I have something I've been waiting to show you." He extends a hand to tug me to the right.

"What is it?" I ask, eyes flitting over the *Fiona*, bobbing in the water in her usual spot.

Evan redirects my attention a little to the right.

Docked next to the *Fiona* is a gleaming pearly-white vessel that leaves me momentarily speechless. It's a good five feet taller and nearly twice as long. The slatted wooden deck is tidy and uncluttered, with brand-new traps, bright red buoys, and ropes just begging to hit the water for the first time.

"Oh my god. You got the second boat." My voice trails off when he nods, confirming. For the past two years, I've been trying to convince him to invest in another boat for his charters to keep up with the demand. He's always been gun-shy, convinced money is too tight.

"*Our* second boat," he corrects.

I shake my head, barely able to speak through my awe. "It's absolutely gorgeous, Evan."

"And the best part . . ." He rips off the white tarp draped over the side of the railing. In glittering black cursive, it reads *Melanie*.

"You named her after me?" My voice cracks mid-question.

He tugs me close to trace his thumb over my jaw, cupping my chin to settle his lips over mine. "Who else would I name her after?"

I'm overwhelmed with gratitude for him and for all the adventures we'll have together on this boat. I pull him tighter, pressing a flurry of tiny kisses to the tip of his nose.

"Come check it out," he murmurs, pulling me over the

threshold to show me around the deck. He's even had a cushiony white leather bench with adequate back support installed along the back so I can enjoy the views in comfort. To my delight, the cabin boasts equally luxurious seating. "It's got about twice as much space as *Fiona*, so we can bring out larger groups of people. And it has other perks too," he says, slanting a mischievous eye at the couple of bunk beds for the crew.

"Other perks, huh? You'll have to be more specific." I raise a brow as he scoops me into his arms, plopping me onto the bottom bunk.

"Specific enough for you?"

I nod, rolling over him. *I love you*, I mouth.

I love you, he mouths back.

I press my face against the warmth of his neck. As I take in his woodsy scent, it occurs to me that Evan is my favorite place in the entire world.

Some people grow up with a sense of home. They know where they were born. They know the family they're born into is who they were meant to be with. My entire life, I've been looking for home. A refuge. A place to belong. Somewhere I can cultivate my hopes and dreams. A light when everything else feels dark.

Now, for the first time, I feel wholly anchored. Whether we're kissing in the middle of a gum-pocked sidewalk in downtown Boston or nestled on the porch swing at the inn, tucked snugly under a blanket of shimmering stars. Wherever I am with Evan, I am home.

acknowledgments

Writing the acknowledgments for *The Catch* is bittersweet for many reasons, mostly because this is the third and final book in the Influencer series. From the outset, I hoped to differentiate the three books to showcase each main character's unique interests, personality, and journey. But in the end, I knew the books' common thread would be the characters' unwavering friendship and support for each other, even if that means a little blunt honesty from time to time. I'm a huge believer in the idea that women should support each other instead of competing—which is exactly what these girls do.

That's why saying goodbye to Crystal, Tara, and Melanie is hard. Crystal taught me self-acceptance. Tara taught me that emotions = strength. And Mel taught me to invest in the people in my life, not material things. I hope they helped you too, and have brought you some comfort during times of loneliness (adult friendships are hard!). I will be forever grateful to them for making me a published author.

Since publishing operates on strange timelines, I am writing this in March 2023, right after the publication of *Exes and O's.* I am filled with gratitude for my talented publishing teams all over the world for their steadfast hard work in getting this series into your hands. A huge thank-you to my Berkley team: Kristine Swartz, Mary Baker, Yazmine Hassan, Jessica Mangicaro, Cat Barra, Lindsey Tulloch, Christine Legon, Vikki Chu, Allison Prince, Alex Castellanos, the Penguin Sales team, Abby Graves, Lisa Davis, and Megan Elmore, as well as my Viking UK team: Lydia Fried, Ellie Hudson, Federica Trogu, Samantha Fanaken, Ruth Johnston, Kyla Dean, Linda Viberg, and Maddy Bennet.

I'd like to give a special shout-out to my Canadian readers. Ever since late 2019, when I started writing this series, I knew this was going to be Mel's story. City girl meets small community is one of my absolute favorite tropes—and it comes straight from experience. Something you probably didn't know about me is that I grew up in a small town with a population of five thousand people, so close-knit communities have a special place in my heart. I also desperately wanted to write a book set in coastal Canada—particularly in one of the most beautiful, cultural, and underrated provinces (Nova Scotia). I hope you enjoyed some of the Canadian references. #TeamPoutine

As always, a massive thank-you to my hardworking literary agent, Kim Lionetti. I still remember how excited you were about a grumpy fisherman romance from our very first phone call. I'm so grateful to the team at BookEnds Literary for helping me

ACKNOWLEDGMENTS

brainstorm the logistics of this *While You Were Sleeping* x *The Proposal* mashup.

Endless appreciation to Dr. Kimi Chernoby for taking the time to provide expert medical input with regard to Evan's boating debacle. Look for her cameo in the hospital scene!

Most of all, thank you to the readers, book influencers, reviewers, booksellers, and librarians for your support and enthusiasm for my books. I can't wait to write more for you!

The
Catch

♥

AMY LEA

READERS GUIDE

DISCUSSION QUESTIONS

1. What was your initial impression of Mel as a side character in the first two books in the series? Did you make certain assumptions about her that may have been challenged upon reading *The Catch*?

2. How did Mel's upbringing and childhood affect her relationship with fashion?

3. At the beginning of the book, what is Mel's relationship with fashion influencing? Do you get the impression she truly enjoys it, or is it a means to an end? How does this change throughout the book?

4. Mel is a lonely, closed-off character who tends to guard her heart. What factors in her childhood and upbringing have influenced this?

5. What do you think Mel's motivations were to pretend to be Evan's fiancée after the boat accident? Would you go to such lengths to repair a family feud?

6. How did Evan and the Whalers change the way Mel approaches relationships with people?

7. Mel's brother, Julian, is a large part of her life. While he has relied on Mel for a lot of his life, in what ways does Mel also rely on him?

8. Do you think it was too much for Evan to ask of Mel to move from her home in Boston to Cora's Cove? Was Mel justified in being conflicted over the decision? Do you think their compromise in the end will work in the long term?

9. Would you prefer to live in a small town or a large urban center? What are the pros and cons of both?

Keep reading for a preview of

Set on You

by Amy Lea, available now!

THE GYM IS supposed to be my safe place. The place I de-stress, reenergize, and ponder random wonders and mysteries, like: how was I delusional enough to think I could rock a middle hair part circa 2011?

That's why I'm equal parts horrified and appalled that my Tinder rebound, Joe, has sprung onto the treadmill to my right.

I brace myself for an awkward, clunky greeting, but thankfully, his attention appears fixed on the treadmill's touch pad. As he presses the dial to increase his speed, I catch a whiff of eau de wet dog. He not-so-subtly glances in my direction before averting his eyes.

Sure, Tinder Joe was kind enough to order me an Uber after our lackluster quarter-night stand two weeks ago. But it's highly coincidental we'd end up at the same gym, in all of Boston. I wonder if he's stalked me. Maybe I blew his mind in bed? So much so he went FBI on my ass, located my gym, and staged a casual run-in? Given my social media presence, it isn't out of the realm of possibility.

At every opportunity, Dad warns me of the dangers of posting my whereabouts on Instagram, lest I be kidnapped and sold into sex slavery, *Taken* style. Except Dad is no Liam Neeson. He doesn't have "special skills," aside from his legendary sesame chicken recipe. And so long as the Excalibur Fitness Center continues to sponsor my membership in exchange for promotion on my Instagram, I'm willing to risk it.

Tinder Joe and I lock eyes once again as I catch my breath post–sprint interval. Our shared gaze lasts two seconds longer than comfortable and I can't help but notice how his perfectly coifed boy-band hair remains suspiciously intact with each giraffe-like stride. Whether he stalked me here or not, my first instinct is to flee the scene.

So I do.

I take refuge in the Gym Bro Zone, aka the strength-training area.

As a gym regular, I exchange respectful nods with the other patrons as I enter. A familiar crowd of 'roid-pumping frat boys loiters near the bench presses while simultaneously chugging whey protein shakes like they're on the brink of dehydration. Today, they're donning those cringey neon tank tops that hang too low under their armpits. To their credit, they're nothing if not devoted to their daily routines. And after catching a glimpse of my sweaty, tomato-faced self in the wall-to-wall mirror under harsh fluorescent lighting, I'm not in any position to judge.

A guy man-splaying on the bench press grunts excessively, chucking a set of dumbbells to the floor with a loud *thud*. Normally this would grind my gears, but I'm too busy bounding toward a majestic sight to care. My treasured squat rack is free. Praise be.

The window squat rack is one of exactly two racks in this facility. It boasts a scenic view of a grungy nightclub across the street, a long-rumored front for a murderous motorcycle gang. The natural light is optimal for filming my workouts, especially compared to the alternative—the rack cloaked in shadow next to the men's changing room, which permanently reeks of Axe body spray.

The window rack is close enough to the industrial-size fan to let me savor a stiff breeze mid-sweat, but not close enough that I'll succumb to wind-induced hypothermia. It's also in the prime position for gawking at the television, which, for unknown reasons, is cruelly locked to the Food Network. I worship this squat rack the way Mother Gothel regards Rapunzel's magic hair. It gives me life. Vigor. Four sets of squats and I'll be high on endorphins for at least a day, fantasizing about the strength of my thighs crushing the souls of a thousand men.

Giddy at the very thought, I stake my claim on the rack, setting my phone and headphones on the floor before heading for the water fountain. The man with a goatee, who rocks knee-length cargo shorts and an actual Sony Walkman from the nineties, approaches at the same time. He graciously waves me ahead of him.

I flash him an appreciative smile. "Thanks."

My back is turned for all of three seconds while I take a sip. Freshly hydrated and eager to crush some squats, I spin around to find an exceptionally broad-shouldered figure stretching directly in front of my window rack.

I've never seen this man before and I'm certain I'd remember the shit out of him if I had. He's tall, well over six feet, with a muscular build that liberally fills out his unassuming gray T-shirt and athletic shorts. One look at his enormous biceps and it's clear he knows his way around a gym. A black ball cap with an unrecognizable logo shadows his face. From the side, his nose has a slight bump, as if it's been broken before.

I shimmy in beside him to pick up my phone, purposely lingering for a few extended beats to transmit the message that this rack is OCCUPIED. He doesn't get the memo. Instead, he proceeds to clasp his massive hands around the barbell, brows knit with intense concentration.

Either he's fully ignoring me, or he genuinely hasn't noticed my presence. The faint beat of his music is audible through his earbuds. I can't identify the song, but it sounds hard-core, like a heavy-metal lifting tune.

I clear my throat.

No reaction.

"Excuse me," I call out, inching closer.

When his gaze meets mine, I jolt, instinctively taking half a step back. His eyes are a striking forest green, like an expanse of dense pine trees dusting untouched misty mountain terrain in the wilderness. Not that I'd know from personal experience. My exposure to the rugged wild is limited to the Discovery Channel.

I'm nearly hypnotized by the intensity of his eyes, until he barks a "Yeah?" before reluctantly removing his right earbud. His voice is deep, gruff, and short, like he can't be bothered with me. He momentarily lifts his ball cap, revealing wavy, dirty-blond locks that curl at the nape of his neck. It reminds me of the scraggly hairstyles worn by hockey players, the kind you just want to run your fingers through. And he does just that. My throat dries instantly when he smooths his thick mane with one hand before dropping his ball cap back over the top.

Deliberately ignoring the dip in the base of my stomach, I nod toward my headphones hastily strewn at the base of the rack. "I was here first."

Expression frosty, he arches a strong brow, regarding me with contempt, as gym bros tend to do when women dare to touch what they deem as *their* equipment. "Didn't see your stuff."

Undeterred by his brush-off, I take a confident step forward, laying my rightful claim. When we're nearly chest to chest, he towers over me like a behemoth, which is more intimidating than I anticipated. I expect him to back off, to see the error of his ways, to realize he's being a prick, but he doesn't even flinch.

Swallowing the lump in my throat, I find my voice again. "I'll only be a few minutes, max. We could even switch in and out?"

He sidesteps. For a second, I think he's leaving. I'm about to thank him for his grace and humanity . . . until he dares to load one side of the barbell with a forty-five-pound plate, biceps straining against the fabric of his T-shirt.

"Seriously?" I stare at him, hands on hips, gaze settling on his soft, full lips, which contrast with the harsh line of his stubbled jaw.

"Look, I need to get to work in half an hour. Can't you just use the other rack? It's free." As he ruthlessly balances the rack with another plate, he barely spares me a passing glance, as if I'm nothing more than a pesky housefly.

I pride myself on being an accommodating person. I wave other cars ahead of me at four-way stops, even if I have the right-of-way. I always insist others exit elevators in front of me, as my parents taught me. If he had just been polite, half-decent, even the slightest bit apologetic, I probably would have let him have it. But he isn't any of the above, and I'm shook.

"No," I say, out of principle.

His jaw tightens as he rests his forearms on the bar. The way he leans into it, stance wide and hulking, is purely a territorial move. He gives me one last, indignant shrug. "Well, I'm not moving."

We're locked in a stare-off with nothing but the faint sound of Katy Perry singing about being "a plastic bag drifting through the wind" over the gym sound system and a man grunting on the leg press a couple feet away to quell the silence. My eyes are dry and itchy from my refusal to blink, and the intensity of his stare offers no sign of fatigue.

When Katy Perry fades out, replaced by an Excalibur Fitness promotional ad, I let out a half sigh, half growl. This guy isn't worth my energy. I retrieve my headphones from the floor and stomp to the less desirable rack, but not before shooting him one last evil eye.

11:05 A.M.—INSTAGRAM POST: "ASSHOLES WHO THINK THEY OWN THE GYM" BY **CURVYFITNESSCRYSTAL**:

Real talk: This morning, an arrogant dickhead with nicer hair than me callously stole my squat rack. Who does this? And if you're guilty of this crime, WHO HURT Y'ALL?

I don't know him personally (and I don't want to), but he struck me as the kind of person who loathes puppies and joy in general. You know the type. Anyway, I ended up channeling all my anger into my workout while blasting my current jam, "Fitness" by Lizzo (trust, this song is fire).

Final thoughts: Most people at the gym aren't assholes. I promise. 99% are super helpful and respectful, even the steroid frat boys! And if you do encounter that unfortunate 1%, just steer clear. Never give them power over you or your fitness journey.

Thanks for listening to my TED Talk,

Crystal

Comment by **xokyla33**: YAS girl! You're sooo right. You do ♡ you!!

Comment by **_jillianmcleod_**: I just don't feel comfortable ♡ working out at the gym for this reason. Would rather work out at home.

Comment by **APB_rockss**: U promote embracing your ♡ curves/size but all u do is work out and live at the gym? Hypocrite much??

Reply by **CurvyFitnessCrystal**: @APB_rockss Actually I ♡ spend one hour in the gym working out each day. Devoting time every day for yourself, whether it's at the gym, taking a walk, or in a bubble bath is hugely beneficial for all aspects of your life, including mental health. Also, you can both love your body and go to the gym. They aren't mutually exclusive.

• • •

AFTER YESTERDAY'S INCOHERENT Instagram rant, I took a much-needed soul-searching bubble bath. My response to the person who called me a hypocrite unintentionally sparked a fierce debate of epic proportions between my loyal followers and my haters. I try not to pay the trolls an iota of attention, but after Squat Rack Thief and two glasses of merlot, I was feeling a tinge combative. And it's been building for months.

For seven years, I've striven to shatter harmful, fatphobic stereotypes in the fitness industry. I've built an Instagram following of two hundred thousand based on my message of self-love, regardless of size. The drama over me being "too big" to be a personal trainer yet "not big enough" to represent the curvy community is typical in the abyss of the comments section. There's no in-between.

The crass body-shaming and occasional racist slurs have become more commonplace with the growth of my following. For the sake of maintaining a positive message, I've ignored the hateful comments. The fact is, I love my curves. Most of the time. I'm only human. Occasionally, the trolls manage to penetrate my armor. When this happens, I allow myself a short grace period to wallow. And then I treat them to a proverbial middle finger in the form of a thirst trap (a full-length body shot, for good measure).

But last night, sometime before my rainbow glitter bath bomb dissolved entirely, it occurred to me that my followers are probably equally, if not more, hurt by the comments. If I want to stay authentic and true to my body-positive platform, maybe it's time to start speaking out.

Today's workout is the perfect time to ruminate over my strategy.

But to my displeasure, Squat Rack Thief is back again, for the second day in a row. He's stretching in the Gym Bro Zone. Must he have such magnificent quads?

He narrows his gaze in my direction as I shimmy through the turnstiles. Instantly, his expression goes from neutral to a deep scowl, as if my mere presence has derailed his entire day.

I eye him sideways before shifting my faux attention to the generic motivational quotes plastered on the wall in an aggressively bold font: *If it doesn't challenge you, it won't change you.*

Evading him for the duration of my workout is harder than I expected. Wherever I go, he's looming in my peripherals, taking up precious space with his gloriously muscled body.

When I woke up this morning, it crossed my mind that he could be an Excalibur Fitness newbie who hasn't grasped the concept of gym etiquette. I fully intended to give him the benefit of the doubt. Maybe he was simply having a bad day. Maybe he spent the entire night staring into the vast distance, roiling with regret. Lord knows I've had my fair share of rage-workouts.

All of these possibilities lose legitimacy when he conspires to out-pedal me on the neighboring assault bike. When I catch him eyeing my screen, I channel my inner Charlie's Angel and full-throttle it.

At the twenty-calorie mark, we both stop, panting, hunched over the handles. My "no-makeup" makeup has probably melted entirely, and I'm seeing spots. But my exertion was worth it—I beat him by a whole 0.02 miles. He practically seethes when he reads my screen. Evidently unable to cope with my victory, he pouts, promptly hightailing it to the machines.

Not half an hour later, it's officially game over when I witness him saunter away from the leg press without bothering to wipe down the seat. The darkest places in hell are reserved for those who don't clean the machines after use.

Compelled to speak up on behalf of all hygiene-policy-abiding gym patrons, I set my dumbbells down and march forth.

He's in the zone as he does a round of effortless pull-ups. I stand, mouth agape, unintentionally mesmerized by the taut, corded muscles in his arms flexing with each movement.

He gives me a Chris Evans vibe, but with slightly longer, luscious locks. I don't know if it's the glint in his hooded eyes or the dimples, but he has a boyish look to him that makes him appear faintly approachable when he isn't scowling at me.

When he catches me gawking at him like a crazed fangirl thirsting for a selfie, he pauses, dangling from the bar. "How's the view from down there?"

I'm about to say *godlike*, both because it's entirely true and because it's my default to compliment people. I do it for a living. But the last thing this guy needs is a confidence boost.

I consciously make a flat line with my mouth, channeling Mom's severe expression when she's supremely disappointed in my life choices. I hold out a paper towel, generously pre-sprayed with disinfectant, for his convenience, of course. "Are you forgetting something?"

He blinks. "Not that I'm aware of."

"You forgot to clean the leg press."

He releases the bar, sticking a smooth landing as he eyes the paper towel pinched between my fingers like it's been dipped in sulfuric acid. "Keeping track of my workout or something?"

"No," I say, a little too defensively. "But you need to wash the machines when you're done with them. It's a rule here. People don't want to touch your dried sweat." I inwardly cringe. I might as well have an I'd-like-to-speak-with-a-manager angled bob. But I can't back down now. In fact, I double down, pointing to the sign on the wall to our right that reads *Please wipe down machines after use.*

He doesn't even glance at the sign. Instead, he appraises me, arms folded over his broad chest. "I'm not done with the machine. Are you unfamiliar with supersets? You know, when you cycle through multiple exercises back-to-back—"

"I know what a superset is!" I snap. Heat rockets from my lower belly to my cheeks when I realize I've unjustly called him out. This is mortifying. I silently will myself to disappear into an obscure, nonexistent sinkhole. Maybe this is cosmic retribution for not minding my own business.

He flashes me a knowing smirk and struts back for another set.

As if this painful interaction never happened, I slink away into obscurity to film my back workout tutorial on the cable machine. It's a prime opportunity to promote my sponsored sweat-resistant activewear.

I'm midway through filming a shot of ten cable rows when Squat Rack Thief materializes out of thin air. He chooses to park his massive body directly in front of the camera, of all places, blocking the shot. In my silent fury, I lose all focus, with zero recollection of whether I'm on the first rep or the tenth.

He leans lazily against the machine, wearing a smug grin that I'm beginning to think is his natural resting face.

"Yes?" I ask through clenched teeth, irritated at the prospect of re-filming the entire segment.

He produces a paper towel from behind his back, swishing it in front of my face. "Here. So you don't forget to wipe down the seat."

His sarcastic tone combined with his sneer tells me he isn't doing this out of the goodness of his heart. This is a hostile act of aggression, cementing our rivalry.

Before I can formulate a cutting response, he drops the paper towel into my lap and waltzes toward the changing room.

Photo courtesy of the author

Amy Lea is the international bestselling author of romantic comedies for adults and teens, including *Set on You*, *Exes and O's*, and Mindy Kaling's Book Studio selection *Woke Up Like This*. Her acclaimed works have been featured in *USA Today*, *Entertainment Weekly*, *Cosmopolitan*, and more. When Amy is not writing, she can be found fangirling over other romance books on Instagram (@AmyLeaBooks), eating potato chips with reckless abandon, and snuggling with her husband and two goldendoodles in Ottawa, Canada.

Ready to find
your next great read?

Let us help.

Visit prh.com/nextread

Penguin
Random
House